GOLDEN TALLY

Vinnie, badly shaken and angry with herself, stared round at the astonished faces which peered at her from all directions between the hop-bines. She straightened her back and opened her mouth to speak, then changed her mind. Perhaps she had said enough already, or perhaps she had said too much. Pity for Mary's predicament outweighed her resentment of the other's harsh comments, for Vinnie recognised in her heart that up to a point everything Mary had said was true. Inadvertently, Vinnie had stolen the men in Mary's life and had enjoyed the affection Mary had wanted. Now she felt intuitively that Mary might lose this last 'man' in her life.

As she walked back to the house she tried to remember exactly what she had said. She felt uneasy and the more she recalled of the exchange, the more anxious she became. She had probably made matters worse. And what was it Mary had said? That she 'pretended innocence'. Could that be true?

PAMELA OLDFIELD

Golden Tally

WARNER BOOKS

A WARNER BOOK

First published in Great Britain by
Century Publishing Co. Ltd 1985
Reprinted 1990
Reprinted by Warner Books 1992
Reprinted 1998

Printed in England by Clays Ltd, St Ives plc

ISBN 0 7515 0375 4

Warner
A Division of
Little, Brown and Company (UK)
Brettenham House
Lancaster Place
London WC2E 7EN

FOR MY MOTHER – JULIE WILSON
to remember her with love, respect and gratitude

CHAPTER ONE: JULY 1909

Cook waddled across the lawn. In her hands she carried a tray; on her face she wore a scowl of disapproval which stemmed from two sources. Firstly, carrying a tray of drinks was *not* her job – preparing it, yes; carrying it, no. That was Edie's job, or even Bertha's, but Edie was sick in bed and Bertha had been sent to the village store with a shopping list. Meanwhile lemonade had been requested and somebody had to carry it. Realising that no one had noticed her approach, she set down the tray on the broad stump of a recently stricken chestnut tree and paused, hands on hips, to catch her breath and consider the scene before her – which constituted the second source of her disapproval.

'Tennis, indeed!' she muttered disparagingly. Whatever was the world coming to, she asked herself. During all the years she had been at Foxearth the front lawn had been laid out with hoops and many an elegant game of croquet had been played thereon. The soft swish of skirts, the light laughter and the steady click of mallet on ball had been a joy. Janet had once described the scene as 'enchanting' which had surprised Cook who did not think she knew such words. But Janet was now nurse to old Colonel Lawrence and maybe he was educating her.

Now a tennis net had been stretched across the grass, although as yet no one had bothered to mark out the courts. Tennis, thought Cook, was a noisy, rumbustious game in which everyone, even the spectators, became hot and bothered; certainly no one could ever describe it as 'enchanting'. She allowed herself a loud snort of disapproval as she considered the antics taking place. On one side of the net, Vinnie Lawrence gathered her long white skirt into one hand and lifted it indecorously as she leaped to hit the ball which Bertie, her brother, had sent over her head. She missed it and there was a roar of laughter from the onlookers and a shout of triumph from Bertie as the ball bounced into the shrubbery and rolled out of sight.

Cook shook her head. That brother of Vinnie's was a mad devil, she reflected. You would never think he had only one eye, the way he carried on. Always up to something and with that loud laugh of his – you couldn't help but smile. He came into the kitchen sometimes, to steal a few currants or try to wheedle her into making his favourite bread pudding. Bread pudding for dessert at Foxearth! Whatever next! But he had a way with him, Bertie did, and Vinnie would miss him when he went away.

'Anyway, it was out!' cried Vinnie. 'It must have been!' As she spoke, James – the eldest of her three children – set off in search of the ball.

'Oh, Bertie, it must have been *out*, I tell you. Miles out! Wasn't it out?' she appealed to the onlookers who sat on a row of wicker garden chairs.

Beatrice laughed. 'Hardly miles,' she said, 'but it *was* out by a good few yards.'

She was Bertie's wife, a small quiet girl with straight dark hair pulled back severely over her ears and plaited into a bun. An odd match, thought Cook, not for the first time: Bertie so full of high spirits and Bea so quiet. Not that she was a mouse – far from it! She could be very strong-willed, could Bea, and her head was screwed on the right way, there was no doubt about that. The attraction of opposites, they called it.

Bertie grinned, undismayed by the verdict. 'But it was a damned good lob,' he said. 'You must admit that!'

'It was a fluke,' laughed William, 'and you know it.'

'A fluke?' Bertie's face assumed an expression of deep indignation. 'That superb shot, a *fluke*?'

'You know it and we know it,' William taunted humorously.

'And we know that you know that we know . . . '

William le Brun, a pleasant-looking, stocky young man, was Vinnie's fiancé and spent a good deal of his time at Foxearth, where he was a great favourite. Cook was particularly fond of him.

'Anyway,' said Vinnie, 'it was out, so that's "vantage" to me.' She positioned herself in the court and cried, 'Next ball, please Bertie! If we don't get a move on, it will be lunchtime and Bea and William won't get a game. So hit it straight into the net and then I shall have won the set!'

Bertie swung his racket and the ball skimmed low and fast across the net.

'Lordy!' muttered Cook, as Vinnie made an unsuccessful attempt to return it. 'I wonder how good he'd be with two eyes!'

At that moment William turned his head and caught sight of her.

'Ah, the drinks!' he said and, jumping up from his chair, crossed the lawn towards her. 'I'll take the tray, Cook,' he continued. 'I'm sure you have better things to do than to wait on us. Bertha should have brought them out.'

'She's gone down to the village, sir.'

'I see. Well, thank you anyway. Aha, what's this? Lemon snaps?'

Cook winked. 'I know they are your favourites, sir.'

'You spoil me,' he said. 'Vinnie swears, you know, that I am not marrying her for love, but for your cooking!'

'Oh, sir, I do hope not,' said Cook, trying to hide her delight at the compliment and failing completely.

'Well, so long as you promise me lemon snaps once a week . . .'

William gave her a wink in return, which sent her waddling back to the house with flushed cheeks. Why *wouldn't* Vinnie name the day, she wondered, and put the poor young man out of his misery? They called it 'an understanding', but how long was an understanding supposed to last? Vinnie had been wearing William's ring for nearly two years now and how long was it since her husband had died – three years or four? Maybe more.

Cook could not be sure, but she knew it was a long time to keep an attractive man like William le Brun dangling.

'I would say "yes" to him tomorrow if he asked me,' she said to herself. 'If she's not careful, he will get tired of waiting and begin to look elsewhere. And who could blame him?'

Reaching the kitchen door, she sighed deeply and turned her thoughts reluctantly to the more urgent matter of a pudding to be prepared for the evening meal.

*

Meanwhile Doll, the children's nanny, was supervising James's search for the lost ball. She found it herself, moved it to a more conspicuous place and then turned away. A plump, cheerful girl with brown hair parted in the middle and pulled back into a bun, she was not a beauty but her eyes sparkled and there was a warmth and softness about her face that men found appealing.

'Well, I'm blessed if I can see that ball,' she said now. 'I'm such a duffer at finding things. It's to be hoped your eyes are sharper than mine, James.'

'They *are*,' James assured her. '*Much* sharper! I can find lots of things when they are lost.' He stopped searching the ground in order to look earnestly into her face with his large grey eyes. 'Mama says I'm the world's best "finder". I found her sewing scissors once when she had looked everywhere and one day I found a button from Louise's shoe!'

'Right, then,' said Doll, seating herself on a fallen tree-trunk. 'I shall sit back and rest while *you* find the ball.'

James, seven years old, was a handsome child with a slim body, soft blond hair that was almost silver and large grey eyes with flaxen lashes. His pale colouring gave him a fragile appearance, but in fact he was sturdy enough: a serious child who divided his affection scrupulously between his mother and his beloved Doll. There were also two younger children of Vinnie's marriage to Julian – a girl of six whose name was Louise Jane and a boy of five, Edward John. Louise was a petite child with the same silvery hair as James and a rare but bewitching smile which she already used to great effect on the men in her life. Edward – or Teddy as he was invariably called – was golden blond with grey eyes and very like his father in looks but not in character, being altogether more excitable and full of fun.

Now Teddy appeared among the laurels in his short breeches, neat boots and frilly shirt, his wide-brimmed hat hanging down his back. His curls were damp with perspiration where they framed his face.

'I'll find it!' he told them eagerly.

'You won't!' cried James. 'This is *my* ball.' They took it in turns to act as ball boy.

Louise followed her younger brother, sedate and immaculate in her white dress with its pink sash, buttoned white shoes and hat.

'It's lemonade time, Doll,' she said. 'And there are lemon snaps.'

Teddy waited to see if the prospect of this treat would persuade James to abandon the search, but precisely at that moment the older boy spotted the ball and snatched it up.

'Well done, James!' said Doll. 'Another ball rescued. Lemon snaps, did you say, Louise? I think I fancy a lemon snap – if it doesn't, that is.'

'Doesn't what?' asked Louise, taking hold of Doll's right hand before Teddy could decide to do so.

'Snap, of course!'

Teddy laughed, leaping ahead of them and making his right hand into snapping jaws.

'How do you make a lemon snap?' Doll asked, giggling.

'Break it in half,' cried James.

'Oh, we are witty today,' said Doll as they emerged from the trees to rejoin the party.

Vinnie was already pouring lemonade into glasses, her straw boater tipped back at a rakish angle. Bertie was drinking with large noisy gulps, his head thrown back; he had loosened the high collar of his white shirt and his tie hung around his neck like a tailor's tape measure. He had put on weight since his return to England and the striped belt that supported his flannels strained at the S-shaped silver buckle. He was hatless, but wore a rakish black patch over his right eye. Beside him, William appeared cool and collected as he nibbled a biscuit. Beatrice offered the plate of lemon snaps to the children and then to Doll.

'A good game!' said Vinnie, flushed with victory. 'And don't pretend, Bertie, that you *let* me win, because you didn't – I could tell you didn't.'

'I am a bit of an actor on the quiet,' Bertie parried, but he was immediately howled down by the others.

'And here is your lost ball,' said Doll. 'James found it.'

Vinnie turned to give her eldest son a playful pat on the head. 'Well done, James,' said William. 'Next year, perhaps you can start to learn the game. At present your hands are a little too small to grasp the racket handle properly, but next year you will be much bigger.'

'I shall be taller too, sir,' said James earnestly.

'Of course you will,' said Bertie. 'You will be taller, fatter, heavier, a lot noisier – and, I daresay, a lot naughtier!'

He put down his empty glass and made a pounce to catch James round the waist, but anticipating this James dodged him, a smile lightening his face briefly.

'Catch *me*, Uncle Bertie!' cried Teddy. 'You can catch me, Uncle Bertie, you can – oh!' He chose not to move quickly enough and Bertie caught him, tickled him and stood him upside down on his head.

'Bertie!' grumbled Vinnie, as Teddy's squeals echoed across the garden. 'You make him worse than he is already. Stop teasing him – look how hot he is!'

Bertie lowered his nephew to the ground where Teddy lay panting and laughing. His sister Louise watched him dispassionately.

'You look awful,' she told him primly, 'and you've got grass in your hair.' He put out his tongue and she turned away in deep disgust.

'You might be next,' Bertie whispered to her, but her pale brown eyes flashed him a stony look that dared him to take such a liberty and she turned away with a toss of her head. Bertie glanced at Vinnie, who laughed lightly.

'Louise takes after grandmother Lawrence,' she told him. 'She will be quite a formidable lady when she grows up!'

'She is formidable *now*!' said Bertie; then, glancing up, he added, 'Hullo, what's up?'

Bertha, the maid, had appeared at the top of the steps and now began to run wildly across the grass towards them, waving her arms to attract their attention.

'They told me at the store,' she gasped, 'and then I saw Mr le Brun arriving and he says it's true . . . ' As she reached them, she put a hand to her side. 'Ooh, I've got a stitch!' she said, raising her hand to her heaving chest. 'He was coming to tell you, but he says I can do it because I was already on my way –'

'Tell us *what*?' cried Vinnie. 'Bertha, what are you talking about? Do calm down and tell it properly.'

Bertha, seizing her moment of glory, gazed round to make quite certain that she had the undivided attention of the entire tennis party. Bea, Vinnie, William, Doll, Bertie and the children all stared at her expectantly.

'You three little ones,' Bertha told the children, 'you listen carefully to this. This is a very special day – that's what Mr le Brun said *and* Jarvis Tupp at the store said it, because someone has flown right over the sea – *our* sea between England and France – and he's landed in Dover! His name's Mr Bellioh!'

She turned to glance over her shoulder. Clive le Brun, William's father, was following her at a leisurely pace, a smile on his lean face. He was a tall, good-looking man, whose wife had died many years earlier; William was the only surviving child of the marriage. Clive le Brun's links with the Lawrence family were on both a personal and a business level, for the firm of le Bruns were hop factors in the Weald of Kent and the Lawrences, with their large acreage under hops, had been clients of theirs for several generations.

Vinnie found herself watching him as he strode towards them and wondered, not for the first time, why he had never remarried. She knew women found him attractive, but he appeared genuinely unaware of the fact and showed no inclination to find another wife. Vinnie envied him his self-assurance, which she had – albeit subconsciously – hoped to find echoed in his son. In this, however, she had been disappointed; father and son were not at all alike, for William had taken after his mother whom Vinnie had never met.

Clive smiled at Bertha. 'Well, did you tell them?'

'I did, sir,' Bertha told him, 'but I don't reckon they believe me.' She turned back to her small audience. 'It's the gospel truth, cross my heart! Mr le Brun will tell you the same as me. Louise, his name is. Louise Bellioh.'

'But Louise is a girl's name,' James objected. 'You said he was called *Mister* Bellioh!'

Bertha looked a little put out by his obvious scepticism. 'It's only a girl's name in our country,' she explained, 'but in France it's a man's name. You tell them, Mr le Brun – isn't that right?'

Clive nodded. 'Bertha is absolutely right,' he said, 'about the flight. It's a very historic day. A man has flown across the English Channel and it took just over half an hour.'

There were gasps of incredulity and Bertha said, 'I told you so!'

Clive continued, 'A Monsieur Blériot, to be exact. He left Calais early this morning, flew through a fog to Margate and then turned back to land at Dover beside the castle. Thirty-seven minutes, they told me at Leysdown.'

Seeing Vinnie's puzzled look, he explained that he had been looking over the Aero Club's flying ground on the Isle of Sheppey when news of the historic flight came through; a friend of William's was working there for the Short brothers and had offered to show Clive round. Everyone wanted to know more, but no further details were available. While they discussed the great event, Bertha returned to the kitchen to break her news all over again to the kitchen staff, Teddy turned a celebratory somersault and Vinnie poured Clive a glass of lemonade.

'Man conquering the air,' said Bea. 'I wonder where it will all end? I must admit I do not welcome change as much as I might do – it's not always for the better.'

'Not always,' agreed Clive. 'But flight could open up communications in a way that has never been possible before. Thirty-seven minutes from Calais to Dover! It's a tremendous breakthrough.'

'I do wish it had been an Englishman,' said Vinnie.

Clive laughed. 'Never satisfied, some people!' he said. 'Here's poor Blériot risking his neck to hop across the Channel in a flying machine and all you can say is "I wish it had been an Englishman".'

She laughed goodnaturedly as Bertie raised his glass.

'Lemonade is hardly the correct drink for toasts,' he said, 'but I propose a toast to Louis Blériot – a brave man and a fine aviator!'

They all raised their glasses and echoed his words. Only Teddy frowned.

'What's the matter with you, young man?' whispered Doll.

He sighed deeply and scowled into his empty glass. 'It's my turn to find the ball,' he grumbled, 'and I want them to get on with the game.'

*

Clive le Brun stayed to lunch and then, while the tennis playing was resumed, he made the rounds of the hop-fields with Vinnie at his side. Together they walked between the rows of hops, which towered above them and met overhead to form cool tunnels of leafy vegetation. The August sunshine made the leaves glow deep green and ripened the pale green hops which hung in clusters along the twisting bines.

'A nice crop,' Clive said again, with a nod of his head. He sounded satisfied, as indeed he was, for it was his guidance which brought the hops to a timely harvest in September of each year and his advice also which ensured their survival from a variety of hazards – for the hops were very vulnerable and suffered from inclement weather, blight and insects. A good hop factor played a vital role in the hop industry, for not only was his expertise needed in an advisory capacity during the growing season but it was also important when the hops, correctly dried and pressed into 'pockets', were offered for sale on the open market; they must be sold when the price was right and when foreign competition was at its least damaging.

'Three weeks to go,' Clive said, 'and then these gardens will come alive.'

Vinnie nodded. 'I love September,' she said. 'Although it is a very anxious time, I must admit that I love the excitement. When the hop pickers' train draws in at Wateringbury station, my heart still gives a great bound – after all these years. The thrill of that moment is as strong as ever!' She paused to reach up and let a handful of hops rest in the palm of her hand. 'The carriage doors crash open and the pickers tumble out on to the platform. Suddenly it's all noise and commotion and I remember that once I was among them – hidden in a roll of blanket so that poor Ma didn't have to pay my fare!'

She let her hand fall to her side once more and they walked on in silence for a while. Then Vinnie looked up at the man beside her. 'I'm looking forward especially to watching the men's faces when they see their new quarters.'

Some years earlier Vinnie had taken out a bank loan in order to build a soundly constructed hut to house most of the women and children. This year she had repeated the operation with a smaller hut to accommodate the men, who never came in such large numbers as the women.

'It won't take all of them,' she admitted, 'but the best of the tents and the small barn will shelter the rest.'

Reaching the lower end of the hop-field, they went through a gate into another field which sloped steeply down to the River Medway gleaming in the valley below them. Around them the hop-bines clung tenaciously to poles and stringing. The hops would soon be picked by hand into canvas troughs known as 'bins' – mostly by the Londoners, although a few local people would take part – and would then be measured into sacks called pokes and carried away to the oast-house to be dried. Eventually they would be sold and the crop would find its way to the brewery, where it would add its pungent bitter flavour to the beer.

At twenty-eight years of age, Vinnie Lawrence was a mature woman, the widowed mother of three children. She had taken over the running of Foxearth after her husband's death and the few intervening years had rounded her personality. Motherhood and business responsibilities had developed her mind and sharpened her ambition and she meant to make Foxearth into one of the largest and most modern hop-gardens in the Weald of Kent, supplying fine hops to the many breweries in the Maidstone area. Clive le Brun – watching her over the past two years with shrewd grey eyes – had grown very fond of her; he admired her spirit and hoped that her courage and determination would be properly rewarded. Only in one respect did his admiration for her falter; his son William still waited impatiently for Vinnie to agree a date for their wedding. So far Clive had resisted the impulse to interfere, daily hoping that William would return to their home in Tunbridge Wells with the welcome news. Today, however, he had decided he would wait no longer. While they chatted of the height of the bines and the price of imported hops, his mind sought a way of introducing the topic closest to his heart.

Suddenly intuitive, Vinnie glanced at him curiously. 'What is it, Clive?' she asked. 'Something is troubling you. Is it bad news? If so, then I ought to hear it.'

'It's not bad news,' he said. 'No, not exactly.' He tugged at a stray bine which, freed from its pole, hung in the air, trembling in the light breeze.

'I have no right to say this – ,' he began.

Her eyes narrowed almost imperceptibly. 'But you will?'

'Yes, I think I must,' he responded.

Vinnie waited, head down, watching the toe of her right shoe as it scuffed the well-trodden earth.

'Why do you avoid my eyes?' he asked.

'Because I know,' she said. 'I know what you are going to say; it's about William.'

'Yes.'

She sighed deeply and her slim shoulders rose and fell.

'He puts on a brave face,' said Clive, 'but you are breaking his heart, Vinnie, and I cannot let it go on.'

'I know,' she said again. Her voice was so low that he had to lean forward in an attempt to catch her words and his expression hardened a little.

'Then you must name a day, Vinnie,' he said. 'You are making a fool of him and I will not stand for it. He loves you and he has waited far too long already. I love you both and I want to see you happy together. Don't tell me it's a question of your independence, for you have proved yourself a dozen times already.' She made no answer and he went on. 'William is not perfect, but I know him as well as any man knows his own son and he will make you a good husband. I am sure of it.'

She greeted his words with another long sigh. 'Look at me, Vinnie!' he said sternly. 'This is not like you at all. You are usually so open, so direct. Tell me what is wrong and maybe I can help.'

Vinnie looked up at him and then hastily lowered her eyes which, to his dismay, had filled with tears. 'I will tell you,' she whispered, 'but I shall lose your respect and that will hurt me dreadfully.'

'Tell me anyway,' he said more quietly.

Vinnie turned away to pluck at the green leaves in nervous agitation. He noted the dejected set of her shoulders and found the sight of her slim neck strangely moving.

Suddenly she turned back to face him. 'I cannot marry William!' she blurted out. 'I don't love him and it would not be fair.'

'Don't *love* him?'

'No!'

'But for God's sake!' he cried, astonished and dismayed by her admission. 'If you don't love the boy why the charade? Why promise to marry him?'

Vinnie shook her head. 'Because I *wanted* to love him,' she said, the tears trickling down her cheeks. 'I know how much he loves me and I wanted to make him happy. Oh Clive, please believe me! I tried to love him, truly I did. I have pretended, to him and to myself, praying that love would come – that I would somehow *learn* to love him. That's possible sometimes, isn't it? One person can *learn* to love another? I know he would make me a good husband and that he would be a good father. The children love him. But would I make *him* happy? I have asked myself a hundred times and still I don't know the answer. Help me, Clive, if you can, because I . . . because . . . '

Momentarily her voice became choked with sobs, her words incoherent, and Clive stood helplessly as she struggled with her emotion. Then, resisting the urge to take her into his arms, he gently patted her shoulder.

'Don't, Vinnie!' he told her. 'Don't cry, it won't solve anything.'

'I can't help it,' she wept. 'I am so dreadfully sorry, but . . . '

He handed her a large clean handkerchief and waited as she wiped her eyes. When at last she could speak again, she said, 'What shall I do, Clive? Either way I shall break his heart and I cannot bear to do that. He means so much to me as a person, as a friend.'

'But not as a husband, Vinnie? Are you quite sure?'

'Quite sure! Yes, I have put off the moment when I should tell him, hoping against hope that if I waited a little longer love would grow. I have tried and tried.'

'Perhaps you have tried too hard?' he suggested. 'Maybe once you were married – '

'No!' she interrupted. 'I will not take that chance, Clive; it would not be fair to either of us. William deserves a loving wife, someone he can adore wholeheartedly and – '

'He adores *you*, Vinnie.'

'I cannot marry him, Clive! I simply cannot do it!' She began to cry again.

He shrugged. 'Well, I don't know what to say, Vinnie. This has been a shock and I will not pretend otherwise. I am disappointed.'

Yet even as he spoke the words, he was aware of a certain falseness in what he was saying. *Was* he truly disappointed? He was arguing William's case, but the words had a hollow ring to them, a disturbing fact which he pushed firmly to the back of his mind.

'Please say you *don't* despise me, Clive! Say that you forgive me.'

Clive longed to comfort her and, putting his arm round her, began to pull her towards him; then, suddenly not trusting himself, he dropped his hands to his sides, trying not to see her bewildered look.

'Of course I don't despise you, Vinnie,' he said abruptly, 'and there is nothing to forgive. But you *must* tell William and the sooner the better. He's young enough to start again and he will find someone else. It's very sad, but these things do happen.'

She stepped back from him, her reddened eyes searching his face. 'And you do truly forgive me?' she whispered.

'I cannot forgive you another person's pain,' he said quietly, recovering his composure. 'Only William can forgive you. But I do understand. You wanted to save him hurt, but you have only delayed it.'

He took her hands in his and for a moment regarded the slim fingers in silence. Then he said, 'Tell him tonight, Vinnie – '

'Tonight? Oh no, let me have time to – '

'To what, Vinnie? To decide how to tell him? No, Vinnie! You have had nearly two years to consider that. You will tell him tonight and then he can learn to live without you. Let him get on with the rest of his life.'

Vinnie tucked up an imaginary strand of her heavy gold hair – a habit which Clive had always found endearing. He turned away.

'Very well, tonight,' she said at last. 'But will I still be welcome at your home? I suppose not. William will not want to see me, will he?'

'Maybe not – at first – but he's a civilised person and he will come round if you give him time.'

There was a long silence.

'I shall miss you,' said Vinnie at last.

'Oh, I shall be around as usual,' he said lightly. 'If I do not see you at Harkwood, then I shall see you here at Foxearth.'

'I am glad of that. Oh Clive – I am so angry with myself. Poor William! I would do anything – '

'Then tell him, tonight,' said Clive.

CHAPTER TWO

On the same day, a woman walked purposefully along Wentworth Street in London. As she turned the corner into Osborne Street, she straightened her back and lifted her chin defiantly. Five years earlier, Mollie Pett had been a vivacious young woman, freckle-faced, with bright ginger hair. Now her small features bore the pallor of ill-health and the freckles on her sallow skin made her complexion seem muddy. She was thirty-one years old but looked forty, for her eyes had sunk back into the bony framework of her face and the lustre of youth had left them. Her expression was grim – her mouth was set in a hard line and her nostrils flared occasionally, betraying the fierce workings of her mind as she rehearsed the speech she was about to make.

Mollie Pett was on her way to visit Mary Bellweather, a highly respectable and well-intentioned spinster of similar age to herself. Some years earlier Mary had adopted Mollie's illegitimate son but, perversely, Mollie had never forgiven her – although she had been wholeheartedly in favour of the adoption and had accepted willingly the generous money settlement Mary had made. However, that was all in the past and now Mollie was in dire need of further financial assistance. It was for this reason that she had steeled herself to approach the house where her son Alexander now shared a very comfortable home with Mary Bellweather. Despite a brave exterior, Mollie's heart thumped uncomfortably as she turned another corner and the house came suddenly into view.

'Please don't let Alex be there,' she begged. 'Let the old cow be on her own!'

God – if he heard this simple prayer – did nothing to allay her nervousness and as she drew within twenty yards of the front door, she faltered and almost stopped. Her instincts were to turn and run from the encounter, but she knew in her heart that if she did not face up to the ordeal now, it would merely be postponed until the next day or the day after.

She paused, however, allowing herself a brief delay while she clung to a row of white-painted railings, trying to catch her breath and compose herself. Below her in the basement, the face of a maidservant peered up over the window-box with wary eyes and Mollie stuck out her tongue in the girl's direction.

'Stuck-up prune!' she muttered, but the girl's expression of distaste had reminded Mollie of her bedraggled appearance and she made a last futile effort to smarten herself, tweaking her old straw hat straight on her greasy curls and smoothing down the faded blue skirt. Tutting, she snatched up the hem and rubbed with some success at a muddy mark, then checked that on her tight-waisted red jacket the remaining buttons were correctly matched with their buttonholes. One button was missing, she noted with dismay, and as the maidservant ducked away in answer to a summons from elsewhere, Mollie nipped quickly down the area steps and picked a blue pansy from the colourful window-box. An enraged shout heralded the opening of the basement door and the appearance of an ageing butler. He shook his fist at Mollie's unrepentant back as she scuttled to the safety of the pavement once more.

'Hope your chickens die!' she shouted, then took to her heels in case he followed her up the steps. She hoped his dignity would not allow him to chase her along the street, for she had no wish to arrive at her destination pursued by an irate butler.

Reaching the safety of Mary Bellweather's front steps, she glanced back and was reassured to see his bald head disappearing below ground level once more. She straightened her clothes for a second time and tucked the stem of the pansy through the second buttonhole in place of the missing button.

Pleased with this additional touch of colour, she drew a deep breath.

'*Please* let Alex be out!' she repeated and, seizing the gleaming brass lion's head, knocked loudly four times.

Mrs Markham, Mary's housekeeper, opened the door and stared at the visitor for a moment without recognising her.

'It's me, Mollie Pett,' said Mollie, aware of the deep dismay which these words would provoke. As she expected, the kindly features of the housekeeper tightened and she uttered a shocked sound that was halfway between a groan and a gasp.

'Yes, it's me, Mollie,' she repeated. 'I can tell you're real pleased to see me. Aren't you going to ask me in? I can stand here all day and wait if you like, but the one thing I won't do is go away, so don't bother suggesting it. Don't even hope it, because I want to see her ladyship!'

Mrs Markham opened her mouth, searched vainly for words and then closed it helplessly. Enjoying the old woman's reaction, Mollie felt the beginnings of confidence.

'Well, go on,' she said. 'Tell her ladyship I'm here – tell her an old friend wants a word or two.'

The housekeeper's dismay gave way to indignation at this distortion of the facts. 'Old friend?' she cried. 'You're no friend of hers!'

They glared at one another like two dogs bristling for a fight; then suddenly Mollie leaned forward, seized the knocker and hammered it against the door. 'If you won't tell her I'm here, I shall do it myself,' she said.

Mrs Markham's hand closed over hers and forced her to relinquish the lion's head. 'There's no need for that sort of behaviour,' she began. 'Of course I shall tell Miss Bellweather that you are here.' Her voice shook with suppressed rage as she added the words which courtesy required: 'Please come in. You can wait in the morning-room.'

Mollie followed her into the spotless room, over which the rays of the afternoon sun lay like a blessing.

'Thank you,' she said sarcastically. 'Tell Miss High-and-Mighty not to hurry herself – I shan't run away.' She laughed

mirthlessly as her gaze moved around the room which she had
last seen almost eight years earlier. It had not changed. The
same antimacassars covered the same well-stuffed chairs. The
grandfather clock still stood in the corner, its spindly gold
hands at twenty-past four. The brass fender shone and so did
the fire-irons. The wooden scuttle was well-polished and filled
with neat nuggets of coal, the fireplace laid with twists of
newspaper and small kindling wood. Large – and to Mollie's
eyes hideous – china ornaments decorated the mantelpiece
and a big aspidistra in a gleaming copper container graced the
window. There was an air of serene gentility about the room
which Mollie found unnerving. Outside she heard footsteps on
the stairs.

'What on earth was all that banging?'

She recognized Mary Bellweather's voice. There was a
flurry of whispered talk and Mollie imagined Mary's constern-
ation on learning that Alexander's mother was waiting in the
morning-room.

Mollie took a quick look at herself in the large oval mirror
above the mantelpiece and her reflection did not inspire her.
She pulled a face at herself in the mirror – pushing out her
tongue, pulling her eyes into slits with her fingers – and then
noticed three photographs, each in an oval velvet frame.

One showed the head and shoulders of a plump elderly
woman in a high-necked dress of a dark material. 'Her Ma,'
Mollie muttered, guessing correctly.

The middle photograph showed what appeared to be the
same woman taken some years earlier, sitting beside a tall man
with a large white moustache. The third was of a young man.

'Alex!' she whispered, recognising her son, and she carried
it to the window to study the likeness more carefully.

She saw a good-looking boy, about sixteen years old, wearing a Norfolk jacket and trousers tucked into thick woollen
socks. He carried a shotgun, albeit self-consciously, crooked
over his left arm.

'Crikey!' she said, awed.

The features were recognisable as those of the young lad she had given up years earlier, but the face had filled out and the hair was combed back and parted into the fashionable centre style. Large eyes stared with candour into the camera and there was a hint of a smile at the corners of the firm mouth.

'Quite a little gent, aren't you?' she said and gave the photograph a hasty kiss before returning it to the mantelpiece. Almost immediately the door opened and Mary Bellweather entered the room. She was still an attractive woman, her dark hair drawn up severely above a face in which fine bone structure and delicate complexion bore mute testimony to her breeding. Mary wore a dress of slate-blue silk and Mollie envied her the soft rustle of movement as she came forward, her right hand outstretched.

'Mollie Pett, this *is* a surprise!' The manner was calm and the tone cool, but inside her head Mary's thoughts whirled chaotically and a hint of fear showed in her eyes. 'Please do sit down,' she said as Mollie, surprised, shook her hand reluctantly.

Mrs Markham closed the door quietly and Mollie waited until the housekeeper's footsteps had faded.

'Well,' said Mollie, as boldly as she could. 'You can guess why I've turned up again like a bad penny. I won't waste your time or mine – I'm skint and you're the only one as owes me.'

Mary's eyebrows rose. 'Owes you?' she repeated. 'I am not aware of any outstanding debt. Perhaps you would be good enough to – '

'*You* know what I mean,' Mollie interrupted. 'I mean you've got my son and he should be out earning for me. So you owe me!'

Mary had seated herself opposite her visitor, who sat facing the window. As the bright sunshine showed up the hollow cheeks and dull eyes of Alexander's mother, Mary felt a wave of pity for the woman which she tried at once to overcome.

'I paid you well when the adoption went through,' she said. 'I gave you enough money to start afresh. Moreover I paid – and still do pay – for your two little girls.'

'Are those girls doing all right?' Mollie asked.

'Yes, they are, but no thanks to you,' Mary told her. 'The Hearns are a kindly family and the girls are happy and well cared for.'

'And Alex?'

Mary stiffened and found her voice with difficulty. If this wretched woman were to – no, she would not think of it!

'Alexander is well and happy also,' she said. 'At present he is in Cherbourg, staying with friends. He will spend six months there and then travel to Italy for another six months. After that he will take up his place at the University of Cambridge.'

Mollie was momentarily silenced by this glittering catalogue of her son's activities.

'I hope,' Mary continued, 'that you did not expect to see him? It is obviously not possible, but in any case it would be most unwise. Surely you can see that?'

'I didn't want to see him,' said Mollie. 'I was hoping he'd be out. I just need some money.' She took a deep breath. 'I'm sick and I can't earn.'

'Sick? Ill, do you mean? You certainly do look pale.' Instinctively she moved back a little in her chair and Mollie smiled sourly.

'Oh, don't fret! It's not catching. Least, not to your sort. It's – '

'Don't!' cried Mary. 'Don't tell me. Don't talk about it!' Her voice had risen with her growing agitation. 'You had your chance,' she said. 'I warned you to make a new start, find a respectable job and keep off the streets. You can't blame me if you have ended up in this state.'

Mollie shrugged. 'I'm not blaming anybody. I'm asking you for some more money, that's all. A hundred pounds and off I go.'

'No!'

Mollie regarded her dispassionately. 'Is that your last word?'

'Yes, it is,' said Mary. 'I gave you a fair chance and I will not be blackmailed. If you didn't like it . . . oh, Mollie, how could you be such a fool? You had such a marvellous opportunity to make something of your life.'

Molly ignored the question. 'Hundred pounds is nothing to you,' she stated.

'I will *not* give it to you.' Mary stood up abruptly, as though she could speak more decisively in that position. 'If I give you money now, you will be back next year demanding more – I know your type.'

'*Do* you?' said Mollie. 'Do you really know my type? What am I then? Go on, Madam Knowall – let's hear all about my type.'

Mary swallowed, regretting her outburst. She had spoken from fear, not anger, but it was too late now. The words were out.

'Go on!' Mollie taunted. 'Let's hear all about my "type". Oh, lost your tongue, have you?'

'No, I have not lost my tongue,' Mary said. 'I will give you my impression of the kind of person I think you are, if that's what you want. I think you are greedy, feckless and entirely lacking in morals. I think you are irresponsible and lacking in finer feelings, or else you – '

It was Mollie's turn to jump to her feet, eyes blazing. 'Oh, no, I've no finer feelings – I can't bloody afford them! I'm just a whore! That's what you wanted to call me, only I expect the words stuck in your ladylike gullet. A whore! That's right! What's more, I'm ill and I'm going to die of what I've got – d'you know that, Miss High-and-Mighty? Yes, that's right – die! So you'll be well rid of me in a year or two. Cling on to that thought!'

'I'm sorry' . . . stammered Mary, her face ashen. 'I didn't know. I mean . . .'

'Course you didn't know!' cried Mary, 'because *your type* never do. They don't like to think about folks like me; it upsets their delicate stomachs! So why not spare yourself some agony of mind, *Miss* Bellweather? Why not pay me my hundred pounds and be rid of me? Then you can forget me.' She took a step forward and Mary recoiled from the hate in the woman's ravaged eyes. 'Because if you don't pay me, I'll tell you what I'm going to do – I shall take myself down to Foxearth and – '

'No! I forbid it!'

Mary put out a hand to the mantelpiece to steady herself. The interview was taking on nightmare proportions. Bertie Harris was at Foxearth – could Mollie possibly know that?

'You can't stop me!' cried Mollie triumphantly. 'No one can. It's a free country. I'll knock on the door and say, "Tell Miss Vinnie the mother of her precious Bertie's child is here." Oh, that'll set the cat among the bleeding pigeons! I can just imagine the look on her face – someone like me and her precious brother!'

Mary sat down heavily, a hand to her mouth. 'How did you find out?' she whispered.

Mollie shrugged. 'A word here – a word there. I've known for nearly a year now. I'm not silly, you know – I may be greedy and feckless and all those other things you called me – '

'I'm sorry,' repeated Mary.

'But I'm *not* silly. I reckon Vinnie Lawrence would be really interested to know she had a nephew. I bet she'd pay a hundred pounds to know that – and another hundred to know who he is and where he is.'

Mary made an enormous effort to pull herself together. Exactly how much did this wretched woman know? If Mollie knew that Bertie was Vinnie's brother, did she also know that he was back from India and staying at Foxearth? Did she know that he had married? Presumably not – or had she reserved her trump card? Was she clever enough?

'So,' said Mollie flatly, 'a hundred pounds or I tell Vinnie Lawrence about Alex. Make up your mind.'

Mary bowed her head, terrified that her thoughts would show in her face.

'Let me think,' she begged. 'Just for a moment. This is all so sudden.'

At all costs she must prevent Mollie from visiting Foxearth. Bertie must never know that he had had a child by this awful woman – nor must he know that the child was now Mary's adopted son. The thought that Bertie might one day discover the truth and reclaim Alexander had haunted her dreams since the day she had discovered the boy's full identity. He was

Mary's life and she could never let him go.

Suddenly Mollie picked up a small china sweet-dish and dropped it into the fireplace where it cracked into two uneven parts. 'Don't take all day,' she said, 'or I might drop something else.'

Mary choked back the furious words which sprang to her lips. Ignoring the broken dish, she stood up slowly.

'I will give you ten pounds a month,' she said, 'for as long as you live. Give me an address and I will post it to you on the first day of each month. But if you ever set foot in Foxearth or attempt to get in touch with Vinnie or Bertie – '

'Twenty,' interrupted Mollie.

'Ten,' said Mary. 'Ten pounds on the first of each month until you die. Not a penny more, and if you break your part of the bargain the money stops. Is that understood?'

'Fifteen,' said Mollie.

'Ten, and pick up the sweet-dish. I may be able to get it repaired; I hope so.' She held her breath as Mollie hesitated.

Mollie gave her a look of pure hate. 'I'll live as long as I bloody well can!' she said. 'You're a hard bitch, Mary Bellweather, so don't fool yourself otherwise.'

'It's agreed, then?'

'I suppose so,' muttered Mollie, picking up the pieces of china and venomously slamming them down on the mantelpiece.

Mary breathed again.

*

When the woman had gone, Mary leaned back against the front door as Mrs Markham came hurrying out of the kitchen.

'Is it all right, ma'am?' she asked. 'Oh, you look dreadfully pale! Is it going to be all right – for Master Alexander, I mean?'

'Yes, Mrs Markham, it's going to be fine. Please bring me a pot of tea – the Lapsang. I will be in the study.'

The housekeeper beamed. 'Very well, ma'am, and I'm so glad. So very, very glad!'

As Mrs Markham bustled off, the fright and rage which

Mary had fought down surfaced suddenly and she let out a stifled cry of defeat. She believed herself to be a good Christian; she distributed clothes to the poor and needy and she genuinely cared for those less fortunate than herself, but at that moment, shaken and humiliated, she wanted only to run after Mollie Pett and strangle her with her bare hands. She stood for a moment, breathing heavily, one hand to her heart. She would *not*, she told herself, allow that pathetic creature to upset her.

Passing the morning-room door, Mary caught sight of something blue lying on the carpet – it was the pansy which Mollie had worn in her buttonhole. Slowly she went back into the room and stared down at it. 'It's only a flower', she thought, but the connection with her unwelcome visitor, gave it hideous associations and Mary fancied its bright face stared back, mocking her. She longed to grind it underfoot, and dared not.

'It's *only* a flower!' This time she whispered the words, but the sound did nothing to reassure her, and, taking up the coal-tongs, she determined to pick up the flower and drop it into the coal-scuttle. With the tongs in her hand, however, she found she could not do it and, instead, stepped across to pour herself a glass of sherry with shaking hands. She sipped the drink gratefully, staring out of the window and waiting for Mollie's hateful image to fade. Then she called Mrs Markham into the room, told her to remove the flower and watched as the house-keeper bore it away, held distastefully between a plump finger and thumb.

CHAPTER THREE

That same evening the kitchen at Foxearth hummed with activity as the evening meal was served. Edie, washing up, pushed a stray lock of hair behind her right ear with a soapy hand and then grumbled as the water ran down her arm towards her elbow.

'Get on with it,' said Cook. 'The sooner it's done, the sooner you can go back to bed.'

'I should never have left it,' said Edie, her tone resentful. 'I should have stayed in me bed. I shall catch me death!'

'Catch your death? Don't talk nonsense, girl!'

'I will,' she insisted. 'Why can't Bertha wash up?'

'Because she's serving at table, that's why.'

'Janet, then. She could've washed up.'

'Janet's looking after the Colonel, as you well know.'

Cook lifted a leg of pork to the meat dish and began to surround it with roast potatoes.

'Well, I've got a tempercher,' Edie protested. 'The doctor said I had. I shouldn't be down here washing up with a tempercher.'

'We've all got *temperatures*,' said Mrs Tallant. 'If we hadn't, we'd be dead. Yours is just a bit high, that's all. You're hardly at death's door, so do be quiet and get on with it. As Cook says, you can go back to bed as soon as the washing-up's done. Bertha will bring up your dinner on a tray – how would that be?'

A broad smile replaced Edie's normally vacant expression. 'What, have me dinner in bed? Like the Colonel?'

Mrs Tallant nodded. '*If* you get on now without moaning.'

Edie rubbed her wet arm with a wet hand and then discovered that soapy water had trickled down the dry arm. For a moment she surveyed her arms despairingly and then, remembering the treat in store, seized the brush, plunged her hands once more into the sinkful of soapy water and attacked the soup saucepan with a rush of energy and enthusiasm. She was *not* moaning and she wanted to be *seen* to be not moaning. Dinner on a tray in bed like the Colonel! The world had suddenly taken on an unusually rosy hue.

Bertha came back into the kitchen with the soup bowls and unloaded them on the draining board. 'What's up with Vinnie?' she demanded.

'Not "Vinnie",' said Mrs Tallant. ' "The mistress" or "Mrs Lawrence", if you please! You've been here two years now and you ought to know better. She may have been Vinnie to you once, but now she is "the mistress", "ma'am" or "Mrs Lawrence".'

' "The mistress," then,' Bertha amended. 'She's got a face like a wet week and she's left half her soup.'

Cook looked up anxiously. 'Left her soup? What's wrong with it?'

'Nothing, I shouldn't think,' said Bertha. 'Everyone else has finished it up.'

Edie took up a half-empty soup bowl and drank from it noisily. 'Nothing wrong with it,' she told them cheerfully.

Mrs Tallant rolled her eyes. 'How many times have you been told not to do that?' she demanded.

'I forgot!'

'You *always* forget. You're worse than a dog! Anybody would think you didn't get enough to eat.' Mrs Tallant turned her attention to the dinner, inspecting it as usual before it was carried in to the dining-room.

'Parsnips,' she said. 'Where are the parsnips, Cook?'

'Parsnips? It was turnips, not parsnips. They're here.' She lifted the lid of one of the three tureens.

'It was parsnips,' said Mrs Tallant, who would not admit that her memory was failing. 'But never mind. The turnips look very nice.'

Cook bit her lip, holding back an exclamation of annoyance. Mrs Tallant was going through her 'funny time,' she reckoned, and excuses had to be made for her but she, Cook, had long since put all that sort of bother behind her.

Bertha disappeared with the tray of vegetable dishes, then scurried back again for the meat and the gravy-boat. When all was safely delivered to the dining-table, she came back to the kitchen with the news that 'the mistress' looked as grim as before.

'Perhaps she's sickening for something,' Mrs Tallant suggested.

'Perhaps *she's* got a tempercher,' said Edie. 'Like me! Perhaps she's caught my tempercher off me.'

'You can't catch a temperature,' said Bertha. 'Can you?'

''Course not!' said Cook emphatically.

At that moment Janet came into the kitchen, giggling. 'The Colonel says top marks for the egg custard,' she told Cook, 'but if you give him steamed fish again he's going to have you court-martialled!'

Edie gave a screech of laughter and the others grinned.

'Doctor's orders,' said Cook, mortified.

Janet laughed. 'I told him that. He said the doctor could face the same firing-squad.'

'He's a game old boy!' said Cook. 'I'd give him anything he wanted if I dared, but I'd have the mistress down on me like a ton of bricks if I did.'

'Don't worry yourself,' said Janet, stacking the dirty plates for Edie's attention. '*He* knows that. He couldn't eat anything else if you gave it to him, but he likes to make a bit of a protest now and again.' She returned the cruet to its place on the dresser and sighed. 'I don't know how he keeps alive on a few mouthfuls of fish and a bit of egg custard. He's become so frail these last few months. I keep wondering how much longer will we have him with us. Nearly ninety! It's a fine old age.'

Bertha said, 'Something's up with Vin – I mean the mistress. She's sitting in there looking as miserable as sin and has hardly touched her food.'

To her surprise, Janet only nodded. 'She'll be giving that poor man his marching orders,' she said. 'I'll wager you that's it.'

They all stared at her in astonishment. 'Whatever makes you say a thing like that?' cried Mrs Tallant. 'Do you know something, Janet?'

Janet shook her head. 'I don't *know* anything,' she admitted, 'but I've got a pretty good idea. Vinnie came up to see the Colonel just before dinner and I was asked to leave the room.'

'And you listened at the keyhole!' cried Edie.

'I did *not*!' said Janet indignantly. 'At least, I didn't actually listen, but I couldn't help catching the odd word here and there. I heard William's name more than once and when I went back Vinnie had gone downstairs and the Colonel looked very upset.'

'You never said.' Cook looked hurt at this betrayal.

'I don't have to tell you everything,' said Janet, 'but he was upset and so was the mistress. I had a feeling something was up.'

Cook settled her large hands on her hips and shook her head. 'Mind you,' she said, 'it's been that long since they got engaged.'

'Oh, poor Mr le Brun!' cried Bertha. 'Why won't she marry him, I wonder? He's such a *nice* man.'

'Niceness isn't everything,' said Cook darkly. 'I wouldn't marry a man just because he was *nice*. Oh, don't give me that old-fashioned look, Bertha. I've had chances in my time and I've turned down some nice young men. There's more to marriage than niceness.'

The others were not convinced. 'Well, I think it's a crying shame,' said Bertha. 'I think Vinnie's real mean. We were all looking forward to having him for master – '

'Hang on a bit!' said Mrs Tallant. 'Don't go jumping the gun, Bertha! We don't know for sure, so let's save the grumbles until we do. In the meantime, Edie, you hurry up with that washing-up and there'll be you-know-what on a tray for you. And Cook, let's have that syrup pudding out of the cloth. There'll be time for gossiping later.'

*

When dinner was over, William and Vinnie walked through the hop-gardens. As usual, they held hands but even while they moved wordlessly through the lacy green aisles, unspoken words leaped between them. William, his heart heavy, felt the tension in the small hand that clasped his and noted the unnatural tilt of Vinnie's head and the reluctant way she placed one foot in front of the other, as though each step carried her nearer to something she wished to avoid. During the meal she had signalled desperation with her eyes and he felt a deep foreboding.

Between the rows of hops the ground was deeply rutted from the wheels of the alley bodge and other carts which had made their way along the rows during heavy rain earlier in the year. A sudden sun and high winds had locked the earth into ridges – a trap for the unwary. Vinnie, her thoughts on her confession, tripped and would have fallen if William had not steadied her.

She thanked him and prepared to walk on, but William's hand restrained her.

'Here will do as well as anywhere, Vinnie,' he said gently. 'I know you have something to say, and I'm trying to help you to say it.'

With an agitated movement, she put up a hand to her mouth in an effort to hide the tremor of her lips.

'Oh, no!' she said. 'Not here. Not yet!'

'Here,' he said, 'and now. I didn't think you were a coward, Vinnie. It's about us, isn't it? Something is troubling you. I can't help you if you won't tell me what it is.'

Vinnie looked up at him, surprised at his quiet manner, and reflected that perhaps he had more of his father in him than she had thought.

'I don't think you can help me,' she said. 'Some things cannot be mended. Some problems cannot be solved.' She sighed heavily and William put an arm round her dejected shoulders.

'Are you wise, William?' she asked. 'Oh, I do hope you are.'

'Try me,' he said, his arm tightening round her. 'Or if you will not tell me, let me guess what it is that makes you frown so dreadfully.'

Vinnie swallowed hard and tried to remember how she had intended to broach the subject. William, seeing her distress, tried to help her.

'It's Foxearth, isn't it?' he said. 'You are reluctant to share Foxearth with me? Is that it, because if so I – '

'No, William,' she broke in, 'it's not Foxearth.'

'Then is it children, Vinnie? I have this dream of a large and happy family, but which man hasn't? But I hear that childbirth is – well, a painful business and if it's the thought of more children that frightens you – '

'Oh, William!' Vinnie said miserably. 'It's nothing like that.'

'Give me just one child of my own, Vinnie,' he pleaded. 'We already have three. Four will be enough – four healthy children and I will be content. Is it the childbirth, Vinnie? No? Oh God, Vinnie, why do you look so stricken? Look, I shall not move from this spot until you have told me what's troubling you. I cannot bear to see you so unhappy. I want to make you happy, Vinnie, and to protect you from the bad things in life.'

Vinnie closed her eyes and blurted out the first words that came to her.

'I don't think I will make you happy, William,' she stammered. 'I'm not the right woman for you. It has all been a mistake.'

'Vinnie!' He was appalled

'William, please!' she begged. 'Call me what you like, I deserve it all. Oh yes I do, William. I should have told you before, but I am so fond of you. So terribly fond of you!'

'You *love* me, Vinnie!'

'No, William.'

'I tell you "Yes," Vinnie.' His eyes were too bright, his voice too sharp. 'You do love me, Vinnie; you have told me so a hundred times. You cannot *not* love me. You are just frightened – of taking the final step. That is not unusual,

Vinnie; a last-minute panic, that's all. Oh God, you *can't* stop loving me now. Everyone knows. Everyone will wonder. They will . . . '

As the full horror of the situation dawned on him, he fell suddenly silent, beseeching her with his eyes. Vinnie suffered with him.

'Vinnie!' he whispered at last. 'Say it isn't true, that you don't mean it. You *do* love me, Vinnie. You *do*!'

With a wild gesture he pulled her into his arms, crushing her so tightly that she bit back a cry of pain. His lips were close against her hair and she heard the choked sob that was instantly stifled.

'Don't leave me, Vinnie!' he begged. 'Don't do it! It will work for us – I know we can be happy because we love each other, Vinnie, you know we do. Don't say these terrible things. Don't break my heart!'

Vinnie's own agony of mind matched his as he pleaded brokenly with her. She was horrified at the effect of her words and utterly dismayed by the extent of his misery. One word from her would rescue him from the depths of his unhappiness, but that would only lead him into another grief – that of a loveless marriage.

'You deserve someone who will love you,' she whispered. 'I am not the one, William. Believe me, I would wed you if I thought we might be happy together, but I know how hard it is for two people to share a life.'

'You are afraid!' he cried.

'No, not afraid, William. Aware.'

'You are afraid!' he said. His wretchedness was turning to bitterness. 'You are afraid you will not be happy with me, because you think it will be the way it was with Julian – but I am not Julian, Vinnie. I am William and I swear it will be different. Julian was not right for you; you told me so yourself.'

Vinnie stared at him. 'I told you *that*?'

'Yes, you did, Vinnie.' He spoke rapidly, recklessly. 'You told me how it was all wrong from the start and that you didn't know he was marrying you. That you were only half-conscious and he thought you were dying, and that was why he married you – he didn't know you would ever live together. Isn't that the truth, Vinnie?'

Too late Vinnie regretted her confidence. 'I – oh, William, it wasn't quite like that,' she stammered.

'Yes, it *was*!' he cried. 'It was exactly like that and it was no way to start a life together. No wonder it failed. No wonder he couldn't make you happy.'

'William, stop it!' Vinnie's voice rose, too, as a note of near hysteria crept into William's words. 'That's not how it was, he did make me happy. I never said that our marriage failed. We were happy for much of the time. I don't think I ever said it failed – did I?'

'You *hinted* at it, then,' he cried. 'You cannot deny it, Vinnie. Oh, don't deny it, for I swear it is the truth. You are afraid to risk marriage with me because your life with Julian was not all that it should have been. Face facts, Vinnie! Look at it the way it is and admit that I am right.'

She looked at him, her eyes dark with pain. 'No, William,' she said, 'I cannot do that. You are painting it blacker than it really was.'

He clutched triumphantly at the slip. 'Oh, then it *was* black! You see, Vinnie! All you have to do is trust me. With us it will be different. With us it will be so good because we will start off in the right way, loving and trusting each other. For God's sake, Vinnie, why do you still shake that stubborn head of yours? Can't you understand what I'm telling you? That marriage failed because you and Julian were not suited. You were both too young, too far apart. You were Cinderella and he was the handsome prince! It was a fairy story, Vinnie! *Our* marriage will be – '

But suddenly Vinnie's eyes had a cold glint in them. His rash words had offended her, for they had come too near the truth for comfort. What he had said about her marriage was true in many respects. She had admitted as much to herself, but to hear it described so ungenerously by another – that was not to be borne. Vinnie told herself she was turning him down because she did not love him and could not risk making them both unhappy by pretending otherwise. Nor would she wait for love to grow, because it might not. There was no reason to discuss her marriage with Julian.

'It's no use, William,' she said firmly. 'I will not marry you. I am truly sorry that you should take it like this. I had hoped against hope that you would understand and trust my judgment.'

'Oh, I understand!' cried William. His face was pale and a variety of emotions struggled for mastery in his eyes. He was in turn bewildered, humiliated and angry. With a flash of insight, Vinnie could see that the last emotion was easier for him to bear. Then let him be angry with her, she decided wearily, for she deserved his anger; she certainly could not bear his despair.

'I tried to tell you as kindly as I could,' she went on, 'but you refuse to understand what I am trying to say. I have come to realise that I don't love you, William. The feelings I have for you are respect, delight in your company, deep affection –'

'To *hell* with your deep affection!' he shouted. 'And to hell with your respect!'

'I mistook those feelings for love, William,' she continued. 'It isn't easy to admit that I have made a mistake and I cannot ask you to forgive me.'

'I'm glad of that!' he cried, 'because I don't believe a word of it, Vinnie Lawrence, and I don't forgive you! You love me, but you are afraid: afraid of love, afraid to trust me, afraid of your own shadow!'

She watched him, helpless to ease his pain and reluctant to dispel his anger because she wanted him to walk away from the encounter with dignity. It was so terribly hard for him. Her own brief anger had faded, leaving her full of self-reproach. She *did* admire him tremendously and she had not wanted to hurt him. Love, she thought wearily, has a lot to answer for.

William broke off and took a deep gulp of air like a drowning man who is surfacing. Vinnie made no effort to defend herself.

Let him work out his anger, she thought. She deserved his scorching words and the hostility in his eyes. 'Just don't let me cry,' she prayed inwardly.

William controlled his anger with an effort.

'Vinnie' he said, 'I will not argue with you any more and I will not plead. I will ask you for one last time. Think carefully, Vinnie, for God's sake, because I shall never ask you again and if you turn me down it will be a mistake which I think you will live to regret. I still love you, Vinnie, and I am asking you to marry me.'

Vinnie did not lower her gaze. 'I am deeply sorry, William,' she said, 'but I don't love you enough.'

For a long moment he looked into her eyes; then he stepped forward as though to give her a farewell kiss and for a moment Vinnie's heart soared, for she believed herself forgiven. But he hesitated and then turned and strode away – his head high, his shoulders set in a hard line. She watched him until he passed out of her sight to be hidden by the dense greenery. She had sent him away and the chance of love had gone with him. The future loomed dark and cold . . . Vinnie was alone again.

CHAPTER FOUR

The following day Mrs Bryce made her way across the dewy grass which was sparkling in the early-morning sunshine. When she reached the hive she laid a clean white cloth on the grass beside it, on which she placed a blunt knife; beside this she set down the smoker. She was already dressed for what she called the 'honeying'. In addition to protecting her face with a piece of net curtain draped over a wide-brimmed hat and her hands with gauntlet gloves which had seen better days, a pair of old leather gaiters which had once belonged to her husband covered the lower part of her legs. Fortunately for her peace of mind, the latter were decorously hidden by her long skirt and petticoat, for although she expected to be unobserved it was always possible that the fish-man might call earlier than usual. Tuesday was his day and she had never known him to miss.

'Now then, let's see what you've got for me,' she murmured soothingly as a few bees deviated enquiringly from their flight path in order to investigate her.

'It's only me,' she told them 'so don't go getting yourselves in a tizzy.'

Taking up the smoker, she lifted the lid to make sure the rags were still smouldering. Then she squeezed the bellows which formed part of the smoker and produced enough smoke to puff around the hive entrance. Having thus quietened the bees, she used the blunt knife to ease off the roof of the hive; then she carefully lifted the roof to one side, lowered it on to the grass and puffed more smoke into the top of the hive.

Now that she had exposed the top chamber with its parallel rows of frames, Mrs Bryce lifted each frame and examined it to see how many of the tiny cells had been filled with honey. This was easy to tell, for each full cell was capped with a pale layer of wax. The frames that were full or nearly full she lifted out and laid on the white cloth; the others were returned to the chamber. In all she took five frames and then, with another puff of smoke – for the bees were getting a little flustered by her activities – she replaced the roof of the hive. Several of the bees clung to her veil, but she brushed them off gently with a practised hand.

Vinnie had given her the hive – complete with swarm – as a birthday present five years ago and Clive le Brun, himself an enthusiast, had initiated her into the mysteries of bee-keeping. Now she could rely on having perhaps twenty jars of soft brown honey most years, half of which she sold to implement her meagre income. There was a strong bond of affection between Vinnie and Mrs Bryce, for it was she who had taken in five-year-old Vinnie when her mother had been drowned. The Lawrences at Foxearth had paid for the child's keep, and although Vinnie had never called her anything but 'Mrs Bryce,' she had looked upon her as a mother.

'Well, you did very well for me, thank you,' Mrs Bryce told the bees. 'We shall be extracting that this evening and then in the morning we'll put on the lids and Bob's your uncle!'

She believed in talking to them. Clive le Brun had assured her that it was essential to have a rapport with them if the bees were to do their best. Mrs Bryce, a little in awe of the tall hop factor, had agreed solemnly and to her surprise had found herself developing a feeling of respect and something approaching affection for the small furry creatures which filled the summer garden with their humming. She worried about them in the winter and watched anxiously for the early spring blossoms, in case the bees emerged from their winter rest to find insufficient flowers waiting for them on their first tentative flight.

As the old lady wrapped the full frames in the white cloth, she thought with a sigh of her only son Tom who had killed himself some years earlier. She had lost her husband and then her son, but still she had Tom's children. Bertha, Tom's eldest girl, was now up at Foxearth as Vinnie's parlourmaid: a nice settled job for her. The Bryce family had been through hard times, she reflected. Who would have thought they could have survived those dreadful years, but they had. All except her husband and poor Tom!

'Still, it sorted itself out,' she told the bees resignedly as she took up the white bundle in her arms and prepared to stagger back to the house with it. The smoker and the knife she would collect later.

'A fine old muddle,' she repeated, 'but it sorted itself out. It could have been worse I suppose, but . . . ' She sighed heavily. 'My poor Tom,' she whispered. 'I haven't forgotten you, lovey! Don't you ever think I have. And don't fret about the kids, for they're happy enough and Rose, too, with her new husband. I'll say that for Andy – he's doing his best for your little family – but we've not forgotten you, Tom. Oh no, lovey, we'll never do that. Never in a million years!'

Once she had talked to her dead husband to ward off the loneliness of widowhood. Now she talked to her dead son and found it brought him back momentarily from the far-off place to which he had gone. This frequent polishing kept his image bright.

As she made her way up the path to the back door, she sighed again. Tom was gone but Rose, his wife, had given her five lovely grandchildren by Tom and another one by Andy Roberts. Mrs Bryce shook her head. She did not blame Rose for marrying again, not with all those children to support; Andy was a good man and it was not as though Rose could help Tom by staying single. He was beyond help now – at peace, she hoped.

Inside the tiny kitchen she put the frames on the table and gingerly began to remove her veil and gloves. The gaiters could stay until she had let out the chickens and fetched in a few beetroot for the salad. On her fingers she counted the people who were coming to the 'honey treading' – Vinnie's name for the process of extraction. There would be Rose's children, including Bertha (Tuesday was her evening off), Rose herself, Vinnie's three children and possibly Vinnie herself. Afterwards they would have a bit of supper and drink some parsnip wine and the children would have home-made ginger beer. In a more cheerful frame of mind, she went out into the garden to pull the beetroot. They were as big as tennis balls – larger than she liked them; she would have to boil them for an extra half-hour.

By six-thirty that evening Mrs Bryce's kitchen was full to bursting point. Tommy (Rose's eldest boy) turned the handle of the extractor, while Rose slid a practised knife upwards across the surface of the next frame to remove the wax cappings and reveal the honey within. Bertha watched from the far side of the kitchen, trying to keep a distance between her second-best dress and the sticky honey which tended to spread in all directions. Louise sat on her lap, watching the noisy proceedings with a slight frown that wrinkled the bridge of her small nose. As always she was immaculate, pert and assured, and she intended to remain so.

Mrs Bryce, standing beside Bertha, put her hands over her ears as the extractor handle whirled and the extractor itself shuddered and boomed.

'Not so fast, Tommy!' she bellowed for the third time. 'I've told you – you'll burst open the frames! Slow down, for goodness' sake!'

He grinned up at her impudently, the image of his father, but made no attempt to obey her.

'Tommy!' cried Rose. 'Have you gone deaf suddenly? Your Grandma says slow down. Now do it!'

Louise added her weight to the argument. 'You're hurting my ears Tommy! Stop it at once!'

Tommy put out his tongue at her and Bertha, nervously aware that Louise was 'from the big house', cried, 'You stop that, Tommy!'

Rose finished the preparation of the frame and held it up for approval.

'That's a good one,' said Mrs Bryce. 'Now Master James can

have a go at turning the handle', (she ignored Tommy's grumble) 'and who wants to get the next frame ready?'

Shyly young Edward put up his hand, but as he was too young Rose offered to help him. While they were thus engaged Tommy was sent out to shut up the chickens, two of the girls were despatched to pick some raspberries and Mrs Bryce and Bertha continued their discussion which had been interrupted yet again.

'But whyever won't she?' cried Mrs Bryce, having learned with dismay of Vinnie's rejection of William. 'Whatever's got into the girl? No one could wish for a nicer young man – good respectable family, money – what more does she want?'

'Don't ask me,' said Bertha, 'but she's been crying her eyes out all day. You should see her face – a proper sight, it is!'

'Oh dear! Poor soul!' Mrs Bryce was torn between pity and exasperation. 'She's always been so headstrong.'

'Who?' interposed Louise, turning her saucer eyes on Mrs Bryce's face.

'No one you know,' said Bertha hastily.

'Who's headstrong?' the child persisted. 'What is head-strong?'

'Never you mind,' said Mrs Bryce. 'Wouldn't you like to go out with the others and pick raspberries?'

'No, thank you.'

Mrs Bryce sighed. 'Well, sit quiet then,' she said, 'and don't keep asking questions. Some things aren't for little ears.' She turned to Bertha and said behind her hand, 'This one's going to be a little madam when she's older. Too clever by half, she is! Vinnie will have her work cut out to keep her in her place in a few years' time.'

Briefly, and with reluctance, she then returned her attention to the honey extractor once more. Inside the large metal drum, the frame was being rotated by the action of the handle and the honey was being thrown off the comb by the centrifugal force. It then ran down the sides of the drum to collect in a depression at the bottom whence it flowed out, when released, through a tap and into a large brown jug. From the jug it went into the newly-washed jars which waited on the tray on the other side of the sink.

'You're going a bit too slow, James love,' Rose was saying. 'Like this, look. Turn the handle a bit faster or the honey won't come out. That's better!'

'Is that jug nearly full?' asked Mrs Bryce. 'I'd better take it. No, I'll do it, thanks, Rose. Pouring's tricky work. It's surprising how heavy a jug full of honey can be and you need a steady hand or it gets everywhere.'

Louise, after long reflection, piped up again. 'Who's been crying?' she asked. 'Mama?'

Bertha's mouth opened and shut and she looked at her grandmother in alarm.

'Now then, Louise!' said Mrs Bryce hastily. 'My big box of ribbons is up in the front bedroom. Would you like to have a sort through and see if you can find one you like?'

'Yes, please.'

Obediently forgetting her awkward question, Louise slid from Bertha's lap and set off at once for the stairs. Mrs Bryce sighed as the small blonde head disappeared.

'She's all ears,' she grumbled, 'and bright as a button. Now tell me quick before she comes down again. What more do you know?'

As she talked she was steadying the big jug from which the warm liquid honey flowed thickly into each jar; it was full of air bubbles, but they would rise to the top overnight and in the morning a thin pale 'crust' would form on top of the honey, speckled yellow and purple from the clover amongst which the bees had foraged.

'Not much to tell,' said Bertha. 'All we know is that she told Mrs Tallant the engagement was off and she didn't want it discussed – poor William le Brun hasn't been seen since, nor his father.'

'She *is* a silly child,' said Mrs Bryce. 'For a widow with three children to behave like that! Sending away a good man. Mind you, it doesn't really surprise me; William's very young for his years, not a bit like his father. Now there's a man with real character, if you know what I mean. I've always *respected* Clive le Brun. Tom did, too. But there you are, Vinnie said, "Yes," to William and now she's blowing hot, blowing cold. If I was William le Brun, I'd stay away – it might bring her to her senses. I mean, she's no chicken, is she? Nearly thirty and – '

'She's only twenty-seven,' said Bertha, 'or is it twenty-eight?'

Mrs Bryce snorted. 'Well, whatever! I had more sense than her when I was *seven*, let alone twenty-seven! Good husbands don't grow on trees – she'll find that out for herself.'

'Cook's that upset,' continued Bertha, giggling. 'These last two years she's been buttering up William with all his favourite foods – lime jelly and lemon snaps – and now it looks as if he won't be master after all!' She dipped a finger into the nearest pot of honey and sucked it.

'Stop that!' said Mrs Bryce automatically, adding, 'What's it like?'

'Like honey,' Bertha grinned.

'Good, is it?'

'Honey's honey, isn't it?'

'Well, that's where you're wrong, young madam! There's thickness and smoothness and colour and flavour and – '

'Well, then, it's thick and smooth and brown and tastes like honey!' She ducked as her grandmother took a playful swipe at her head. Then upstairs in the bedroom, Rose's new baby began to cry and Bertha was on her feet immediately.

'I'll see to her, Ma,' she told Rose. 'I bet Miss Louise has woken her up.'

James complained that his arm ached and his place at the handle was immediately taken by Edward. Tommy came in from the garden and prepared the next frame and Bertha brought down the baby to Rose to be fed. Honey flowed on until nineteen of the jars were filled. A twentieth jar was half-filled and traditionally this was shared by the children – a large spoonful each. When at last all the cleaning-up was done, the big demijohn of parsnip wine was opened and the little party squashed itself round the table for a salad supper with crusty home-made bread. Only Mrs Bryce missed Vinnie's presence at the feast and she, raising her eyes heavenwards, urged God to bring the silly girl to her senses before it was too late.

*

Colonel Henry Lawrence was a very pale shadow of his former self but Janet, devoted to the frail old man, made regular references to the more exciting periods of his past life. She would seize whatever chance presented itself to remind him about his youth, his years in the Army as a cavalry officer and what he loved to call his 'naughty' weekends when he was on leave with fellow officers, sampling the heady delights of the London music halls and the less heady but equally satisfying delights of the popular eating-houses.

Having outlived Queen Victoria, whose birthday he shared, the Colonel no longer boasted about his age and Janet was careful never to refer to dates when they reminisced. Daily she saw signs that he might not be with them much longer, although she did not put this impression into words, nor did she share it with anyone else. His appetite was bird-like and he had no real interest in his food, so occasionally Janet would spoon-feed him, pretending that he was a fractious child and she an exasperated parent. On this occasion, the Colonel's meal consisted of steamed plaice, carrots and creamed potatoes, followed by semolina and jam. The old man ate slowly, his appetite further diminished by a small but persistent ache in an upper right molar which was not responding to Janet's frequent applications of oil of cloves.

'Fish and more fish!' he said. 'I'm beginning to feel like an ancient tom-cat, too old to catch a decent mouse.'

'But I reckon you had a fair old appetite when you were younger,' said Janet.

His pale, watery eyes lit up at her words, as she had known they would.

'A fair old appetite? I should say I did, eh? When I was soldiering I would out-eat the lot of them! Where the devil d'you put it all, they'd ask me. Hollow legs, I'd tell 'em! Hollow legs, eh?' He laughed, began to cough, then laughed again. 'Game pie, that was one of my favourites. Oh, and pork – a nice leg of pork with crackling! Oh, I used to enjoy a bit of crackling!' He laughed again, cheered by the memories. 'We'd go to the music halls and then afterwards we'd eat. Oysters, a couple of steaks or a plate of roast beef – but it had to be just right, mind. Pink and bloody in the middle, or I'd send it back. I didn't order leather, I'd tell 'em! Appetite? I could eat like a horse in those days. Like a damned horse, Janet!'

Janet nodded. She could not imagine life without him and the certainty of his approaching demise weighed down her own usually high spirits. To the Colonel, however, she presented a cheerful face, but the other servants suffered increasingly from her bouts of depression and irritability. She had no family or husband of her own, having devoted herself to the job of caring for the Colonel.

'Just one more spoonful,' she told him, scraping the last of the buttered carrots into the remaining mashed potato. 'Open wide, now! I don't want any of your old nonsense. You've been very good today.'

Obligingly he opened his mouth and Janet slid the spoon between his worn teeth. His eyes smiled at her as he turned over the food in his mouth and then swallowed it.

'Do I get a pat on the head?' he asked mockingly, 'for being a good boy?'

She patted the bald and freckled head with its wispy fringe of white hairs. What she *wanted* to do was hug back some life into him, but she knew it was impossible – out of the question. She was merely his nurse. The sad thing was that nobody hugged him but, grieved though she was by the fact, she understood how it had come about. In his younger days he had been a formidable figure and the children, Julian and Eva, had been greatly in awe of him. His wife, Christina, had not loved him, reserving her affections for her lover. The pattern of physical affection had never been established and now it would seem out of place. She returned the plate to the tray which stood on top of the blanket box and exchanged it for the dish of semolina and raspberry jam. The old man screwed up his face in an expression of disgust.

'Take it away!' he told her. 'I can't bear it. Mish, mash, mush! That's all I get these days. What's wrong with a nice bit of beef and some fried onions, eh? What's wrong with *that*?'

'Doctor won't allow it,' said Janet. 'Now do be good and eat this up – I shall catch it from Cook if I take it down again.'

He winked a pale eye. 'You eat it, there's a good girl!' he told her. 'You always do and you know you love it.'

Janet sighed. 'But look at me! I'm as fat as a pig already. Eating up your semolina every time . . . oh well, all right then. But this is the very last time and I mean it.'

She gave the mixture a brisk stir and began to eat the resultant pink mess with great relish.

'Oh, I nearly forgot,' she told him between mouthfuls. 'The mistress is coming up to see you tonight. She's got some news for you.'

'News? What news?'

'She doesn't tell me everything,' said Janet, 'but I do know it's about a letter that came this morning. I heard her telling her brother that she would discuss it with you later on.'

'Hmm. A letter, eh?'

'Sounds exciting,' she said, finishing the semolina and putting the empty dish with the dinner plate. She took his table napkin, folded it neatly and rolled it into the silver ring, then brushed the counterpane for non-existent crumbs.

'Shall I brush your hair, sir?'

'Brush my hair? Janet, I haven't got any hair – '

'You have got a bit round the edge,' she protested, but just then there was a knock on the door.

'Oh goodness – here she is, sir! Now, are you comfortable?' He nodded and she called, 'Come in, ma'am. We're all ready for you.'

With a last smile at the Colonel, Janet picked up the tray and departed with it as Vinnie came into the room, pulled a chair up to the bedside and sat down.

A week had passed since her conversation with William and during that time she had heard no word from him. Clive had telephoned once, but she had not been at home to take the call. To some extent she had mastered her emotions and only her eyes gave the lie to her apparent composure – they were dark with remorse and still luminous from her earlier tears. However, today she smiled cheerfully enough and held up a letter for the Colonel to see. She explained that it came from a firm of estate agents in London and concerned a certain building in Whitechapel which had recently come on to the market and was available for the sum of eight hundred pounds. The property consisted of a former brewery – 'Now extinct, but much of the equipment is still there,' Vinnie told him – and a small tap-room at ground level.

'The tap-room is called the "Barley Tap" ' said Vinnie. 'It's been closed for nearly a year but the agent says there would be no problem in getting a new licence. We only have to contact them and they will arrange to show us over the property.'

For the past nine months Vinnie had been looking for a small brewery in London which Bertie and Beatrice could manage and which Foxearth could supply with hops. The original idea had been hers, but the Colonel's approval was necessary since he was to fund the venture and to Vinnie's relief he had given the proposal his enthusiastic support. Bertie, too, was in favour of the idea, although his wife had some reservations. Her main objection was that she did not wish to live in London and certainly not in the poorer areas where the smaller breweries were to be found, but Bertie had brushed aside these objections as being of no real consequence. Dutifully she had withdrawn her protests and the search for a suitable property had begun. So far three had been rejected – on grounds of price, position or reputation. The one which Vinnie was discussing with the Colonel was the fourth.

'Whitechapel?' he repeated. 'Isn't that where Mary Bellweather does her good deeds?'

Vinnie smiled. 'You're right,' she agreed. 'The Brothers in

Jesus have a soup kitchen in one of those back streets. I had forgotten that!'

The old man laughed wheezily. 'Bertie will have to watch his step,' he said, 'or he'll have Mary on the doorstep with a banner or marching up and down outside with a pair of sandwich-boards! Down with the demon drink!'

His laugh became a cough and Vinnie watched anxiously as the thin shoulders jerked convulsively and finally relaxed. 'She will frighten away all your customers, that one!' He shook his head wonderingly. 'But she's a handsome woman, I'll grant her that. A very handsome woman! She ought to be married with a family of her own, eh? The demon drink! Poor old Bertie!' He began to chuckle and then thought better of it.

Vinnie read out the estate agent's particulars and he listened intently, nodding from time to time. When she had finished he said, 'Go up and take a look – it sounds promising. If you don't look, you won't know! The price seems a fair one, but you will know more about that when you see what sort of state it's in. We can always make them an offer.'

'It's only been empty a year or so,' said Vinnie. 'It can't be derelict, can it?'

'I should hope it isn't derelict, for eight hundred pounds!' he snorted. 'You go up and have a look at it – you, Bertie and that funny little wife of his. And if you need another opinion, ask Clive le Brun to go with you if he can spare a day.' He looked suddenly weary, as though the decision had been an effort.

Vinnie stood up. 'Thank you,' she said. 'I shall keep my fingers crossed. It would be *so* good to see Bertie settled at last.'

The Colonel allowed himself to slip further down the pillows. 'A very handsome woman,' he repeated, 'and Vinnie, send Janet back to me, will you? This infernal tooth is playing me up again.' He sighed tremulously. 'Yes, a handsome woman, Mary Bellweather, but one I should not care to cross!'

CHAPTER FIVE

Dora Wilks, who should have been Dora Carter but was not, eased the old wicker perambulator down the kerb and waited for a chance to cross the road. From her right a market cart was approaching, the driver singing out an almost incomprehensible cry of 'Ra-a-g a' bo-o-n-e!' Behind him a milk-float rattled unevenly and behind that, and overtaking it, came a hansom cab drawn by a black horse. Dora looked left and groaned. A yellow motor car, which she did not recognise as a Standard, was being driven slowly along the road. It was flanked on one side by a brown horse-van offering 'Sutton's High-Class Bread' and on the other by a railway parcels van, its horse blinkered against the surrounding traffic. The baby in the pram began to wail and she jiggled the handle crossly.

'And you hold your noise!' she told the little boy. 'Perishing sight too much of your racket these last few days. I've had about all I can take from you!'

She glanced down at her other son, a boy of two who clung timidly to her grey worsted skirt. 'Hold tight now, Sam,' she said. 'When I say, "Go", I mean "Go". You 'ang about and you'll get run down, so stick close to me.'

She jiggled the pram again and saw that one of the front wheels was loose and out of line. 'A little job for your Pa,' she said. 'Good thing he's clever with his hands!' She gave a quick glance in both directions as the last of the hansoms passed them.

'Go!' she shouted, but as she moved forward the toddler overbalanced and with a curse she grabbed him with her right hand and tugged him back on to his feet.

'What did I *say*?' she nagged. 'It's time you learned to stay on
your perishing feet! Get us all killed, you will, one of these days.'

A huge Shire horse, pulling a heavy coal-cart, narrowly
missed them as Dora managed to push the pram up on to the
opposite pavement and heave Sam up beside her. The driver of
the coal-cart shouted at her retreating back and she paused just
long enough to retaliate with a rude gesture. Then she changed
direction with a yank of the pram-handle and inadvertently ran it
into a woman in a smart black hat trimmed with a creamy silk
rose.

'Watch where you're – '

'What the hell – '

The two women stared open-mouthed.

'It's never Mollie Pett!' cried Dora.

'Christ!' said Mollie. 'Is it Dora Wilks? I don't believe it!'

Neither would admit that the six years since they were last
together had wrought drastic changes in them both. Mollie had
lost a lot of weight; her face was gaunt and the smart hat sat
incongruously on her ginger hair.

'You look very dashing!' Dora lied, eyeing the hat.

'You don't look so bad yourself,' said Mollie generously,
'except for – '

'Oh, I'm a bit of a pudding at the moment,' Dora laughed,
patting her swollen belly. 'Due in December!'

'How many's that, then?'

'Just the three,' said Dora nonchalantly. 'Sam here' – she
indicated the toddler – 'Billy in there – and don't start bawling
neither!' she added, tilting the pram so that Mollie could
admire her youngest child. Mollie clucked encouragingly,
but a wizened face with its halo of pale hair stared back
unhappily from the pillow.

'What's happened to *your* kids?' Dora asked. 'The little girls
and young Alex?'

'They're fine.' Mollie avoided Dora's eyes. 'Alex is a bright
boy – well, he's a young man nearly – seventeen!'

'Still with that lah-di-dah Miss B, is he? The one that gives
you the money?'

'Yes, he is, but I see him regular. The girls, too,' Mollie lied, deciding to brazen it out. 'Real pretty, they are. I wanted to have them back with me, but they're used to the country life, you see, and it wouldn't be fair.'

'That's only natural, I suppose,' said Dora kindly.

Mollie nodded dispiritedly and said, 'So you found yourself a husband after all? You said you never would – said you never wanted kids.'

Dora shrugged. 'I didn't have no choice, did I, with *him* on the way? Still, it's not so bad. We've got a room in Bourne Street near where you used to live. Sid Carter – that's his name – he's a porter up at Smithfields. He does OK. Leastways, we manage. Haven't had the bailiffs in yet, so you could say we manage.'

'What's it like?' asked Mollie curiously. 'Being married, I mean?'

Dora shrugged. 'It's not all it's cracked up to be,' she admitted. 'He can be a bit of a swine when the mood's on him – a bit of a bully.'

'What? Knock you about, d'you mean?'

'Oh, he doesn't mean it,' Dora said hastily. 'It's just if he's had a few pints or if he's skint, or he's had a barney with one of his mates. Gave me a real black eye one day, he did, and I had to have a stitch in it. Still, no one's perfect and he can be OK. We've had some fun, the two of us – he's not all bad.'

'No one is,' said Mollie. 'We've all got our bad points. And good.' She turned to Sam and smiled. 'Hullo, young Sam. I'm your Auntie Mollie. Aren't you going to say "Hullo"?'

'He won't,' said Dora. 'He's shy – leave him be. So how's life treating you, Mollie Pett? I like your titfer.'

Mollie patted her hair and straightened her hat proudly.

'An admirer,' she lied again. 'Give me a ring on me birthday, but I lost it. Diamond, it was. He was hopping mad, but . . . ' She shrugged expressively. 'No good crying over spilt milk, I told him. I'll have another birthday.'

'Going to marry this one, then?' Dora, recalling the old Mollie, was not entirely convinced.

'Never on your life,' said Mollie. 'He's married already.' She was rather pleased with this last invention, because now she could hardly be expected to produce him. 'Where are you off to then, Dora?' she asked, changing the subject.

'Fetch some washing from Sid's mum. I do a bit for her on Wednesday. She looks after the kids for me sometimes on a Sunday morning, while I go down to the "Five Bells" with Sid for a drop of stout.'

Mollie grinned at her. 'I'll pop in there one Sunday. Might see you?'

'That'd be a laugh. I'll keep me eyes skinned!'.

They looked at one another, wistfully conscious of shared exploits in the past.

'We did have some fun in them days,' said Dora.

'Not 'arf!'

'He's married, you say, Mollie – your chap?'

'Yes,' said Mollie. 'Well and truly married.' She sensed Dora's suspicions and cast about in her mind for a way to convince her. 'He's a doctor,' she said, lowering her voice to a conspiratorial whisper. 'Very well-known and highly thought of. I *daren't* tell you his name. It would ruin him – the scandal, I mean. If his wife ever found out about us . . .' She left the sentence unfinished, suggesting unimaginable horrors.

Dora's infant started to cry.

'Well, I must fly,' said Mollie, seizing her chance. 'Keep your pecker up and I'll keep an eye out for you in the "Five Bells".'

'I will, and you!'

They hesitated again, both longing to renew the friendship but aware that it could never be the way it had been before.

'You sure you're all right, Moll?' Dora asked. 'You look a bit peaky.'

'Peaky? Me?' Mollie laughed.

'Well,' Dora shrugged, 'as long as you're all right?'

"Course I am. You always was a worry-guts, Dora Wilks.'

There seemed nothing more to say. 'Bye, then.' Mollie raised a hand and fluttered her fingers in the way that she imagined a doctor's mistress might make her farewells.

'See you soon,' said Dora, leaning forward to tuck the crying baby more firmly into the threadbare blankets. 'And stop bawling!' she yelled, suddenly aware of her defeat and pretending not to notice Mollie's departure. Then with a loud sigh, she clamped her other son's hand on to the pram-handle and continued her journey.

'Doctor, my fanny!' Dora muttered. 'You must think I was born yesterday, Mollie Pett!' She sighed again. She hadn't much cared for Mollie's hat – black made Dora think of funerals – but secretly she coveted the cream silk rose.

*

Three minutes after Dora had turned the street corner, the yellow Standard motor pulled up outside the 'Barley Tap'. Bertie was in the driver's seat, complete with goggles, stout windproof coat and leather gloves. Behind him Vinnie and Beatrice shared the back seat, their sober motoring clothes contrasting with the bright red leather upholstery.

'I told you it must be along here somewhere,' said Vinnie triumphantly. 'We must have gone right past it the first time round.'

They remained in the motor, staring up at the tall thin building which towered above the 'Barley Tap' for another four storeys, its sooty exterior rendering it as unattractive as the rest of the adjoining properties. The 'Barley Tap' was clearly untenanted and as such rather inhospitable. The glass in the large windows was heavily decorated in a design of scrolls and flowers, making it impossible for anyone on the outside to see in; brown paint peeled from the window-frames, littering the broad stone sills. The doors were recessed into a porch and the small area above the step had accumulated street rubbish and smelt strongly of urine. Dismay mingled with alarm showed on Beatrice's face and Vinnie, seeing this, was determinedly enthusiastic.

'I bet those door handles are solid brass,' she said. 'A bit of polish and they'd shine up a treat!'

Bertie nodded, then he took out his watch and frowned. 'That chap is late,' he said. 'He's supposed to meet us here at three and it's ten-past already.'

A Mr Sparks from Hammonds Estate Agents had agreed to show them over the premises. He would bring the key and without him there was nothing the prospective clients could do but wait and impatiently stare up and down the street.

The property was in fact a tower brewery, in which the brewing process begins at the top of the building and proceeds downwards, relying on the force of gravity to move the large quantities of developing ale and thus removing the need for the installation of expensive pumping equipment.

Bertie glanced back at his wife. 'D'you understand, Bea?' he asked excitedly. 'It's water at the very top,' he pointed upwards, 'and then as it comes down from floor to floor it's gradually turned into ale!'

'Of course I understand,' she said flatly.

Beatrice was depressed by the greyness of the street which compared so unfavourably with the beauty of Foxearth. She also resented Vinnie's obvious enthusiasm, although she knew in her heart that this was unfair of her. With great generosity, the Lawrences were offering to set Bertie up in a business of his own and she knew she ought to feel grateful. She *was* grateful – for their generosity and for the wonderful opportunity which had so delighted Bertie. He had never doubted for one moment that his wife shared his enthusiasm and she had not had the heart to express her reservations about the scheme, consoling herself with the thought that some parts of London were attractive or had 'a good atmosphere'. This mean street, however, with its stark houses and dingy shops, was not at all attractive. In fact it was a realisation of her worst imaginings and for a moment panic flared within her as she visualised herself trapped in this sombre building in a way of life that was quite alien to her.

However, she set her mouth into a tight line and imperceptibly straightened her back. She was Beatrice Harris, Bertie's wife. She loved him passionately and she would live anywhere he wished – if it would make him happy. Presumably he *would* be happy in this dismal street? As Bertie and Vinnie chatted on, unaware of her dismay, she studied the faces of the people who passed them. Their eyes went first to the bright paintwork of the car with its gleaming brass trim, and then to its three well-dressed occupants. In their different expressions she read envy, curiosity, resentment, even a half-veiled mockery.

'We don't belong here,' she thought fearfully. 'Can't Bertie see that?' But then reason and common sense came once more to her rescue. The car was Vinnie's and it was Vinnie who no longer belonged to the drab side of life; Vinnie who, despite her humble origins, no longer needed to work for her living! No, that was unfair too and Beatrice was ashamed of herself. They owed Vinnie so much and would be for ever in her debt. She had made them both so welcome on their return from India and Foxearth truly had been home for the past two years. Vinnie had insisted that they rest and 'build themselves up' and Bertie had cheerfully abandoned himself to a life of unexpected luxury, but Bea had watched jealously as the relationship between brother and sister grew stronger. She did not want to share her husband, not even with his sister, but she could never tell Bertie about her feelings. So it was at Beatrice's insistence that they had finally made plans for their future and thus the idea of the brewery had been born.

'So you've brought this on yourself, Bea Harris,' she told herself sternly. 'This is the price you pay for having your husband to yourself once more.'

'What a big sigh!' She realised suddenly that Bertie was smiling at her. 'You're miles away, Bea!'

'Am I? I'm sorry.'

'Where is that wretched man?' Bertie went on. 'He's nearly twenty minutes late.'

'Perhaps this is him,' said Vinnie as a small man in a dark suit and curly-brimmed bowler approached along the pavement at a half-run. The man stopped beside the car, lifted his hat with one hand and put the other to his chest.

'Do forgive me,' he began. 'Oh dear! An unfortunate delay. I came as fast as I could. Mr Bertram Harris?'

Bertie nodded as he clambered out of the car. The two women lifted their motoring veils, were introduced and allowed themselves to be helped down to the pavement.

'Mr Sparks, at your service! I have all the details here – ' the little man patted his pocket. 'A most desirable property this, which has just come on the market.'

Bertie looked at him. 'But it's obviously been empty for ages,' he protested. 'Look at the state of it!'

'Ah!' Mr Sparks smiled nervously. 'It has indeed,' he agreed, 'but that's not to say it has been on the market all that time. Oh, dear me, no!'

Vinnie nudged Bertie. 'Don't waste time arguing!' she hissed. 'I want to see inside.'

'It's a matter of probate,' explained the agent, producing a key from his jacket pocket. He read the cardboard label which was tied to it by a piece of string and nodded with satisfaction. A small boy lingered, eyes popping, beside the motor.

'There will be twopence for you,' Bertie told him. 'if you stay here and see that no one touches it.'

The boy nodded without answering, then stationed himself beside the bonnet and folded his arms in an unconscious desire to give more substance to his puny body.

Mr Sparks looked up, shading his eyes from the light. 'Very sound property,' he told them. 'Built less than a hundred years ago. Brickwork in good condition, no repointing required. Windows intact, door and step in first-class condition. You've got a bargain here, sir! A real snip, as they say. Sound as a bell, this little property. A pleasure to sell a building like this.'

With a flourish, he opened the door and pushed it inwards. It creaked on rusty hinges and Vinnie laughed, but Beatrice felt depressed as she followed her sister-in-law into the public bar of the 'Barley Tap'.

Mr Sparks knew his job. He specialised in properties connected with the brewing industry and had sold no fewer than three similar breweries in the previous nine months. He led them to the top of the building where he paused, breathless from the number of stairs. His nervous manner hid a good brain, for he understood the market and Bertie found his professionalism reassuring. Mr Sparks knew that clients *wanted* to be convinced that here was the very property they sought and he did not consider it his job to disappoint them. Minor flaws would be dismissed with an airy, 'A small matter of no import'; major faults would be ignored altogether or, if discovered, dealt with by the phrase, 'That can easily be made good.' The entire inspection would be carried out in an atmosphere of great optimism on the part of the agent and with frequent hints from him that no one in their right mind could afford to turn down such a wonderful opportunity.

The tour began where the water supply was held in a vast wooden tub, below the sloping roof-beams. Mr Sparks slapped the tub and it rang hollowly. He pointed to the letters L.B. engraved on its side.

'Here's your liquor back – that is, store,' he told them. 'Never call it water, ma'am!' He smiled at Beatrice, having already established that she was Bertie's wife. 'Empty now, but the liquor is pumped up from an underground well. You'll buy in the malt, of course, and here's your malt store.' They ducked their heads and followed him through a small doorway on which the door hung sideways from one rusting hinge. 'Best take the door right off, sir, I'd say,' Mr Sparks suggested. 'Not necessary at all, that door!'

Before Bertie could comment, the agent was explaining how many quarters of malt could be accommodated in the store.

'Where do we keep the barley?' asked Beatrice.

Mr Sparks smiled at her paternally as he shook his head. 'Oh, the ladies always ask me that,' he said. 'The malt *is* the barley. The grains of barley are allowed to germinate for a period and then they are dried. We don't call it barley any more then; we call it malt. Your sacks of malt will go there . . .' he pointed. 'Your mill is there . . .' he pointed again. 'You do the milling, of course, and it's collected in this container, which we call a hopper.'

Mr Sparks opened a lid at the front of the hopper. 'Empty

now, of course,' he said, 'but that will be full of ground malt ready to be fed into the "mash tun" below.' He pointed to wooden 'pipes' which led from the hopper and disappeared through an opening in the floor. 'The ground malt is called grist. Now, if you'll please follow me . . .'

Their footsteps clattered on the bare wooden floor and down the steps, echoing in the silent airless rooms. Beatrice, last to leave, glanced back in time to see a mouse scuttle along the wainscot and into a hole beneath the grimy window. Ahead of her she heard Mr Sparks say, 'You can still smell the ale, sir. It lingers, as they say. No mistaking the purpose of this establishment – that rich smell says "brewery" to anyone with a nose.'

They found themselves beside the 'mash tun', which proved to be a large circular vessel with a domed copper lid. Mr Sparks rapped on it proudly with his knuckles.

'In first-class condition,' he insisted. 'A bit of elbow grease and you'll have that shining like a new pin, as they say. Beautiful, that copper! This is your mash tun, where the hot liquor and the grist are blended and heated to a temperature of, I believe, one hundred and fifty degrees. From here, it's run out into the copper – over there, marked with a 'C'. At this stage, ladies, it's called 'wort'. You see, the starch in the malt has turned into sugar.' He laughed at the looks on their faces. 'Oh yes, I'm quite learned in these matters – it's my special field, you might say. I had it all explained to me many years ago, by an expert. I may slip up now and then, but I've a good general grasp of the whys and wherefores of brewing.'

'It's all very interesting,' Vinnie told him, glancing at Beatrice for her comments.

Beatrice could only nod and Bertie, mistaking her silence for confusion, took her hand and squeezed it cheerfully.

'Don't worry,' he told her, 'you'll soon get the hang of it. I'm sure it sounds much more complicated than it is and Clive le Brun has promised to find us an experienced brewer. I shall soon pick it up.'

She nodded, forcing a smile, and returned the pressure on his hand.

Mr Sparks continued, 'In this copper, hops are added to give it that bitter flavour – but you don't need me to tell you about hops!' They all laughed. 'And then it's boiled for a certain period. I do forget for just how long, I admit. An hour, maybe, or two. If you will follow me downstairs again, please?'

'It's all stairs!' Vinnie complained, manipulating her skirts with difficulty as they made their way down another flight of worn steps. The agent glanced back. 'Ah! That's the secret of it, ma'am! The gravity, you see. It all just flows down. Well, now we have the hop back; this is a storage vessel where the hops are separated from the wort, then the liquor goes over a cooler to reduce the temperature ready for fermentation.'

The cooler was a 'wall' of parallel copper pipes through which cold water was pumped while the hot wort flowed down over it and was cooled. On the floor below they saw an open rectangular vessel which would contain the cooled wort. Here, Mr Sparks told them, the yeast would be added and up to a week would elapse while the process of fermentation took place.

'That's quite a sight, ma'am,' Mr Sparks told Beatrice. 'A sight for sore eyes, as they say – if you're a beer man, that is. The yeast fluffs it up into a creamy froth which floats on the top. Oh, you'll have all the old biddies round with their jam-jars when they know you're fermenting – and they'll know by the smell!' He tapped his nose with a meaningful gesture.

'Jam-jars?' said Beatrice, intrigued in spite of herself.

'Oh yes, ma'am. They'll want a jar full of froth, you see. Full of goodness, that yeasty froth is, and they know it. Very nourishing stuff – and it's free.'

'I see.' Beatrice stared around. Dust lay everywhere and cobwebs hung from every corner. The small window was partly greened over with mildew and one pane was missing, allowing a damp patch to form below it on the floorboards.

'A small matter of no import,' Mr Sparks said, seeing the direction of her gaze and reading the unspoken criticism in her expression.

'It's over-priced,' said Bertie firmly, 'but no doubt we can come to an arrangement if we *do* decide to buy.'

Mr Sparks looked hurt. 'I cannot agree with you there, sir,' he said, 'but no doubt the owners will consider any reasonable offer.'

'I'm sure they will,' said Bertie. 'Well, Bea, what do you think? You're not saying much.'

'I'm sure it's very nice,' she stammered, the question taking her by surprise. 'I mean . . .'

'*Nice?*' cried Bertie, slapping his forehead with a comic gesture of despair. 'All this,' he waved his arms 'and all you can say is "nice"! Bea, it's marvellous! Take my word for it.'

Bea felt herself blushing and Vinnie looked at her in surprise.

Mr Sparks hurriedly intervened. 'The racking room is this way,' he said and they followed him down the last flight of steps. The ground floor of the premises extended back to include the living accommodation.

'Racking,' Mr Sparks explained, 'is the process of running the beer into the casks.' He waved a hand to indicate a large area, in the furthermost corner of which a few split and rotting barrels could be seen.

'There's no stable,' he told them, 'but the previous owners hired a dray and a team of horses to make their occasional deliveries. They sold most of the beer in the tap-room, of course, but sometimes they would have a surplus and would want to sell elsewhere.' He inhaled deeply. 'What a fine smell, or should I call it an aroma? A year since the brewery was last in production, but we can still smell it.'

The living quarters were very cramped – a tiny kitchen, living-room and one bedroom – but Bertie appeared quite unconcerned and Beatrice made no comment. How could she query the single bedroom, she reflected bitterly, when the doctor had told her she would never be able to give Bertie a child? If he thought one bedroom was enough, she would not argue the matter. Obediently she followed the others out into the back-yard and watched as Mr Sparks unfastened the gate to show that it led into a back street.

'It's a narrow property, sir, but with height and depth. Tall, and goes back a good way. With your tap-room at the front, you are all set up with a good business and a cosy little home.'

He directed his smile towards Vinnie and Bertie, ignoring Beatrice's obvious lack of enthusiasm. 'A nice little business, sir, as many men would envy.'

The tap-room he saved until last, but they finally stood on the dirty sawdust and surveyed the room which one day might be filled with the cheerful noise of working men, drinking a hard-earned pint of beer at the end of a hard day.

'Fancy yourself behind the bar, Bea?' Bertie teased.

This was a large wooden counter, with chipped china pump-handles. Beatrice shrank back uncertainly but Vinnie darted forward, lifted the flap and took up her position behind it.

'And what's for you, sir?' she asked Mr Sparks. 'A pint of our best bitter, perhaps, or a half of porter? And you, sir?' She grinned at Bertie. 'Your usual, Mr Harris?'

Bertie stepped forward and leaned one elbow on the dusty counter-top.

'Why not?' he said. 'I've a thirst on me like a fish in a desert. A pint of brown, please, love, and a half of stout for the missis here.' He pulled Beatrice towards him and put an arm round her waist.

Vinnie took up an imaginary glass and pulled on one of the pumps which moved convincingly.

'Get that down you, sir,' she said. 'Best drop of beer in London, although I say it as shouldn't. What do you think, Bertie? Do I make a good barmaid?'

'You're not fat enough,' Bertie told her.

'I'm fatter than Bea!'

Mr Sparks, disapproving of this levity, took out his half-hunter watch and glared at it.

'Well, sir,' he said pointedly, 'time's getting on.'

'And you're a busy man,' said Bertie. 'Come on out from there, Vinnie.'

But his sister was exploring. 'There are shelves down here,' she called. 'There's even a sink – to wash the glasses, I suppose. Can I come up sometimes and help you, Bertie?'

'*If* we buy it.' The words were out of Beatrice's mouth before she could stop them.

Bertie gave her a hug.

'Don't worry,' he said, 'of course we're going to buy it!' He glanced at Mr Sparks. 'If we can agree a price, I think the 'Barley Tap' has found a new owner.'

CHAPTER SIX

Blériot's landing near Dover was by no means Kent's first introduction to the advent of the flying machine. The sport of flying was becoming increasingly popular and a band of enthusiasts had formed the Aeronautical Club, while the Royal Aero Club had the first 'flying ground' at Leysdown on the Isle of Sheppey. Two brothers by the name of Short had an aircraft factory in Battersea and Frank McClean ordered a tailless biplane from them – the 'Shorts No.1'; it was taken to Sheerness Field, but could not be persuaded to take off. At the beginning of August, a modified version was under construction and this was being discussed by two men outside one of Shorts' workshops at Leysdown. One of the men was Clive le Brun, who had been introduced that morning to the other – a young French flier, Philippe Delain, who went on to explain that he had heard the news of Blériot's Channel crossing with a feeling of deep chagrin.

'I was *désolé* . . . ' he told Clive with a disarming smile and an expressive wave of the hand. '*Désolé*! Like others, I wished very much to be the first. I have my own machine, a Voisin, and I am certain I too can do it. I too can cross the Channel! You are not a flyer, Monsieur le Brun? Does not the air hold any charm for you?'

'One day, perhaps,' said Clive. 'I am willing to be persuaded; I have an open mind on the subject of aviation. But you will meet plenty of enthusiasts here in this part of Kent; they frequently visit Sheppey, or you may see them if you go to the Shorts' factory in Battersea. There's Charles Rolls, of course, Dr Lockyer, a chap called Griffiths – oh, and Frank Butler too.

You are in very good company here, Monsieur Delain!'

The young man laughed. 'Perhaps we shall yet convert you, Monsieur le Brun. And of course there is much money to be made. I see this morning that one thousand pounds has been offered by your newspaper, *Daily Mail*, for a flight of one mile. Am I not right?'

'That's correct,' Clive told him. 'The circular flight must be over English soil, must be undertaken in an all-English plane – and of course, by an Englishman.'

Philippe shrugged. 'How sad for me when my own plane will arrive in Britain tomorrow.'

'For what purpose?' Clive asked, surprised.

'Why, to make a *return* flight. I mean to cross the Channel from Dover to Calais, to prove to myself that I can do it.' He glanced around at the collection of workshops, hangars and sheds and beyond them to the large field which served as the flying ground. 'This is like wine to me; I find it good to be alive at such a time!' he said simply 'The flying machine is here to stay – like the motor car before it. Man has conquered the skies!'

'Has he? So soon?' Clive was amused by the young man's enthusiasm. Philippe Delain was a handsome man – his olive skin, modest nose and sensitive mouth added up to a pleasing whole. He *looked* like a Frenchman, thought Clive, and he behaved like one with his expansive speech and expressive movements.

'You speak very good English,' he remarked. 'How has that come about?'

Philippe smiled. 'Ah, my mother, she is English and at home we speak both languages. Also, as a boy I spent much time in Sussex with my mother's family in Hastings. I am very much at home in England. Have you ever been to my country, Monsieur le Brun?'

Clive nodded. 'Oh, yes, many times. To Paris, of course, and to the Loire valley.'

Now it was Philippe's turn to laugh. 'Our wines appeal to you, perhaps, Monsieur le Brun?'

'Most definitely! But France, too, is a beautiful country with great charm.'

They began to walk towards Muswell Manor, a large house nearby where the Royal Aero Club had its headquarters.

'I will introduce you to a few friends,' said Clive, 'but then I am afraid I must leave you to your own devices. But maybe one day you will come to Harkwood, my home in Tunbridge Wells, to have dinner with me and my son William. He is very interested in flying machines and he often comes down here. I am surprised you haven't already bumped into him.' He raised a hand as a man passed them at a run, obviously in too much of a hurry for introductions.

'That's Moore-Brabazon,' he told Philippe. 'Short is building a second biplane for him and he'll almost certainly have a try for that *Daily Mail* prize you spoke of just now. They have added a kind of tail to the plane, which he believes will provide that vital lift. Let's hope so!'

They parted half an hour later with a firm date for dinner later in the month, but as Clive drove home he was somewhat chastened by the sudden realisation that he could no longer invite Vinnie to share the meal. He must therefore resign himself to the fact that without any female distractions, the talk on the occasion of the dinner would centre inevitably on flying.

*

Vinnie knocked on the kitchen door and walked straight in; she was in her outdoor clothes and looked very tired. Everyone stood up except Edie, who was scrubbing the floor; Mrs Tallant, who was standing beside her, pushed her with the toe of her black lace-up boot and Edie scrambled hastily to her feet just as the others, receiving a nod from Vinnie, sat down again.

'It's all right, Edie,' said Vinnie. 'I am only here for two minutes,' she turned to Cook, 'to see if you have any calves' foot jelly. Ned Bray's little boy is still very poorly. Coughing himself sick. I think perhaps he needs building up a little.'

'The Colonel's wife used to swear by calves' foot jelly,' said

Cook. 'I'll put some in a clean jar. Will you be taking it down to them yourself?'

Vinnie shook her head. 'I thought maybe Bertha could pop it in to them on her way past.'

'I will, ma'am,' said Bertha with a quick glance at the large clock beside the dresser. It said five minutes to four – only another hour and she would be off duty at last and on her way to her grandmother's.

'Take a jar of honey, too,' said Vinnie. 'And half a dozen eggs. Poor Ned – he's having a bad summer. First he breaks his arm and now his little boy is sick. And only a month before we start picking!'

Ned Bray was well known as chief 'pole-puller' at Foxearth, but the actual title dated back to the latter part of the previous century when the hop bines were grown entirely on poles and a pole-puller did in fact pull up each pole – laying it across the bins to be stripped of its hops by the quick-fingered pickers.

'All that coughing,' said Mrs Tallant. 'Sounds like asthma to me.'

'Croup, more like,' said Bertha. 'Our Grace had croup years back. Real nasty, it was. Hack, hack! She nearly shook herself to pieces.'

Mrs Tallant clapped a hand to her mouth. 'Oh ma'am! I nearly forgot. Mr Samm's here with the hoppers' list. I put him in the morning-room half an hour ago with a pot of tea and some sandwiches and told him you wouldn't be long.'

Vinnie put a hand to her head and sighed. 'I had quite forgotten he was coming,' she confessed. 'Take in a fresh pot of tea, will you? I'll take off my coat and tidy myself – tell him I'll join him shortly.'

When she had left the room, the staff resumed their various tasks. Edie scrubbed away at a piece of cabbage that someone had trodden into the stone floor; Mrs Tallant returned to her kitchen accounts, a frown darkening her face; Bertha took up a dab of silver polish and worked it into the back of Vinnie's hairbrush. 'Young Harry', middle-aged and growing taciturn, tried patiently to reassemble a door-lock which he was supposed to be repairing.

'The mistress will wear herself out,' said Cook, spooning the delicate meat jelly into a screw-topped jar. 'All that visiting she does – and giving an eye down at the school. Never a moment to call her own!'

'She's filling the hours,' said Mrs Tallant wisely. 'I've seen it before – when a woman's husband dies, as like as not she takes to spring-cleaning the house, even in the middle of winter.'

'But the master died years ago,' Young Harry argued.

'Ah!' Mrs Tallant waved her pencil at him. 'But when did she give poor Master William his marching orders? A few weeks ago, that's all.'

'I had the croup once,' said Edie.

'You never did,' said Mrs Tallant. 'You get on with that scrubbing and don't talk so much.'

Cook screwed down the lid, stuck on a label and wrote 'Carves Foot Jelly' in careful letters. Then she fetched a jar of honey from the larder, giving it a quick wipe with the tea towel, and picked out six brown eggs from a crock in the larder. She arranged everything in a small basket and covered it with a small cloth.

'There you are!' she told Bertha. 'And go careful with the eggs.'

'Of course I will,' said Bertha. 'What d'you take me for?'

'Wear a red cloak,' said Young Harry, 'and they'll think you're Red Riding Hood!'

They all laughed except Edie who paused in her scrubbing. 'Well, it was asthma, then,' she said hopefully. 'I *know* I had something.'

*

Harry Samm, the hoppers' agent, had worked for the Lawrences for over twenty years. He was now nearly sixty, but Vinnie did not want to replace him. Although unprepossessing – small-eyed, long-nosed and thick-lipped – he nevertheless knew his job inside out and could deal firmly with the more obstreperous families on the Foxearth list. Each year his work began in the Spring with visits to every family on the list, and gradually he worked his way along the streets of Whitechapel, Shoreditch and Poplar. At each call he checked whether or not the same members of the family would be picking in the coming September. Sometimes the name of a neighbour would be put forward and these people would be added to the list on a provisional basis. Theoretically bad language, immoral behaviour or dishonesty would result in the permanent removal of a name from the approved hoppers' list. However, a blind eye was often turned to these offences if the person picked exceptionally well. They were casual labourers and unless they were likely to create a serious disturbance, they could be tolerated for the four or five weeks of the hopping season.

While Mr Samm sucked his tea noisily, Vinnie tried to concentrate on the list of names he had given her. Most were familiar to her, but here and there she spotted a discrepancy.

'Annie Green's missing,' she said. 'Not ill, is she?'

'Dead,' said Mr Samm. 'Got drunk and fell under a horse.'

'Dead?' Vinnie was shocked. 'Poor old Annie! How dreadful.' Her finger moved on. 'And Daniel Goodbody?'

'Gone off his rocker.'

'Off his head?' Vinnie looked startled. 'Rather sudden, isn't it? He was all right last year.'

Mr Samm shrugged and rattled the empty cup which Vinnie refilled for him. 'Well, he's not all right this year,' he said. 'Daft as a brush – didn't even recognise me.'

Vinnie hesitated. 'Was he sober?'

'Oh, yes, sober as a judge,' he told her. 'Sober but barmy.'

Still Vinnie was unconvinced. 'But did he want to come down? How will he get through the winter?' She was answered with another shrug.

'I shall make a note of him,' she said, 'and notify Mary Bellweather. Perhaps the Brothers in Jesus will look after him.'

Her fingers proceeded slowly down the list and then she stopped again.

'Dora Wilks?' she said. 'Do we know her?'

'No. Lady-next-door's bringing her – that's Mrs Gorringe, as comes with the twin boys. Proper little perishers, they are! This Dora Wilks has got two and another on the way, but she's leaving the kids with her so-called mother-in-law.'

'She's not married, then?'

'No – not many of them are.'

Vinnie sighed. 'And what's happened to the Browns from 26, Brune Street. There used to be five of them –now there are only three.'

'The old boy died and the old girl's gone into the work-house.'

'Oh, dear!' Vinnie's concern was genuine for it was based on her own experience in the workhouse. That had been a long time ago, but she had not forgotten.

With another shrug, Mr Samm helped himself to the last coconut biscuit which he dipped into the dregs of his tea. His personal view was that 'people got what they asked for' and that disasters were sent by the Lord to punish sinners. He was not a religious man, nor even a regular church-goer, but a belief in divine dispensation made it easier for him to ignore the many calls for help that were made to him in the course of his duties. A conviction that the unfortunates deserved their difficulties obviated the need for any pity or compassion on his part and thus made his own lot easier. His own 'wife' had run away years ago and Harry Samm had not bothered to run after her, preferring to live alone and save his money.

Vinnie came to the end of the list and handed it back to him. 'A hundred and forty,' she said. 'If the weather's fine, we may finish picking in four weeks. Last year we were into the sixth week, but we had so much rain it slowed us down. Where are the cards?'

From his canvas bag Mr Samm produced several bundles of cards tied with string. These were already addressed, one to each family or group, and would be sent off when it was known on exactly which date picking would commence. The date would be entered on the back of the card, as would the time of the train from London Bridge. These 'Hoppers' Specials' left London in the early hours of the morning when normal rail traffic had ceased, carrying thousands of Londoners into the 'wilds' of Kent to deposit them, tired and fractious, on various station platforms. There, harassed officials would herd them with all speed into the carts and waggons provided by the hop-growers to take them to their respective destinations.

Quickly Vinnie did some mental arithmetic to see how many vehicles they would need for one hundred and forty pickers and all their accompanying baggage. Finally she nodded and made a further note on her pad.

'And they all have their letters?' she asked. 'Last year four families came without them and it caused a lot of bother.'

He looked aggrieved. 'Don't blame me,' he said. 'I can't help it if they lose the letters – thick as planks, some of them.'

'They all claimed you had not given them letters.'

'Well, they would, wouldn't they?' he argued. 'Stands to reason they're going to blame me.'

Vinnie knew she was on uncertain ground and did not pursue the point. Once their names were on the official list, each family received a letter authorising them to travel to the appropriate hop-garden on receipt of the card. The hoppers' letter gave them the status of approved pickers and most growers were reluctant to take on anyone who turned up without one.

Vinnie reminded herself of the other tasks urgently awaiting her attention. She must tell Ned Bray to purchase clean straw for the pickers' bedding and see that there were sufficient hop-pokes (loosely meshed sacks) to serve as mattress cases. Faggots must be ordered for the camp-fires and the latrines must be dug. Then there was anti-cholera medicine to be ordered from the chemist in Maidstone, as well as basic first-aid equipment which Vinnie provided each season for the Brothers in Jesus' mission tent. She wondered if a box of 'Dr Holloway's Pills' would be a useful addition to the selection of bandages, cough syrups and liniments she normally provided. Thinking about cough syrups raised in her mind's eye the image of Ned Bray's son, bent over the old tin bowl as a fierce paroxysm of coughing brought up the gruel his mother had just given him. Exhausted and shaken, with his eyes streaming, the boy had looked up at Vinnie and tried to smile. The little face had been so pale, the trembling lips so grey . . .

Vinnie frowned, unaware that her agent was speaking to her. Was it really croup, as Mrs Bray believed? Or asthma? Could it be whooping-cough? No, there was no distinctive 'whoop.' Yet she felt uneasy and an indefinable fear nagged at the back of her mind.

Abruptly she stood up and tugged the bell-rope three times.

'I *said*,' repeated Harry Samm, 'that if that's all, then I'll take my money and be on my way.'

'Oh?' Vinnie regarded him vaguely.

'My *money*,' he said loudly. 'I said if that's all, then I'll – '

'I'm so sorry – your money, of course.' Vinnie opened a drawer in the desk, withdrew the money she had prepared for him and watched as he counted it laboriously with much licking of his forefinger. As he stood up, satisfied, there was a knock at the door and Mrs Tallant came into the room.

Vinnie smiled at Harry Samm and bade him good-bye. 'Please show Mr Samm out,' she told the housekeeper, 'and then telephone Doctor Jerome. Ask him to call at Ned Bray's cottage first thing tomorrow morning and look at their little boy. I'm not quite happy about him.'

'Will that be at your expense, ma'am?'

'At my expense? Yes, of course.'

*

Doll saw to it that breakfast in the nursery was never a hurried affair, for she believed a day should begin slowly and then gather speed. The three children came to the breakfast table washed and fully dressed, with combed hair and gleaming teeth. Having supervised their ablutions, she would leave them to dress while she went down to the kitchen to collect the breakfast tray. This consisted invariably of four boiled eggs, a plate of thin bread and butter, a jug of milk and a pot of jam, marmalade or honey. The crockery and cutlery were kept in the nursery and since Doll was responsible for washing them up after each meal, one corner of the room had been redesigned for this purpose with a large sink, draining-boards and cupboards. A heavy wooden ironing-board was a permanent feature also, for although the children's clothes were washed downstairs with those of the rest of the family, Doll preferred to iron them herself. There was a gas-iron and several clothes-horses over which the newly-ironed clothes were hung to air, before being folded and put away in the large chest of drawers in the children's bedroom.

Doll's own room was between their bedroom and the nursery and in this small corner of the house she reigned supreme, with the welfare and happiness of her three small charges as the focus of her life.

On the morning following Harry Samm's visit, Doll waited outside the nursery door with the breakfast tray and called out, 'Knock, knock! Let me in! It's the big bad wolf come to gobble you all up!' She growled loudly.

Teddy, giggling, looked at Louise. 'It's your turn,' he told her.

'I don't want to go,' she said. '*You* go.'

'I'll go,' said James.

'She said *me*!' cried Teddy. 'Didn't you say I could go?'

The two boys looked at their sister, waiting. Opening the door for the breakfast tray was another task taken in strict rotation; if Louise was not going to use her 'turn', then she must nominate someone else. Meanwhile Doll growled again and tapped impatiently at the door with her shoe.

'Teddy,' said Louise and he slid from his seat with a triumphant glance towards his older brother. He threw open the door, giggled and said, 'Come in, wolf! We're not scared'.

Doll put the tray on the table and looked at Louise. 'What's up with you, then?' she asked in surprise. 'It was your turn today.'

She transferred bread and butter, strawberry jam and milk to the table, then set the eggs into their respective egg-cups.

'Whose turn to pour?' she asked.

'Mine,' said James and with great concentration, he filled the four mugs without spilling a drop of milk.

'I don't want my egg,' said Louise.

'It's not a case of want,' said Doll in her briskest tone, 'it's a case of what's good for you – and it's good for you to eat an egg every day for breakfast.'

As she handed round the plate of bread and butter, James began to batter his egg with the spoon.

'Steady on!' Doll told him. 'You'll hammer that egg right through the table if you go on like that!' She reached across and removed the broken shell for him. 'And not too much salt this morning,' she said. 'You overdid it yesterday and then what happened?'

'He left it all,' cried Teddy.

'Exactly – and Cook wasn't at all pleased. She seemed to think it was *my* fault!' She glanced at Louise. 'Come on, lovey – get a move on.'

'I don't want it.'

'You won't have any bread and jam,' said James, 'if you don't eat your egg.'

'He's right,' said Doll. 'You won't and it's strawberry jam – your favourite.'

'I don't want any,' said Louise. 'I'm not hungry.'

'Mama has bacon for breakfast,' said James. 'I wish we could have bacon.'

'You will one day,' said Doll, 'when you're bigger.'

'But *when*?'

'When pigs can fly.'

Teddy giggled. He made flying motions with his arms and said, 'I'm a pig and I can fly. Look, Louise. I'm a pig and – '

'Your egg's getting cold,' said Doll. 'Stop acting daft and eat nicely.'

'He can't fly,' said James, 'but he *is* a pig.'

'Don't talk with your mouth full, James, there's a love.' Doll turned her attention to Louise, concerned by the child's indifference. Usually she was only too quick to criticise her brothers for their lack of manners or boisterous behaviour.

'Are you feeling all right?' she asked. 'You do look a bit pale.'

'My throat hurts.'

'Open wide and let me see.'

There was certainly a slight inflammation. Doll put a hand to the child's forehead and shook her head. 'You're not feverish,' she said.

Downstairs the telephone shrilled and then stopped abruptly.

'Perhaps it's Uncle William,' said Teddy hopefully.

James shook his head. 'He doesn't come to see us any more,' he said, 'because Mama sent him away.'

'Now then,' said Doll hastily, 'it wasn't quite like that.'

'I wish he *would* come,' said James. 'Soon Uncle Bertie will be gone to London and we shall have nobody to play with us. It's not fair, Doll; why does Uncle Bertie have to go to London? I don't want him to go.'

'He's got to earn his living,' said Doll, 'same as the rest of us. Maybe he'll invite you to go and stay with him one day and help him make all that beer! How would you like that?'

'*I'd* like it,' said Teddy. 'I'd drink it all! Gobble, gobble.'

'You mean glug, glug,' said James, scraping out the last scrap of egg. 'Gobble is eating and you don't *eat* beer, silly.'

'I'm not silly! I'm not, am I, Doll?'

At that moment the door opened and Janet slipped into the room looking upset. She stood with her back to the door, beckoned to Doll and then put her finger to her lips.

'What on earth – ' Doll began. She left the children at the table and crossed the room to Janet.

'The telephone just now,' Janet whispered. 'It was the doctor to say Ned Bray's little boy died in the night.'

Doll's hand flew to her mouth. 'Died? Oh, dear God in Heaven! But how?'

'Collapsed, apparently. He just coughed and coughed until his heart gave out. There's a couple of cases in Hunton and another one in Coxheath.'

'Oh poor, *poor* Ned!' gasped Doll. 'He worshipped that little

boy. But whatever was it? What killed the poor little mite?'
'It was diptheria,' said Janet.

CHAPTER SEVEN

Mary Bellweather stared at the speaker and tried to concentrate on what he was saying. The small missionary group that called itself the Brothers in Jesus was meeting in Roland Fry's parlour to finalise plans for their month in Teesbury, when they would be working in the hop-gardens at Foxearth. Every year they followed the Londoners down to Kent and set up a missionary tent to cater for the physical and spiritual needs of their 'flock'.

Lydia Grant, a nurse, had outlined the medical provisions she considered necessary in addition to those being supplied by the Lawrences and the group had approved the expenditure. Gareth Brooks, also a founder of the Brothers, had borrowed a magic lantern and slides from a friend of his mother and they hoped that this entertainment would successfully compete with the attractions of the two public houses in Teesbury – the 'Horse and Cart' and the 'Blue Fox'. These establishments, although welcoming the extra money which the hopping season provided, found it difficult to cope with the large influx of rowdy Londoners and fights frequently developed between them and the sadly outnumbered locals.

As usual Roland Fry, the group's leader, would run the evening prayer meeting, but this year his wife Emily would remain at home with their child. To encourage regular attendance at the prayer meeting, the Brothers proposed to introduce a 'points' system whereby anyone attending a total of fifteen meetings in the four-week period would qualify for a free outing to the seaside at Camber Sands when the hop-picking ended.

In addition to this novelty, the usual services would be provided for the pickers – help and advice would be given about family matters, second-hand clothing provided for the needy and cheap tea and buns served twice daily. There would be story times for the children and sing-songs for the adults – anything, in fact, which the group believed would improve the lot of the pickers and hopefully keep them out of mischief at the same time.

Mary was deeply involved with the mission and had been for a long time, but now she allowed her mind to wander from the familiar problems. Alexander was due to leave France in a few weeks' time and travel to Italy; his extended travels were primarily intended to keep him out of reach of Mollie Pett and away from Bertie Harris, but Mary had missed him with a passionate intensity which astonished and dismayed her. The boy meant too much to her – she acknowledged the fact with reluctance. She had allowed her life to centre around him and the past few months had been the loneliest she could remember. Only his frequent letters had sustained her.

In his absence Mary read more, visited more art galleries and went frequently to the theatre. She also devoted extra time to the Brothers in Jesus, giving up three mornings a week to serve breakfasts at their base in Whitechapel and in her 'spare time' organizing fund-raising events for their benefit. She went about these various activities with a brisk and efficient cheerfulness that deceived all but her closest acquaintances. Roland Fry knew that she missed her adopted son but he had no idea of the terrible ache in her heart, the desperate counting of days and the agonised daily wait for the postman.

Mary knew that next year Alexander must go up to Cambridge to study for his degree – but what then? She dared not think about it. He would be twenty-one, a man, with the world at his feet – a foolish phrase, thought Mary. He could earn his living as a teacher, perhaps, but would he want to do that? Would he still wish to live with her or would he want his independence? Three years at university might make him dissatisfied with the life he had shared with her for so long.

Mary fought down panic. If Alexander wanted to go abroad again, she would go with him; her money would open doors for both of them. At twenty-one he would still be very young, she reassured herself – they could still be together, enjoying each other's company . . .

Roland Fry stood up to bring the meeting to a close and Mary forced her attention to the matters in hand.

'Any other business?' he asked. 'Have we covered everything?'

His glance moved from person to person – Lydia, Emily, Gareth and Mary. She smiled at him and nodded in answer to the second question, but almost at once her thoughts reverted to Alexander. He had come to her as an awkward sullen boy when Mollie had run away from Foxearth after smashing a window. Mary had a sudden vision of him after Mollie's disappearance: sitting at the trestle table in the mission tent, a scowl hiding his nervousness. He had not been at all pleased to hear that he was to live with her, and she had sweetened the pill with the promise of riding lessons! She smiled faintly at the memory. Now he was a handsome boy – no, a young man – with Bertie's height and colouring but Mollie's features. That she could not deny, recognising the broad cheekbones, well-shaped mouth and fine eyes.

There was a scraping of chair-legs as the meeting ended and Mary rose also. Once, many years ago, she had loved Roland Fry but Vinnie, a helpless waif of fifteen, had come between them. Later Mary's heart had gone out to Julian Lawrence, and even briefly to William le Brun, but always and inevitably – though unintentionally – Vinnie had come between them. Always it seemed that Vinnie enjoyed the love that Mary craved – until Alexander had come into her life. Now Mary's relationship with the boy was close and rewarding and she did not need anyone else, wanting only that they should be together always. The word 'possessive' was never admitted into her thoughts, although she was uneasily aware that outsiders might use it, though never to her face. A friend of her mother's had offered to take Alexander for a six-month stay in Cherbourg, assuring her that the lad would benefit from the company of his own two sons of similar age. He had not included Mary in the invitation but, though hurt by the exclusion, she had reluctantly accepted the offer as a way of keeping Alexander well away from Mollie, whom he had not seen since he was eleven. Another invitation had followed and Italy was dangled before the boy as a carrot to a donkey. Sick at heart at the prospect of so long a separation, Mary had given in gracefully . . .

Buttoning her coat, she began to pull on her gloves.

'Not long now,' said Gareth.

'No.' She smiled at him.

'Then it's "into battle"!' They both laughed.

'You're going to have fun with that magic lantern,' she said. 'It's a splendid idea and the pickers will love it, especially the children.'

'I hope so. Yes, I'm sure they will.' He hesitated. 'May I walk you home?'

Mary shook her head. 'Thank you, but that's not necessary these light evenings,' she said. 'In the winter I must admit I don't relish the dark streets, and I'm very grateful for your company, but the summer presents no problems.'

They made their farewells and Mary set off for home, her thoughts firmly fixed on a more immediate problem. She had agreed to accompany the hop-pickers on the train down to Wateringbury, an idea that had been mooted the previous year but too late to put into practice. This year Roland's enthusiasm had inspired them and Mary, Gareth and Lydia had all agreed to go.

She was pushing her key into the lock of her front door when a tall shadow darkened the glass on the other side. The door opened and for a moment she stared in disbelief and joy: it was Alexander.

*

Later that day they sat over their dessert with a glass of Muscatel. They had talked about Cherbourg, the members of the family who had been Alexander's hosts and the charm of the French way of life. Mary had told him about the mission's plans for the hop-picking season and various innocuous items of London gossip. All the while she steeled herself to ask him why he had come home, but she feared she already knew the answer. There was a new softness in his voice, a glow in his eyes and an increased assurance in his manner which were not simply attributable to his holiday. Mary knew intuitively that he had fallen in love for the first time and she was devastated.

'So,' she said at last, 'tell me your *real* news!'

'Oh!' He laughed. 'Is it so obvious, then?'

'Yes, Alexander, I think it is.' She could not lift her eyes to meet his.

'Mary, look at me,' he said. 'I *will* tell you, but I was going to wait . . . to choose the right moment.'

'Now is the right moment,' she said. 'Please, Alexander! We have never kept secrets, you and I. Why should we start now?'

'I don't know,' he said. 'I did not mean . . .'

She waited, giving him no help, her eyes still on the glass as she willed her fingers not to tremble.

He took a deep breath. 'Oh Mary, I've met someone – a marvellous girl – '

'Yes?'

'Do look at me, Mary,' he insisted. 'I want to see your eyes; I want to know you are pleased for me.'

Mary put the glass to her lips and drank the wine that remained without tasting it.

'How can I know if I am pleased', she said, 'if you tell me nothing about this girl?'

'I will tell you, Mary, only I do so want you to understand and to be pleased for me. For us, I mean.'

'What do you mean – "for us"?' Mary felt a great coldness.

He hesitated. 'Nothing . . . at least, yes, I do mean something. I mean that she feels the same way about me. That's why it is so unbelievably wonderful – it's incredible, Mary! Her name is Sylvia.'

Mary looked at him at last. 'She is English?'

'Why, of course.'

'You did not say.'

'Didn't I?'

Now that she faced him she saw the joy in his eyes and was herself torn by conflicting emotions: a delight in his happiness and a terrible jealousy that threatened to overwhelm her.·

'Well,' said Mary, playing for time and hoping to control herself, 'so now we have established that you have met a girl called Syliva. So far, so good. Is there more?'

Some of the light faded from his eyes and she regretted her words and the tone in which they had been uttered. Alexander was no fool, nor was he a child. Since he was fifteen she had watched him hovering on the brink of manhood and now this slip of a girl had tripped him headlong into adulthood.

Alexander was recovering his poise. 'She's English,' he said calmly, 'and her name is Sylvia Barrett. She's eighteen and her parents come from Godalming in Surrey – Sylvia is their only child.'

'What do they do, these Barretts?' Mary replaced the wineglass on the white tablecloth and began to roll up her napkin.

For a moment he made no answer and again she cursed her stupidity. Whatever her feelings, she must tread carefully with this young man who had reappeared so unexpectedly to shatter her composure.

'Her father is an engineer. He has a small company and they are currently building bridges for the railways.'

'I see.'

'Do you?' Alexander pushed back his chair and stood up, but just then Mrs Markham came in with the coffee and he sat down again. They both watched in silence as the housekeeper poured two cups and then withdrew, obviously puzzled by the charged atmosphere.

Mary lifted the cream jug, but Alexander put a hand over his cup.

'I take it black now,' he said with an attempt at lightness.

'I suppose you have been converted?' said Mary.

He laughed. 'Sylvia has convinced me that – '

'Is Sylvia pretty?'

'Yes.'

'Very pretty?'

'She's quite beautiful, Mary, and I love her desperately.'

Mary swallowed hard, then added sugar to her coffee and stirred it slowly. She wanted to scream out, 'Don't tell me about her! I don't want to know', but she knew she dare not and fought to conceal her mounting panic. It was irrational, she knew – all young men fall in love and she had known it must happen some day. She had not expected it quite so soon however. Alexander had gone away a boy, she thought bitterly, and now Sylvia had transformed him into – what? A lovesick man! No, she was being unfair. 'Be careful,' she told herself. 'Watch what you say or you will lose him for ever!' But then a new and fearful thought struck her. Was this love merely spiritual or had he . . . had they . . . the idea was too terrible to contemplate and she resisted it, pushing it to the darkest recesses of her mind. She herself had no experience of physical love and no understanding of sex.

'Please don't be this way, Mary,' Alexander pleaded. 'You will like her when you meet her. She is so sweet, so truly kind and thinks only of others. Sylvia is so much like you, Mary – you will love her as I do. Believe me, you could find no fault in her!'

'A paragon, then. How rare!'

'Don't, Mary!' He stood up again, pushing himself to his feet so abruptly that the table shuddered and the coffee was spilled into the saucers. 'Don't sneer at her, Mary! I won't have it and it does you no credit!'

Mary stared at him open-mouthed. He was *daring* to tell her how to behave? She was lost for words.

'We are very much in love, Mary,' he went on, 'and we don't want to be parted. I came home to tell you that I am not going to Italy – '

'Not going . . .' she faltered.

'With your permission, I want to go to Switzerland where Sylvia's grandparents have a small house. She will stay there and they have offered to find me a room nearby.'

'No!' cried Mary. 'You are going to Italy.'

'I am going to Switzerland.'

Mary rose to her feet also and allowed herself a brief glance at his face, which was white and anguished.

'Mary!' He was shouting at her. 'Don't try to part us – don't you understand what love is? I love her, Mary. I would *die* for her! Why can't it be Switzerland instead of Italy? What difference can it possibly make to you? I want to be near her; we want to be together. *Her* parents understand this so why not you? I told them that you would be so pleased for us, because I believed you would.' He came round the table towards her, his eyes full of appeal. 'Mary, please, if you love me at all . . .'

But Mary drew back, ignoring his outstretched hand. 'If I love *you*,' she said. 'What about your love for me? I had such plans for you – Venice, Rome – and you want to throw it all up for the sake of some twopenny – '

Without warning Alexander brought his fist crashing down on to the table and the tall coffee-pot tottered and fell onto its side, spilling a stream of dark liquid which flowed across the cloth and dripped on the carpet. Mary, horrified, watched helplessly as he made ineffectual efforts to staunch the flow with his table napkin.

'I will not hear a word against her, Mary,' he said, dabbing at the spilt coffee. 'She does not deserve such spiteful remarks. She's a lovely girl and I'm *so* lucky. I won't allow you or anyone else to spoil our love.'

'Love? What do you know of love? You are seventeen – a child! You are *besotted* with her,' cried Mary, struggling to hold back the tears of rage and helplessness that pressed against her closed eyelids. 'Oh, leave the cloth alone, for heaven's sake! You are making it worse!'

She snatched the dripping napkin from his hand and threw it on to an empty plate. For a moment they both stared at the spoiled tablecloth; he looked very vulnerable as he stood beside the table.

'I love her,' Alexander repeated dully, but Mary hardened her heart towards him.

'I will not send you to Switzerland,' she said. 'You will go as planned to Italy; you cannot go to Switzerland without my money and I warn you that I shall not – '

Alexander played his trump card. 'Her parents have invited me to go at *their* expense,' he said. 'I told them it would not be necessary, but if it is, they will be willing. Mary, for the last time, do *please* give Sylvia a chance. I have a photograph of her upstairs to show you.'

'And a lock of her hair, I suppose!' said Mary. She knew she was making a fool of herself, but the words tumbled out as she turned away and hot tears spilled down her cheeks.

'Oh, please don't cry, Mary,' he begged. 'I don't want to hurt you.' He put his arm round her shoulders, but furiously she shook it free and pushed him away.

'Don't pretend!' she cried wildly between her sobs. 'Don't pretend you love me. How can I mean anything to you, with this Sylvia turning your head with all her nonsense. It's Sylvia you love, not me!'

'But Mary,' he protested, 'Sylvia's different. I mean, I have loved you all these years. You have been everything to me – the mother I never had. I love you both but in different ways, that's all.'

'I don't want you to love her!' cried Mary recklessly. '*I* love you. Don't you understand?'

There was a long horrified silence and Mary closed her eyes. She heard Alexander move away and the door slammed. He had gone. Still sobbing, Mary gazed round the room and then slowly lowered herself to her knees.

'Don't go, Alexander,' she whispered. 'Don't leave me. *Don't*! I can't bear it!' She rocked backwards and forwards consumed by black despair. 'Don't go to Sylvia . . . don't go,' she muttered brokenly. 'I'm sorry, Alexander – I'm truly sorry. Only don't go away, Alexander. I love you. Please don't go . . .'

Dimly she was aware that the front door had opened and closed violently and a moment later Mrs Markham was beside her, her plump kindly face full of concern as she knelt beside her, whispering words of comfort and urging her stricken mistress back on to her feet.

*

It had finally been arranged that the 'Barley Tap' should be taken on a lease for a period of twelve months, with an option to purchase at the end of that time for a sum which was mutually agreeable. The preliminaries were thus expedited and on the twentieth of August Bertie and his wife would leave Foxearth to take up temporary residence in a small hotel in the vicinity of their brewery. This would enable them to supervise the preparation of the living quarters, discover a man suitable to be employed as head brewer and conduct various other lines of enquiry necessary to the commencement of the enterprise. A licence must be applied for, Customs and Excise must be notified, supplies of malt and sugar must be negotiated and further monies must be raised.

These were all Bertie's particular problems, but Beatrice had her own. She would have to advertise for a healthy, hardworking woman to undertake some of the cleaning. Furniture and furnishings had to be chosen – they had none at all – and there was a part-time barmaid to be engaged. Beatrice still suffered agonies of apprehension about the entire project – not least about her own contribution – but still she had not revealed her doubts to her husband. He was immersed in discussions and obsessed with figures and calculations, remaining quite unaware of her reluctance to exchange the security of Foxearth for an unfamiliar life at the 'Barley Tap'.

When finally the day came to leave Foxearth, Beatrice stood on the doorstep with dread in her heart as they made their farewells to Vinnie and the children.

'And you promise you will write,' Vinnie urged Bertie. 'Or telephone – or both. Oh, do make him promise, Bea! I am going to miss you both so dreadfully and the children will have no one to play with them.' She turned towards James and Edward who stood behind her on the steps, watching the scene with anxious faces, aware of the enormity of the occasion.

'I'll write to Uncle Bertie,' said James. 'I am a good writer – Doll says I am. I'll write you a letter.'

'Thank you very much,' said Bertie, seizing the child, swinging him up over his head and lowering him, squealing, to the ground.

'*Me*!' cried Teddy. 'Lift *me* up, Uncle Bertie, it's my turn!' He ran from the steps with arms outstretched and Bertie took hold of his hands.

'Will you write to me?' he asked and, when the boy nodded, swung him off his feet and round in a circle in a 'twister'.

Bea looked round for Louise. 'Where's that other little poppet?' she asked. 'And Doll? I haven't said "Good-bye" to them.'

Vinnie stepped out on to the gravelled drive and pointed to a first-floor window from which Doll and Louise leaned to watch the proceedings.

'Louise is still fretful,' said Vinnie, 'and Doll thought she should stay in the nursery.' She waved up at the two smiling faces.

'I'll go up to them,' said Bea, snatching the opportunity to delay their departure by a few more minutes. She gathered up her skirts and hurried up the steps, leaving Vinnie staring forlornly at Bertie and then beyond him to the horse-brake which had been hired to take them to the station. Vinnie had wanted to accompany them and see them safely on to the train, but Bertie had refused, maintaining with some truth that platform partings were even harder to bear.

'Cheer up, Vinnie!' he teased. 'We're only going to London, remember. How would you feel if we were off to India again? Ah, that made you think! I promise to keep in touch and as soon as we are straight, you will be invited to see a day's brewing and sample the famous Harris beer. What shall it be – a good dark stout or a drop of porter? And I have promised to let you play barmaid, remember?'

She laughed shakily. 'If only we weren't so near to September, I would insist on coming with you,' she told him.

'Perhaps in October when we're finished-. . . '

'We shall see,' he said. 'I'm hoping a couple of months' work will break the back of it. Don't worry about us, Vinnie – we shall take to our new lives like ducks to water, you'll see! You have worries of your own, with the picking about to start. I feel we are deserting *you* in your hour of need.'

'Oh, Bertie, what fools we all are!' cried Vinnie and hugged him again.

Beatrice reappeared and after kissing Vinnie and the boys 'Good-bye' for the third time, climbed into the carriage with Bertie behind her. They moved away at a walking pace and then at a trot as the driver whipped up the horses. Bea and Bertie waved energetically to the subdued group on the steps and the two faces above them at the window.

'I don't want them to go to India', said Teddy, his lips trembling.

Vinnie knelt and put her arms round him. 'They're not going to India, darling,' she told him. 'Only to London. Don't cry, Teddy.' She wiped away two large tears which rolled down his cheeks. 'It's always a bit sad when people we love go away, but we will see them again soon, I promise you.'

'*I'm* not crying at all,' said James, who looked as though he might. Vinnie put an arm round him also.

'I know,' she said, 'we'll play a game to cheer ourselves up until it's time for your tea – how about "Hide-and-Seek"? Shall we play that?'

Teddy nodded, his face unsmiling, but James shook his head. 'There's not enough,' he said. 'Can Louise play – and Doll?'

Vinnie shook her head. 'Not today,' she said. 'Louise is a bit grizzly, so Doll is helping her with a jigsaw.'

The corners of James's mouth drooped. 'It's no good with only three,' he insisted. 'I want Louise and Doll to play too.'

Vinnie stood up and straightened her skirts, trying to conceal her irritation. 'And I have just told you that they can't,' she said firmly. 'So we'll forget about the "Hide-and-Seek" and go back indoors. We can play "Happy Families" instead and save the "Hide-and-Seek" for tomorrow when Louise *can* join us!'

She was not to know that by the following day Louise's sickness would be more pronounced and that by the end of the week the doctor would be calling daily, his expression and manner becoming increasingly concerned.

CHAPTER EIGHT

On the doctor's first visit Bertha opened the front door to him and was immediately impressed by his appearance, particularly his youthful good looks. Doctor Lucian Jerome had taken over the old doctor's practice on his retirement two weeks earlier, having moved to Teesbury straight from London where he had been a junior partner in a small general practice in Highgate. He came with glowing references and the highest recommendations. Certainly nobody could fault his personal looks and though he was very familiar with the expression of admiration on Bertha's face, it was to his credit that he was not a conceited man. In fact, on occasions he found his handsome features a distinct disadvantage, having suffered acute embarrassment from the unwelcome attentions of some of his female patients. He had studied mainly at Guy's Hospital, but had spent a short period at Great Ormond Street where he had later held the appointment of Registrar for two-and-a-half years.

He smiled politely at Bertha as he stepped through the door and she smiled radiantly in return, unable to take her gaze from the clear grey eyes with their long dark lashes, smooth-shaven skin, aquiline nose and fine cheek-bones. He handed her his cane and began to remove his white gloves, easing off one finger at a time as he avoided her eyes and glanced round the tastefully-furnished hallway. Handing her the gloves, he removed his silk top-hat to reveal a well-shaped head and short brown curls. For a moment Bertha continued to stare at him, memorising every feature so that she could give the rest of the kitchen staff an accurate description of this paragon of manhood.

Vinnie now appeared at the top of the stairs. 'Doctor Jerome?' she called.

He nodded and as he went up the stairs she came down to meet him half-way, though Bertha saw only the lithe figure of the doctor, elegantly clothed in the regulation grey coat and pin-striped trousers. Receiving Vinnie's nod of dismissal, she put the doctor's cane, gloves and hat on the hallstand and then hurried back to the kitchen.

On the stairs Vinnie said, 'I am Mrs Lawrence,' as they shook hands.

'Ah, yes,' he said, 'you asked me to see the little Bray boy. That was a great tragedy – as you know, he was dead by the time I reached them.'

Vinnie's face was pale and drawn and she sighed heavily. 'I blame myself,' she said. 'I visited them earlier in the week, but did not suspect for a moment that it was not croup.'

'Please do not think that way,' he told her. 'You called me in promptly as soon as your doubts materialised – you have no medical knowledge, so how could you expect to diagnose the disease? Who would expect diptheria in summer? It is very uncommon. You must not blame yourself, Mrs Lawrence.'

'At least you do not pretend it was God's will,' she said.

He shrugged. 'We cannot tell,' he replied.

'But if I had called you in earlier – '

'Probably it would have made no difference,' he assured her. 'There is no certain cure for the disease, only the best possible skilled nursing, a great deal of luck and an iron constitution. Even with all three, diptheria can still prove fatal.'

He regretted his words as soon as he had uttered them, for Vinnie's eyes widened with fear although she made an effort to control herself.

'Doctor, I was there!' she said. 'I was with Ned's little boy and then . . . ' she swallowed. 'And then I came home to my own children. The infection – I'm afraid I may have passed on the infection. Oh, if I had only known! And now Louise is poorly. I want you to look at her, doctor, and tell me that I'm letting my imagination . . . ' She faltered to a stop.

He saw the tears gathering and said quickly, 'Well now, let's go and have a few words with your little girl. It's by no means certain that you will have carried the infection.'

Vinnie led the way to Doll's bedroom, explaining as they went that Louise was so fretful in the night that Doll had taken her into her own room.

'Very sensible,' he said as he followed her into the bedroom where Louise lay propped against the pillows, her face pale. Her hands rested limply on the patchwork coverlet and she watched their approach with indifference. Doll sat beside the bed, a story book in her hand.

'This is Doctor Jerome,' said Vinnie. 'Dorothy, our nanny.' Doll nodded and he bowed briefly in her direction.

'And you are Louise,' he said to the little girl, smiling. 'And you're not feeling too well, is that right?'

The child's mouth drooped and she looked at Doll for reassurance.

Doll smiled cheerfully. 'The doctor is going to make you better,' she said. 'He knows all about little girls and boys and when they feel ill, he makes them well again.'

'That's right,' said the doctor. 'Your nanny has hit the nail right on the head. Now, I want you to tell me where it is you feel so poorly. Is it your head? Your tummy? Where is the pain?'

'Nowhere,' she said with a slight frown.

Vinnie explained that Louise was listless, irritable and had no appetite. There was no fever so far as they could tell. Doll added that in the night the child had complained that her neck hurt.

Dr Jerome nodded, then took one of Louise's hands in his.

'Well, Louise,' he said, 'I want to examine you. That means I shall look in your mouth, feel your poor old neck and listen to your heart. It might tickle a bit, but it won't hurt you in any way.'

Louise looked at Doll again.

'It's all very exciting,' said Doll. 'The doctor has come to visit you and now he's going to examine you. What a lot we shall have to tell the boys when they come back!'

James and Teddy had gone with Tim Bilton, the head groom, when he took the bay mare to the smithy to be shod.

The doctor opened his Gladstone bag and took out his stethoscope; then Louise's nightdress was rolled up and he listened carefully to her chest and back.

'Has she been coughing at all?' he asked, his tone deliberately casual as his slim fingers felt for the glands on either side of her neck.

'No!'

The women spoke simultaneously and the same thought leaped into both minds.

'Good!' he said. 'And you say she has no appetite? Is she taking any fluids?'

Doll shook her head and the doctor smiled at Louise.

'I want you to open your mouth as wide as you can,' he told her. 'Oh, that's splendid! What lovely white teeth – I can see you use your toothbrush every day. No, keep it open a little longer. Good girl!'

He felt for the pulse in the small wrist and took a watch from his waistcoat pocket – 'Aha! That's fine' – then laid a hand across her brow. While the women waited, he sat back and gave Louise a long appraising look before patting her cheek gently.

'We shall soon have you well again,' he said. 'You do everything your nurse tells you and – '

'*Nurse?*' cried Doll, startled. He gave her a warning look, closed his bag with a snap and stood up.

'I shall call in again tomorrow to see you,' he finished. 'You and I will soon be good friends.'

As the doctor turned to leave the room, Vinnie asked Doll to stay with Louise and followed him out on to the landing and down the stairs to the hall.

'A nurse?' she echoed. 'Oh no, doctor! She doesn't need a nurse – Doll is very capable and – '

'Mrs Lawrence,' he interrupted. 'I'm afraid your fears were well-grounded. Your little girl is very sick and she will need very expert care. I don't doubt that your nanny is a capable woman, but – '

'Is it diptheria?' cried Vinnie. 'Oh God, I can't bear it! How can it be? She has no cough and yet poor Ned's boy was coughing.'

'I'm afraid it *is*,' he said gently. 'Can we talk somewhere?'

'In the morning-room,' she whispered. She led the way and they stood on opposite sides of the fireplace. 'Tell me the worst,' Vinnie said dully. 'I don't want you to keep anything from me. I think I can bear it – if only you tell me the truth.'

'I am quite certain it is diptheria. The cough will develop soon, I'm afraid, but there is plenty of hope.'

'Hope? But you said – '

'With Mr Bray's son it was not diagnosed in time,' he reminded her. 'No one recognised the disease and because of that he had no proper nursing. Thanks to your vigilance and that of your nanny, Louise's illness *has* been diagnosed and we can take all the proper steps. We must, for instance, keep a close watch on the two little boys. Also, it is important that you try not to distress yourself, Mrs Lawrence – you will need all your wits about you. You have asked me for the truth and I will give it to you; your little girl has all the symptoms – swollen glands in her neck, a pulse rate that is high in relation to her fever, a pallor, no appetite and, most significant, a greyish look about the tonsils which will almost certainly develop into the membrane so characteristic of the disease.'

'The membrane?'

'It's like a grey skin which forms in the throat and inhibits the breathing. In extreme cases it blocks the air passage. We shall have to remove it at intervals if we can.'

'Oh, dear God!' Vinnie's eyes were large and frightened and her voice shook.

'As I said earlier, there is as yet no positive cure, but hundreds of lives are being saved by skilled nursing and you will have an expert nurse – I believe a Nurse Ramsey is sometimes available.'

'Yes, that's right. She came once when Colonel Lawrence first became bedridden, to teach Janet – ' She broke off and covered her face.

The doctor continued, 'Louise must have *complete* bed rest. She must be fed and washed with a minimum of movement, because the heart can be easily damaged. The throat membrane makes breathing difficult, so the body has to make greater efforts to suck air in and out through the constricted airway. That in turn strains the heart.'

'Then Ned's boy . . . '

He nodded. 'Heart failure,' he said. 'It is a very real danger. I am telling you all this not to frighten you, but because if your daughter is to pull through you must understand exactly what is happening. I believe Nurse Ramsey is most experienced, so your little daughter will be in good hands.'

'And Doll?'

He shrugged. 'She may assist if the nurse is agreeable – some nurses prefer to have sole charge. Oh, and she must remain in strict isolation. Can your sons stay elsewhere temporarily? With a relative, perhaps?'

Vinnie thought rapidly. Eva, her sister-in-law, lived in Bromley with her own family.

'But the risk of infection?' she said.

'I shall satisfy myself that the boys are free of the disease before I allow them to go, of course.'

'Or they could stay with Mrs Bryce, perhaps, in the village.'

'I'm sure you will be able to make suitable arrangements. Don't worry on that account. It's your daughter who must be our main consideration. A light diet, please, and plenty of fluid. The nurse will monitor her urine output. No laxatives. Plenty of glucose. And at all times *complete* rest on her back.' He stood up. 'It may be a long fight, Mrs Lawrence, so do take good care of your own health. I believe your busiest month is coming up shortly.'

Vinnie looked at him blankly. 'The hop-picking,' he said.

'Oh, yes.' She laughed shakily. 'I had forgotten. Doctor Jerome, you *must* save my daughter – please say you will.'

'I will do my very best, Mrs Lawrence, and we will pray it is a mild case and that her resistance is good.'

In the hall he pulled on his gloves and picked up his cane.

Tucking it under his arm, he took up his bag and hat.

As he stood on the doorstep, Vinnie said, 'Oh dear! I haven't offered you any refreshment. A cup of tea, perhaps? Do forgive me – I am so terribly worried! This dreadful thing – doctor, she must get better! We'll do anything. Expense is of no importance, so please ask for anything you need.'

'Thank you, Mrs Lawrence. I appreciate your feelings entirely and of course I will do everything I can to ensure her recovery. I shall contact Nurse Ramsey on your behalf and if she is not available, I will find someone equally experienced. Now I must go, but I will call again tomorrow at the same time unless there is a change in her condition and you feel it necessary to send for me this evening. And remember, take care of your own health, Mrs Lawrence – I don't want another patient on my hands!'

*

Doctor Jerome kept his word and at quarter-past-seven that same evening, Nurse Ramsey arrived and took over the spare room on the other side of the nursery. Now nearing sixty, she remained as efficient as ever and was not looking forward to her retirement. She was a small woman who had put on rather too much weight and her uniform strained at the seams. Her grey hair was pulled back into two thin plaits which encircled her head and dozens of broken veins covered her cheeks and nose; these gave her a tipsy appearance, but she was in fact strictly teetotal and high-principled. As Vinnie had told the doctor, Nurse Ramsey had trained Janet to take care of the Colonel who still recalled her stay at Foxearth with great amusement, assuring Janet that the nurse's bedside manner had been more frightening than anything he had experienced in the Boer War.

But the Nurse Ramsey who had dealt with the cantankerous old man was not the same person who now took Louise's life into her hands. With the child she was gentle but firm and within an hour of her arrival – and to Doll's great relief – had persuaded Louise to eat a few spoonfuls of milky rice pudding and a little puréed apple. The nanny's initial dismay at being replaced by the nurse soon gave way to ungrudging admiration for the older woman and secret relief that the burden of responsibility was no longer hers. She remained in daily attendance as Nurse Ramsey's 'right hand', and fetched and carried for her without a word of complaint. Nurse Ramsey, equally tireless in her devotion, agreed to take two hours off in the middle of the afternoon for a refreshing 'nap' and to go off duty at nine o'clock at night, remaining on call in case of any emergency.

Teddy and James spent two days with Mrs Bryce until the short incubation period was safely past and they were declared free of infection. Then they travelled to Bromley to stay with Aunt Eva and their cousins.

The passage of several days saw Louise's condition deteriorating as the deadly membrane spread from the tonsils to the larynx. As it spread, it thickened and the child's breathing became laboured; paroxysms of coughing began to exhaust her strength. The nurse checked her pulse hourly – any change in the rhythm of the pulse-rate was to be reported immediately to the doctor, who waited also for a tell-tale drop in the urine output which might signal the beginning of heart failure. No one except Vinnie was allowed into the sick-room, but by the fourth day even she made only rare visits, for the sight of her excited Louise and provoked further bouts of coughing.

'What can you do,' Vinnie asked Dr Jerome on the fifth day, 'if the membrane closes her throat completely? You cannot let her choke to death; there must be something you can do!'

The doctor nodded. 'We shall do all we can, you may rely on that,' he said. 'In the meantime, you can pray. I will call again tomorrow morning.'

When he had gone, Vinnie stood uncertainly in the hallway. Then she pulled a shawl from the hall table, threw it round her shoulders and went out of the front door, making her way round to the side of the house and then through the gate into the upper hop-garden. A light rain was falling, but she adjusted the shawl to cover her head and went on through the garden.

The hop-bines towered above her on both sides, dripping greenly and hemming her in, reaching out to pluck at her hair and clothes with long delicate tendrils. Underfoot her light shoes were soon wet through and muddy from the well-trampled grass over which she walked. Overhead, heavy grey clouds scudded past, blown by winds that fortunately were too high to disturb the acres of hops that were so nearly ready for picking. But Vinnie walked on without even seeing them, her eyes wide with nameless horrors, her hands clutching the wet shawl across her chest.

'Louise is going to die,' she whispered. 'I know she will die and I don't know how I shall bear it.' She felt a terrible remorse that when Ned Bray's son had died, she had not even *begun* to understand his parents' anguish. She had paid for the funeral but found an excuse not to attend, reluctant to share their overwhelming grief.

'And now it will be my turn,' she thought. 'I shall lose my little girl.' Already she felt Louise slipping away from her, surrendered to the nurse's more competent hands. The knowledge that she had two healthy sons did not console her – Louise, her tiny elfin girl, was going to be taken from her. Vinnie believed she could see through the doctor's encouraging manner – could read between the optimistic phrases. Silently the rain fell and the shawl slipped down; her hair was soon wet and bedraggled, but Vinnie neither knew nor cared. She thought of nothing but the helpless lungs being starved of air and the small heart labouring under its tremendous burden.

'Keep beating, little heart,' she whispered. 'Please keep beating.'

The hop-garden sloped down towards the river and Vinnie made her slow, stumbling progress between the rows of hops and out of the lower gate on to the river bank. There she stood for a moment, her face upturned to the rain. Panic started up in her mind and she made no attempt to suppress it. She was so very weary of pretending and it would be such a relief to throw herself face-down on the wet grass and give vent to great animal howls of fear and misery. Only a last vestige of self-control kept her upright and silent.

With a deep sigh she turned to the left, walking towards the ancient stone bridge where so many years ago her mother's drowned body had been discovered. Reaching this, she leaned against it, relishing the feel of the cold damp stonework against her body. Indirectly, five-year-old Vinnie had brought about Sue Harris's death, for she had fallen into the water while looking for Vinnie who had hidden herself away in a gipsy cart.

Now Vinnie turned suddenly and stared at the smooth clean water with its treacherous weed – weed which had caught and held her mother's body.

'Ma!' Vinnie whispered. 'I need you – where are you?'

She let her knees buckle and allowed her body to slide down until she was crouched on the wet grass, hugging her knees, her back against the bridge.

'What's it like, Ma, being dead?' she whispered, trying to imagine a dark, silent void where there was no anguish, no fear, no striving. Rest in peace, they said. 'Is that how it is, Ma?' Was her mother peaceful, warm, protected? Vinnie almost envied her.

'I'm cold and frightened,' she muttered. 'Help me, Ma!'

A few slow tears trickled down her face, but she did not know that she wept. Her knowledge of death and beyond was a hazy one and she had no faith to guide her, only the vague notion that a spirit might linger in this world until it passed over into another. Such spirits were surely ghosts, she argued, but could a ghost comfort the living?

'I suppose not,' she said aloud, opening her eyes to survey her ruined shoes.

Another phrase occurred to her, increasing her anxiety. 'The sins of the father . . . ' Was Louise's death to be Vinnie's punishment for all her past sins? Frowning, she tried to rationalise this new worry. If she *had* sinned in the past, it had not been intentional, but she had made many mistakes and had hurt many people. Tom Bryce's death still haunted her; his image flitted in and out of her dreams, reproaching her, but she had not killed him. He had taken his own life and no one could blame her for that, yet she *had* been involved in his downfall. Others might declare her innocent, but in her own eyes she would always be guilty.

Roughly she brushed both rain and tears from her face. 'I didn't mean to hurt anyone,' she said loudly, as though to put the record straight. 'I got it wrong, but I didn't *mean* to hurt anyone.' Julian – her husband – and now William. She hadn't loved them in the way they had wanted to be loved. Was that a sin?

Aware suddenly of her discomfort, she stood up awkwardly on her cramped legs. Glancing under the bridge, she remembered herself on that first hopping, as though the twenty years that had passed since had never been. The children had played beneath the bridge – shrieking, laughing, jostling each other on the narrow edge of ground uncovered by the low summer level of the river. Above, *on* the bridge, they had leaned over to toss sticks into the water and the boys – daring or dared – had walked along the narrow parapet with arms out-stretched to preserve their balance. Bertie had done it, his body silhouetted by the sunlight, and her terror had been real. The older boys had 'fished' with home-made rods, silent and earnest in the twilight after the day's hopping was done, grumbling at the girls for 'disturbing the fish' when they ventured too near the river. The women had taken water from it in clanking pails to provide a quick wash morning and night – what Sue Harris had called 'a lick and a promise'. Further along, Vinnie had stood in the shallow stream that fed the river to give herself an extra good wash with a sliver of borrowed soap. With a faint smile, she remembered how she had first seen the young Julian Lawrence, resplendent in a crisply laundered sailor-suit, as he strolled among the pickers with Eva, his sister. A prince and princess, Vinnie had thought them as, dirty and bedraggled, she had stared back at them in the dappled green light.

'You smell, Vinnie Harris!' Julian had told her, his fingers to his nose. 'You need a wash.'

She recalled the water, cool to her feet as she chased the

elusive soap across the pebbles at the bottom of the stream. Yes, she had *washed* for Julian Lawrence, but she had fought for him too when a group of London boys had rolled him on the dirty ground. Then Vinnie had thrown herself into the fray regardless of her own safety; in the mêlée she had lost a penny and his mother, the cool and elegant Christina Lawrence, had given her another. Christina, the Colonel's wife, had loved Tom Bryce. Much later Christina had died too ... Vinnie bowed her head as the past returned to torment her.

'It all just happened, Ma,' she whispered. 'I didn't mean it to happen – not any of it.' She blinked rapidly as fresh tears gathered.

Impulsively, Vinnie ducked under the bridge and began to search along the stonework. Here countless names had been scratched by generations of hoppers – some children, some lovers. Somewhere Bertie had scratched hers, but now she could not find it among the confused jumble of names – ANNIE ... DF ... S loves GW. ... Was that George Walker from Whitechapel? Vaguely she saw the Walkers – a noisy, quarrelsome family. And plump Mrs Batty, who had hidden the Harrises in her cellar when the rent man called. Further along she found the letters 'MP' contained within a lopsided heart – possibly the awful Mollie Pett who had caused so much trouble and then disappeared, leaving young Alexander to fend for himself.

'Vinnie? What on earth are you up to? Come out of there, for heaven's sake!'

She whirled to see Clive le Brun beside the bridge.

For a moment she stared at the familiar figure framed against the curved arch. In spite of her wretchedness she was aware of a lightening of heart, almost a surge of hope, and realised with a shock of excitement the depth of her pleasure at seeing him again. She appreciated for the first time how much she had missed him. Obediently she took his proffered hand and allowed him to help her out from under the bridge and up the slippery river bank to level ground. She saw the surprise in his eyes as he noted her wet clothes, muddy shoes and the dripping hair which clung to her head. Without speaking, Clive reached up to brush back a tendril of hair from her forehead, his eyes expressionless.

'The housekeeper told me Louise is ill,' he said at last.

'Did Mrs Tallant tell you it's diptheria?' Vinnie whispered.

'Diptheria?' She saw the shock in his eyes. 'No, she didn't.'

'I expect she thought you already knew.' Vinnie looked into the familiar face and tried to read the expression in the grey eyes, but failed. 'I couldn't bear it any longer – I had to get out of the house and be alone. Oh Clive, I'm so frightened – and so helpless. I upset Louise if I go in . . . it's Doll she wants. There is nothing I can do except wait.'

'I am so sorry,' he said simply. He took her arm and began to lead her back towards the house.

'And the boys?' he asked.

'Both all right, thank God! They've gone to Eva's at Bromley, but it's so terribly quiet without them.'

'You have a nurse, of course?'

'Nurse Ramsey,' she told him.

He nodded. 'You must be brave, Vinnie. We all find hidden resources at such times.'

They walked in silence until Vinnie remembered that she had not spoken to Clive since she and William had gone their separate ways.

'How's William?' she asked him.

He shrugged. 'He'll survive, but these things take time.'

Clive continued to hold her arm and the pressure of his fingers comforted her. For a while they walked in silence and then, at his request, Vinnie gave him an up-to-date account of Louise's illness.

'It all seems very hopeful,' he reassured her. 'Louise was diagnosed very early and she is receiving the best treatment money can buy. Doctor Jerome sounds first-class – it's most important for you to have confidence in your doctor.'

'I do,' said Vinnie. 'He seems very experienced – and Nurse Ramsey, too. She is a bit of a dragon, but Doll thinks the world of her and I have no worries on that score.'

They had reached the front steps and Vinnie offered him some refreshment, but Clive declined.

'I just wanted to reassure myself that you were all right,' he told her. 'And do get out of those damp clothes,' he added. 'You look like a scarecrow.'

Vinnie laughed shakily. 'I will,' she promised. 'But I wish you would come back when you've finished your calls and have dinner with me. I should be very glad of some company.'

'I accept willingly,' he said. 'I have three calls to make in Hunton, but then I shall be back. About seven? Will that suit?'

'Yes. I'll tell Cook.'

Clive's carriage waited in the drive, the horse tossing his head restlessly.

'And no more rolling about in wet grass,' said Clive. 'You're too old for that sort of thing!'

'No, sir,' she mocked and he allowed himself a smile, pleased to see a little of her spirit returning. When the carriage had gone Vinnie stood for a long time gazing after it. She was ridiculously glad that he was coming back later.

*

That evening, for the first time since Louise had been taken ill, Vinnie felt the panic within her subside slightly and a little warmth crept into her cold and shivering soul. Some of Clive's strength reached out to her wordlessly – in the firm set of his mouth, the calm look in his eyes and the even tenor of his voice. Sitting opposite him at the table, Vinnie felt her own courage returning and was unutterably grateful for his presence. He talked positively of the future without giving false hope and her admiration for him deepened with each passing hour. To distract her thoughts from Louise, she asked him about his own family and listened with fascination as he described them. He spoke with affection and humour of his mother, who had defied her family's wishes in order to marry Charles le Brun; obviously he adored her and Vinnie envied them the closeness of a relationship she herself had missed. Of his father, Charles, Clive spoke with respect; it seemed he had been a reserved man who found it hard to communicate with his only child. His wife's death from consumption had had tragic consequences.

'My father died of a broken heart,' Clive told her. 'A little hard to believe, but I saw it with my own eyes. He simply lost the will to live.' He smiled suddenly and Vinnie thought, 'He doesn't smile enough,' and wanted to make him happier – to bring more laughter into his life.

'Why are you smiling?' she asked.

'You look so earnest. And I am talking too much. Now it's your turn, Vinnie.'

But she shook her head resolutely. While Clive talked she could take comfort in his voice and keep some of the horrors at bay.

'You haven't told me about your grandparents yet,' she reminded him, 'or your great-grandparents!'

Clive laughed. 'I shall be here all night,' he joked.

The moment he spoke, Vinnie knew that that was what she wanted.

'Stay with me!' she blurted out, giving herself no time to think. 'Just for tonight? I would feel so much better if I knew you were here – Mrs Tallant can easily make up a bed.'

Clive hesitated, greatly taken aback by her invitation. 'I don't know . . . ' he began.

'*Please*, Clive! You could telephone William, so that he doesn't worry. It is selfish of me, I know, but I feel so much braver tonight because you're with me. Does that sound very silly?'

He shook his head. 'Not silly at all, Vinnie. It would be churlish to refuse – I'll stay overnight.'

Vinnie stretched out her hand and put it over his lightly-clenched fist as it rested on the table.

'You are a good man, Clive, do you know that?' Her voice was soft.

'A good man?' He shrugged. 'Is there such a creature? Is there a good man or a good woman anywhere in the world? I doubt it! We are all a mixture of good and bad, aren't we? Some bad in the best of us and some good in the worst of us!'

'You are being very profound.'

Seeing Clive glance at the table, where her hand still rested on his, for a few seconds Vinnie was aware of a tension between them. Then he turned over his hand so that hers rested in his palm and closed his fingers gently around hers.

'What a little hand,' he said.

Vinnie's heart was very full as she looked at him. She longed to walk round the table, put her arms around him and hold him close to her as a mother holds a child. Why, she did not know. Or perhaps she could hold out her arms to him and say, 'Comfort me', and he would stroke her hair with those long fingers. She did not want to be separated from him by the width of a table.

'Oh, Clive!' she whispered, then shook her head. Clive le Brun was hop factor to the Lawrences and a family friend. She told herself sternly that she was letting her imagination run away with her; she was mistress of Foxearth and as such must behave with dignity and good sense.

'What is it?' he asked.

'Nothing. I'm sorry.' Gently she withdrew her hand. 'But you will stay, Clive? You promise? Just for tonight.'

'Of course I will.'

A deep sigh shook her slim frame and Clive said again, 'Vinnie, won't you tell me what's troubling you?'

'Nothing apart from my anxiety over Louise,' she said, smiling in an attempt to dispel the heightened tension between them. 'I'm just so pleased that you will stay. Now I have an idea – let's have a game of chess!'

'At this hour!' he exclaimed. 'And after a good meal, wine and brandy!'

Vinnie laughed. 'If I can't beat you now, I never will!' she teased and jumped up to fetch the board.

*

Nurse Ramsey's bedtime routine had remained unaltered for the past twenty years of her life, ever since she had taken up private nursing on the death of the widowed mother whom she had nursed devotedly for six-and-a-half years. Her professional duties made it necessary for her to spend most of each year in other people's homes, in temporary – often makeshift – quarters, but she saw in this no excuse for relaxing her standards. Whenever the patient's condition allowed, she retired to her room promptly at nine o'clock and began her preparations for rest. Tonight was no exception. First she brought out from beneath her pillow a high-necked, long-sleeved flannelette nightgown, which she laid out on the bed. She wore flannelette winter and summer, being convinced that the British climate should never be trusted and believing that a sudden fall in temperature during the night could have dire consequences for the lightly-clad sleeper.

Taking up a small hand mirror, she then separated the sheets of the bed, held the mirror between them while she counted to ten and then withdrew it. The glass had not misted over, therefore the bed was not damp. With a nod of satisfaction, she replaced the mirror and sat on the wicker chair beside the bed to unbutton her shoes. She took them off carefully, straightened them out and placed them side by side beneath the bed. In the morning she would rub them over briskly with a soft yellow duster. Shoe-polish was applied once a week on Thursdays.

Panting with the effort of leaning so far down, she straightened up slowly and waited for the slight dizziness to fade, then stood to take off her white apron and blue starched uniform. Both were hung on a padded coat-hanger. Then she moved across the room in her stockinged feet and hung the coat-hanger on a hook behind the door, first giving the uniform a shake to loosen the creases. Catching sight of herself in the long swing mirror, she gave her dumpy figure a disparaging glance and turned away. Off came the petticoat, the stockings and stays, and on went the nightgown. From the large blue and white jug she poured a small amount of cold water into the matching bowl and washed her face, hands and neck. Cleaning her teeth took a few more moments. She emptied the dirty water into the pail and then it was time to unplait her sparse grey hair. Standing by the window, which was partly open, she began to brush the crimped hair with long firm strokes, counting as she did so – fifty strokes for each side.

Nurse Ramsey stared out over the shadowy grounds, thinking of her brief visit to the Colonel earlier in the afternoon. Janet was not firm enough with him, she reflected. He was not a child – he was a contrary adult and should be treated as such. All that coaxing to take a spoonful of medicine! And the silly woman was a sight too fond of him, that was quite plain. A nurse should be detached from her patient – it was better for both of them. Not that the old man would last much longer; she had seen plenty like him and recognised the final frailty which allowed life to glow like a wavering flame waiting to be extinguished by the slightest breeze.

Hairbrush poised, she listened intently as the sound of coughing reached her through the connecting door, but she heard Dorothy's voice, cool and comforting, and then the child was silent again.

She visualised the child slipping once more into sleep and then deliberately cast around in her mind for another subject with which to distract her thoughts. It had long been her practice to exclude concern for her patients whenever she could legitimately do so, because it did not do to become too involved. Involvement led to heartache and she could not allow herself the luxury of affection. Louise Lawrence was just another patient. Perhaps the more permanent Dorothys and Janets of this world were to be envied in that respect.

With an effort, she thought about the house in Pimlico where she had been born, and now lived alone – except for her cat, which had to be cared for by good neighbours during her frequent absences. The large tortoishell was all she had in the way of family and on the brief occasions when she was at home, she would smother him with love. Soon, however, she must retire and spend all her time at home – talking to the cat, cleaning the house and tending the garden. She viewed this prospect with mixed feelings.

Reaching the hundredth stroke, her hair was finished and

she pulled on her night-cap and pushed the hair up into it. Clumsily she knelt beside the bed and with closed eyes and clasped hands, recited the Lord's Prayer and then her own:

Most merciful Father, look down on Thy servant and give her the wisdom and skill to do Thy healing work. Bless Louise Lawrence and if it be Thy will, restore her in fitness and health to the loving arms of her family. Amen.

Getting up was not as easy as getting down these days, but she managed it. The doctor was only a few miles away and, thanks to Mr Graham Bell, could be reached very quickly by telephone if Louise's condition became acute. That could be tonight or tomorrow night – she knew it was very close and that she must snatch a few hours' sleep while she could.

*

Later that night Nurse Ramsey awoke to hear someone calling her name. The door handle was being rattled and a flurry of blows against the panel drowned her reply.

'Nurse Ramsey, wake up!'

She recognised Doll's voice. 'I'm coming!' she shouted back. 'I've said I'm coming!'

She was already half out of bed and reaching for her blue woollen dressing-gown, glancing at the clock which showed nearly two o'clock.

'Nurse Ramsey! Oh, for God's sake, come quickly!'

With hasty fingers, she brushed the remains of sleep from her eyes and unlocked the door. It was tonight – so be it. She ran into Louise's room, where one glance at the child told her all she needed to know. The little girl's face was blue and she was fighting for breath; her eyes were dark with fear and her mouth wide open as she struggled desperately to suck in air through a throat already constricted by swelling and now almost totally blocked by the fatal membrane.

'Fetch the mistress,' she told Doll. 'She must ring for the doctor at once – and rouse one of the servants for hot water. Quickly!'

'Is she going to die?' stammered Doll.

'She will if you don't do as I say. Now move yourself!'

Doll ran out of the room and almost collided with Vinnie. 'It's Louise ma'am,' gasped Doll. 'We must telephone for Doctor Jerome.'

At that moment Clive le Brun came out of the guest-room, fastening Julian's dressing-gown around him.

'I'll do it,' he told Vinnie. 'You go to Louise.' He hurried downstairs as Vinnie ran to her daughter, staring ashen-faced at the child in the bed. Louise could not speak, but she stared up in mute appeal as she tossed restlessly from side to side. Tendrils of pale hair clung damply to her head and the small hands were clenched into frantic fists.

Nurse Ramsey knew with a dreadful certainty that without a tracheotomy the child would die. If the doctor did not arrive promptly she would have to perform the operation herself. The scalpel and tube – discreetly covered with a cloth – had already been placed on the bedside table, in preparation for just such an emergency. Now she prayed that the doctor would arrive and her prayers were answered.

Bertha opened the door to him less than five minutes later. Fully dressed – but without gloves, hat and cane – he ran up the stairs and into the room. He took one look at Louise and noted the loud tortured breathing.

'A tracheotomy!' he said. 'Nurse . . . '

Vinnie put a hand to her mouth. 'Oh God!' she whispered. Seeing the scalpel which the doctor took up, a faintness swept over her and she swayed on her feet as Doll stepped forward to steady her.

'Take her out of here,' said the nurse. 'Leave her with Mr le Brun and come back – we may need you.'

At that moment there was a banging on the wall further along the passage.

'Now we've woken the Colonel,' said Doll, steering Vinnie out of the room. 'Never mind, Janet will attend to him.'

Clive led Vinnie downstairs and into the drawing-room.

'She's too young to die!' Vinnie whispered. 'I know she's going to die.'

'You know nothing of the kind,' Clive told her firmly, 'and I won't have you saying such a thing. She is in the best possible hands – I have every confidence in Doctor Jerome and Nurse Ramsey, and so have you. Now sit down and I will ask Bertha to heat you some milk.'

'No, Clive, don't go,' she begged 'Stay with me; I am so glad you are here.' She stood with her hands over her face and Clive regarded the small huddled figure with deep compassion.

'She's going to pull through, Vinnie,' he told her. 'I feel sure of it. Call it intuition – call it what you like, but I know she will recover.'

Slowly Vinnie uncovered her face. 'Do you mean it, Clive?' she asked. 'Or are you just trying to comfort me? Do you *really* mean it?'

He nodded. 'Yes, I do.'

'Oh, Clive! Then I do, too. Please God – oh please God – I feel so helpless.'

In spite of her resolve to the contrary, Vinnie felt the tears well up and as they began to roll down her face, Clive took her into his arms and held her close.

*

Upstairs doctor and nurse wrapped the little girl in a blanket to keep her as still as possible and pushed a lightly-rolled pillow under the back of her head. Moving expertly and without undue haste, the doctor made a small incision at the base of the throat. Louise made a slight sound as the blade went in, but Nurse Ramsey smoothed her forehead and spoke briskly to her to distract her attention as the end of the tube was inserted.

'Brave girl!' the doctor told her cheerfully. 'Soon be all over. Just keep as still as you can.'

As soon as the tube was in place there was a marked change in Louise's breathing as air, bypassing the constriction in her throat, flowed freely once more into the lungs. A look of great relief passed over her small face and she closed her eyes, exhausted from the long fight.

'Good,' said the doctor. 'We were in time – just.' Nurse

Ramsey nodded. 'Now for the main tube,' he said.

A second and narrower tube was now fed through the first one. If it became blocked with mucus or any other matter, it could be easily withdrawn for cleaning with a solution of bicarbonate of soda and replaced without difficulty or risk of damage to the original incision.

Doctor Jerome straightened his back and wiped his forehead with the back of his hand. Then he took Louise's wrist between his fingers and checked the pulse with a satisfied nod for Nurse Ramsey.

'I think we've saved this little one,' he said. 'We'll let the mother in shortly, but first I shall bandage the neck lightly so that it doesn't look too unsightly. She must now sit up all the time and someone must be with her constantly, day and night, to see she doesn't dislodge the tube. Fortunately she is old enough to understand. I expect she will sleep now – she's been through a great deal.'

Bertha knocked at the door and came in with a jug of hot water, looking fearfully towards the bed.

'She's going to live,' the doctor told her. 'You can tell Mrs Lawrence and say that I will be with her as soon as I've finished here. I'll wait for her downstairs in the hall. As for you, young lady,' – he smiled at Louise, who was staring up at him wide-eyed and uncomprehending – 'you will soon be well again and able to play with those harum-scarum brothers of yours.' He leaned forward and began to secure the tube with a bandage. 'You have a little tube in your throat to help you breathe. I want you to be a good girl and not touch it. Your neck may be a little sore for a while, but don't touch that either. A lot of don'ts, eh?' He put out a hand and gently ruffled her hair. 'You do what Nurse Ramsey tells you and I will come and see you in the morning. When little girls are ill they need plenty of sleep, so you remember that. You have been very brave. Goodbye for now, Louise. I'll see you in the morning.'

She blinked at him, but made no sound.

He turned to the nurse. 'You see, her normal colour is returning, thank goodness! I should like you to stay with her for the rest of tonight if you would – it will take Dorothy time to get used to the tube. Maybe you can change your hours, so that you do the night duty and Dorothy does the days.' He poured out some hot water and washed and dried his hands. 'Well, thank you for your assistance, nurse. It was, as always, most professional.'

Nurse Ramsey's tired eyes glowed with pleasure as she mumbled her thanks for the compliment.

'I'll be getting along now,' he said, 'and will have a word with Mrs Lawrence as I go out.'

When Doctor Jerome had left the room, the nurse settled herself on the chair beside the bed and took Louise's hand in hers. The child still stared, wide-eyed and silent.

'Now you close those peepers of yours,' said the nurse. 'It's all over now and time to forget it. You heard what the doctor said – lots of sleep. No, don't try to talk – just sleep.'

Obediently Louise closed her eyes and Nurse Ramsey looked at the slim fingers which rested in her own stubby and unlovely hand. Strange, she thought, that she had never wanted a child of her own. These little ones that came so fleetingly into her care were all the family she needed.

CHAPTER NINE

Maisie Hunter, drying glasses behind the bar of the 'Horse and Cart', watched critically as Sam Glover carried in what he called his 'paraphernalia' – bamboo canes, brushes, cloths and sacks – and set them down before the fireplace.

'You'll have to stir your stumps,' she told him. 'We open in fifteen minutes. You should have come back tomorrow and done it.'

Sam shook his head without bothering to look at her. 'Booked up solid,' he said. 'It's now or never.'

'Well, you should have been here on time, then. Three-thirty we said, not a quarter to six. I mean to say, all the sheeting I put over the chairs has been taken off again. We gave you up as a bad job when you weren't here by five-thirty. We can't have folk coming in and finding old sheets spread over everywhere.'

Sam Glover ignored the rebuke in her voice. Her husband had understood his reason for being later and *he* had said to go ahead. So go ahead he would, and Maisie Hunter could nag all she liked. Spreading a large grey sheet over the floor immediately in front of the fireplace, he began to whistle cheerfully to let her know that he was not in the least put out by her comments. He was a small, bent man with eyes like currants and he wore a curly-brimmed bowler – he had never been known to take off this hat in public, but rumour had it that he was bald. Maisie glared at his back, put away the last of the glasses and draped the wet cloth over the bucket which stood below the pumps to catch the drips. The sweep unfolded a large sooty blanket with a small hole in the centre and this he draped across the fireplace, holding it in place by two canes wedged between the fender and the mantelpiece. Having pushed the circular brush behind the blanket, he took up the first cane from the bundle beside him.

'Well, see there's no mess!' said Maisie. 'Our customers are used to a clean pub and I've no time to start dusting and polishing at quarter-to-six.'

The sweep paused to look pointedly at the clock on the wall. 'Clock wrong then, is it?' he asked. 'Says eighteen minutes to.'

Maisie snorted. 'Well, eighteen then. Eighteen, fifteen, what's the difference?'

'Three minutes, to my way of thinking. Leastways, that's what we was taught at school.'

Reaching under the blanket, Sam lifted the brush to the hole in the middle so that the end extended through it and he could screw on the first cane. This was accomplished with a few deft turns in an anti-clockwise direction and he pushed it up the chimney, twisting it as he did so, taking care always to work the brush in the same direction. Only once, as a young lad, had he made the mistake of turning it the wrong way and he could still remember his chagrin as the canes worked undone and fell back into the hearth, leaving the brush stuck in the chimney.

A second cane followed the first and in turn was pushed and twisted in the chimney. There was a spattering of soot in the hearth as the bristles scoured into the accumulated deposit inside, whereupon Sam gave a satisfied nod.

Ted Hunter came into the bar from the yard and stopped half-way across the room, watching him.

'Been smoking something awful, I hear,' said the sweep smugly.

Maisie bridled as he knew she would. 'Something awful?' she repeated. 'Who says so? Who says it's been smoking something awful?'

'Everyone,' said Sam as another cane disappeared through the hole in the blanket and more soot fell.

Maisie looked at her husband furiously. 'D'you hear that?' she demanded.

Ted shrugged. 'Damn chimney's always smoked,' he said. 'You know it has.'

'We had a brand new cowl fitted – ' she began.

'That was *years* ago,' said Sam. 'And it didn't stop it smoking.'

Maisie's eyes narrowed and she wondered whether she dared forget the customary free pint which they usually served him as a bonus to his charges.

'You can't blame us for that,' she said. 'We paid good money for that wretched cowl.'

'Nobody's blaming us,' said Ted. 'It's the chimney. Damned thing has never been right! I can remember it as a kid – remember my father cursing and carrying on about it, and my grandfather before him.'

'Chimneys are funny things,' said Sam as the last rod disappeared. 'Some'll go for years. Others – you can sweep 'em and a month later there's soot dropping.'

Coal fires were used by most of the villagers, for heating water all year round and to warm their homes in winter. The sweep was busy for twelve months of every year with the exception of Easter and Christmas and his small cart, pulled by an ancient grey mare, was a familiar sight in Teesbury and the surrounding villages. He had once aspired to be a jockey, but had been thrown after only a few months and the damage to his spine had been permanent.

As the brush reached the top of the chimney and broke free, he felt the changed tension on the canes.

'She's out!' he said and began to reverse the proceedings.

Still working anti-clockwise, he gradually worked the canes back downwards and unscrewed them one at a time, laying them neatly beside him while the soot pattered down like heavy rain behind the blanket.

Maisie exchanged an exasperated glance with her husband, jerking her head towards the clock which now showed five minutes to six. A shadow appeared beyond the glass pane of the door and the handle was turned enquiringly.

'Typical!' grunted Ted. 'When you're not quite ready, there's always someone turns up early.'

'Looks like Young Harry from Foxearth,' said Maisie. 'Let him in, Ted! He'll know how young Louise is after that nasty do the other night. Poor little mite!'

Ted pulled back the bolt and Harry was admitted. Seeing that he was the first, he grinned sheepishly and explained that he had been strawing the hoppers' huts.

'Straw dust gets in your throat,' he said, as Maisie pulled him a pint of his usual porter. He smiled at Ted and turned to the sweep. 'Now then, Sam? How's business?'

'So-so,' said Sam.

'It's always so-so with you, Sam,' said Ted. 'With other folks, it's good or bad, but with you it's always so-so.'

With the final cane unscrewed, the sweep released the canes that held the blanket in place and Ted moved forward to marvel at the amount of soot which had collected.

'Mind how you go with that filthy blanket,' cried Maisie, coughing loudly. 'The soot's going everywhere – I can smell it from here.'

Her husband gave her a warning glance. 'Don't fret, Maisie,' he said. 'Sam's doing fine.' He turned to Harry. 'And how's the little girl getting on? Nasty business that. Very nasty business. Could have been another goner.'

'Terrible thing, that diphtheria,' Maisie added. 'Poor Ned. I feel for him, I do really. How's he taken it, Harry? He's not been in here since it happened.'

Harry shrugged. 'Doesn't say much. Very quiet. Getting over it a bit now, I reckon. Cheers!' He drank deeply. 'Doll says our Louise is on the mend.'

'Just imagine having a tube in your throat,' said Maisie with a shudder. 'Ugh! The thought of it makes me go all funny. Still, it saved her life, they say.'

'Oh, it did that all right.'

'And is the nurse still there?'

'Yes,' Harry told them, 'and likely to stay a few weeks longer from what I hear. Poor Vinnie – she must have gone through hell that night. Good job Mr le Brun was there; sort of Providence the way he stayed on that night – almost as though it was meant to be, Doll says. He's a good man to have around in times of trouble. Like a rake, she is, poor soul. The flesh has just fallen off her these last weeks and we start hopping in three days' time. If it's not one thing, it's another.'

'Seems so,' said Maisie. She coughed loudly again as Sam began to shovel up the soot, holding the sack open with a practised hand.

'You been burning logs again?' the sweep asked.

'A bit of both,' said Ted.

Sam shook his head. 'You can always tell,' he said. 'It's the resin in the wood, you see. It burns sticky, not like coal.'

He folded over the top of the first sack and reached for the second. 'You want this for the garden?' Ted nodded. 'I'll leave it by the shed, then.'

The door opened and Jarvis and Joan Tupp from the village stores came in, closely followed by Andy Roberts.

Maisie greeted them cheerfully and said, 'Where's your wife, then, Andy? Up at Foxearth?'

Maisie's smile was a trifle supercilious, for it pleased her to know that she did not need to lower herself to such menial work in order to earn a few extra shillings.

Ted laughed. 'Rose let you off the lead, has she, Andy?'

Andy shook his head. 'She's still at Foxearth, giving a hand. They're all behind, what with Louise and all. Rose and her mother and a couple of others are at the oast-house.'

There was always casual work available at Foxearth. Even before the hops first showed above the ground, there was a constant war to be waged against weeds, blight and voracious insects. At intervals the hop-bines themselves had to be tied to poles or strings; this work could be pleasant enough if the day was mild and there were friends to chat to. By the end of August the hops had reached the tops of the poles; then there were only two jobs left for the women and these could be carried out in the comparative comfort of the oast-house. The so-called 'bins' into which the hops were picked were actually deep canvas slings which were tacked on to wooden frames to form long troughs; this canvas frayed eventually and had to be patched or re-tacked on to the frame. In addition to this task many of the pokes would need darning; these were large loose-meshed sacks in which hops were carried from the bins to the oast-house, and they had to stand up to a fair amount of rough handling.

'Well,' said Maisie, 'it's a nice bit of pin-money. You have to make it while you can. Will Rose be in later?'

'By and by,' said Andy. He turned to the sweep. 'How's tricks then, Sam?'

'So-so.'

'Didn't expect to see you in here so late in the day.'

'I didn't expect to *be* here,' said Sam. 'Real held up I was this morning and never caught up. Had a bit of a collison, like, with some old fella's motor. I'd make them motor cars illegal if I could.' He stood up wearily, one hand to his aching back. 'Just after six, it was, and you don't expect too much traffic on the roads as early as that.'

Seeing that he had everyone's attention, he warmed to his story. 'Just coming up to the cross-roads at Wateringbury, I was, and this green motor's coming from the right – I can hear the danged thing clunking and spluttering – and next thing he sees me coming and blasts his horn. To 'let me know he was there', he tells me! 'Know you was there?' I says. 'I could hear you half a mile back!' So anyway, my poor old mare's frightened half out of her wits and gives an almighty leap and then bang! We goes right into the side of his motor. Dents his door and wrenches off my wheel. And *me*, I'm thrown out and fell almost on top of him, with me legs up in the air and him hollering and swearing like a trooper. ''Tis your own fault,' I told him, 'sounding your horn like that.' He didn't like it, but I told him straight!'

There were appreciative comments and laughter.

'So neither of you were hurt,' said Maisie, pouring a port and lemon for Joan Tupp. 'No prosecutions or anything unpleasant like that?'

Sam shook his head. 'Not as I know of,' he said. 'Leastways, I'm not prosecuting him. Not worth the rigmarole, is it?'

'Who fixed the wheel?' asked Andy.

'Man named Tapper. John Tapper. Took over at Wateringbury when old Martin died.'

'Any good?'

'So-so.'

Sam carried the sack of soot outside and Maisie took the opportunity of his absence to apologise profusely for his presence in the bar. He returned for the rest of his things and then went to wash his hands and face at the pump in the back-yard. When he came back into the bar Ted gave him his money, plus a Guinness on the house, and a few more people drifted in. Maisie detached herself from the bar to run a duster over the mantelpiece and a few of the nearest chairs and tables, but the sweep had worked efficiently and there was very little for her to complain about.

Harry called across to Ted, 'Did you know Bertie Harris has gone into the brewery business?'

'I did hear something,' said Ted. 'True then, is it? In London, I heard.'

'That's right enough. Whitechapel, I believe – least, that's what Janet heard from the Colonel. The "Barley Mow", it's called. Brewery *and* tap. That must have set someone back a pretty packet. Fallen on his feet there, if you ask me!'

' "Barley Tap" ' Andy corrected him. 'Bertha was telling Rose.'

Maisie snorted. 'What in the world does Bertie Harris know about brewing beer, I'd like to know? Soldiering's all he knows about.'

'He'll be getting a man in,' said Ted. 'He'll need to have a brewer in to show him the ropes. It's a tricky business getting a brew right, for it all depends on temperature, all the way through. You can ruin a brew if the temperature's wrong. It's not just a case of bung in some malt and a handful of hops and hope for the best.'

'And yeast,' said Harry.

Ted ignored the correction but Maisie, feeling disloyal, said, 'What do you know about brewing, Ted Hunter? You've never brewed anything in your life.'

'I can know it without doing it,' replied her husband. 'You don't know anything about running the country, but you're always putting the politicians right.'

Everyone laughed except Maisie, who gave Ted a withering look.

'And I could!' she said. 'You wait until we get the vote – you'll see a thing or two then.' She glanced across at Joan Tupp. 'We'll show the men a thing or two, won't we Joan, when we get to vote?'

There was an amused roar from the men as Joan raised her glass and said, 'We certainly will. You men have had it all your own way for far too long.' She winked at Maisie.

Andy shook his head. 'You'll never get the vote, my duck,' he told Maisie. 'The suffragettes are their own worst enemies. All this carrying on and so forth – they just make fools of themselves and lose sympathy. What man in his right mind will give the vote to women like that? Shouting and marching and waving banners . . . they should know better.'

'What's wrong with marching and waving banners?' Maisie wanted to know. 'Men march and wave banners – *and* they do plenty of shouting.'

'Ah, but men are *men*,' said Harry. 'Women are *women*!'

'Oh, Lord!' said Joan. 'Don't you chime in, Harry. I thought you'd be on our side – you're a reasonable man.'

He grinned uncertainly, enjoying the compliment but unwilling to alienate the men.

Ted said loftily, 'I never lose a moment's sleep over women and the vote. They'll never get it but if it amuses them to try, why then, let them!'

Diplomatically, Maisie changed the subject. 'All ready for the hopping, are you, Jarvis? I see you've got the barricades up in good time.'

A few days before the annual 'invasion' of Londoners, the Teesbury shopkeepers took precautionary steps to prevent pilfering. The vast majority of visitors were scrupulously honest, but among so many people there were bound to be a few light-fingered souls and the local tradesmen had learnt the hard way that prevention was better than cure. Jarvis Tupp erected wooden boards around his shop counter, so that the goods could not be removed by innocent-faced children or voluble and disarming adults.

'It's always the ones you least expect,' said Jarvis. 'Last year there was this bonny lass, no more than sixteen – '

'Not-so-sweet sixteen!' added his wife.

' – telling me this sob story about her ailing mother took ill in the hop-garden and shivering with fever and could I sell her a hot-water-bottle. Well, I mean! Hot-water-bottles in September? I'd got them all out the back in the stock-room. While I was gone she made off with all the rest of her shopping without paying for anything!' He shook his head sorrowfully. 'Really bonny, she was. Lovely blonde hair . . . '

'She got your number all right," said Joan. 'It's amazing what a man will do for a pretty face. *Any* man, not just Jarvis. And then there was that little lad, no higher than this' – she held her hand table-high – 'crying his eyes out and telling me how his mother had sent him with a sixpence to buy some eggs, and he'd lost it, and his mother would wallop him when he got back. Well, Jarvis was out and I was sorry for him so like a fool I *gave* him the eggs.'

Jarvis took up the story. 'I'm walking back along the road and I hear this lad, all smiles, not a tear to be seen, telling his pals how he'd pulled a fast one over the shop-lady. He didn't know me, of course; first year they'd been down here.'

'What did you do? asked Maisie.

'Gave him a clip round the ear,' said Jarvis ruefully. 'Trouble was, the eggs flew out of his hand and they all smashed!'

A roar of laughter greeted this story as more people came into the bar – Liz Parsloe, Andy's wife Rose, and Mrs Bryce; Steven Pitt, the head drier, his wife Ellen and John Burrows, Steven's assistant. There were greetings, good-natured banter and a further exchange of news and gossip as full glasses and foaming mugs were carried to various corners of the room.

'All the hopping cards gone out, Steven?' someone asked.

'Oh, aye. They sent them out a week back – not that it means much to some of them. There are always a few who come down early to get a good bed, as they say. We've a dozen or so already – Vinnie's put them in the barn – and the gipsies turned up yesterday. They always do come early, same old crowd.'

'Crop's fair, I hear?'

'Aye.'

'Let's hope for fine weather then.'

'Aye.'

'Kids are going on an outing, I hear. When's that, then?'

Steven Pitt scratched his head. 'Don't rightly know,' he confessed. 'The last Sunday, most likely. Last Sunday is it, Young Harry?'

Harry nodded. 'They're going to Camber Sands – all those that go regular to the prayer meetings, that is. The mission's running it and good luck to them, I say! I want no part in it.' He shook his head. 'All that lot let loose on the beach – they'll be drowning each other, like as not. Real terrors, some of them. Up to all sorts of mischief. Picnic and a paddle in the sea and then back to Foxearth. That's the plan.'

'I've been asked to do the food,' Ellen Pitt put in. 'Depends how many goes, I said. I've only got one pair of hands.'

'And who's paying for it all?' someone enquired.

She lowered her voice confidentially. 'Well, they say it's the Brothers in Jesus, but I reckon it's Miss Bellweather – she's the one with the money.'

Sam had a second pint to wash down the first and then announced that he would be going, but before he did so the door opened and four Londoners came in, all men. They looked round warily as Maisie greeted them, aware of the stares of the locals. When the rest of the pickers arrived the inside of the 'Horse and Cart' would be out of bounds to everyone except the regulars. Then drinks for the pickers would be served outside in the yard from a makeshift bar –

barrels would be set up on a trestle table and a returnable deposit charged on every glass. Home-brewed ginger beer and lemonade would also be sold to those children who brought along their own mugs.

The Londoners' visit in September was a time of noise and excitement, of shared labour, of mutual suspicions and respect. For one month of the year town and country met in an uneasy alliance which called for tolerance and understanding. When they first arrived in the village the Londoners would prove too many and too boisterous, but when they left they would be greatly missed and village life would seem uneventful.

Andy Roberts raised his glass to the four Londoners. 'Here's to you lot!' he grinned.

Surprised, the four men raised their glasses in return. They looked alike, an elderly father perhaps and his three sons. The older man said 'Cheers,' and the younger men nodded.

Sam Glover wished everyone, 'Good night' and left them to it.

*

A few days later, Mary Bellweather stood in the hall making a last-minute check of the contents of the suitcase she was taking with her to Foxearth. Mentally she listed the items she had always found most necessary for her month's stay among the hoppers. Every year she determined to travel with less luggage, but when it was actually time to pack she was reluctant to leave anything behind. This year she had *added* to the list, for Roland had suggested that to show good faith with their flock, the Brothers in Jesus should occasionally take part in the picking.

Previously they had restricted their activities to what Roland called 'ministering' but this year they would occasionally soil their hands – busying their fingers among the hops, leaning over the bins or perching awkwardly on the sides of the wooden frames like ladies riding side-saddle. Mary heartily approved the idea, on the grounds that it would bring workers and missionaries into closer contact and hopefully encourage mutual respect. So in addition to clothes, toiletries, a copy of the bible, stationery, smelling salts, violet cachous and a photograph of her mother, she had included a pair of stout shoes, an old cotton dress, long black mittens and an apron borrowed from Mrs Markham. She also had a square of calico which, if the weather was too hot, she could attach to the brim of her hat to protect the back of her neck from the sun.

The mission's medical stores were going down in the horse-van specially hired for the purpose, which would also carry the folding beds, blankets, toys, the magic lantern and general provisions for the first few days. Roland would also take a purse full of money, for there were always some hoppers who spent their last shillings on the train fare and arrived at Foxearth destitute and starving; they would be subsidised by the Brothers in Jesus until the first week's money was paid out. This was a practice of which Mary disapproved, for too often she suspected they pretended poverty, relying on Roland's kind heart, and on several occasions the money had never been fully recovered.

Mrs Markham hurried into the hall from the kitchen, her normally cheerful features drawn into a frown.

'I do *wish* you would take a few sandwiches with you for the train, ma'am,' she said. 'There's a nice piece of York ham – or even a slice of madeira cake. I'm sure you shouldn't travel all that way on an empty stomach, and so late at night too. It's not at all natural for a woman of your upbringing. If your poor mother was alive, she'd wring her hands – she'd be that worried. Gallivanting off with all those wild people!'

'They are not wild people, Mrs Markham,' Mary said patiently, 'and I am *not* gallivanting. I am merely accompanying the pickers on the train. There is no way I can come to the slightest harm and I just may be able to help someone who is in trouble or, better still, ensure that there *is* no trouble. Roland Fry is quite right: the pickers *do* need a little supervision . . . '

The housekeeper tightened her lips. 'If Roland Fry thinks it's such a good idea, he should be going with you.'

'Lydia will be there and so will Gareth. Roland had to go on the van with the stores and equipment – someone has to be responsible for them.'

Mrs Markham was not convinced. 'You've got that nice motor car,' she said 'and yet you let yourself get talked into a train ride in the middle of the night, crammed in with all sorts of undesirables.' She waved her hands in a gesture of despair. 'Well, I've had my say – '

'Yes, you have,' said Mary shortly, 'and on more than one occasion. I appreciate your concern, but I consider it to be my duty and I am going. So let's say no more about it, if you don't mind. Now, you've telephoned for a cab?'

'Yes, ma'am. It will be here on the stroke of midnight. 'Like Cinderella's coach', he said, cheeky wretch! I don't know what the world's coming to and that's a fact – they're all getting so uppity these days.'

'*Please*, Mrs Markham!' Mary was rapidly losing patience. 'Now I think I have everything I need. I shall telephone you regularly, as I always do, and you can forward any correspondence that comes for me. The large envelopes are on my bureau. Let me see – is there anything else, I wonder?'

'If I may suggest a hot-water-bottle, Miss Mary?'

'In September?'

'It can turn cold of an evening, ma'am.'

'I don't think so. Remember I sleep in the house, not in the marquee, and I'm very grateful for that. The dubious pleasures of the marquee are reserved for the menfolk.' She opened the front door and looked out into the dark street which was lit only by the light of the gas-lamps.

Mrs Markham, looking past her mistress into the street, said, 'Oh, *do* be careful! The streets are no place for a woman after dark.'

Hastily Mary closed the door. 'I shall not be in the streets,' she said. 'I'll be in the cab and quite safe. Now, I've given you your wages for the month, haven't I? Is there anything I have forgotten? I do so hate the last ten minutes – I'm always sure I must have overlooked something.'

For a moment they looked at each other in silence, for they were running out of time and it was the housekeeper who plucked up the courage to ask the question which was uppermost in both their minds.

'And Master Alexander, ma'am?' she asked. 'What if he should come back – or call up on the telephone or . . . ' Her voice faltered as she saw Mary stiffen, but then she plunged on. 'He will come back, Miss Mary, won't he? This is his home, but it's been so long now since he – that is, I know it's none of my business, but I can't help worrying about the boy. He will come back, won't he?'

Mary turned away, but not before the housekeeper had seen the tell-tale tremble of her mouth and realised she was not as hard-hearted as she pretended. Mrs Markham had listened in on the argument which had ended so disastrously, but Mary had not mentioned the boy's name since that day. The house-keeper's one attempt to raise the matter with her mistress had earned her a firm request that she should concern herself no further.

Now Mary said levelly, 'I'm sure he will come back in his own good time.'

'But he's only seventeen!'

'Nearly eighteen.' Mary turned and Mrs Markham saw the pain in her eyes. 'It's this foolish nonsense about the girl – really, I gave him credit for more sense.'

'But young men do get these fancies.'

'Apparently. I find it rather ridiculous.'

'But where is he, ma'am?' the housekeeper pleaded. 'He's got no family, only us – I beg your pardon, only you. Unless . . . '

'Unless what, Mrs Markham?'

'Unless he's gone to look for his mother, ma'am,' she faltered.

Mary's face paled, but she spoke calmly. 'I'm sure he would never be so foolish.'

'But he is headstrong, Miss Mary, and maybe if he found himself with nowhere to go . . . '

'But of course he has somewhere to go. He can come home. No one is stopping him. He can go to Italy as we planned and no one will be any the wiser, but I will not allow him to go to Switzerland to be with this . . . ' She stumbled for words ' . . .

this Sylvia. I do feel her parents are behaving very foolishly in encouraging the relationship. They are much too young.'

'But if he goes to his mother – that awful woman, Lord knows what would become of the boy. I do wish – ' She stopped as the horse's hooves clattered to a halt outside the house.

'Oh ma'am, the cab's here! What *am* I to do if he comes back?'

Mary hesitated. It was only with the greatest difficulty that she had refrained from cancelling her trip to Kent, for her instinct had been to stay at home, waiting and praying for Alexander to return. Nobody could have guessed at her agony of mind as the days passed and there was no communication from him. She went about her daily life as though he no longer existed, but her pride masked a harrowing sense of loss which deepened into terror when she allowed herself to consider that he might never return. Mary had confided in no one, preferring to let everybody believe that he was still in Cherbourg. That way she could avoid the pitying looks and anxious enquiries which would so easily undermine her brittle composure. She felt she could bear anything but pity and a sympathetic word or glance would be enough to demoralise her totally.

'Make him welcome, give him a meal and then telephone me at Foxearth,' she said crisply. 'And if by any miracle that happens,' she thought to herself, 'I shall come back to London on the next train. I shall make up some excuse and come back – and he will tell me his story and I shall forgive him and he'll ask me to go to Italy with him.' It *could* be like that. Of course the boy loved her and of course he would never go in search of Mollie Pett. That 'awful creature'! No, she was worse than that – she was a slut, a street woman, a whore.

'Well, then, Miss Mary, have a nice time.'

The housekeeper looked at her helplessly as the cab driver knocked impatiently on the door.

'I must go,' said Mary reluctantly. She opened the door and the driver came in to collect her suitcase and hat-box.

'He *will* come back, ma'am,' whispered Mrs Markham.

Mary's eyes were full of unspoken fears. 'Of course he will,' she said.

CHAPTER TEN

Dora sat on her 'bundle' in the middle of the platform and sucked a pear-drop. It was pink and tasted of raspberries. She had one left after that – her favourite, which was white and tasted of pears. In her arms she held a small sack containing a tin kettle, a battered saucepan, half a loaf of bread, a 'screw' of sugar and another of tea, a plate, knife and spoon and a chipped tin mug. Her coat pockets bulged – one with an onion, the other with two herrings wrapped in an ancient copy of the *Daily Mail*. The bundle on which she sat consisted of a rough grey blanket and a somewhat threadbare Axminster rug bought second-hand a year or so earlier; these two items would serve her as a bed. Her one good dress had been laid between the blanket and the rug and also rolled up. Mrs Gorringe had assured her that straw would be provided and Dora planned to lay the rug over the straw and cover herself with the blanket. She hoped she could beg, borrow or steal an old sack which, rolled up, would make a passable pillow; if not, she would do without. According to Mrs Gorringe she would 'sleep like a log' after a day picking hops. Hops, she had assured Dora earnestly, were 'sopporific things' which made folks sleepy and the absence of a pillow was 'neither here nor there'.

Now Dora stared around her at the milling throng of people. The train was not due until twelve-forty but already the platform was crowded, more people clamoured at the barrier and others were still arriving. The noise was incredible – mothers shouted at children, children shouted at each other. Here and there groups sang songs from the music halls, swaying to and fro in time to the music, hardly able to hear what they sang for the noise which rose to the high roof and bounced back. Childen ran and tripped and howled and were smacked for their pains, while elderly women sat amid their piled belongings and surveyed the surrounding chaos with indifference for the majority of them had seen it all before, many having been hopping since childhood. They had hopped as giggling young women and irritable mothers and were now resigned grandmothers. Those who remembered so far back knew that hopping had changed for the better over the intervening years, slowly but inexorably. The living conditions had gradually improved and so had the rates of pay. Now it was a shilling for eight bushels and that was not to be sneezed at for the old ladies knew their worth – their fingers were as nimble, if not nimbler, than many a younger, less experienced picker.

To Dora's right she saw a mother with five boys who presumably were her sons. The boys were close together in age and like peas in a pod, with open mouths, vacant blue eyes and careless hair-cuts. Their mother attracted no interest from those around her as she suckled the youngest, a baby, her dress unbuttoned to the waist. Dora was impressed by their luggage, which consisted of a hopper's 'waggon' – a deep wooden crate set on four small wheels and with a pram-handle. This waggon was full of kitchen utensils, spare clothing and bedding and tied to the handle was a chamber pot! Looking behind her Dora saw an elderly couple sitting together on a rolled-up mattress – single size – and the man's arm was round his wife's shoulders. Catching Dora's eye, the man smiled but did not speak.

A young man in his early twenties sat on a small tin trunk to Dora's left. He had short-cropped ginger hair under a flat cap and a complexion marred by acne scars. His long arms were wrapped round his knees and he watched his fellow travellers with a shy expression that Dora liked. She gave him an encouraging smile.

'You look a bit lonely,' he said, after she had smiled at him several times. 'Where's your old man?' He looked knowingly at Dora's swollen belly and she giggled.

'Oh, you noticed then!' she said.

'Couldn't hardly miss it!' he responded.

'He's working,' she told him. 'He's a porter at Smithfields.'

'All on your lonesome, then?'

'Seems like it.'

'Bit off, isn't it, in your condition?'

She shrugged and an aggrieved look settled on her face. 'Mrs Gorringe couldn't come – leastways, not yet. She's my neighbour, see, and I was coming with her, but one of her twins was took bad and can't keep nothing in his belly. Straight through him, it goes, and she wasn't feeling so chirpy herself but she'll come on down as soon as she – here, watch it!' She broke off to address a small boy who, chasing past, had fallen over her feet. 'Serves you blooming well right!' she added as he sprawled on the ground. 'You should look where you're going.'

The boy, about ten years old, scrambled to his feet and stuck out his tongue.

'And don't you sauce me,' said Dora, 'unless you want a clout.'

He stood defying her, just out of reach. 'And who's going to give it me?' he demanded.

To Dora's surprise, the young man said, 'I will, so do yourself a favour and clear off.'

The boy hesitated and then took a step backwards. 'You and who else?' he taunted.

The young man made an elaborate pantomine, scowling fiercely, rolling up his sleeves and rising slowly to his feet as the boy braced himself for flight.

Dora felt unequal to any kind of hostilities. 'Don't hit 'im,' she said wearily. 'He's only a kid.'

The boy, noticing her shape for the first time, cried, 'What you expecting then – an elephant?' and darted off, pursued by the young man. Dora watched them go and then, having lost sight of them in the crowd, crunched up the remaining sliver of pink pear-drop and popped the white one into her mouth. 'An elephant,' she thought. It certainly felt like an elephant. But did elephants kick, or was she expecting a kangaroo? Did kangaroos kick or did they only box? Maybe they just jumped. Elephant, indeed. Cheeky little sod! She looked up as the young man returned. He said something which she did not catch as a woman with a laden pram and a brood of children pushed between them. When they had passed he pulled over the tin trunk and sat down next to Dora.

'I'm on my own too,' he said.

'Is it your holiday?' she asked.

'Lost me job two weeks ago,' he confided. 'I thought I'd do a bit of hopping before I look for another.'

'What was you doing before?'

He shrugged. 'Mucking out stables and all that. Guv'nor give me the push one morning – said I was idle, but I knew it wasn't that because he give the job to his sister's boy and I'd seen it coming. He was always round Saturdays, his sister's boy, and getting under me feet, making out he was helping. I never give it a thought at first and then one day I thought, "Hullo! This kid's up to something." He was going to leave school, see.' He smiled at Dora. 'What's your name, then? Mine's Albert Crittenden.'

Before Dora could answer a woman stopped in front of them. She had dark hair and a friendly face, but she was wearing the kind of clothes that immediately set her apart from most of the people on the platform. Her high-necked blouse was of white lawn with a pale blue tie, her jacket was well-pressed and the skirt of navy blue serge looked new. On her head she wore a straw boater with a red band round it, her hair being drawn back to hide her ears and form a chignon at the nape of her neck.

'I'm Lydia Grant,' she told them, her manner at once friendly and authoritative. 'I'm trying to check up on the Foxearth pickers.' She waved the list she held in her hand. 'Are either of you ... ' She waited, not bothering to finish the question and Dora looked anxiously at Albert.

'I am,' she said and saw his face brighten.

'Me, too!'

'Names, then, please?'

They gave the details and Lydia marked her paper and then glanced around. 'Where are Mrs Gorringe and the twins?'

Dora explained that she had had to come on without them.

'Oh dear,' said Lydia, making another note. 'So you're alone, Miss Wilks?'

'Mrs,' said Dora, with a hasty look at Albert. 'Well, you know.'

Lydia smiled. 'When's your baby due?'

'God knows. I don't!'

'Hmmn.' She pursed her lips. 'Is it your first?'

'Me third. Sid's mother's minding the others.'

Dora was aware without actually looking at Albert that he was rather disappointed by these disclosures, so she added sharply, 'What's it got to do with you, any road? It's none of your business. There's no law against it and I can still pick hops, can't I? Haven't lost the use of me hands, have I?'

She appealed to Albert, who said, ''Course you haven't.'

Lydia smiled. 'I am not suggesting for a moment that you cannot pick. I'm only asking so that I know the situation and we can keep an eye on your health. We wouldn't want you to get overtired and we mustn't have you overdoing it. Will you come and see me when you've settled in? On the second day, perhaps, when we've had time to get ourselves organized?'

'Come and see you?' Dora regarded this suggestion with suspicion. 'What for? I can pick the same as everyone else. You can't tell me what to do – I've been tired before, you know. In fact, I've spent most of me life tired, come to that. Your sort don't know what "tired" is!'

Lydia kept her patience. 'I just want to look after you, that's all. A girl in your condition – '

'I'm a married woman,' Dora broke in, waving the ring she had bought for herself from a stall in Petticoat Lane. 'This is a wedding ring, in case you hadn't noticed.'

'It's just that you look . . . ' She lowered her voice so that Albert could not hear too clearly. 'Your pregnancy looks well-advanced and I'm a nurse with the Brothers in Jesus, so it's my job to care for the – '

'Oh, stuff the Brothers in Jesus!' cried Dora. 'You just leave me be and pick on someone else. I'm on the list to pick hops and that's what I'm going to do, so you can like it or lump it. Some of us have to earn a few bob, you know!'

'But you will come and see me?' Lydia persisted, adding, 'There may be a few extras for those in particular need.'

Dora's expression changed rapidly. 'Extras? What sort of extras?'

'I'm not sure exactly but an occasional free meal, perhaps, or free milk.'

Overhearing these last words, an old lady who had been standing nearby shuffled forward. She was small and wiry with a face like crushed leather and black beady eyes.

'Here,' she interrupted, 'I could do with some extras if there's any going. I'm in pertikler need too – same as her.'

'I don't think – ' began Lydia politely.

'I might be in the club for all you know,' the woman insisted. Albert sniggered, but she pretended not to hear. 'I might be in a "delicate condition". You can't prove I'm not, 'cos it's my word against yours, see?' She cackled suddenly with laughter and began to cough. 'I might be in pertikler need. I reckon I *am*!'

'What's your name?' asked Lydia, humouring her.

'Alice Ellen Mary Smith.'

'Who are you picking for?'

'Mr Hobden, Church Farm, just beyond Beltring.'

'I'm sorry,' Lydia said thankfully, 'but you're not with us – we're Foxearth.'

The old woman clutched at her arm. 'Maybe I could change over. Come to Foxearth with you? I'm a good picker, but I am in need and I could do with some extras.'

Lydia gave up and tried to ignore her, addressing herself once more to Dora and Albert. 'I shall put you in the new accommodation,' she told Dora. 'You, Mr Crittenden, will be in the small barn with the other single men.'

Alice Smith came to the end of another bout of coughing and said, 'Have you got any cough syrup? That's what I'm in need of.'

'I'm afraid not,' Lydia told her.

The woman scowled. 'Why not, then?' she demanded. 'You said you were a nurse, didn't you? I should think cough syrup is an extra, isn't it? I reckon I'm entitled, same as her.'

'I'll see you two later,' Lydia said to her two charges; Dora and Albert nodded without any great enthusiasm as Lydia moved away with the old woman trotting behind her.

'That old girl!' said Albert. 'Nutty as a fruit-cake. Did you hear her? Delicate condition! Who'd put an old bag like her in the club?'

'Blind man on a dark night?' suggested Dora.

He thought that very witty and laughed. Dora was flattered and also secretly relieved. He seemed to have accepted her recent revelations and he wasn't bad-looking, though a bit wet behind the ears. And he had stuck up for her.

'Pity about the small barn,' she said. 'Not a lot of fun for you in there.'

Albert stared at her and his heart skipped a beat. He was astonished at how easy it was. He, Albert Crittenden, virgin, of 19 Poplar Way, London, had found himself a lady-friend – a *pregnant* lady-friend at that! – and all in the space of ten minutes. It was too good to be true – too good to last, perhaps.

'Don't you worry about Lydia – What's-her-name,' he said. 'If she starts on at you, she'll have me to reckon with. I'll soon put *her* in her place.'

'Really?' breathed Dora. 'Would you? That's ever so kind. Stuck-up cow! They're all the same. Still, I wouldn't say no to a free meal.'

'Of course you wouldn't.'

In the distance they heard the clatter of wheels and the chuff of steam as a train rounded a bend in the track and a murmur of excitement ran round the thousand or more people waiting on the platform. As one they rose to their feet, conversation giving way to a desperate seizing of bags and bundles and a last-minute flurry of instructions to the children to, 'Get back from the edge' and, 'Hang on to me' – along with dire threats as to what would happen to them if they got themselves lost. Albert rose, tucked the tin box under his right arm and helped Dora to her feet.

'I'll take that,' he offered and, before she could object, her bundle had been tucked under his left arm. 'You stick with me,' he said. 'I'll see you are O.K.'

Dora clutched the sack and nodded. It seemed almost too good to be true, she thought. One minute she'd been on her own, deserted by the Gorringes, with less than a shilling in her purse. Now here she was with a gallant young man to look after her and a promise of free meals. There had to be a catch in it somewhere!

The train came to a halt with a deafening rush of steam and a grinding and locking of wheels and brakes; then the mad scramble began. Dora found herself buffeted and jostled as she and Albert edged closer to the carriage door, then somehow she was inside the train and to her surprise, Albert was still beside her. She stumbled, but there was no room to fall, and then she was squashed into a seat with a fat woman on one side and a very old man on the other. The old man had a young child on his lap, presumably the son of the girl who stood beside him and called him 'Grandpa'. Albert stood in front of Dora with the rolled-up blanket between his legs and the tin trunk in his arms.

'Here, you give me that,' she told him, indicating the trunk. 'It can go on my lap and my stuff can go on top of it.'

He relinquished it gratefully and they exchanged conspiratorial glances. Every seat in their carriage was full and people sat and stood in every available space. Now that they were on the train the atmosphere changed as tensions relaxed. The worst was over, they were safely ensconced and nothing would budge them until they reached their various destinations and were deposited, dishevelled but triumphant, on tiny station platforms in what always seemed to be the middle of nowhere. For most of them it was a familiar routine, but for a few it was a new experience.

Albert leaned down. 'I've never had a holiday before,' he told Dora.

'Me neither,' she said.

She caught a glimpse of Lydia outside on the platform, conferring earnestly with another woman and a man, but a whistle blew and their discussion was hurriedly abandoned. There were shouts from the guard and a great slamming of doors along the whole length of the train, which then lurched violently, throwing everybody standing on top of all those sitting down. While they were sorting themselves out amidst the beginnings of hilarity, the train lurched again and then began to gather speed and Dora, with another smile at Albert, settled down in her seat and prepared to enjoy herself.

*

One hundred and thirty pickers arrived at Foxearth during the early hours of the morning and, thanks to the efforts of the Brothers in Jesus, were all safely installed in their allotted accommodation with a great deal less confusion than had been the case in previous years. Ellen Pitt produced hot milky cocoa and a current bun for everyone, children and adults alike, and after the initial excitement – greeting old friends, making up the makeshift beds, settling the children – the weary hoppers finally succumbed and silence gradually descended as one by one they slipped into an exhausted sleep.

Early the next morning they were roused at five-thirty by the furious ringing of a bell and scrambled blearily into their clothes to queue for the only breakfast that would be provided for them. On this one occasion the Brothers in Jesus offered free hot tea and a thick slice of bread and dripping for everyone. In future the hoppers would do their own cooking, either in families or in whatever groups they chose to arrange among themselves. Free faggots were provided for their fires and it was the job of an elderly local man – one Dan Dobbet – to tend the fires so that they would be alight when needed. Dan would rise even earlier than they did in order to throw small twigs and kindling wood on to the still-glowing embers of each fire, so that the hoppers could heat water for their early-morning tea, make porridge or even, if they were lucky, fry a few rashers of streaky bacon and a slice or two of bread. As each afternoon drew to a close, he would make the rounds once more, ensuring that the hungry hoppers would be able to brew up their tea and cook their supper. For many, breakfast and supper were their only meals. Local pickers from the village – people like Mrs Bryce – would bring a token lunch: a hunk of bread and cheese perhaps, and an onion or a slice of meat pasty baked especially the previous weekend.

At six-thirty, after the tea and bread, Vinnie greeted the hoppers as they crowded round to hear the regulations read out. To the regulars this was a waste of valuable time, for they were not earning any money as they listened to Ned Bray gabbling the familiar Rules. To newcomers like Dora and Albert it was also a waste of time, for Ned Bray's words ran together incoherently and they were no wiser when he had finished. His voice droned on.

' . . . to pick hops clean from strings and poles and free from bunches of leaves – for every breach of these regulations to forfeit one bushel of hops . . . all who leave before picking is finished to be paid at half the agreed rate . . . Signal to commence to be given by ringing a bell . . . No lucifer matches . . . No pickers allowed in adjoining orchards . . . '

After the Rules came the inevitable haggling, but the tally was fixed at one shilling for eight bushels, exactly the same as the year before. The pickers had wanted more, but Ned offered less. There were rarely any surprises, but to accept the first rate offered would have been unheard of, for the tally had been negotiated afresh each year for as long as anyone could remember.

Vinnie then gave her short speech of welcome, introduced the Brothers in Jesus and outlined their role. She wished everyone a pleasant stay in Kent and expressed a hope that the weather would be fine.

When Ned rang his bell it was time to follow him to the hop-gardens for the allotting of bins and within a surprisingly short while the pickers settled to work in a buzz of cheerful conversation and an initial rush of enthusiasm for the work.

Bines were cut down and carried to the pickers, where eager fingers searched among the leaves to pluck the small greeny-yellow cones and drop them into the canvas bins.

When Vinnie was finally satisfied that another season's picking was under way, she made her way back to the house to find two letters awaiting her attention. The first, from Clive le Brun, was brief and to the point.

I shall be calling to see you on Monday and hope you will not mind if I bring a friend with me. He is Philippe Delain, a young French flyer based temporarily at Leysdown.

My best wishes for your first day's picking, it is always an anxious time.

Vinnie noticed with a smile that he had signed it, 'Your friend and servant, Clive le Brun.' However, the second letter filled her with dismay and having read it once, she took a deep breath before sitting down to read it again. It was from Eva, her sister-in-law in Bromley.

Dearest Vinnie, whatever am I to do? Alexander Bellweather arrived on my doorstep an hour ago in a state of great distress – not having washed, slept or eaten for several days. He will say only that he has left Mary's home in London and has searched unsuccessfully for his real mother. He has become very friendly with a young woman he met in Cherbourg. The poor young lad is quite infatuated with her and has been invited to share a holiday with her family when they go to Switzerland. He speaks of her with such passion (her name is Sylvia) and looked so young and entirely vulnerable that I must confess I would like to help him, but Gerald is away and cannot advise me. Perhaps Mary has spoken to you on the subject? I think she must be told that the boy is safe, although Alexander begs me not to contact her. I therefore send this letter instead of using the telephone, not wishing him to know that I have broken his confidence. Do please advise me.

In great haste – Your Affectionate Eva.

P.S. James and Teddy send their love. We are all so relieved that Louise is on the mend. By the time this reaches you, no doubt you will have started picking. One of these days we shall join you – I'm sure my boys would find it great fun! Eva.

Vinnie cursed silently and was immediately ashamed, reminding herself that the world did not stand still just because hopping had started in Kent! Other people had problems too and she must help if she could; at least she must tell Mary that the boy was safe.

She marvelled that Mary had allowed no hint of her personal problems to affect her work. She had travelled down on the train with the Londoners, supervised their accommodation when they reached Foxearth, and finally gone to bed just before three o'clock in the morning. The Brothers in Jesus had risen early to prepare the breakfasts and Mary had appeared as calm and efficient as ever. Poor Mary, thought Vinnie, and wondered if she would ever marry. Having read Eva's letter for the third time, she slipped it into her pocket and went out into the sunshine, across the lawn and through the gate.

The hop-gardens of Foxearth sprawled below the house, which stood on the left of the road running from Maidstone to Tonbridge. They extended down the slopes of the valley and were bounded at the bottom by the river Medway which wound its way eastward through West and East Farleigh, into Maidstone and on to Allington where, beyond the lock, it became tidal and flowed into the estuary where it met the Thames and finally the North Sea. Most of the land between Teesbury and Maidstone was under hops, but here and there apple and cherry orchards formed a recent addition and a few acres had been turned into pasture for cattle and sheep.

As Vinnie walked between the rows the hop-poles, twelve feet high, towered above her and the sun shone through the leaves, dappling the little groups clustered round each bin. Many children picked also and those who could not reach the bins picked into other containers – an upturned umbrella or an old wooden box – which later would be emptied into the bins. As Vinnie walked past the pickers the cheerful chatter died away self-consciously and the women looked up to greet her with a cheerful, 'Here we are again, Mrs Lawrence,' or 'Good morning, ma'am'. A few merely smiled. Word had spread of Louise's illness and several people enquired after 'the poor little mite' and were pleased to hear that the danger was past.

Young children toddled aimlessly among the discarded hop-bines or crawled around the feet of the pickers. It was the first morning, Vinnie reflected, and everyone was pleased to be in the country breathing in fresh air and enjoying the sunshine. Their 'holiday' was just beginning. Later, as the weeks passed or the weather deteriorated, their attitude could change. Other years had brought problems – arguments over money, quarrels among the pickers, trouble with neighbouring farmers or friction with the local people. It could all turn sour, Vinnie reflected, or it could be a good year; she devoutly hoped for the latter.

'Morning, Mrs Lawrence, ma'am. Nice bit of sunshine! Do my poor old back the world of good – it's the warmth, you see.'

'Good morning,' Vinnie smiled. 'Mrs . . . ?' She didn't recognise the woman's face.

'Knapp, ma'am. Edie Knapp. I came last year.'

'Oh, yes, I remember,' said Vinnie. 'Yes, let's hope it lasts – the sunshine, I mean. Have you see Miss Bellweather, by any chance?'

Mrs Knapp jerked a thumb. 'She went down to the lower field,' she said, 'but that was half an hour ago. She could be anywhere by now.'

Vinnie thanked her and walked through into the lower field which sloped more noticeably. A young man and a woman were picking into a half-size bin and they both nodded shyly as she approached. The woman was pregnant, Vinnie saw, but she looked healthy enough. Not for the first time Vinnie was grateful for the presence of the Brothers in Jesus, for a trained nurse removed a great responsibility from her own shoulders.

'You're new, aren't you?' Vinnie asked them.

They both nodded and she noticed that the man was much younger than the woman.

'Our first trip,' he said. 'I'm Albert Crittenden.'

Vinnie smiled. 'And your wife's name is – ?'

'I'm Dora Wilks.'

'Oh.' There was an awkward silence.

Dora said, 'It's not his – the baby, I mean. I mean he's not my husband. We met up at the station and he helped me – carried my bedding for me and that. We're just friends and we thought why not pick together.'

'I don't know anyone else,' Albert explained.

'We're not doing any harm,' said Dora defensively. 'It's not what you think.'

'I don't think anything,' said Vinnie. 'Really I don't. . . . Is your accommodation satisfactory?'

Dora nodded and Albert said, 'I'm in the small barn with the men.'

'I've got a husband, you know,' persisted Dora. 'His name's Sid and I've got two more kids.'

'That's nice.' Vinnie was relieved. Suddenly she remembered the letter in her pocket and asked them if they had seen Mary Bellweather. Albert pointed: 'She went on that way about ten minutes ago – she's getting some free milk for Dora.'

'Good,' said Vinnie. 'They're very good people, all of them. So – are you getting the hang of the picking? Has anyone shown you how to do it?' She glanced into the bin, where a very thin sprinkling of hops covered the canvas. 'You'll get faster as you get used to it.'

Dora smiled. 'Mr Wickens showed us; he was ever so nice.'

Vinnie said, 'Toby Wickens – he's our new measurer. He'll be round later with another bin to measure out how many bushels you've picked and make a note of it.'

Dora and Albert peered into the bin. 'What *is* a bushel?' Dora asked.

'A basket-full,' Vinnie told her. 'A bushel basket. When you've picked enough to fill eight baskets, then you've picked eight bushels and earned a shilling.'

'My Aunt Nelly used to go hopping,' said Albert. 'She's dead now, but she could pick very quick – one of their best pickers, she was. Merryon Farm, that's where she went; it's not far from here, so she used to come down to the same station. Made a mint of money, she did, but she died of her lungs. They said it was bronichal like her husband, my Uncle Tom who died the year before – very sudden, and they said *that* was bronichal because it runs in our family, you see. My ma – '

Vinnie could see that he was about to launch into a history of the entire Crittenden family, so she interrupted as tactfully as she could and left them to continue their work. Judging from the amount they had picked so far, she guessed they were doing a lot of talking and not much picking.

At last she found Mary, talking to an elderly woman; she drew her to one side and gave her the letter to read. The colour drained suddenly from Mary's face but then returned, burning hotly in her cheeks. Her hand trembled slightly as she slowly folded the letter and returned it.

Vinnie began, 'I thought you would want to know that he's safe.' She searched her mind for a comforting phrase. 'Young people are so impulsive, aren't they?'

'Yes, they are,' said Mary. 'They don't think of the worry they cause. I'm sorry Eva has been put to so much trouble.'

Vinnie hesitated. 'I'm sure she didn't mean to intrude on a private matter, but I don't suppose she felt she could turn him away.'

'I suppose not. Eva is obviously impressed by all this nonsense about the girl.' Mary avoided Vinnie's eyes. 'It's quite absurd at his age and to be truthful I am rather disappointed in him.'

Pretending not to notice the agitated way Mary's hands were clasping and unclasping Vinnie continued with an attempt at lightness, 'I was only five when I fell in love, the first time I set eyes on Julian! By the time I was fourteen, I just adored him. He was older, of course, but he felt the same way about me and I suppose he was about Alexander's age then. It's one of those things that happens – very wonderful at the time and over-powering. It can be desperate.' She hesitated, then added gently, 'I don't think it is ever absurd.'

'So you take the boy's part, too,' said Mary, bitterly.

'Oh, not really. I just wondered if you would like him to come to Foxearth,' Vinnie suggested, 'and then you could talk it over – '

Mary stiffened. 'What is there to talk about? Really, Vinnie, I know you mean well but as you say, it *is* really a private matter and not open to general discussion.'

Stung by the obvious snub, Vinnie bit back an angry reply.

'Then we won't discuss it any further,' she said, 'but what is Eva to do if Alexander asks to borrow some money for his fare to Switzerland? Do you want her to do that or would you rather – '

'I have told you that I don't wish to discuss it. If the boy is foolish enough – '

Vinnie's patience expired. 'Oh, for pity's sake!' she burst out, 'don't keep calling him "the boy". His name is Alexander and you've never called him "the boy" before. If you must know, I think *you're* foolish! You're just being stubborn and what's more you know it – but you're too proud to admit it. Alex has got pride, too, you know; I expect he's worried to death *and* longing to see his young lady again.'

'*Young lady*!'

'Yes, young lady! Why shouldn't she be? It sounds as though she comes from a nice family. At least they're doing their best to understand their daughter's feelings for him and to offer Alex their friendship.'

The old lady to whom Mary had been talking had drifted back and now stood only a few feet away, listening to the argument with her mouth wide open. Mary, seeing her, said furiously, 'That's quite enough, Vinnie! I have no wish to hear any more from you. If you will excuse me, I have work to do. People need my help.' She turned to the woman. 'I'm sorry . . . ' she began.

'You promised me some shoes,' said the old lady in an aggrieved tone. 'Good stout shoes, you said, 'cos these poor old things of mine are rubbish.' She lifted one foot to show the sole parting company from the rest of her ancient boot. 'Rubbish, these!' she said 'You promised me – '

'Oh, do go away!' Vinnie interrupted impatiently. 'Can't you see that Miss Bellweather and I are talking?'

'We are *not* talking,' said Mary coldly. 'Not any longer,'

Vinnie's exasperation gave way to anger. 'I said go *away*,' she told the old woman, 'and get back to your picking. I'm sure Miss Bellweather will see about the shoes later.'

Mary opened her mouth to protest but the woman, recognising Vinnie's superior authority, shuffled away muttering resentfully to herself. Mary and Vinnie were left regarding each other furiously.

'For the last time,' said Mary, tight-lipped, 'I do *not* wish to discuss the boy with you or anyone else. He has a comfortable home and he is welcome to return to it at any time he chooses and that is my last word – '

'Then I hope you realise what might happen,' cried Vinnie. 'He might borrow the fare and disappear. Or he might go back to London and continue looking for his mother until he finds her. You don't want either of those things to happen – you know it and so do I. So for God's sake, be sensible. You will lose him, Mary, if you're not careful. I am sure he loves you deeply – '

'He has a funny way of showing it!' cried Mary, on the verge of tears.

'He's *young*, Mary. You were young once.'

'I was never stupid,' protested Mary, 'and I was never ungrateful! I was brought up to know how to behave – '

'Well, you are not behaving very well *now*!'

Mary's eyes blazed. 'For the last time, Vinnie Harris,' (the old name slipped out) 'will you stop meddling in my affairs?'

'I am not meddling – I'm trying to *help* you, Mary,' cried Vinnie. '*You* will be the one who is hurt by all this, not me. These things easily get out of hand.'

Mary tossed her head. 'Get out of hand? Well, you certainly ought to know all about that,' she said. 'No one can have done more harm than you in your time. And you dare to lecture *me* on how to behave!'

Vinnie became aware that heads were turning in their direction. 'Keep your voice down,' she hissed. 'Everyone is listening.'

'Whose fault is that?' Mary demanded. 'You were the one who insisted on this conversation, so you have only yourself to blame. Now, will you please go away and let me get on with my work!'

'No, I will not!' cried Vinnie. 'Eva has written to me for advice about Alexander and you are his legal guardian, so you should at least – '

'Don't you dare to tell me what I should and shouldn't do!' Mary's voice trembled with suppressed rage. 'Why can't you leave me in peace? Haven't you done me enough harm in the past? First Roland, then . . . ' She bit back Julian's name, adding more quietly, 'And then William! Oh, you can pretend innocence, Vinnie, but all I know is that . . . ' Her voice broke suddenly. 'You have ruined my life, Vinnie Harris, one way and another. Oh yes, you have!'

To Vinnie's dismay she began to cry – deep ugly sobs. Full of remorse and aware that perhaps she had been too outspoken, Vinnie tried to put an arm round her shoulders, but Mary shook her roughly away.

'For God's sake, leave me alone,' she begged and half-ran, half-stumbled away in the direction of the mission tent.

Vinnie, badly shaken and angry with herself, stared round at the astonished faces which peered at her from all directions between the hop-bines. She straightened her back and opened her mouth to speak, then changed her mind. Perhaps she had said enough already, or perhaps she had said too much. Pity for Mary's predicament outweighed her resentment of the other's harsh comments, for Vinnie recognised in her heart that up to a point everything Mary had said was true. Inadvertently, Vinnie *had* stolen the men in Mary's life and had enjoyed the affection Mary had wanted. Now she felt intuitively that Mary might lose this last 'man' in her life and sincerely hoped that by trying to help she had not been instrumental in bringing about a similar outcome.

As she walked back to the house she tried to remember exactly what she had said, endeavouring to reassure herself that she was not entirely to blame for the disastrous course of their argument. Yet she felt uneasy and the more she recalled of the exchange, the more anxious she became. She hoped desperately that her well-meant intervention had not strengthened Mary's resolve, but her uneasiness crystallised slowly into a certainty that probably she had made matters worse. And what was it Mary had said? That she 'pretended innocence'. Could that be true?

'Dear God,' she whispered, 'please don't let it be like that. I have never intended her any harm – I'm sure I haven't. I have never intended anyone any harm, so why do I feel so terrible? And how am I supposed to advise Eva?'

She was vaguely aware that several of the pickers spoke to her as she strode past, her face set in a frown, but she did not answer them. What could she do to make amends, she wondered. Who could she turn to for advice now that Bertie had gone? She considered for a moment whether she should take the next train to London in order to see Bertie, but that meant involving another person in the matter and she was sure Mary would not thank her for that. Vinnie wished heartily that Eva's husband had not gone away on business and hoped with a sigh that he would soon return.

CHAPTER ELEVEN

Vinnie was going up the steps to the front door when it was opened by Bertha.

'Mr le Brun's in the morning-room, ma'am,' she said, 'with a French gentleman.' She lowered her voice. 'I forget his name, but he's ever so handsome!'

'Clive? Oh, thank goodness!' Involved with Mary, Vinnie had forgotten that they were coming, but the knowledge that he was at Foxearth cheered her up immediately and she resolutely put Mary Bellweather out of her thoughts as she went in to greet them. Clive le Brun had been so supportive while Louise was critically ill, calling in or telephoning every day to enquire after her.

'Vinnie, it's good to see you.' Clive took her hand briefly and then turned to his companion. 'May I introduce Philippe Delain? He is one of these misguided people who like to view the world from a great height.'

Vinnie smiled. 'So you're a flyer, Monsieur Delain? I am so pleased to meet you. I've never met a flyer before. You are a rarity!'

'*Enchanté, madame,*' he said and taking Vinnie's hand, he bowed his head and kissed her fingers.

She was flustered, aware of Clive's eyes upon her, and drew back her hand a little too quickly. 'It must be very exciting to fly, Monsieur Delain.'

He smiled and she acknowledged to herself that Bertha had been right: Philippe Delain was very good-looking in a foreign way. No one would mistake him for an Englishman, she thought. No one had kissed her hand that way before and she found the courtesy a charming one. For a moment her grey eyes met his brown ones and she saw unfeigned admiration in his gaze.

'Philippe's own machine is at the flying ground at Leysdown,' Clive told her. 'He plans to fly back to France in it.'

The young man shrugged humorously. 'Who is this Monsieur Blériot?' he mocked. 'My machine is as good as his, but he was so fortunate with the weather. The wind was kind and it *blew* him across.'

'You speak English very well,' commented Vinnie.

Philippe spread his hands. 'Ah yes. My mother is from England, many years ago – from Wimbledon in London. Always she speaks to me in English and my father, he speaks to me in French. When I am a boy I visit often my grandparents in Wimbledon, but today' – he shrugged again – 'Alas, they are both passed away, as you would say.'

'How sad,' said Vinnie. 'They would have been so proud of you.'

It occurred to her that perhaps she could talk to Clive about the problem of Alexander. He might know what to do for the best and if she could speak to him in confidence Mary need never know.

Clive was addressing her, but she caught only the tail-end of his sentence.

' . . . to initiate him into the mysteries of hop-picking.'

Vinnie smiled at Philippe. 'You want to pick hops, Monsieur Delain?'

'A few,' he said cautiously and they all laughed.

'And will you,' Vinnie asked, 'initiate me into the mysteries of flying?'

'*Mais non!*' he exclaimed, genuinely shocked at the idea. 'Flying is not for women.'

'It's much too dangerous,' Clive agreed quickly. 'Quite unthinkable!'

'And the Voisin, my machine, is built only for one person,' Philippe told her.

Vinnie laughed. 'Don't look so upset,' she said. 'I didn't

mean it. I have no wish to go up in the air. Instead you can tell me how it is done, how a machine that is heavier than the air can ever get off the ground. I am a coward, I'm afraid, and I certainly don't want to risk my life a hundred feet up in the air!'

Clive looked relieved. 'I was hoping to leave Philippe in your capable hands while I make a few more business calls in the area,' he told her. 'I have promised to look in at Merryon and John Barker at Longford Farm is having some trouble with blight – not much, but it has come at a bad time. I had hoped you would give Philippe a "guided tour" of Foxearth.'

'I shall look after him, of course,' said Vinnie, hiding her reluctance. 'I can show him round the hop-gardens while you are away and then give you both some lunch. Don't worry, Clive, I will entertain Monsieur Delain until you return.'

'You English are so hospitable,' said Philippe with a small bow.

Well, I must go' said Clive, 'or they will wonder where I am – but first tell me, how is Louise? Still making good progress?'

'Very good,' said Vinnie. 'The doctor wants her to convalesce by the sea as soon as she is well enough to be moved. We shall rent a cottage in Cornwall and Doll will take all three children there for a holiday. I shall join them there as soon as I can.'

When Clive had gone Vinnie offered Philippe some refreshment, after which she took him upstairs to meet the Colonel.

'He loves having visitors,' she whispered before they went in. 'He was a very active man and hates being confined to bed. His hearing is not very good, but do talk to him about flying. He follows all the reports in the newspapers.'

Once inside the Colonel's room Vinnie made the introductions, inviting Janet to stay.

'Monsieur Delain is a flyer,' she told them. 'His plane is at Leysdown.'

The Colonel said, 'Leysdown? Ah, the flying ground on Sheppey. I hope they're looking after you, young man?'

'They are, sir. I have been most fortunate.'

'Short Brothers,' said the old man. 'You've heard of them, of course? Oswald and Eustace Short?'

'I have met them both, sir, and I visited their factory in Battersea!'

'Still making balloons for the military, are they? What would we have done in the Boer War without the balloons, eh? Damned useful, they were. For observation, you see. You've got to know what's going on – got to see what the blighters on the other side are up to. Not that I've ever been up in one myself, though. The Cavalry was my line.'

Janet took her cue and brought the Colonel's photographs for Philippe to see.

'I am most impressed,' he said. 'There is nothing quite so beautiful as the – how do you say it – mounted military?'

The Colonel beamed at him. 'Ride, do you, Monsieur Delain?'

'I do, yes sir.'

'Then ride any of our horses,' he told Philippe. 'The poor beggars don't get enough exercise. Vinnie doesn't care to ride, although she is improving. You need to be born to the saddle, I always say.'

'Like you, sir,' Janet said and the old man smiled.

'Like me, Janet,' he agreed, adding to Philippe in a loud stage whisper, 'She's a good girl, this one, you know. Humours me. Thinks I don't know what she's up to, but I do. We understand each other, don't we, Janet?'

'We do, sir.' She smiled at the Colonel and then at Philippe.

'Hmn! So you're hoping to fly your own plane back to France. When will that be, d'you think?'

'It is not easy to say. The weather . . .' Philippe shrugged. 'And there are still adjustments to be made to the Voisin; I am not entirely happy about her yet. Then there will be a test flight, maybe more than one.'

Janet's eyes widened. 'A test flight, sir? Will it be anywhere near here? Might we actually see you flying, sir?'

'I had not thought about *where* to fly,' he admitted. 'But why not? If it is possible, I will fly over Foxearth and wave to you all.'

'Vinnie, d'you hear that?' said the Colonel.

Vinnie's thoughts were revolving once more around Mary, Alexander and Eva, for Mary's bitter words had affected her deeply and she still struggled to exonerate herself from blame. Now she looked up guiltily.

'I beg your pardon?'

'Monsieur Delain is going to fly his machine over Foxearth,' the Colonel told her. 'Give the pickers a bit of a fright, eh! Give 'em something to tell their grandchildren about in years to come. A Voisin. You remember that, Janet – Monsieur Philippe Delain in a Voisin.'

'But I haven't got any grandchildren,' Janet reminded him.

'No grandchildren? Well, that doesn't matter, girl! You can tell somebody else's grandchildren. You must remember it, that's all.'

'I'll try, sir,' she said.

*

Later, as they walked round the hop gardens, Vinnie found Clive's friend a very attentive listener. This surprised her a little, for she had imagined that he would not really be interested in anything but flying and had started her 'guided tour' almost apologetically. Philippe, however, had insisted that he wanted to know and understand everything. As they walked he looked at her with a humorous, half-mocking smile, his head tilted slightly to one side as he spoke, his delicate hands moving expressively.

'Foxearth is your world,' he told her. 'Flying is mine. I enjoy my world with a great passion and I want to share that passion with anyone who will listen to me. I want them to understand what it is about flying that so – how you say? – exhilarates me. I want *you* to understand because if you do not, how will you share my excitement? So I shall talk about my machine, my plans, my problems.' He paused and Vinnie nodded, finding his enthusiasm appealing. He continued, 'Foxearth is your world and you have a passion for it, no?'

'Yes, I suppose so.'

'But of *course* you do,' he exclaimed. 'Hops are your life, your *raison d'être*! How shall I share that with you if you do not talk to me, explain to me, inspire me!' He laughed. 'We must not be half-hearted about life. Time is so precious and life is short. We *must* be passionate or we are only half-alive.'

'Oh!' Vinnie stared at him, surprised by his eloquence and what she imagined to be his 'foreign' way of thinking. All thoughts of Mary, Alexander and Eva had been swept away by his words.

Seeing her reaction he laughed gently. 'You do not agree? They say the English are not a passionate people, but I cannot believe that. My mother tells me the English are – what is her word? – oh yes – reserved.' He shook his head. 'But it is not true. Since I am in England with the Voisin, everyone is so friendly and so helpful and they are not reserved at all. It is all a wicked lie!'

'Are you laughing at us?' she asked suspiciously, but he threw up his hands in pretended horror.

'Would I do such a thing?'

'I don't know,' she laughed. 'You might, but I *will* tell you about my hops. Now let me see, we have three-quarters of our acreage under hops; the rest are apples, cherries and a few pears. It is the hops that make beer bitter. Do you like our English beer?'

He hesitated, then said gallantly, 'In France we drink wine but beer, I am sure, is excellent also.'

'You will have to try some of my brother's beer one day,' she told him. 'He runs his own brewery in London. But where was I? We grow hops called Fuggles and we pick them in September. Most of our pickers are from London, but some are gipsies and others live in the village. When the hops are picked they are taken to the oast-house – you can just see the pointed roof through the trees – where Steven Pitt and John Burrows dry them on a sort of blanket of horsehair.' She glanced at him and he nodded intently. 'Then they are pressed into pockets,' she went on breathlessly, 'which you would call sacks, and off they go to be stored or sold to the brewery – but I shall sell some of mine to my brother. Clive le Brun is our factor and he will sell all the rest. Hops are our lifeline at Foxearth and I have loved them ever since I was five years old. To me they are quite beautiful.'

Philippe laughed. 'So you can be passionate!' he said, taking her hand in his.

'Monsieur Delain!' Vinnie withdrew her hand, feeling the hot colour in her cheeks and annoyed with herself at her inability to cope with such teasing. What had he said earlier? He spoke too easily of passion, she thought nervously.

'I have offended you?' His brown eyes were anxious. 'You are angry with me? What can I say except that I am sorry?'

'No, please,' Vinnie protested. 'Of course I'm not angry – why should I be? I was just . . . I don't know. But I am certainly not offended.'

'That is good.' He paused, then went on, 'I should not wish Monsieur le Brun to be angry with me.'

'Clive? Why should he be?'

He shrugged. 'Because I show my admiration for you and you and he are . . . ' He left the sentence unfinished.

'Clive and I?' Vinnie was astonished. 'Oh no, you are wrong. We are just very old friends. I have had some bad times – some *very* bad times – and always Clive has been there for me to lean on.' She went on earnestly, 'When Louise was ill of course, he was a tower of strength – and years ago when my husband died he was marvellous, travelling to London with me every day and then finding me a room near the hospital because the daily journey was too much for me. Julian, my husband, was in a coma for weeks and it was so terrible.' Her eyes darkened at the memory, then she shrugged. 'But that's all over now. Clive is a *strong* man, do you know what I mean? Not just strong in the physical sense but he . . . ' She paused, searching for the right words, and frowned, suddenly wanting to convince this young Frenchman of Clive's true worth. 'Clive is always in control of his feelings,' she said slowly. 'He has standards and' – suddenly she smiled triumphantly – 'he is a real English gentleman!' she exclaimed. 'That describes him perfectly: a true gentleman with great integrity.'

Philippe Delain was watching his hostess with barely concealed surprise, but Vinnie was scarcely aware of him.

'Clive le Brun *is* a very attractive man,' she concluded, 'but there is nothing between us, at least not in the way you mean.'

Yet even as she spoke a small doubt niggled at the back of her mind. Was that all Clive meant to her? Was he just a good friend? She became aware that Philippe was regarding her with a half-mocking smile.

'So,' he said, 'Monsieur le Brun is a good friend, no more, no less, as you say in England.'

'That's right.'

'Then he will not be angry with me – he will not be jealous?'

'Of course not.' She felt the colour burning her cheeks and was certain that she was making a fool of herself. Why on earth had she spoken at such length about Clive, she thought. No wonder Philippe Delain was laughing at her.

'I hope,' Philippe said softly, 'that one day I may deserve such a glowing tribute. I would like very much for us to be such good friends.'

'I'm sure we will be, Monsieur Delain.' Vinnie struggled to regain her poise.

'Will you call me Philippe?' he suggested. 'It would seem a good beginning.'

'Oh! Should I?' She hesitated momentarily and then nodded. 'Perhaps I could, but then you must call me Vinnie.'

'Oh no! Not "Vinnie",' he protested. 'That is not your name. I shall call you Lavinia. And we will be good friends.'

'I am sure we will. Yes, of course we will.' The look in his dark eyes confused her.

'Perhaps we shall be more than good friends.'

Unused to such directness, Vinnie was startled. Was the young Frenchman flirting with her on such short acquaintance? She was also immensely flattered.

'I don't know,' she stammered in some confusion. Perhaps the French *were* more direct; she would give him the benefit of the doubt. Seconds passed in silence and Vinnie was aware that he spoke to her with his eyes. Bertha's words came back to her:

'He's ever so handsome.' Yes, she thought with a sense of shock, he is handsome but he is also desirable! His brown eyes shone with unexpressed emotion as though willing her to respond in some way, and she felt powerless to resist the pressure.

She wanted to cry out, 'Stop! Give me time to think. I don't understand what is happening.' Desperately she tried to rationalise the sudden whirlwind that was threatening her senses.

Philippe said gently, 'Won't you speak to me, Lavinia? Won't you trust me?'

Her heart pounded so treacherously that she was embarrassed in case he might hear it and could only shake her head helplessly.

Philippe smiled at her. 'Perhaps we should continue the guided tour,' he suggested.

'Oh yes!' cried Vinnie gratefully. 'I think perhaps we should.'

*

Vinnie's tour was as comprehensive as she could make it in the time which remained before lunch. She described the various stages of cultivation which culminated in the ripening of the cone-like hops in September and explained the layout of the hop-gardens, pointing out the rows of bins arranged in 'drifts' which were moved along as each section of the field was picked clean, leaving piles of wilting hop-bines minus the hops littering the ground.

Together Vinnie and Philippe watched the measurer and bin-man at work, the former taking baskets full of the freshly-picked hops from the bin and emptying them into the poke held open by the bin-man.

'Five bushels for Mrs Day's lot!'

Bertha's young sister Grace, acting as 'booker', licked her pencil earnestly and recorded the total in the ledger.

At the far end of the field they saw young Amos Bead urging the horse along at a walking pace, stopping at intervals to lift the full pokes on to the cart. When at last it was fully loaded,

Vinnie and her companion climbed up to share the rickety seat with him as they bumped and bounced their way towards the oast-house.

Philippe asked suddenly, 'Why do you call them gardens? Are they not *fields*?'

'A good question,' said Vinnie. 'A long time ago people brewed their own beer and grew their own hops in their back gardens. If you grew hops in your garden, you paid no tax on them. But if you grew them in your fields in large quantities, you were growing for profit and had to pay tax. So farmers had very large "gardens" in order to try to avoid paying the tax.'

Surprised, Amos said, 'I didn't know all that.'

'Actually the Colonel told me,' Vinnie confessed. 'He knows all there is to know about hops; the Lawrence family have grown them for generations. Ah, the oast-house. Here we are.'

Quickly Philippe jumped down and reached up with both hands to help Vinnie from the cart. She felt his hands tighten round her waist and for a moment their eyes met – his sensual yet still touched with humour, hers wary. It seemed a long time before he released her.

'Thank you,' she said breathlessly.

'But it was *my* pleasure.'

Amos had jumped down on the other side and now he tossed the reins over a post and shouted to let Steven Pitt know he had arrived. A door opened in the oast-house wall above them and John Burrows appeared; Amos climbed back on to the cart and between them the two men manhandled the pokes into the large upper storey. Philippe stepped back to look up at the oast-house, shading his eyes from the sun. The building consisted of a large barn with a conical kiln in the middle. Vinnie explained that the barn was divided into a lower storey – for storage of the dried hops – and an upper loft into which the hop-pokes were delivered so that the hops could be tipped out and spread over the drying area.

'The fire is below the drying area and the hot air rises and goes through the hops and up out of the top of the kiln,' she explained. 'That's a cowl at the very top – '

'A cowl?'

'Yes. That swings round and stops the wind blowing back down into the kiln.'

Philippe nodded but, despite his earlier insistence that he wanted to learn, he found himself considering Vinnie instead as she stood beside him with her head tilted back, a few strands of her heavy gold hair blown by the breeze.

'When the hops are dried to the right texture, they are raked off the heat and spread to cool,' she went on earnestly. 'Then they are pressed into another very large sack – we call it a pocket – and that is lowered down to the ground floor to await collection.'

'You are very knowledgeable, Lavinia,' he told her. 'I am truly impressed. I knew that English women were very beautiful – I did not know they were also intelligent.'

Vinnie looked at him suspiciously. Was he seriously paying her such a compliment or was he mocking her again?

'What is the matter?' he asked.

'Nothing.'

'You look – how do you say? – puzzled.'

'No, I'm not,' Vinnie told him, looking at Amos to see if he was registering their exchange.

'Well,' she said, 'shall we go on? I'll introduce you to our head drier, Mr Pitt. He will baffle you with facts and figures – like how many sacks of charcoal it takes to dry a ton of hops!'

She took a few steps forward, but when he did not follow she turned back. 'What's the matter? Don't you want to look inside?'

'I think I would rather look at Lavinia Lawrence,' he said quietly.

'Philippe!' She laughed to hide her delight. 'You must not talk like this,' she said. 'I don't know how to answer you.'

'But do you not receive compliments from your English admirers?'

'I don't have admirers – at least, I do but no – they don't pay me such compliments.'

He walked towards her, closing the small gap between them.

'Then that is very sad,' he said softly. 'How is a woman to know she is beautiful if a man does not tell her so?'

'I think . . . ' she began, then stopped. 'The oast-house,' she said. 'I thought you – '

'If I come back to earth again in another life, I shall not be a flyer,' he told her. 'I shall be a painter – an artist. And I shall paint your portrait. Ah! I have an idea – I shall engage a photographer with your permission, and he shall take a portrait of you.'

'Oh dear, I don't know . . . ' said Vinnie.

'You will not allow it?'

Vinnie capitulated. She thought she would find it difficult to refuse him anything.

'Of course I will. Yes, you may arrange for a photograph if you wish.'

'I *do* wish,' he said. 'How will it be? A portrait of you for me to carry home to France and another portrait of Lavinia Lawrence with her staff and some of the pickers with a row of hop-poles in the background – a present from me to you!'

'And won't you be in the picture?'

'Yes, I would like that,' he said. 'Perhaps in a day or two, Monsier le Brun may be able to recommend a photographer. I will ask him. Oh, he told me you were a remarkable woman and now I see he was right. To be a widow with three children to raise, yet stay alone rather than marry for the wrong reasons – that takes great courage, Lavinia. And you manage Foxearth – that also is a great responsibility for a young woman. I think you must be very brave and very lonely.' He looked at her steadily. 'I know what it is to be lonely.'

'You are not married, then?' She held her breath.

'No.'

'You will marry one day,' she said.

'Who knows?' He shrugged lightly. 'And will you marry again, Lavinia?'

'Maybe,' said Vinnie. 'One day.'

He took her hands and held them against his chest. 'I have an idea,' he said. 'Suppose we delay our visit to the oast-house?

Let us walk by the river instead, just until lunch-time. Dare you be away from your beloved hops for so long? Will they survive without you?'

She laughed. 'I suppose so.'

'Then I will tell you my life story and you will tell me yours.'

'Oh!' Vinnie remembered her past with some dismay. 'Perhaps not today'.

'Lavinia Lawrence! You are not so brave as I thought!' he smiled. 'Then tell me only *some* of your past. Or invent a new past if you wish. I promise to believe every word of it.'

'Just until lunch, then,' she agreed. 'You have a watch? Because we won't hear the gong down by the river.'

He patted his pocket by way of answer. 'Then you will walk by the river with me?' he asked and Vinnie nodded. 'Good. We shall play truant, as you say.' He held out a hand and after a moment's hesitation, she took it. Together they walked away from the oast-house and down towards the river, engaged in earnest conversation.

*

During their walk Philippe told Vinnie that his family were wine producers with a considerable reputation in the Dordogne. His father, Jean, was one of twin brothers – the sons of Marcel Delain – and the twins had inherited the business jointly, but the other twin had died in a riding accident and Philippe's father was now sole owner of the large vineyards. Jean Delain had come to England on business and had met and married Constance Jay after a whirlwind courtship and despite dire warnings of the folly of such indecent haste. Fortunately the marriage had been a happy one and three children had been born – Jean-Paul, the elder son; Marie, the only daughter; and Philippe, the younger son. The three children had spent frequent holidays with their English grandparents and all spoke both languages fluently.

'And are you good friends with your brother and sister?' Vinnie asked.

He shook his head ruefully. 'We once were,' he said, 'but now we are older . . . ' He shrugged, the movement slight but elegant in a way that Vinnie found very attractive. 'Jean is like my mother and so very English. So – what is the word? – earnest. Yes, he is earnest and so serious. He works but he does not play. Me, I play with my flying machine whenever I can. Sometimes I work, but life is so short. And he is jealous of me because I am the baby brother.' He laughed. 'Is it not always so?'

'Oh yes, it is,' agreed Vinnie. 'When I was a little girl I so adored my brother Bertie; then Emmeline was born and I was so jealous. I couldn't bear him to fuss over her and I used to sulk. Poor Emmeline! She died and then of course I felt so terrible, thinking that maybe I had not loved her enough. Don't you get along with your sister either?'

He considered for a moment, his head on one side. 'I think we are good friends, yes, but we are too much alike. We both are quick to anger, quick to tears. We fight, as my mother says, like cats and dogs! Marie will shout at me and stamp her feet and her arms wave like windmills – then it is all over and we make up and are friends again. It is the same with me. We are *passionate*.' He regarded her quizzically, on the point of saying something else but then apparently changing his mind.

'So while you are in England with your aeroplane,' said Vinnie, 'is your brother working?'

'*Mais oui*! They all work very hard, for they are harvesting the grapes and I should be there also. But instead I am here in England, walking beside the river with a beautiful woman. Because I am not earnest and serious, but idle!' He laughed. 'Jean-Paul will complain of my absence and my mother will support him but my father will say, "Let him be. He is young. Life is short".'

'And your sister?'

'Marie? Oh, she will want me to go back to France, for without me who will she fight with? You would like Marie.'

'And when will you return to France?'

'Very soon. In three or four days, maybe a week.'

Vinnie looked at him, startled. 'But I thought it would be longer. I thought . . . '

'I had hoped to stay longer, but the weather is set fair and my beautiful Voisin is almost ready. Shall you miss me, Lavinia?'

'Of course,' she stammered.

'Then perhaps I shall come to England again.'

'I hope so, Philippe . . .' She hesitated, eyes downcast.

'Yes?'

'Nothing.'

'Oh, but there is something,' he said gently. 'I can see it in your eyes. Won't you tell me? Won't you trust me? We are friends, are we not?'

Vinnie took a deep breath. 'Is there anyone special in your life Philippe? A woman, I mean?'

She saw the gleam of amusement in his eyes as he nodded slowly. '*Mais oui*,' he said. 'A very special woman! She has hair like golden corn and eyes as grey as a cloud. She twists her fingers together when she is nervous and she is walking beside me now.'

'Oh!' Vinnie hoped he would not see how pleased she was. 'Do the women in your life become "special" so quickly?' she asked him. 'We hardly know each other.' She managed a light laugh.

'How long does it take to feel at ease with another person – to know that your minds are in tune?'

'I don't know,' she said.

'How long did it take you to fall in love with your husband?'

'About five seconds!'

'So you see – you can become special to me in as many minutes.'

'But I was only five when *I* fell in love,' she protested.

'And I am only twenty-five!'

They laughed together and then Philippe said, 'Well, Lavinia, I have told you my life story. Now you must tell me yours.'

Vinnie stopped walking to stare out across the smoothly-flowing river, scattered with almond-scented flowers. Dense green turf grew to the sloping edges of the river bank and then gave way to clumps of wild mint and slender reeds. A fish jumped close by and from somewhere above them a skylark rose higher and higher into the blue dome of the sky. Vinnie thought, with a sudden rush of resentment, that it was easy for Philippe to tell his story – he had nothing to hide. But her own story? Did she want to tell it? Did she *dare*? To him she was Lavinia Lawrence, wealthy mistress of Foxearth. He had never known Vinnie Harris and he might not like her. He had said that Lavinia was special to him – Vinnie might not be so special. The silence lengthened uncomfortably until Philippe took her hand.

'Let us sit here,' he said. 'I am too lazy to walk far. That is why I like to fly – it is so much easier.'

'If you don't crash,' said Vinnie.

'If I don't crash,' he concurred.

He sat down and leaned back, resting his weight on his elbows. 'A river is a river wherever it is,' he said. 'You could take this river to France and I could bring the Dordogne to Kent and no one would be much the wiser.'

'Is it very beautiful in the Dordogne?'

'It rains a lot,' he said.

Vinnie sat beside him, arranging her skirts decorously around her knees. Somehow she felt that by agreeing to sit with him she was committed to tell her story. Philippe pulled a long grass stalk and nibbled the end of it.

'Is it so dreadful?' he asked. 'This life story of yours?'

'Yes,' she said, 'I think perhaps it is.'

'And you don't want to share it with me?'

Vinnie swallowed hard and plucked nervously at the grass, rolling and crushing the blades in her fingers.

'I was born in London,' she said, 'in Whitechapel. That is not a very nice place. My father was with us then, but I hardly remember him at all. There were quarrels and he got drunk and spent all the money. Then he went away.'

She looked at Philippe, unable to hide her anxiety, but he was watching something on the water.

'A wild duck, look!' he whispered.

'We call it a moorhen,' said Vinnie, relieved that he did not appear to be paying too much attention to her story. 'Often there are swans, too, but this year we haven't seen any – I don't know why.'

'A moorhen,' he repeated. 'How can you tell?'

'The red flash on the beak. Do you see it?'

'Ah yes.' He glanced up at her. 'Go on with your story.'

'Oh!'

'Your father went away,' he prompted.

So he *had* been listening!

'I used to hide under the table,' Vinnie told him, 'and Bertie would tell me when it was safe to come out. Then we came down here to Teesbury for the hopping and one evening my mother and her friend quarrelled and I ran away to hide. My mother went to look for me and fell in the river.'

'And that is how she was drowned.'

Vinnie nodded, then sighed. 'The Colonel's wife, Christina, arranged for me to be looked after by a woman in the village called Mrs Bryce. She is a widow and at that time she lived with her son, Tom. He was Christina's lover, but I didn't know that then – no one knew.'

Suddenly she knew that she had his full attention, although his eyes were fixed upon the moorhen which dabbled among the reeds. For a brief moment she wondered if she could twist the truth a little, but then she determined stubbornly to tell it all exactly as it had happened. It was all in the past and there was no going back. In her heart she knew that she had never wittingly done wrong – certainly she had never intended anyone harm.

'Is that the end?' Philippe teased. 'Have you told it all?'

'No, there is more.'

He turned towards her and took her hand in his. 'Don't tell me,' he said, 'if you do not wish it. I will not press you. But I would like to hear it and whatever they are, these terrible secrets of yours, they will not make any difference. You will still be very beautiful to me and very special.'

He bent his head and the sun gleamed on his dark hair as she felt his lips brush her fingers. Then he lay on his back once more, looking up at the sky, and closed his eyes.

'I am imagining the young Lavinia,' he said, 'hiding under the table!'

Vinnie smiled nervously. 'It was a very long time ago,' she reminded him.

'So this lady brought you up as her daughter?'

'Mrs Bryce – yes, she did and she was very good to me. Then Tom married Rose Tully and I had fallen in love with Julian, the Lawrences' only son.'

'The handsome prince! It is a fairy tale, your story!'

'Not exactly.' She searched her memories, trying to put the events in their correct sequence. 'One day a man in the village – at least, then he was only a boy – tried to . . . ' She could not finish, but Philippe gave a slight nod to show that he understood and she rushed on, 'I ran away to Rose's cottage, but only Tom was there. He and I – well, something happened and Christina found out – and I was sent back to London. I told you it was a dreadful story,' she ended breathlessly.

He opened his eyes. 'From here you still look very beautiful,' he said, '*and* very special. Go on.' His tone was gentle and Vinnie felt an illogical surge of gratitude that there was no trace of reproof in his voice.

'In London I ended up in the workhouse, but Julian sent people to look for me. When my poor baby was born it was dead, and I was so ill with a fever that I hardly knew what was happening. Julian found me and took me to a doctor who said I would die, so Julian married me.'

Philipe rolled over and sat up. 'And you didn't die.'

'No.'

'Then it *is* a fairy story,' he said softly.

'Not really,' Vinnie told him. 'It gets worse after that.'

'My poor Lavinia.' He put his arm lightly around her shoulder. 'It is a fascinating story and puts my poor little tale to shame. You have great courage, Lavinia. Won't you tell me the rest?'

'I told you – it's all dreadful,' she said. 'Julian and I were happy enough and we had the three children, but then he was killed.'

'Ah, yes. That was very sad.'

'That's all,' said Vinnie, although she had not quite told everything. Her voice trembled with emotion and she felt naked and defenceless, not at all beautiful or special.

Philippe, however, pulled her down closer to lie with him and put both arms round her. His lips were brushing her ear and the words he murmured were full of admiration. Vinnie closed her eyes, luxuriating in the sudden release from anxiety and the knowledge that her past really was of no significance to him. Philippe Delain was not repelled by her story – she truly was still beautiful in his eyes, as he had promised she would be. His fingers moved to her neck and face, exploring and gentle, then back again to her shoulders and down to her arms and hands. He kissed her hands and then her neck and Vinnie's protests, incoherent and unconvincing, went unheeded. His words became words of love and desire and when at last his lips met hers she was already lost.

CHAPTER TWELVE

'Pass the chutney,' said Edie.

'*Please*,' said Cook. 'How many times do you have to be told?'

'*Please*, then!'

Cook passed the jar to her. 'And don't take too much! You're always wasting it – eyes bigger than your belly, that's your trouble.'

She glanced up at the clock and then laid down her knife and fork. 'It's no good,' she said, 'I just can't eat anything. It's choking me – going down like sawdust.'

Her plate contained a thick slice of pork, creamy mashed potatoes and thinly-cut runner beans. Edie looked covetously at the slice of pork. 'If you don't want it . . . ' she began.

'Mind your manners!' snapped Mrs Tallant. 'If Cook chooses to leave her lunch, that's her affair. You eat yours and keep quiet.'

Bertha and Janet exchanged meaningful glances, but said nothing as Cook pushed some mashed potato on to her fork and lifted it to her mouth. It was now after two o'clock and Vinnie and Philippe had not returned for lunch.

'Something *must* have happened,' said Mrs Tallant.

Young Harry reached for another chunk of bread and began to butter it. 'He'll look after her,' he said. 'It's not as if she's on her own.'

'Perhaps she's drownded,' said Edie, 'like her Ma did.'

Mrs Tallant glared at her. 'Drowned? Don't be so stupid, girl, of course she's not drowned!'

'Lost, then,' Edie persisted. She spread the apple chutney on the remains of her bread and stuffed it into her mouth.

'*Lost?*' Bertha broke her silence. 'How can she be lost at Foxearth? She knows every inch of the place – she's lived here so long she must know it like the back of her hand.' She sighed. 'Mind you, I wouldn't mind being lost with Mister Delain. There's something about the way he talks with that funny accent – and he's so handsome.'

There was a pause while Young Harry helped himself to more potatoes and Cook managed to eat another forkful of peas.

They had all reacted differently to Vinnie's non-appearance. Cook took it as a personal affront that apparently neither Vinnie nor her visitor wanted to eat the meal she had prepared. Clive le Brun, returning to find Vinnie and Philippe missing, had declined to eat alone and – obviously annoyed – had left Foxearth looking very grim. Mrs Tallant had her own opinion about what was happening; she disapproved strongly of the mistress of Foxearth absenting herself with a foreigner, no matter how handsome he might be, and adamantly refused to do anything about finding them. Janet was rather scandalised by what she imagined might be happening and Young Harry was indifferent, but Edie positively revelled in the mystery.

'More pork, anyone?' asked Cook. 'More beans?' But it seemed they were all adequately fed. 'Clear away then, Edie.'

Edie pushed back her chair and reached awkwardly across the table to collect Bertha's plate, leaning in the butter as she did so. Cook shrieked at her and she jumped back, rubbing at the greasy mark on her apron.

'Clean on this morning!' Mrs Tallant glared at her. 'You really are the most clumsy – stop rubbing at it! You're making it worse, girl! Oh, for heaven's sake leave it alone and clear the table.'

Harry had seen the fruit jelly. 'I suppose if they're *not* going to be back for lunch *we* could eat that?' he suggested tentatively. 'Shame to waste it.'

'It won't *be* wasted,' said Mrs Tallant. 'It will do for the meal this evening – and anyway, who said they're not coming back for lunch?'

'What, at quarter past two!' Janet exclaimed.

'Oh, don't you start!' said Mrs Tallant, beginning to feel the first prickling of unease.

Edie stacked the plates as noisily as she could. 'I bet they *are* drownded,' she said. 'Both of them, in the river.'

'Well, they could hardly be drowned *out* of the river,' said Young Harry with an attempt at humour. 'It's not easy to drown on dry land, you know, Edie.'

'Oh, very funny!' said Edie, putting her thumbs in her ears and waggling her fingers at him.

'That'll *do*!' cried Cook. 'It's no joking matter. We're all sitting here doing nothing and the mistress might be in trouble. People don't just disappear, you know.'

'They do if they want to,' observed Mrs Tallant grimly. 'We know they left the oast-house together, so it's reasonable to suppose they are still together.'

'It's his eyes,' said Bertha, a dreamy expression on her face. 'They're so dark . . . and those lovely crinkly lines at the corner as though he smiles a lot.'

'Oh yes?' said Janet. 'You seem very smitten, Bertha.'

'Crinkly eyes?' said Edie. 'How can he see with crinkly eyes?'

Bertha groaned. 'It's not his actual *eyes* that are crinkled,' she began, but then the bell jangled on the board above the door and they all turned hopefully towards it.

'It's only the Colonel,' said Janet. 'He's awake again, bless him, and wants me to read to him, I expect. Can I borrow your *Daily Mail*, Cook?'

Cook nodded. 'It's on the dresser.'

Janet hurried upstairs and Mrs Tallant pushed back her chair to show that as far as she was concerned lunch was officially over, and there would be no fruit jelly for anyone but Vinnie and her guest *if* they came back in time for a meal.

'I could pop down to the river,' Harry offered, 'Just to be on the safe side, like?'

Cook looked at Mrs Tallant, who hesitated.

Bertha giggled. 'You might find more than you bargained for,' she said. 'If I was "lost" with Mister Delain, I wouldn't thank you to come spying on me. I'd want to *stay* lost!'

Both Cook and the housekeeper opened their mouths to reprimand her, but at that moment the telephone rang and they all jumped visibly.

Cook put a hand to her mouth fearfully. 'The police!' she whispered. 'Something *has* happened!'

But it was Clive le Brun and Bertha, Cook and Edie leaned out of the door to listen as Mrs Tallant spoke to him.

'I am sorry, sir, but they're still not back . . . I'm afraid I can't, sir. We don't know where they are. We are getting a *bit* worried, sir, to tell you the truth – Mr le Brun? Are you still there? Oh, I thought we'd lost the connection. I hope nothing's happened to her – nothing bad, I mean.'

Bertha clapped a hand over her mouth to stifle a giggle at the housekeeper's tactless wording. 'Do you want to leave a message, sir?' Mrs Tallant continued. 'Oh you don't? Very well, sir. No, I will try not to worry. Good-bye, sir.'

She replaced the receiver and walked thoughtfully back towards the others.

'He's furious,' she told them. 'I could tell by his tone of voice. Mr le Brun may not say a lot, but he doesn't miss much either. He knows what's going on with those two all right and he's hopping mad.'

'It takes a lot to get him upset,' said Bertha. 'He's always so calm and collected. You know where you are with a man like that.'

'I don't know why he's never wed again,' mused Cook. 'After all these years alone. . . . '

'He's not alone; he's got William,' said Bertha. 'I like William; I'd have married William if he'd asked me.'

Harry grinned. 'You'd marry *anyone* who asked you,' he told her. 'You'd probably marry *me*!'

'I would *not*!'

'Maybe I'll ask you and then we shall see.'

'Save your breath because I shall say "No".'

'That will do, you two,' said Mrs Tallant. 'Bertha, you go and clear the dining-room table and re-lay it for the evening meal. That will let her know that I'm not expecting to serve the lunch at this hour. I don't know what's come over her, behaving like this. And as for offending Mr le Brun like that, well, that really is too bad. I'd like to put her over my knee and spank her – and that's the truth!'

Bertha snorted. 'It's Mr le Brun ought to spank her, not you!'

'I wish he would,' said Cook. 'It might bring her back to her senses, silly girl!'

'You're just jealous,' said Edie, ''cos she's out with Mr Delain. I wish I was.'

'She needs a good talking-to,' said Cook, 'that's what she needs. Oh, I do hope that Frenchman hasn't gone filling her head with silly notions. Frenchmen aren't like us – they have a way with them.'

'A way?' Edie looked baffled.

'How d'you know?' asked Bertha.

'I just do,' said Cook. 'They're known for it, Frenchmen are. They all have mistresses and suchlike – it's the thing to do in that country. It's not wrong in their eyes, you see, because they're foreigners.'

'Well, it's wrong in my eyes,' said Mrs Tallant. 'This is England and there is no way the mistress should be gallivanting around with a foreigner, no matter how handsome he is. I didn't know where to put my face when Mr le Brun turned up. I felt terrible, telling him they weren't back – and the lunch all ready and waiting.'

'He could have eaten his,' said Harry. 'I would have.'

'You're not Mr le Brun,' Mrs Tallant told him. 'Mr le Brun is too much of a gentleman to eat lunch alone in someone else's house – it's just not done.'

Cook sighed heavily. 'All that effort to cook a nice dinner and then it's all wasted. That's what gets me! We could have had a bit of an easy morning for once if we'd known. I shall let her see how put out I am when she does get back.'

'*If* she gets back,' contributed Edie lugubriously.

'Of course she'll get back,' said Mrs Tallant. 'The question is, *when?*'

*

Vinnie returned alone at five-past-three, flushed and apologetic, and was mortified to learn that Clive had left.

'Oh, dear. You should have insisted that he stayed,' she said.

Mrs Tallant folded her arms. 'He refused to eat alone, ma'am,' she said coldly, 'and I'm sure I understand how he felt. I expect the food would have choked him.'

Vinnie, in her remorseful state, accepted the rebuke. 'Was he *very* angry?' she asked.

'Not so much angry,' Mrs Tallant improvised, 'as worried that something had happened to you. An accident of some kind. We all were, of course. In fact we were on the point of notifying the police when we saw you coming back. Mr le Brun said he would telephone again later to see if there was any news.'

'Oh dear, poor Clive!' she hesitated. 'Perhaps I should telephone *him.*'

'I'm sure it would set his mind at ease.'

Crestfallen, Vinnie hesitated and the housekeeper continued, 'We took the liberty of clearing the luncheon table. We waited until three o'clock. I could ask Cook to make you some sandwiches.'

'It doesn't matter, Mrs Tallant.' Vinnie was not listening properly, for she was trying to imagine what she could say to Clive that possibly would excuse her irresponsible behaviour.

'What about Mr Delain?' asked the housekeeper. 'Is he hungry?'

'I beg your pardon?'

'Mr Delain, ma'am. Your *visitor.*' Mrs Tallant put a lot of meaning into the word. 'Would he like some sandwiches?'

'He's not here,' said Vinnie. 'He decided not to stay to lunch, as he wasn't hungry. Neither of us was hungry.'

'I see, ma'am. Will you be wanting dinner at the usual time or a little earlier?'

'Half an hour early, please. And I shall invite Mr le Brun.'

'So that will be three for dinner?'

Vinnie shook her head. 'Only two. Mr Delain already has a dinner engagement, so it will be just myself and Mr le Brun. I shall telephone him now. And Mrs Tallant, please convey my apologies to the staff about the lunch. Say that we didn't realise how late it was . . . that we decided to . . . No, just apologise, Mrs Tallant; there is no need to go into long explanations. But I am sorry and it won't happen again.'

When the housekeeper had returned to the kitchen, Vinnie went slowly upstairs. She wanted to use the telephone in the study so that her conversation with Clive would not be overheard by anyone.

Clive, however, was not at home. She tried calling at intervals throughout the day and finally reached him just before six o'clock.

'Clive? It's me – Vinnie. I've been 'phoning you all the afternoon.' There was an uncompromising silence and her heart sank.

'Oh Clive, I don't know what to say,' she stammered. 'I mean, I wanted to apologise – and to explain about this morning . . . Clive, are you there?'

'Yes.'

'Oh. You're not saying anything.'

'I thought it was *you* who had something to say.' She could hear the restrained anger in his voice.

'Yes, of course it is,' she said. 'I am so dreadfully sorry, Clive. It was quite unforgivable, I don't pretend otherwise, so I know I'm asking a lot – but I do hope you aren't too angry with me and I do want to apologise.'

'You're not hurt at all?'

'No.'

'I'm very relieved,' he said. 'I imagined that perhaps an accident had delayed you.'

'No, Clive, there was no accident. Oh Clive, please do believe me, I am so sorry! It just happened. When I got back and you had gone I felt so terrible and Mrs Tallant said you did not have any lunch . . . ' She faltered to a stop and waited for Clive to say something reassuring, but he remained silent.

'Clive, *please* say you forgive me,' she begged.

After a brief pause he said, 'So what happened to Philippe Delain? I naturally expected to meet him again. How did he get home – or is he still with you?'

'No, he went back to Leysdown; I sent him in the carriage. He had arranged to meet someone at the Aero Club and didn't want to be late.' She realised her mistake as soon as the words were out of her mouth.

'How considerate of him!' said Clive. 'I'm glad he has *some* manners, even if he does not display them in his dealings with me.'

'Oh, Clive,' cried Vinnie desperately. 'Don't be angry with him. It was my fault as well as his. Please try to understand. It's not like you to be like this. Please say you are not still angry.'

'Well, of course I'm damned well angry!' he shouted suddenly, his control deserting him. 'I'm angry with both of you for behaving like a pair of – ' He stopped abruptly and the ensuing silence lengthened ominously between them.

Finally Vinnie said nervously, 'I was going to ask you if you would come to dinner instead, but I suppose you won't.'

'I think not,' he said, curtly.

'I don't know what else to say,' said Vinnie. 'I can do no more than say how sorry I am. I wouldn't have hurt you for the world.' Receiving no answer, she made a final effort. 'I wish you *would* come to dinner, Clive? I hate us to be like this.'

'Don't let it bother you,' he replied.

'But when *will* I see you?' she asked.

'I shall be in the area again before too long and I will telephone you in advance to make sure it's convenient to call in.'

'Telephone in advance? But you know that's not necessary.'

'I think it might be best,' said Clive. 'Now, if you'll excuse me I have a few reports to write up.'

There was a click and she realised with a shock that he had

hung up on her. She stared at the receiver in her own hand and then carefully replaced it on its rest.

*

That night Vinnie lay in bed staring at the ceiling, trying unsuccessfully to regret the day. She had behaved very badly, she knew, and very imprudently. The staff were no doubt gossiping about her and she had upset Cook. Moreover she had alarmed everyone by her protracted absence with Philippe and Clive was furious with her. She hoped the Colonel had not learned of her fall from grace – Janet was normally discreet and would not want to worry the old man unduly. But the pickers? Did they know? Was the wretched affair being discussed all round the village, she wondered. And had it reached Mrs Bryce's ears? She wondered how she could face everyone.

'Oh, Philippe!' she whispered into the darkness. 'It was so wonderful, but now that you've gone away it seems so dreadfully wrong. And yet I can't wish it undone – I don't *care* what they say. No, that's not true. I *do* care, but I don't wish it hadn't happened. My very *dear* Philippe! Oh, this is madness, but you're so very beautiful.'

Closing her eyes she recalled his caresses, his endearments and the touch of his lips on hers. She remembered the smell of grass and the feel of his hair warmed by the sun and the gentle way he had teased and coaxed her out of her reluctance. Several times he had lapsed into French and the unfamiliar words like a whispered love-chant had held a certain magic which inflamed her senses.

With a deep sigh she opened her eyes and stared at the pale grey rectangle of the window. Was it so wrong? Afterwards everyone had behaved as though it was, but Vinnie acknowledged that it had been a long time since she had experienced such joy.

'I don't *care*,' she insisted. 'I felt like a young girl again. Is that so terrible?'

Their parting had been a physical blow to her and she had wanted to run after him and call him back – but she was no longer Vinnie Harris; she was Lavinia Lawrence, mistress of Foxearth, and such behaviour was not suitable. She thought wearily of Christina Lawrence, the Colonel's beautiful wife who had taken a lover and scandalised the neighbourhood. Vinnie did not want to become such a byword – but she and Philippe had not been lovers, she reminded herself.

'We were just loving,' she whispered. 'Tell me it wasn't wrong, Philippe,' she begged. 'Julian is dead and I'm alone. Who am I wronging, except myself, and it didn't feel wrong. Just very beautiful and I was so happy.'

She allowed herself to remember Philippe's touch; her body ached for him and her pulses raced. She wondered desperately, not for the first time, whether she would have given herself to him if he had wished it – if he had pleaded for her body. Yes, she admitted, she would have given him anything he wanted and willingly. Perhaps it was wrong, but it was true nonetheless. She had neither the power nor the inclination to deny him anything. And she was going to see him again, for they had arranged to spend an afternoon together. He had suggested they might go for a swim if the fine weather lasted – on Sunday, perhaps, when the hop-pickers took a day's rest. Just to be with Philippe, that was all she craved. Preposterous, she knew, after so short an acquaintance. Dangerous, even, to be so vulnerable and at the mercy of her emotions.

'Philippe, I want you,' she confessed. 'Right or wrong, I want you and nothing else matters. Let them talk if they must and let them disapprove – why should we care?' His name was an aphrodisiac: Philippe Delain. She whispered it again and again until she knew that only his body could satisfy her. It was impossible but true that in a few brief hours she had fallen hopelessly in love with him.

*

Beatrice Harris was doing the washing. The small fire beneath the copper glowed red still, although most of the wash had been done and piles of sheets, towels and tablecloths had been rinsed clean and the water wrung out of them. They now

awaited their turn on the washing line which Bertie had
stretched across the yard for her. The small area reserved
for domestic use led immediately into the coopers' yard, so
Beatrice was careful never to hang out their underwear until
the two coopers had finished work, as she had no intention of
allowing her personal undergarments to become a source of
ribaldry amongst 'the men'. 'The men' were something
Beatrice had not bargained for and she was somewhat piqued
by the close and easy camaraderie which existed between them
and from which she, as a woman, was excluded. There was
Arthur Meach, the head brewer; Ben Billings, his young
assistant and personal dogsbody; Stanley Lovatt, the cooper
and Ernie, Stanley's father, who had once retired from the
profession but now had been persuaded to help his son out at
the 'Barley Tap' whenever the pressure of work demanded it.
Art, Ben, Stan and Ernie were names that jangled discordantly
in Bea's head as their demands on Bertie's time increased and
her own share of her husband's attention dwindled daily.

Wiping the perspiration from her face, she lifted the lid off
the copper, leaning back as she did so to avoid the rush of hot
soapy steam that billowed up to mist the window-panes and
condense upon the whitewashed walls and ceilings of the tiny
scullery. She poked the boiling clothes with a stick, then lifted
one of Bertie's shirts from the water to see if it was clean
enough. Deciding that it was, she set the lid to one side and
began to lift out all the clothes, allowing them to drain for a
moment or two before dropping them into the pail. When this
was full, she carried it out into the yard to the large mangle.
Placed strategically below the wooden rollers was a tin bath to
catch the soapy water which was forced out of the clothes. She
eased one of Bertie's shirts between the rollers, careful that the
buttons were on the inside, and turned the handle vigorously.
When they were all done, she carried the clothes back into the
scullery and rinsed them in the deep sink before carrying them
outside again to repeat the mangling process.

Ben looked across at her and touched his red pull-on hat –
the distinctive headwear of those connected with brewing –

and called out to her, 'Nice drying weather, missus!'

Bea straightened her back. 'Yes, it is, thank goodness.'

'I reckon that's a job my missus'll be doing right now.'

'I expect so.'

When most of the rinsing water had been wrung out of the clothes, she took down from the line two sheets which were almost dry and pegged up in their place four shirts, two towels, a sheet and two tablecloths. These began to flap and dance in the wind and she went inside with a feeling of satisfaction that only a lineful of newly-washed clothes could produce.

The water in the copper would not be wasted. Now that the washing was done, she would ladle out some of the hot suds and scrub the floor. So far they had not found anyone suitable to do the rough work, but Bea would be very thankful when that time came. She was on her hands and knees scrubbing when there was a knock at the door. Glad of the excuse to rest, she stood up and opened it to see a woman standing outside with a jam-jar in her hands.

'Any froth, ma'am?' she asked.

'Froth?'

'Off the beer.' She jerked her thumb in the direction of the top of the building. 'You're brewing, I can tell. New, aren't you? Used to be a nice little pub, this. Always full of a Saturday night. Fridays, too mostly.'

Beatrice, drying her hands on her apron, cast a discreet glance over the woman on the doorstep: about forty years old, ginger hair that was fast losing its colour, a well-made coat, buttoned shoes and a straw hat adorned with a selection of artificial poppies. The woman's face was thin, the cheek-bones protruded and her eyes glittered unhealthily. Her complexion was dappled with freckles.

'We shall be opening the 'Tap' shortly,' said Beatrice. 'In another week or so, I think.'

The woman glanced past her into the scullery. 'Done it up nice, I must say! The other people let it go something chronic. Real shame it was, but then she had trouble with her back and he was blind as a bat. Old couple, they was. You're not from these parts, then?'

Beatrice had no wish to waste time talking, but she felt some compassion for the pathetic creature who talked so jauntily but was so obviously ill.

'We're from Kent,' she said. 'Near Maidstone. Do you know it?'

'Oh, I know Maidstone. Used to go hopping, but now I don't have to – bit of a private income, you might say.'

'That's nice,' said Bea. She held out her hand for the jam-jar. 'I'll find out for you,' she said. 'I won't be long.'

She returned a few moments later to hand over the jar – now full of creamy coffee-coloured 'froth' – and watch the woman drink it down with loud slurping sounds.

'You want to try it, love!' she told Bea. 'Builds you up, yeast does. Gives you stamina. My name's Mollie Pett, by the way. I'll put the word around that you'll be opening the 'Tap' again. Might bring you in a few customers.'

'Thank you. My name's Beatrice Harris.' She held out her hand and Mollie gave it an embarrassed shake.

'I knew a man called Harris once,' she shrugged. 'They come and they go. Ships that pass in the night, he told me, but it's not always that simple, is it? I had his kid, but he never knew.'

'I'm so sorry.'

'Not your fault, love.' Mollie laughed and then sighed. 'Well, I'll be on my way. See you some time. Don't want a barmaid, do you?'

Bea shook her head. 'We've already found one,' she said, 'but she'll only be temporary until I can get the hang of it.'

'You don't look like a barmaid, if you don't mind me saying so,' Mollie told her. 'You have to be tough with this lot round here. They're a rowdy crowd but good-hearted in their own way. It's the beer that does it. Coo, have I seen some fights in here! I hope your husband knows how to use his fists, 'cos they'll walk all over him if he doesn't. And don't you stand no lip. Cheeky sods, some of them! You know how it is. There are some real villains too, some who'd cut your throat as soon as look at you – but if you make a friend of one of them, you've got a friend for life. That's how they are round here, and I ought to know since I've lived here all me life.'

She seemed suddenly to run out of breath and began to cough, one hand held to her chest. Bea waited for the spasm to end and then said, 'Well, I must get on with my work. Nice to have met you, Mrs Pett.'

'It's mutual, I'm sure,' Mollie told her. 'I'll put the word around and drum you up a bit of trade. Thanks for this.' She raised the empty jam-jar and began to walk away across the yard.

'You're welcome,' said Bea and closing the door, she returned to her scrubbing.

*

Nurse Ramsey hated saying 'Good-bye'. She stood beside Louise's bed and looked down at the little girl.

'Now, you remember what I've told you,' she admonished, wagging a finger to emphasise the importance of what she was saying. 'You eat up all your breakfast – '

'And my dinner?'

'Yes, dinner too, and tea. Every bit! And drink up all your milk, swallow your medicine without any fuss and be a good girl for Dorothy.'

Louise giggled, as she always did whenever she heard Doll's real name. Doll, waiting beside her with the nurse's small leather trunk, nodded her head. 'I'm sure she will, won't you, Louise?'

It was Louise's turn to nod.

'And before long,' Nurse Ramsey went on, 'you'll be going down to Cornwall for a holiday. What a lucky girl you are! Lots of girls and boys have never seen the seaside, you know. Never seen the sea and never made castles in the sand. They don't even know what a sand-castle is! Can you imagine that?'

Louise nodded again. The crisis was over and the worst of the illness behind her. The tube had finally been removed and now she was on the way to a full recovery Nurse Ramsey's services were no longer needed. The Nurse hesitated – it was time to go, but as usual it was a wrench. It was not so bad if she was moving immediately to another patient, but this time she was going home for a week's rest before taking up a month's temporary work as relief nurse to an elderly woman in Tonbridge. Parting, it seemed, became increasingly difficult as she grew older and she supposed this was because of the knowledge that when at last she gave up nursing she would be quite alone. Also she had grown too fond of the child, which was a mistake she made frequently. For days after the parting, Louise's face and voice would remain in her memory like a ghost.

'Did you say "Good-bye" to Grandfather?' Louise asked. 'He likes to say "Good-bye".'

'Yes, I did – I've said all my "Good-byes".' She wanted to kiss the small face upturned to hers, but Doll was watching and would no doubt see it as a sign of weakness, maybe regaling the kitchen staff with proof that the nurse was not such a dragon as she pretended.

Doll, intuitive, said suddenly, 'Well, this trunk has to go down. I'll pull it out on to the landing and give a shout to Young Harry.' She departed, closing the door behind her.

Louise said. 'Are you going in the motor then?'

'Yes, I am.' Nurse Ramsey would have preferred the dogcart, having a deep suspicion of all motor vehicles, but Tim Bilton had taken one of the horses to be shod and Harry, commissioned to drive her to the station, had jumped at the chance to act as chauffeur.

Louise pouted. 'I wish I could go in the motor. Mama *never* lets me! She never lets any of us go in the motor.'

'Now, that's not true,' said the nurse. 'Doll tells me otherwise.'

'Well, not very often. She says it's a squash with the three of us and Doll and Mama *and* Young Harry. She says – '

'Who's she? The cat's mother? How many times has Dorothy told you – "she" is not polite.'

The child's pout became a scowl. 'I don't want you to go,' she said.

'Well, I must, so there's an end to it. And quickly, or I shall miss my train.' She leaned forward to press a light kiss on to the blonde head but Louise's arm fastened round her neck, holding her while the little girl kissed her fiercely.

'Now then!' cried the nurse. 'Mind my poor hat! You'll knock it off if you don't watch out.'

She pulled herself free as tears threatened, and made a great show of straightening her hat. 'And remember, eat up your food and take your medicine. No nonsense! Dorothy will send me a letter to let me know how you are behaving.'

'No, she won't,' said Louise. 'She hates writing letters because she can't spell the words – she told me so. I'm a much better speller than Doll. I can spell anything, even long words. I'm *much* cleverer than Doll.'

'Hm! So you may think, young madam. You'll certainly have a bigger head than Doll if you talk *that* way! Now, I'm off and you remember what I've told you. No nonsense!'

She wagged a final admonitory finger but Louise wagged hers in return and when Nurse Ramsey closed the door there was a smile on her face.

'When they start being cheeky, they're getting better,' she told herself as, with the happy knowledge of a job well-done, she made her way downstairs.

*

Later that day Vinnie wrote to Alexander:

'My dear Alexander,

Eva has written to me about your problem with regard to Sylvia and Mary. I hope you will understand that Eva was not betraying your confidence, but asking for my advice. I tried to talk to Mary about you, but she would not discuss it with me. However you are welcome to come to Foxearth to talk to her yourself. It is all very sad because Mary is very fond of you and obviously means well, and I am sure she has your best interests at heart. If you do not want to come to Foxearth, then I can only suggest you go to see my brother Bertie Harris who now lives in Whitechapel. He and his wife have recently taken over the brewery there called the 'Barley Tap'. I'm sure he will give you good advice.

Eva says you have been trying to trace your mother; while I do not think this is a wise thing to do, it is not my business, so I should not try to advise you.

Please excuse this short letter, but we are now beginning the third week of the picking and I am dreadfully busy as you can imagine.

I do hope you can make up your quarrel with Mary. I think she is very unhappy.

With sincere best wishes for your well-being,

I remain your good friend, Lavinia Lawrence.

She read through the letter again, changed the word 'quarrel' to 'disagreement' and then slipped it into the envelope and sent for Edie to take it down to the post-box.

*

Mollie Pett opened her eyes and then closed them again hurriedly. She put a hand to her head, groaned and said, 'God Almighty!'

Her head throbbed and her mouth was both dry and sour. A frown settled over her drawn features as memories of the previous night filtered back into her consciousness. The same old story, she thought wearily: too much to drink and too little to eat. She was not as young as she once was, and her stomach couldn't cope with the unsympathetic diet. Groaning again, she became aware of a faint but persistent nausea. Oh God! She was going to be sick! Slowly she levered herself upright and opened her eyes a little, then swore beneath her breath as she discovered a fully-clothed man sprawled on the bed beside her. In the pale light from the attic window he looked even worse than he had done the night before, when at least the subdued lighting of the public house had been kind. She stared with distaste at the fleshy face with its stubbled chin and slack mouth; he lay on his side so that his face was distorted into unflattering folds.

'Not that you're a handsome bastard at the best of times,' she muttered. It was not the first time she had woken to find him beside her and presumably it would not be the last. There were others less ugly, she reflected, but also less generous with their hard-earned wages. This one, Evans, was a coal-man. The black dust was ingrained in his skin, except round his eyes where his spectacles acted as a protection. No amount of scrubbing would remove it, he had assured Mollie.

With a sigh she slid out of bed and stumbled to the door, then down two flights of bare stairs to the lavatory she shared with the other occupants of the house.

Climbing upstairs again was a lot harder than going down. She frequently found herself panting with effort and had to stop several times to catch her breath and fight down the desire to cough. Miss Gray on the floor below the attic would come out and complain about her early rising and the fact that her coughing disturbed other people's sleep. Miserable cow, thought Mollie – she'd be ill herself one day and then she'd know! Back in her room, Mollie slumped into a chair and wondered whether or not to waken George and get rid of him. Sometimes she gave him a quick cup of tea, but this morning she felt unable to drink anything and disinclined to put herself to any extra trouble on his behalf. Dispassionately she surveyed the shapeless mass of humanity that went by the name of George Evans. He still wore his boots – 'straights' that would fit either foot – and one of these was thrust incongruously through the rusting iron rods which formed the foot of the bed.

'Silly sod!' said Mollie without rancour.

He would get up and go home to his fat little wife and six kids and his elderly mother. And good riddance to him, she thought with another sigh. She wouldn't want him, not for good. A bit of a knees-up at the pub was one thing, and maybe a cup of tea next morning, but she wouldn't want George Henry Evans as a husband. Nor as a son or a father or a brother, come to that. In fact, she wouldn't want him at all.

'You're 'orrible, George Evans,' she told his prostrate form. 'Really 'orrible and that's the truth.'

But so am I, she added inwardly. She glanced surreptitiously towards the little swing-mirror that stood on the chest of drawers, but resisted the temptation to look at herself in its discoloured surface. That was always a mistake, because she was always disappointed by what she saw reflected in it. The pale lined face frightened her anew each time, making her realise with a cold knot of panic just how quickly her life was running out. She didn't want to die, but she knew that she would and that it was only a matter of time. Sometimes she didn't even care. Like now . . . Now it didn't bother her that she would soon be rid of her raddled body. Life held few and dubious pleasures and the faulty workings of her physical self caused her continual discomfort and pain. She could only pretend a sort of happiness when she was drunk. When sober, she was disgusted with the poor creature she had become and appalled by the knowledge that everything about her way of living could only get worse.

'Oi!' she shouted, suddenly angry with life. 'You! George Evans!'

The man in the bed stirred, grunted and heaved himself over on to the other side. Mollie's stomach churned suddenly and she bent her head with one hand to her mouth, but her stomach was empty and after a few moments the nausea passed and she felt slightly cheered by a small triumph. If only she really *had* got a wealthy doctor friend, she thought wistfully. Damn Dora Wilks and her stupid Sid. A rich doctor would set her up in a nice little flat – he might even cure her free of charge! This glittering prospect held her attention as she allowed herself to imagine a life of luxury, cared for by the devoted doctor.

Once she had been a beautiful woman – no, not quite beautiful but attractive, certainly. Well, maybe not attractive, but definitely desirable. Perhaps she had been too generous, she reflected sadly. Perhaps in her youth she had given away too much. The George Evanses of this world had never seen her at her desirable best; they had never met the young Mollie Pett with her vivacious smile and flaming red hair. Many a young man had longed to span her tiny waist with his hands – the trouble was that she had let too many of them do it – and all for love.

'If I'd had a shilling . . . ' she began aloud, then became aware once more of the man on the bed who now began to breathe stertorously.

'Oi! Georgie!' she called again. 'Stir yourself, can't you? Your wife'll be wondering where you are, the poor little cocker! Rather her than me. Wake up, George Evans, for crying out loud! You deaf or something?'

Pushing herself to her feet she crossed to the bed, seized him roughly by the shoulder of his dark coat and shook him. He belched suddenly and she wrinkled her nose in disgust.

'Oh, get up and go home, George,' she begged. 'I'm sick of the sight of you and my bloody head's banging like nobody's business. GEORGE EVANS! D'you hear me? Wake up, I tell you!'

He opened his eyes briefly. 'Mollie,' he muttered. 'It's Mollie – '

''Course it's me! she snapped. 'Who d'you expect? Joan of Arc? Stir yourself, George, for Pete's sake. No, don't close your eyes again. Here . . . ' She tugged and pulled him into a sitting position. 'I'll make you a cuppa tea and then you've got to push off home. Got it?'

She was aware of his bleary eyes watching her shortsightedly as she filled the tin kettle and lit the only burner that still worked on the second-hand cooker. She had filled the kettle right to the top because it leaked badly and if she half-filled it, it would be empty before the water was hot enough to make the tea. Mollie sighed again. A rich doctor friend would buy her a decent kettle. He might even buy her a decent cooker! If only she hadn't been so generous with her favours, she could have been a wealthy woman.

As she rinsed a chipped mug at the sink there was a knock at the door and she turned in dismay. 'Now who the hell's that?'

Experience had taught her that unexpected callers invariably meant trouble of one kind or another. Looking at George, she put one finger to her lips to silence him while she tried to decide what to do. She could pretend to be out, but the door wasn't locked and whoever was there might try it. As she hesitated the knock was repeated. The sound galvanised George into activity and he stood up and began to tidy his clothes with clumsy movements. Mollie did the same, patting her dishevelled hair and smoothing down her gaudy red skirt and jacket.

'Hang on!' she called out, her voice superficially bright. 'Won't keep you a second.' She turned to George. 'Well, get away from the bloody bed!' she hissed.

'But where – ?'

'Sit over there,' she told him, pointing to a chair by the table.

'My specs!' he cried. 'Where are my specs?'

'You don't need them right now, do you? Just shut up and try and look as though you *belong* here – God forbid!'

As soon as he was seated Mollie crossed to the door and pressed her left foot against it, for you could never be too careful and an irate Mr Potter had been known to try to force an entry. Mr Potter was the rent collector. With a warning glance in George's direction, she patted her hair once more, straightened her back and called out, 'Is that you, Mr Potter?'

There was a brief pause before her question was answered in the negative by an unfamiliar voice. Cautiously Mollie removed her foot and opened the door a little to peer out at the owner of this voice. She recognised him instantly: it was her son, Alexander, who stood there! The shock robbed Mollie momentarily of speech and impulsively she slammed the door shut.

George Evans looked at her in alarm.

'Who is it?' he gasped. 'Not my wife?'

'My kid!' hissed Mollie.

'Your kid?' echoed George. 'What, the boy, you mean?'

'The boy, yes,' she repeated frantically. 'Christ! Let me think.' Her mind raced, headache and nausea forgotten. Her own son, Alexander, stood not a yard away from her on the other side of the door, as tall and good-looking as he had been in the photograph on Mary Bellweather's mantelpiece. Oh God, he mustn't see her like this – he must never know what she had become. The knocking was repeated and Mollie leaned her back against the door, her eyes signalling in silent desperation to the man at the table who looked at her blearily.

'What d'you want?' she called through the closed door.

'My name is Alexander Bellweather. I'm looking for someone – for a Mrs Pett. Mrs Mollie Pett.'

'She's not here,' Mollie told him. 'There's no one called Mollie Pett here.'

George Evans rolled his eyes, but Mollie mouthed at him angrily. There was another pause and then Alexander began, 'But the boy in the ground floor flat said – '

'Him? He's barmy,' said Mollie. 'You don't want to listen to the likes of him – doesn't know his arse from his elbow.'

She wanted him to go away for his own good. Intuitively she knew that if he 'found' his mother, it might well ruin his life. But her son, it seemed, was a persistent young man.

'May I talk to you for a moment?' he asked. 'I would make it worth your while.'

Mollie hesitated, reluctant to let him go without the chance to take a proper look at him. 'Hang on,' she said, 'I'm not quite dressed.'

She rushed over to the window and pulled together the tattered curtains, darkening the already gloomy room. Then, as an inspired afterthought, she snatched up George's thick-lensed spectacles from the table and put them on.

'I'm Mrs Evans, your wife,' she told George in a fierce whisper. 'So keep quiet. Let *me* do the talking. Put your head down on the table – make out you're poorly or something.'

At last she opened the door and Alexander stepped uncertainly into the darkened room.

'My husband's took bad,' Mollie told him quickly. 'I'm Mrs Evans.' She kept her face half-averted so that he could not see her clearly.

'Oh, I see,' said Alexander. 'I'm sorry about your husband.'

'He'll live,' she said. 'It's only his gut. No, that boy you said you saw downstairs – daft as a brush!' She tapped her forehead. 'Nice kid but funny in the head. Gets things a bit . . . well, you know!'

'Yes, I see.'

The thick glasses blurred Mollie's vision so that she could not make out Alexander's features clearly and she felt a pang of disappointment. If she took them off to get a good look at him, he might recognise her. She hesitated. It was ten years since they had last spoken together – ten years since she had run out on him. He might not know her now, but she dared not take the chance. She saw his eyes travel round the room, taking in the unmade bed, the sink littered with dirty pans, the rickety table and the stained and peeling walls. She was thankful for the gloom which hid the worst of the squalor from the shrewd young eyes.

'We have to keep the curtains pulled,' she invented. 'The light hurts his eyes.' She turned away her head and went on, 'She *used* to live here, that Mrs Pett, that's all I know. She was a nice woman – kept herself to herself, if you know what I mean.'

Alexander said eagerly, 'You know her, then?'

Mollie shook her head. '*Heard* of her,' she amended. 'When I moved in I heard this and that about her. You know the way people talk. She was a very nice woman, by all accounts. Well-respected, as they say. You a friend of hers?'

'In a way,' he laughed shyly. 'Actually, I'm her son, but . . . we lost touch some years ago and now I'm trying to trace her.'

'Well, I never!' said Mollie. 'She did have a son – very fond of him, she was, and very proud. A clever lad by all accounts.'

'Was she?' said Alexander. 'Fond of me, I mean?'

'That's what they said.' Gaining confidence, she addressed George suddenly. 'You remember, don't you George? That Mrs Pett what had this room before we come here.'

George nodded awkwardly without lifting his head. 'That's right. So she did,' he mumbled.

'I really would like to find her,' said Alexander. 'I don't

suppose you know where she's gone, by any chance?'

His hand strayed to his pocket, for he had found during his search that money set loose reluctant tongues.

'Gone to America,' said George. Having been allowed to join in the conversation, he now felt tempted to contribute more fully and lifted his head. 'Don't you remember, Mo – '
He stopped in the middle of the word.

'America!' said Alexander. 'Good Lord!'

'He will call me Moggie,' Mollie said hastily. 'He knows how I hate it. I mean, Moggie is a cat's name, isn't it? Margaret I was named – and I'll thank people to remember it. Yes, America. That was it, like my husband says, she had this admirer, a doctor he was, and one day he married her and off they went. He got offered this job there, you see. That's all we know, isn't it George?'

George nodded.

Alexander took a florin from his pocket and handed it to her. 'Well, thank you anyway, Mrs Evans,' he said.

'So you can stop looking,' Mollie told him. 'I mean, if she's gone to America probably you'll never find her. She'll have a new name, you see. And she *was* a very private sort of person, so they said.'

She pocketed the florin and moved towards the door, afraid to prolong the interview in case it turned sour on her. Something might slip out and that would not do at all. She rather liked the Mollie Pett she had described to Alexander.

The young man hesitated, then reluctantly took the hint and nodded 'Good-bye' to George.

'I hope you're feeling better soon,' he said.

'What?' said George. 'Oh, feeling *better*. Yes, I'll be all right by and by.'

'And thank you again for your time,' Alexander said to Mollie. 'You have been most kind.'

'Not at all,' Mollie replied, holding open the door. 'You get along out and don't talk to that kid downstairs nor anyone else. This lot will tell you anything you want to hear if they think you'll pay them well enough.'

She watched his blurred outline as he made his way carefully down the narrow stairs. Once he was out of sight she snatched off the spectacles and ran down to look out of the landing window to catch a last glimpse of her son, as he emerged into the street and crossed over on to the opposite pavement. She whispered his name and sighed deeply.

'You turned out a nice lad, young Alex,' she said, swallowing hard and blinking furiously. 'A real nice lad. If your mother wasn't proud of you, she'd need her bloody head examined.'

Her pride mingled with regret as she went back upstairs. George had pulled back the curtains and now stood in front of the mirror, combing his hair with his fingers. The boiling kettle began to steam up the window, but he ignored it.

Mollie looked at him. 'America!' she said. 'I like it! That was clever of you, George Evans. So what d'you think of my son, eh?'

'Nice-looking kid.'

'Takes after his mother!'

'Don't I get a cup of tea, then, before I go?'

''Course you do' She crossed to the shelf and took down a grimy tea-caddy. 'America!' she said. 'Not bad at all. You're not as daft as I thought you were, George Evans.'

CHAPTER THIRTEEN

By seven-thirty on the third Wednesday of the hopping, the long day's labour was already forgotten. The local pickers had long since departed to their respective homes and the three ladies picking for charity had been whisked away by an ancient brougham. The gipsies had quietly withdrawn to their own corner of the nearby meadow, where their caravans were ranged as usual along the hedge in the lee of the prevailing wind. The Londoners, after a cursory wash to remove the day's dirt from faces and hands, had made preparations for their evening meal, descending in dozens on Tupp's Store to buy bacon scraps (specially bought in from one or two high-class grocers in Maidstone), eggs, potatoes, carrots and onions. A few lucky ones had been able to purchase a rabbit from the local poacher, who regularly scurried among them in the hop-gardens when no one in authority was looking. A very few had caught fish from the river – an eel or grey mullet – and one enterprising lad had snared a wood pigeon. Robbie, the local fish-man, had done a roaring trade in kippers, bloaters, herring and haddock. This year the postman's wife had finally given up picking and now found it lucrative to make and sell meat and vegetable pasties.

While the children scampered freely with instructions to 'keep out from under me feet', the adults concentrated their efforts upon the serious problem of filling empty stomachs with a cheap but nourishing supper and the scene was one of great conviviality as more than a dozen bonfires sent bright flames and glittering sparks up into the air. There was no wind, and flames and sparks shot skyward crackling and hissing, scenting the still air with the inimitable smell of wood-smoke plus a variety of appetising smells of stews, baked fish, jacket potatoes and the like. Around each fire little groups of people clustered cheerfully talking, laughing and teasing together. It was the best time of the day, when rivalries, arguments and cross words were forgotten and everyone could look forward to an evening's entertainment. For some this would mean a meal, a sing-song or a chat round the fire followed by an early night. For others less careful of their pennies, it would be a meal followed by a few 'jars' at the 'Horse and Cart' where they would sit around on the ground or lean back in the hedge, thus blocking the roadway and causing a nuisance to any vehicle wanting to pass through. Only rarely did they provoke a breach of the peace which would necessitate the hasty summoning of the local policeman.

One young couple who did not wish to share these forms of entertainment were Dora and Albert, who knelt beside one of the fires toasting thick 'doorsteps' of bread and spreading them with dripping. A family of four women shared the fire with them and one of these, shapeless but with a ready laugh, was stirring the contents of a large but grimy saucepan in which bacon scraps, potatoes and onions bubbled noisily. Dora and Albert had contributed a few pence towards this treat and each looked forward to a generous bowlful in the not-too-distant future. Meanwhile they satisfied their immediate hunger with bread and dripping.

'Watch out! It's burning!' shrieked Dora as a sudden spurt of flame licked the edges of Albert's bread where it hung precariously on the end of a peeled stick which served as a makeshift toasting-fork.

Her warning made him jump and the bread fell off the stick and into the fire, from which it was rescued with great hilarity. He surveyed the bread with a resigned good humour and blew off the surplus ash which clung to one side.

The shapeless woman grinned at him. 'Eat a peck of dirt before you die,' she said. 'Bung some dripping on nice and thick and you won't even notice it!'

Albert nodded and did as he was told. He had more important things on his mind and was not going to be distracted by such trivialities. He had seen one or two couples sneaking off in the darkness to lose themselves among the shadowy hop-poles and was trying to persuade Dora that this might hold possibilities for them also.

'Feel like a walk later?' he asked, his voice low in case the others grouped round the fire should hear. 'Walk your dinner down.'

'A walk!' Dora protested. 'I've been on me feet all blooming day. What d'you take me for?'

'I just thought . . . ' he said lamely. 'You know, just the two of us!' She gave him a sharp look, inspected her own toast and began to spread it with the last scrapings of dripping.

'We'll have to get some more of this,' she said. 'It's tasty.'

'Yes, good idea,' said Albert with his mouth full. His teeth met ash but he scrunched on manfully without complaint. 'I mean, there's nowhere you can be private here. Know what I mean?'

'No,' said Dora, who *did* know. 'I thought we might go for a drink. The 'Horse and Cart' seems to be the favourite.'

'I'm not thirsty.'

'Not now, you daft ha'p'orth! Later on when we've eaten.'

It amused Dora to pretend innocence and watch him flounder. He really was a very nice young man, she thought, but men were all after one thing. Still, it couldn't do any harm in her condition and she was not entirely averse to the idea.

'I thought,' he ploughed on, 'that we might – well, we seem to get along . . . I mean, I really like you, Dora. We could have a bit of a cuddle – well, you know. I mean, how long have we known each other now?'

'Only three weeks,' she said demurely, 'and I *do* have a husband.'

'I know you do and I wouldn't want to – '

'And two kids.'

'I *know*, but what I mean is, you're here with me and there's no one to see. Your husband's miles away and he'd never know and I'm – '

'D'you want any more toast? There's no more dripping.'

'What? Oh yes, I'll have another one. Thanks.' He watched as she cut a last thick slice, leaving only a thin crust.

'What about you?' he asked. 'Don't you want any more?'

'I'll chew the crust – do me teeth good. You toast that.' They busied themselves, Albert toasting and Dora eating her dry crust. There was a long silence.

'That smells good,' Albert said to the shapeless woman, referring to the stew.

'You can't beat a bit of bacon for flavour,' she agreed. 'Takes a lot of beating for flavour, bacon does. Sixpence, that lot. I didn't think that was bad.'

'No. Not bad at all.' Albert's heart was not in this conversation as he wrestled with his conscience with regard to Dora. She did have a husband, it was true, but . . . he decided to make one final attempt.

'Look, Dora, what the eye don't see,' he whispered to her, 'the heart don't grieve over! Your old man's not going to know, is he, the way you are? I mean, nothing can happen like a baby or anything, 'cos it's already happened.'

'Too right it has,' said Dora. 'You don't have to tell me – I *know* it's happened.'

'So you and I – we could have a bit of harmless fun. Well, it *would* be harmless. Not just like last time, I don't mean. Not just a kiss.'

'No? What then?'

Albert looked anxiously towards the four women who were taking no notice, chatting and giggling among themselves.

'You know,' he hissed.

'Do I?'

'You must do – you've got that!' He jerked his head towards her bulging abdomen.

'Oh that! Honestly, Albert, you are awful!'

'But we could.'

She sat back, grinning at him, then leaned forward and

whispered in his ear. 'I bet you never have.'

A deep blush spread over his good-natured face. 'I *have*,' he lied. 'Of course I have.'

'It'd be the first time. Tell me the truth.'

'I tell you I *have*,' he blustered.

'Oh well, then I won't,' said Dora. 'I thought if you was a virgin I just might have.'

Albert's colour faded as quickly as it had come and one of the women looked at him.

'Are you all right?' she asked. 'You look a bit funny.'

'He's O.K.' said Dora, coming to his rescue. She watched as he considered the point.

'You mean,' he hissed, 'that if I never have, you will.'

She nodded.

He swallowed. 'Cross your heart?' he asked. 'Dora, do you cross your heart and hope to die?'

She nodded again and Albert took a deep breath. 'Well then,' he said. 'I never have. So you will? Tonight? You really mean it? Cross your heart and hope to die?'

'I've *said* I will.'

He struggled to hide his excitement. 'Oh Dora, you won't be sorry. It'll be so . . . ' He shrugged. 'Well, I'll see that it's the best time you've ever had, I promise you I will. And first we'll jump over a hop-pole, like they say, to make us man and wife. A hopper's wedding, to make it sort of legal.'

'Legal! A hop-pole's not legal,' Dora objected mildly.

'*Sort* of legal, I said. Anyway, what is legal? Are you and your old man married *legal*? In a church and everything?'

'Not exactly, no.'

'Well then, what's the difference? A hop-pole's as legal as anything else, everyone says so. They all do it. It'll be just for the hopping, you see – just for the rest of the month. Oh Dora, we've only got another ten days! I wish – '

'Don't start wishing, Albert,' she advised soberly. 'Just ten days together here and then that's it. My Sid can be a real bastard and he's as jealous as hell. So after the hopping, it's over. Done with! Agreed?'

'Agreed. Oh Dora!' He hid his face in his hands, over-whelmed by her generosity and thoughts of the delights ahead.

The shapeless woman looked at his bowed head and then at Dora. 'Is he all right?' she asked. 'Up here?' She tapped her forehead and Albert looked up, his eyes gleaming as he glanced at Dora.

''Course I'm all right,' he said jubilantly. 'As a matter of fact, I've never felt better in me life!'

*

The mission meeting that evening was well-attended. Roland Fry regarded his little flock with pride as they sat in rows outside the tent on an assortment of benches and rickety chairs. The children sat on the grass right at the very front. Behind them Gareth was making last-minute adjustments to the 'magic lantern' which was later to provide the high spot of the evening's entertainment. Lydia Grant was inside the tent setting out forty-five tin mugs – she had done a rough head count – and filling a basin with sugar. Roland, book in hand, was calling out the names of the pickers and putting a tick against those present. It was important for the pickers to be seen and to be counted for the accumulation of ticks, since only good attendance would ensure a coveted place on the outing to Camber Sands on the final Sunday.

The last name was ticked and Roland closed the book.

'I would like to welcome you all,' he began, 'to our humble entertainment. We have a splendid programme for you tonight and cocoa will be served, free, in the interval. First we have a selection of songs from a lovely lady – Miss Ellen Willett, accompanied on the mouth organ by her brother Mortimer. Then a rendering of a sad poem about the sea – I'm assured you will need handkerchiefs for this one! – by Miss Ada Knight, who tells me that she learnt all seven verses from her grandfather at the tender age of eight years.'

He waited for murmurs of interest to die down and then continued. 'After that three little sisters – Meg, Amy and Lizzie Crump – are going to dance the hornpipe; then their uncle, Mr Edward Crump, will tell us a few jokes. All these good people have given up their spare time today in order to practise for our little show, so I'd like you to join with me in showing our appreciation!'

During the wildly exaggerated applause which followed, Lydia slipped out of the tent to ask Roland the exact numbers for cocoa.

'Thirty-nine,' he told her after consulting his list. 'We're five up on last night, but seven down on Monday. Still, I'm not complaining; we're doing very well on average. It really is quite heartening. So thirty-nine plus three of us makes forty-two.'

As the applause faded, he held up his hand for silence.

'Before we start though,' he began, ignoring one or two groans and giggles from the children, 'I should like you to join with me in a short prayer. We must never forget we are all in God's hands. Will you all stand, please, and bow your heads.'

Three young lads had been sitting on the end of one of the forms gleefully anticipating the familiar request. Now they stood up abruptly, allowing the form to be upended and depositing two elderly women on to the grass. Roland, eyebrows raised, waited patiently for the noise and hilarity to come to an end, then he placed his hands together and closed his eyes. This was the signal for nearly a dozen people in the back row to abscond. They crawled away on their hands and knees, greatly preferring the 'Horse and Cart' to the mission show but hoping to share in the expedition to Camber. They reckoned they had attended long enough to earn a tick against their names.

Roland was aware of their subterfuge, but did not see how he could forcibly restrain them. Better, he thought, to let them go and pretend innocence. He would remove the ticks from their names later on.

'Dear Father in Heaven,' he began, 'look down on us, we pray You. Bless Thy children gathered here. We thank You for work to do and strength to do it, for fresh air and sunshine, for cheerful company, food to satisfy our hunger and a bed in which to sleep. We praise Thee – '

'That'll do, Mr Fry,' interrupted a loud voice from the back. 'I'm sure He's got your drift, so do let's get on with it!'

' – for Thy great goodness,' Roland persisted, 'for the harvest of the hops and the bounty of the orchards. Teach us to know that Thou art beside us, to love and cherish us – '

'Amen!' cried the same voice.

'Amen!' chorused all the others and they promptly sat down as one man, struggling to keep their faces straight, nudging each other and wondering what Roland Fry would do about their termination of his prayer.

After a brief hesitation, Roland finished '. . . and give thanks O Lord. Amen.' He kept his eyes closed a moment longer than was really necessary, then opened them again. He would *not* let them see he minded, he decided. Smiling cheerfully, he ignored the incident and held out his right hand.

'And now our little show begins. Ellen and Mortimer Willett will sing a September Medley, so give them a big hand, ladies and gentlemen!' Ellen was a plump young woman no more than seventeen years old and Mortimer looked even younger, with light curly hair, but he was very proficient on the mouth organ. Ellen's voice was not of the same high standard as her brother's playing but she sang, tunefully enough, 'After The Ball Was Over', followed by 'Come Into The Garden , Maud' and finished with a song which began, 'If Daddy Hadn't Married Mummy, He Might Have Married Me'. Only a very few cat-calls mingled with the cheers that followed their performance and after an elaborate bow from Mortimer and a shy curtsey from his sister, they returned to their seats to enjoy the congratulations of their family.

After introducing Mrs Ada Knight, Roland left her to her recitation and joined Lydia, who remarked on Mary Bellweather's absence.

'I am sorry,' said Roland. 'I quite forgot to tell you. I suggested she take an evening off, as she looks so very strained. Something is troubling her, I'm sure. I have never known her so edgy. Has she spoken to you, by any chance?'

Lydia, looking for the kettle-holder, nodded. 'She is not

herself at all. I did hear on the grapevine that she and Vinnie had been arguing. I have tried several times to give her an opportunity to tell me what's wrong, but you know how Mary is. I said she looked rather pale and she told me she wasn't sleeping well. She's hardly eaten anything this last week and she does look quite drawn. I wonder if it's her boy, Alexander, but if he were unwell I think she would tell us. She usually talks so much about him, but this year she has hardly mentioned him. She's such a private person, I'm afraid; it's never been easy to get close to her.'

Roland's good-looking face puckered with anxiety. 'Should I speak to her, do you think?' he asked. 'I hate to intrude, but really I am beginning to worry about her.'

'I wish you would,' said Lydia. 'She's always had a deep admiration for you and she might confide in you.'

At that moment Gareth came in to collect the kettle-holder and went outside again, to return a moment later with the large kettle which had been heating over an open fire well to the rear of the tent. Outside, the garrulous Mrs Knight had reached the end of her poem and Roland hurried out again to thank her and introduce the next act.

By the time the forty-two cups of cocoa were served only thirty people were there to claim them.

Gareth grinned. 'They've done it again,' he told Lydia. 'I don't know how it happens – I never see anyone leave.'

'Never mind,' she laughed. 'We can let the children have the extras, poor little mites. They're skinny as sticks, some of them.'

The children needed no second bidding and the remaining mugs were soon emptied down eager throats. The audience resumed their seats for the magic lantern show, staring hopefully towards the 'screen' which consisted of a white sheet stretched over a square wooden framework. After a last-minute check to see that everything was in place, Gareth addressed the crowd which had shrunk even further in number now that the free cocoa had been consumed.

'My little show tonight,' he began, 'is entitled "The Sad

Tale of Sarah Tuck" and the story will be read by Miss Lydia Grant.'

There was furious clapping from the children, who liked to feel they were participating to the full, as Lydia sat down beside Gareth at the rather unsteady card table on which the diascope was perched and began to read from her script by the light of a candle.

'This is the tale of a poor young woman,' she began, 'who lived with her invalid mother Agnes Tuck to whom she was devoted . . . '

The first transparency fell into place and a slightly undulating picture of a young lady appeared on the sheet to rapturous applause. The audience were nothing if not appreciative, thought Lydia.

' – in a small cottage on the edge of the New Forest where her father, Matthew Tuck, a good and honest man, was gamekeeper to the cruel-hearted Squire . . . '

The picture of the young lady was replaced by the head and shoulders of a beetle-browed man in a top-hat, which immediately called forth from the sympathetic audience a mixture of hisses, boos and cat-calls.

'One day good Matthew Tuck sickened and died . . . '

The coffin surrounded by the stricken mother and daughter was greeted with a respectful silence broken only by a few 'Ahs'.

' . . . and mother and daughter were left alone, at the mercy of the Squire – oh dear!'

The next picture appeared upside-down to show mother and daughter clinging together apparently suspended from the ceiling, and shrieks of delighted laughter drowned Gareth's hasty apology. He corrected the slide and the audience fell silent again. Lydia read on as the tale unfolded and Gareth slotted the pictures in and out. A slight breeze made the candle flicker and rustled the 'screen', so that at times the characters appeared to be shuddering but by this time the audience was totally involved in the drama and no longer critical. As the innocent Miss Tuck and her mother were about to be turned out into the snow, a hush fell.

'Supporting her mother with one arm,' Lydia read, 'poor Sarah stepped out into the snow and cast a last look behind her at the little cottage that had once been home. Tears glistened in her eyes as – '

At this point the story was interrupted by a piercing scream which came from somewhere behind them. Lydia stopped abruptly and glanced at Gareth, then all heads turned in the direction of the hop-gardens to their left.

'What the blazes – ' said Gareth and stood up, almost dislodging the diascope which wobbled precariously but finally righted itself. Roland cried, 'What was that? It sounded like a woman.'

Just at that moment, as everyone began to talk at once, a dishevelled figure ran towards them out of the gloom from the direction of the scream.

'It's Albert Crittenden!' gasped Lydia.

'It's coming!' he gabbled breathlessly. 'You must help. Someone must help. I didn't mean it.' He was gasping for breath and there were tears on his cheeks. 'I swear to God I didn't mean no harm. I just thought, you know, to make it legal but she tripped over it. Oh, help her someone, for pity's sake!'

'Help *who*?' cried Roland, grabbing him by the arm. 'What *are* you talking about? Who is it and what's happened?' He turned to Gareth. 'Where's my torch? You had it last night.'

'I'll get it.' Gareth ran into the tent.

'Please,' begged Lydia, 'just tell us who it is and what has happened.'

'I told you,' cried Albert, long sobs punctuating his speech. 'It's the baby – it's coming. I never meant it – she was jumping over the pole and she tripped and fell and then it all just started about half an hour later.'

'It's Dora!' cried Lydia as Gareth returned at a run with the torch and handed it to Roland.

'What's started?' asked Roland, confused.

'Dora . . . Dora Wilks' baby,' stammered Albert. 'She's having the baby and it's hurting her. I think she's dying! She said to run and fetch Miss Grant.'

'The baby?' cried Lydia. 'Oh, dear God! Show us where she is at once. Oh, that poor girl!'

Another scream rent the air.

'I'll go with Lydia,' Roland told Gareth. 'You see that no one follows us. Get on with the show if you can, but for heaven's sake don't let them all come swarming after us.'

Leaving Gareth to try to calm the excited pickers, Roland and Lydia set off at a run, following the distraught Albert who led them through the rows of hops, eerie in the moonlight, to where Dora lay doubled up on her right side on the damp ground.

'Christ, you took your bleeding time!' she greeted them. 'It won't be much longer. Oh, here it comes again.' She gritted her teeth but in spite of her efforts a long-drawn-out scream escaped her, making Albert cover his ears.

'I'm so sorry, Dora,' he sobbed. 'I never thought – I mean, I didn't know it could happen like that, I swear I didn't.' He turned to Roland. 'You gotta believe me!'

'We do believe you,' said Roland. 'But do pull yourself together – you're helping nobody by these hysterics.'

Lydia knelt to examine Dora, propping the torch at an angle so that it gave as much light as possible.

Dora turned her head sharply at Roland's words. 'Don't you get on at Albert!' she snapped. 'He never meant no harm. He's a really nice lad, is Albert. I tell you I'm not going to die, Albert – I shall be fine, honest I shall. It's not your fault, so do quit bawling.'

Roland, agitated, ran his fingers through his hair. 'We must get her into the mission tent,' he declared. 'She can't have the baby out here. Can she walk that far, d'you think?'

'Can you walk, Dora?' asked Lydia. 'It's not very far and we will help you.'

'There's no time, I tell you,' cried Dora. 'I've had two kids already and I'm telling you. There won't be time – ' Another contraction seized her and once more she fell to biting her lip and clenching her hands in a desperate effort to keep silent.

'We could carry her,' said Roland. 'You know, if we cross hands and she puts her arms round our shoulders. Albert and I could carry her, couldn't we, old chap?'

Albert was leaning against a hop-pole and sobbing quietly, his shoulders heaving.

'It's no good,' said Lydia. 'He won't be any help and I think Dora's right – there isn't enough time. Perhaps a blanket, Roland – could you fetch one from one of the mission beds? I'll examine her as best I can, but I really think the birth is imminent.'

Roland ran off without the torch, blundering heavily through the darkness while Lydia tried to persuade Dora to lie on her back and part her legs. Dora's pains were now coming at twenty-second intervals and she had hardly recovered from one before the next one began. Perspiration ran down her face, her mouth hung open and her eyes were wild with pain.

'It's coming!' she gasped. 'Christ Almighty, it's coming, I tell you!' Another shrill scream was torn from her. 'Where is he with that ruddy blanket?' she grumbled. 'It's going to be too late.'

'It's all right,' said Lydia soothingly.

Albert was peeling off his jacket. 'Here,' he said, holding it out while averting his eyes from Dora's prostrate form. 'Have this instead.'

'Thank you,' said Lydia. She managed to ease the jacket under Dora's writhing body so that the child would not be born on the bare ground.

'Now then, Dora, I want you to hold back and breathe slowly,' she instructed. 'Do you hear me? Do you remember how it was before, with the other two? Breathe in and out and don't push too hard. Take it slowly if you can . . . that's the way. Here, take hold of my hand. Breathe deeply and try to slow it down. No, *don't* push, Dora. Don't push until I tell you.'

Dora gulped for air, her face contorted. 'It's not me who's bloody pushing,' she argued, 'it's the baby! Can't wait to be bloody born – aah! This is it! It's coming – '

Albert watched from a safe distance in helpless fascination, the way that a rabbit watches a stoat, not wanting to see but unable to look away. It was dark and all he could see was one woman crouching beside another. Dora's groans and his imagination did the rest.

'Oh God!' gasped Dora, 'that must be the head. It must be!'

'Yes, it's the head and shoulders. Push now, Dora, but steadily, slowly – that's the way. Oh, good girl!'

'It's a girl?' Dora demanded.

'No,' said Lydia, 'you, I meant. *You're* a good girl and your baby's here, safe and sound and it's a little boy.'

'A boy?' cried Dora, enraged. 'Not another boy? Oh, it *can't* be!'

'Well, I'm afraid it is.' Lydia held the baby in her arms for a moment and then wrapped it up in Albert's jacket. 'We'll see to the cord in a minute,' she said. 'Lie back, Dora. Relax. It's all over except the afterbirth.'

She wiped Dora's face and was surprised to discover that her hand was trembling. 'Oh, God,' Dora grinned faintly. 'You're in a worse state than me!'

Just then Roland came back with a blanket, accompanied by the shapeless woman who had shared the bacon stew with Dora and Albert.

'This woman says she knows you,' said Roland. 'She insisted on coming.'

'I should think I would insist,' said the woman. 'An extra pair of woman's hands is always useful at a time like this.'

Clumsily she knelt beside Dora, who smiled up weakly.

'You'll need these,' she told Lydia producing a pair of scissors from her apron pocket.

'It's a boy,' Dora told her. 'Another blooming boy! Just my rotten luck.'

The woman grinned. 'I had four girls,' she said. 'Every time I told my hubby, "trust you to get it wrong again". Well, you made enough noise about it, ducks! I should think they heard you in Maidstone! Scared the wits out of us, you did – poor Mr Brooks nearly dropped his magic lantern.'

Five minutes later Dora was sitting up on the blanket, the

baby in her arms, with Albert kneeling beside her on one side and her new-found friend on the other.

Roland and Lydia had gone to fetch one of the camp-beds to use as a stretcher to carry mother and child back to the mission tent.

Dora turned to the woman. 'I couldn't half do with a cup of tea,' she whispered. 'I don't suppose . . . '

As she had hoped, the woman at once began to struggle to her feet. 'Cup of tea?' she said. 'I should think you could do with a cuppa tea. I should've thought of it myself. I'll go and brew up and bring you one in the tent. Cup of tea, she says, bless her! I should think you can have a cup of tea after what you've been through. Good job the men don't have the babies – we'd have died out long ago!'

Dora waited until her ample figure had vanished into the darkness and then she turned to Albert.

'I wanted to get rid of her,' she said. 'I wanted you to meself for a minute, because there's something you must get into your head. What we did together didn't make the baby come, see? I don't want you to think that.' She reached up with one hand and ruffled his hair. 'You're a great big baby yourself,' she told him, 'but you're not to fret over it, see? I'd have had it sooner or later, so might as well be now. It was jumping that bloody pole that did it and that was me own stupid fault. You didn't force me – I could've said "No", but I never give it a thought and that's the gospel truth, silly bitch that I am.' She peered at him in the darkness. 'Well, say something, or has the cat got your tongue?'

'I don't know what to say, Dora,' he stammered. 'I was that scared, I thought you was dying.'

'Dying? You don't get rid of me that easy. Look, stop worrying about me, you great lemon. You didn't do nothing to hurt me. Quite the opposite, in fact.' She gave him a nudge with her elbow.

'What? Do you mean when we – '

'Yes! It was very nice, Albert, honest it was. You're very good at it, you know that?'

In the dim light of the torch she saw a huge grin spread over his face. 'Am I?' he mumbled. 'Was I? I mean, was it really how it should be?'

"Course it was,' she told him. 'Top marks, Albert Crittenden! I wanted to tell you before the others got back. If it hadn't been for that ruddy hop-pole and this little lad here . . . ' she dropped a kiss on the child's head, 'I reckon I'd be asking you for some more of the same! Second helpings, as you might say.'

'Second . . . ? Oh, I see.' He laughed shakily.

She sighed. 'I suppose now I shall be stuck in that blooming tent for the next week, so you'll have to come and visit me. Bring me grapes and all that!' She giggled, then pulled his head down and kissed him. 'And I'm calling him after you,' she told him. 'This young 'un's going to be called Albert.'

'Oh, Dora!' cried Albert as the last of the nightmare finally faded, giving way to elation.

'What a night!' he whispered. 'What a blooming night!'

CHAPTER FOURTEEN

Rose poured strong black tea into a mug, added milk and three spoonfuls of sugar and glanced into the pram which stood just outside the kitchen door to satisfy herself that the baby still slept. Then she carried the tea through into the forge. Andy stood at the anvil hammering a horseshoe into shape with steady blows, his eyes screwed up against the noise, sweat glistening as always on his face. Rose stood for a moment watching him, comparing him as she often did with her first husband, Tom Bryce, who now lay in his grave in the churchyard. Tom had been a good worker and so was Andy. Tom had been a good father; Andy did his best to cope patiently with Tom's five children plus his own and they all muddled along together without too much friction. Tom had been weak where women were concerned and had been unfaithful to her for years with the Colonel's wife – and then with Vinnie Harris – but Andy was as honest as the day was long and Rose knew intuitively that she need have no fears on the subject of his fidelity. Tom had been moody and liable to deep depressions and sudden angers, whereas Andy lived his life placidly and with mild humour.

She had adored Tom since she was a young girl, while Andy in turn had adored her. It was strange, Rose reflected, how fate had finally brought the two of them together. Now Andy stopped hammering, picked the horseshoe up with the tongs and plunged it into the small water trough beside the hearth. Rose, watching the water bubble and steam, envied him his work and the obvious satisfaction it brought him. Andy glanced up, smiled and wiped his forehead with his forearm.

'Thanks, love!' He took the mug from her and drank deeply. 'The Lawrences' Shetland,' he told her, referring to the owner of the horseshoe. 'Tim Bilton will be in about three.'

Her arms folded, Rose leaned against the large table on which a variety of metal shapes jostled together in apparent confusion – steel mesh, copper strips, sheets of brass and iron rods.

'Tommy not back yet then?' she asked unnecessarily, for there was no sign of her eldest boy who had been sent down to a big house in West Farleigh with a newly-finished weather vane.

Andy shook his head and smiled. 'He'll take his time,' he said. 'I did when I was his age. Something very precious about stolen time. Little 'un all right?'

Rose nodded. 'Asleep,' she told him. Andy had had no children by his first marriage and their baby was the apple of his eye.

'What did your Ma-in-law have to say?' Andy asked.

Mrs Bryce had called in earlier in the morning, as she often did on her way to the shop.

Rose laughed. 'Still on about that picker who had the baby. Over the moon about it, she is!'

'Let me guess,' said Andy. 'She's knitting something for it?'

'A bonnet,' said Rose. 'Blue, of course. I should think everyone in the village is knitting for that baby – it'll be better dressed than royalty. Albert, she's called it – after the King, I suppose. According to Ma, who got it from Bertha, she tripped over a hop-pole and that's what started it off. Nearly a month early, it was. Might have died, poor little scrap. Still, they're in good hands. That Lydia Grant's a proper nurse; they've put mother and baby in the mission tent and they're feeding her up on milk and everything. By the way, what time d'you want your dinner?'

He glanced at the clock on the wall. 'Another hour will see me done with this lot,' he said, 'and Tommy will likely be back by then. I've an axle to do for Jarvis Tupp later, and that new chap from Merryon was in again about his fancy fireguard.

Impatient devil, that one! I'll get round to it, I told him, but it's "when" and "how long" with him. There's more urgent work than his, I told him, for folks that have a living to earn – but he didn't like that one bit. Thinks money talks, but it doesn't . . . Leastways, not with me.'

Rose picked up a curly twist of metal and turned it in her fingers.

'Our Bertha's got the hump with Mary Bellweather, so Ma says.'

'Oh?'

'Seems she took a telephone message for her from London and got her head snapped off for her pains. Right touchy, she is, so Bertha says. Everyone says so in fact.'

She pulled at the metal, drawing it out in a long thin spiral, while Andy watched her. He was vaguely aware of a slight artificiality about Rose's apparently normal chatter.

'Funny she's never married,' Rose went on. 'Nice-looking woman like she is. They all tried to matchmake last year, with her and Mr Brooks, but nothing came of it.'

'Maybe that's it, then,' suggested Andy. 'Maybe she's willing and he's not.'

Rose was silent, concentrating her attention on the metal in her hands. He finished the tea, tossed the dregs into the fire and handed back the mug.

'Thanks, love.'

This was normally his way of saying that their brief chat was at an end and he would be getting on with his work. Usually Rose took the hint and departed, but today she dropped the metal, took the mug and stared moodily into it. Suddenly her interest quickened and she began to examine the tealeaves that remained, turning the mug in all directions in order to identify the shapes.

'Well, I'm blowed!' she exclaimed. 'That's as clear as a bell. Oh dear!'

'Oh dear what?' he asked. 'What's as clear as a bell?'

She gave a nervous laugh. 'I'd best not tell you.'

'Tell me what?' Andy demanded, reaching for the mug.

'What can you see?'

Rose held it out of his reach. 'Best for you not to know. You won't want to hear it – you'll be mad!'

'Mad? Rose, what are you on about? When am I ever mad? Out with it, girl – what can you see?'

Rose considered. 'I'll only tell you if you promise not to be mad at me. Cross your heart?'

''Course I won't be mad at you,' he insisted. 'Look, are you going to tell me or not, because I've got work to do.'

He was calling her bluff – she knew it and he knew it. To hurry her, he reached for the tongs and retrieved the cooled horseshoe from the trough. Hastily Rose handed him the mug.

'Down at the bottom, just below where the handle joins on,' she said. 'It looks like a two. Can you see it?'

'Yes, I can see it. So what?'

'Well, you've got one baby . . . ' She couldn't go on and for a moment he frowned, uncomprehending, then as her meaning registered he looked up slowly.

'You mean – Rose? You're not . . . '

Rose stared fixedly at her right shoe as it cleared a small patch in the dusty floor. 'I'm two weeks late,' she said breathlessly, 'and my breasts are all tingly like always, so I don't think there's much doubt about it.' She looked up. 'You promised you wouldn't be mad, Andy, and you crossed your heart. Blame that girl in the hop-fields. She was broody. She must have flapped her wings! Oh Andy, please don't be cross!'

'Another one! Christ, Rose!' He shook his head in disbelief.

'You *are* cross!' she cried.

Andy's face relaxed into a grin and he carefully laid down the tongs before holding out his arms to her. She flung herself into them and he hugged her close.

'Another one!' he repeated. ''Course I'm not mad but, Christ Almighty!' He gave a triumphant roar. 'Wait until I tell 'em down at the "Horse and Cart"! Another one!'

Rose looked up at him. 'Then you're truly not mad and you don't mind?'

'I *don't* mind and I'm *not* mad,' he grinned. 'Just don't let it become a habit! What's your Ma-in-law going to say, eh? She'll have to start knitting for you now, never mind some blooming picker! You haven't told her yet?'

'No. I wanted to tell you first.'

'I'm glad you did. Christ, Rose. Another one!'

She laughed. 'Is that all you can say?' she teased.

'I'm stunned!' he admitted. 'Knocked all of a heap. Tell you what, love . . .'

'What?'

'I could do with another mug of tea!'

*

Janet pushed up the window of the Colonel's bedroom and leaned out to check on the weather.

'Still fine, sir,' she reported cheerfully. 'I don't think Mister Delain's got any excuse for cancelling the flight.'

The Colonel snorted. 'Cancel the flight? I should hope not indeed, with everyone on their toes watching for him. Mind you, you can never tell with the French. Unpredictable, the lot of them! Same as the Italians. Germans, too. They're foreigners, you see, Janet, and they don't have our ways. Not the same standards at all. An Englishman's word is his bond, that's what they say. Where the devil has Young Harry got to? I shan't see a thing stuck back here – not a damned thing!'

'He'll be up shortly, sir. I expect he's finishing his lunch.'

'Finishing his lunch? Goddammit, a young chappie is going to fly his machine over Foxearth and Harry's worrying about his *lunch*! A chance to see an aeroplane in flight right overhead – a unique occasion – and all he can think about is food. I begin to worry, Janet, about what the world is coming to. Young people today have some very funny ideas. Lunch, indeed!'

Philippe Delain, as a tribute to Vinnie, had offered to fly his Voisin on a route that took him directly over Teesbury when he took it up on its final test flight before attempting the journey back to France. Vinnie had telephoned Clive le Brun and had also alerted Roland Fry, who had passed on the information to all the pickers so that everyone could share in the excitement. It was planned that Philippe would be airborne about one-thirty and flying at a top speed of fifteen miles an hour. He would make a circular flight, crossing the Swale west of Faversham, flying south-west across country to pass south of Maidstone and returning to Eastchurch on the Isle of Sheppey via Rainham. The round trip, he estimated, would very roughly equal the distance he would fly when crossing from Dover to Calais.

Colonel Lawrence, although bedridden for many years, had followed the advent of powered flight with the same patriotic fervour with which he had eventually embraced the motor-car. As long as the British were first in the field he was happy, and it had not pleased him at all that the Wright Brothers were Americans. He had only been reconciled to their success when Janet slyly suggested that probably the Wright family had originated in Britain. Blériot's flight across the Channel had not been entirely welcome either.

'You know, Janet,' he said, '*we* should have crossed the Channel first. There's simply no excuse – we've got the right men made of the right stuff and we've been in the flight game a long time. Take Hiram Maxim, now . . . '

'I know, sir. You told me.'

Intending to tell her again, the Colonel ignored her comment and continued.

'He built a machine at Baldwyn Park years ago, before the old Queen died. Lovely thing, it was. Beautiful! Based it on Cody's kite design and should have flown, you know, that machine. It should have flown! We might have been the first, then. Damned Americans! Any sign of young Delain? It must be nearly time.'

Janet, still at the window, scanned the sky anxiously. 'No, sir,' she told him, 'but I can see the mistress going down towards the river. I hope Mr le Brun gets here in time – there's no sign of him so far. I wonder what the river looks like from up in the air? That's going to be the landmark, the river, so he'll know exactly where he is.'

The Colonel grunted impatiently. 'Where the devil is Young

Harry? I'll give him a piece of my mind when he gets up here. If I miss it because he's eating his lunch . . . '

Harry had been instructed to help Janet push the Colonel's bed over to the window, so that he would be able to see the aeroplane as it flew past. The Colonel had wanted the move carried out first thing in the morning, so that he was in place in good time, but Janet had objected – pointing out that if the weather turned cool the Colonel might catch a chill.

'There's plenty of time, sir,' said Janet. 'Young Harry won't let you down.'

'Hiram Maxim,' the Colonel repeated. 'He should have been first into the air. Trouble was, he was too cautious and that doesn't pay. You've got to take chances in this world if you want to get anywhere. He ran it on rails, you see, to test it and the damned rails broke up. Mind you, even *he* was an American!' He frowned. 'Now who the blazes was that other chappie over at Sevenoaks? He should have done it; he was British. Something Smithers his name was. Built a monoplane only last year. What the devil *was* his name, Janet?'

'I don't know, sir.'

'I know you don't, girl! Langley! That was it. Langley-Smithers. Pretty little plane, but it never did fly properly. It was in all the papers at the time. When I say it didn't fly, it *did* leave the ground; it hopped a bit, you know, in fits and starts and then went sideways like a flying crab!' He chuckled. 'Poor old Langley-Smithers! Still, it was an achievement to get the ruddy thing off the ground at all. And there was another fellow quite near here, at Mereworth Castle. Lovely machine, Janet. Looked just like a bird, you know, with struts along each wing that looked like feathers. Balston, his name was. Of course, you need money to be a flyer – to build a flying machine. This Delain's machine must have cost him a pretty penny.'

'Doll says he's got pots of money,' Janet told him, 'or rather his family has. They grow grapes and make wine.'

'Ah yes, so he does. Told me so himself. Where is Doll these days? Haven't seen her lately. She usually brings in the children to see me.'

'She's gone down to Porthleven, sir, in Cornwall, for Louise's convalescence. She popped in yesterday to say "Good-bye". You've probably forgotten, sir.'

'Have I, Janet? Oh, well, maybe I have. Funny thing, my memory. Ask me about old Hiram Maxim and I can tell you time and place, but ask me about yesterday and it's a damned blank. Funny, that! Where on earth is Young Harry?'

As if in answer to his question, there was a knock on the door and Harry's cheerful face appeared.

'And about time too,' the Colonel muttered irritably. 'I thought you'd forgotten.'

'No sir, I didn't forget.'

'You won't see a sight like this again in a hurry, Young Harry, I can tell you. A flying machine over Foxearth! Jolly decent of him, if you ask me. Whoops! Steady how you go with this bed – you're not pushing a pram, you know.'

Between them, Harry and Janet manoeuvred the Colonel's bed up to the window, where he would have a first-class view.

'I hope he comes, sir, after all this,' said Janet.

Young Harry left them to it, preferring to sneak down to the river bank with the rest of the kitchen staff. Janet, with the Colonel's permission, sat on the end of his bed while together they waited.

'Exciting, sir, isn't it?' she said.

But the Colonel, now that he was safely installed in a favourable viewing position, pretended indifference.

Finally, after what seemed an eternity, they heard the 'pop-popping' of an engine and suddenly saw the aeroplane approaching, hugging the line of the river as Janet had predicted. It was flying very low, possibly no more than sixty feet, and looked terribly fragile.

'Oh, sir!' cried Janet, her hand to her mouth. 'It looks so *little*! Oh go on, Mr Delain! Go on!'

The Colonel watched excitedly. 'He's a bit damned low,' he said. 'I hope he knows what he's doing.'

'Look!' she cried. 'He's waving, sir!'

'So he is!' They both waved back furiously. 'He's a cocky

young devil – you've got to hand it to him, Janet. Nerves of steel, these young flyers, you know. My God, he *is* low! And getting lower!'

'Sir! You don't think – Oh! I can't hardly bear to look, sir. What on earth is he doing?'

The engine note changed suddenly to a whine and then the regular 'popping' sound became *irregular*.

'It sounds all funny, sir!' cried Janet. 'He's never going to land, surely? Not on the river bank.'

The Colonel leaned forward anxiously and Janet's eyes widened in horror as the tiny plane seemed to waver uncertainly in the air. One wing dipped, was corrected, then dipped again. A great roar of dismay went up from the direction of the hop-gardens as the pickers groaned aloud.

'Sir!' cried Janet. 'It's going down! He's going to crash!'

The Voisin dropped out of sight behind the rows of hops and almost at once they heard the sound of disintegrating wood, tearing cloth and the snapping of wire struts. Janet, two fists pushed against her mouth, struggled to keep back the tears, while the Colonel stared at the spot where the machine had gone down and then cleared his throat.

'There was no splash,' he said shakily, 'so he missed the river. Poor chap – what a terrible thing! There was no splash, you see, Janet. The water might have broken his fall.'

They stared at each other for a moment, shocked and distressed.

'Oh, sir,' whispered Janet. 'He was such a nice young man. He can't be . . . I can't believe it. Not *dead*!'

With an effort the Colonel rallied his thoughts; he couldn't bear tears.

'Stop that, Janet,' he said as briskly as he could. 'That'll do no good at all, d'you hear me? It may not be as bad as it sounds – best go and see!'

'Oh, no, sir! I couldn't'

'Go and *see*, girl,' he insisted irritably, 'and don't start blubbering. If he's killed himself, it's no concern of ours. They're all the same, these young flyers, all as mad as hatters!

They will take these risks. Go down and find out what's happened to him and then come back and tell me. Well, go *on* Janet. Are you deaf or something?'

*

Vinnie, watching Philippe come down, was in an agony of dread. The plane wobbled at it lost height and the steering was obviously giving trouble.

'Oh, Philippe!' she whispered. 'Please God, don't let him die!' she prayed. Standing beside her, Roland Fry missed the words but caught the sharp intake of breath and saw the terror in her eyes.

The plane hovered over the water and then suddenly veered sideways, wings tilted at an alarming angle. It was so low that the watchers on the river bank instinctively ducked and began to run as it skimmed over their heads, no more than twenty-feet above the ground, to crash into the edge of the nearest row of hop-poles, disintegrating at once into a tangled mass of wreckage.

'Oh, my God!' whispered Vinnie. 'I can't bear it.'

She covered her face with her hands and it was Roland who saw the first slight movement from the pilot's seat and then Philippe raising his right arm to reassure the spectators that he was still alive.

'He's alive,' Roland told her. 'Oh, thank God!'

Vinnie uncovered her face and turned to him with glowing eyes. 'He's alive!' she said, flinging her arms around his neck and kissing him. Then she was away, running along the river bank towards the crashed machine, her skirts held high as she stumbled over the rough grass. Her hat was shaken loose and fell off, allowing the long golden hair to tumble free. Roland watched her for a moment and then slowly followed her across the grass. By the time he reached the wrecked plane, Vinnie and Philippe were in each other's arms as the hop-pickers recovered from their fright and converged cheering furiously on the crashed Voisin, greatly astonished and relieved to find the young pilot miraculously alive. He was badly shaken and there was a small cut below his left eye, but otherwise he appeared unhurt.

Janet ran up to Roland, and he saw the tears drying on her cheeks.

'He's alive, Janet,' he told her as she came to a breathless stop beside him, one hand clutching her side. 'Don't ask me how, but he's alive!'

'Thank the Lord!' she panted. 'Oh, I've got such a stitch. The Colonel sent me out to find out what had happened. I was expecting the worst. He is alive then? Thank goodness for that!'

'Very much alive,' Roland laughed as the young man in question waved a triumphant right arm to the gathering crowd, while his left arm remained firmly round Vinnie's waist.

'But the poor machine!' cried Janet. 'Just look at it!'

The wreck of the Voisin was a sobering sight – its wheels askew, the nose badly crushed and the strutless wings collapsed together like playing cards.

'It's a miracle if you ask me, sir,' Janet marvelled. 'How anyone could get out of that in one piece beats me, it really does. But I'm so terribly glad and the mistress is too by the look of her!'

She watched proudly as Vinnie and Philippe made their way arm-in-arm towards the house, leaving Tim Bilton and Harry to guard the crashed machine, with strict instructions to allow no souvenir hunting. Philippe's engineer would be sent for from Sheppey to organise the plane's removal.

After a closer look at the wreckage, Janet hurried back to the Colonel to give him a first-hand account of the near-tragedy. It was only later that evening that Vinnie realised Clive had not been present to witness the event.

CHAPTER FIFTEEN

Mary got off the bus near the bridge and walked across, pausing to lean over and stare down into the brown water which moved sluggishly beneath her. Then slowly, almost aimlessly, she began to walk up the hill. Maidstone High Street on a Saturday morning was a thriving, bustling place: the pavements crowded with shoppers, the streets chaotic with transport of all types and sizes, horse-drawn as well as motorised; hand-carts and even wheelbarrows were being propelled deftly among the larger vehicles, while several intrepid cyclists weaved in and out with apparent unconcern. Immediately below the cannon an open-topped bus waited, its upper deck already crowded with passengers laden with shopping baskets and large paper parcels. A row of covered horse-carts was parked in front of the bus, some with their respective horses. An elderly horse snuffled noisily in his nosebag, sending out a small cloud of husks. Vans, motor cars and wagons rattled and hooted as Mary dodged between them and finally managed to reach the safety of the right-hand pavement.

She glanced into shop windows as she passed, but her brain registered very little of what she saw for her thoughts were centred on Alexander and her face was drawn into a frown of misery as she made her way through Bank Street. At the first alley she walked through Middle Row and into the upper part of the High Street, where the Queen Victoria Jubilee monument rose in pale splendour below the junction with Week Street and Gabriel's Hill. Gleaming landaus waited in line in the middle of the road, their drivers immaculate, whips at the ready, while the wealthy owners made their Saturday purchases.

Alexander had been home! The knowledge had thrown Mary's thoughts into a turmoil. According to the housekeeper, he had arrived unannounced, had collected a few more clothes and then returned to Bromley. Mrs Markham had tried to persuade him to stay, or at least to contact Mary, but he had refused to do either. So, thought Mary, he was still angry, still unwilling to forgive her. Presumably he was still resolved to join his Sylvia.

Tentatively Mary considered the possibility of travelling to Bromley to confront him, but what would she do if he would not see her? She felt unable to face the humiliation – she would break down and cry, she knew, and Eva would be a witness to the whole miserable scene and would tell Vinnie; then everyone would know that Mary Bellweather had been scorned by young Alexander. No, the prospect was unbearable and Mary hardened her heart. A trip to Bromley was out of the question, she decided.

She wondered if she could write frankly to him, pointing out the folly of his behaviour, but she reminded herself reluctantly that the present estrangement was the result of speaking her mind frankly. With a despairing sigh, she crossed the road again and turned along Week Street, keeping to the left-hand side and ignoring the occasional buffeting she received from impatient people who elbowed or pushed her aside in their eagerness to pass. They were nothing to her, she told herself, merely ignorant specks of humanity on the fringe of her existence and as such of no significance. All that mattered was her grief at the loss of Alexander. She had brought him to manhood, she reflected bitterly, and now he had turned against her, replacing her with a twopenny schoolgirl whose love meant more to him than Mary's years of devotion. She had dedicated her life to him and to his future happiness and he had deemed it worthless.

For a moment the thought coloured her cheeks and her face burned; a fine perspiration broke out on her skin, to be followed almost at once by an icy coldness.

Did he really care for her so little? Did she exist in his small world, or had Sylvia taken her place completely? Mary paused to lean against a shop window, overcome by a great weariness of spirit. Her reason for living had gone and she felt like a drowning man without a straw. Her life was of no importance if she could no longer share it with Alexander.

'You all right, miss?'

A young woman pushing a pram full of shopping stopped to stare at her, concern on her face.

Mary nodded. 'Yes, thank you.'

'Not faint or nothing?'

'No.'

With a nod the woman moved on and Mary pushed herself upright and continued walking. She thought of Alexander and remembered the traumatic first few months with him – his awful tantrums, his lies and deceits. Poor Mrs Markham had threatened on more than one occasion to leave her employ, finding the boy's rough ways unacceptable, his morals abysmal and his language shocking. Mary, too, had experienced serious doubts about keeping him, but very slowly the relationship had changed as Alexander surrendered to his new life. Mrs Markham was won over, Mary felt the beginnings of affection for him and in turn his respect for her grew.

By the time Alexander was twelve, their relationship was one of mutual dependence. Mary, having found someone to love, lavished time and money on his education and together they visited art galleries and museums and attended concerts, taking great pleasure in each other's company. Alexander's sharp edges were rounded off until at last Mary considered him a 'son' of whom she could be justly proud. And he *was* her son, by legal adoption. Now she wondered what Alexander would do to hurt her, to repay the harsh things she had said about Sylvia. Love in a young man, Mary now knew to her cost, could be passionate to the point of obsession. Desperately in love and separated from the object of his affection, he could behave in an irrational way and Mary feared that he might continue his search for Mollie as an act of revenge.

Turning left again, she made her way down Faith Street.

Today she had needed to get right away from Foxearth and the well-meaning enquiries after her state of health and mind – to walk and lose herself among the crowds where no one knew her. She needed to think calmly and positively but now, unable to control her dark thoughts, she swam in an emotional whirlpool of despair.

Eventually she reached the river once more and leaned over the water, now letting her thoughts centre on Vinnie Lawrence. What was it about Vinnie, Mary wondered, that made her so attractive to men? It seemed to Mary that, even without trying, Vinnie inspired devotion. Julian, Roland, William – and now this Frenchman was in love with her and their joy was obvious to even the most jaundiced eye.

She raised her head wearily and took stock of her surroundings. Beyond the old Bishop's Palace she saw the church and impulsively made her way towards it. Surprisingly it was empty and she sat down. She had not meant to come to church and was suddenly ashamed of the fact. Why had she not turned to God in her hour of need? Why hadn't she taken her troubles to Him as a source of help and inspiration, as she urged others to do? She pulled a hassock towards her and knelt down, pressing her clenched fists against her forehead. Slowly and reluctantly she faced up to the truth. She had stayed away from God because she was ashamed of herself – ashamed of the false pride that would not allow her to admit she might be wrong. Was she wrong? Even now it was a difficult admission to make, but in the shadowy seclusion of the empty church Mary felt able to admit her fault. But, she amended quickly, Alexander was not blameless. She would not take all the blame upon her own shoulders but some of it, certainly, for she was older and wiser than the boy and should have been more in control of herself.

Nearly an hour later, when the organist arrived to practise his music for the Sunday services, Mary was still there. She uttered a hasty prayer, then stood up and made her way outside where she stood blinking in the sunshine, her mind much clearer. With a lightening of her heart she came to a decision:

she would go to Bromley as soon as the hop-picking ended and there she would talk to Alexander. She would do whatever was necessary to win back his love, for she could no longer endure their estrangement. Mary took a deep breath as her despair lifted – she would see Alexander again and life was worth living once more. It seemed to her that she had narrowly escaped disaster and she walked back to catch the bus for the return journey with a feeling of intense relief.

*

Brewing at the 'Barley Tap' had started promptly at seven-thirty as usual, but for Bertie it was a special day. A small boy had appeared at the back door at seven o'clock, with a message to the effect that Arthur Meach was 'in bed with a funny back' and hoped to be at work the following day. So, for the very first time, Bertie was solely responsible for the success of the brew – a fact which he digested with mixed feelings. He was still very inexperienced and a lot of time and money would go to waste if he failed to control the brewing process correctly. He took his watch from the pocket of his white coat and regarded it intently. At present he was only seven minutes behind Arthur's schedule. So far, so good!

Later on he double-checked his morning's work to reassure himself that he had not overlooked anything vital. Young Ben Billings had ground the malt and the resulting grist had been mixed with the hot liquor in the mash tun. Bertie had watched the temperature, never allowing it to vary by more than a degree above or below 150°F, and he felt satisfied that it had not done so. Thus the starch had been converted into sugar and the sweet wort had been run out of the mash tun and into the shallow rectangular vessel, where the brown solution of cane sugar had been added to the frothy mixture. By nine o'clock Bertie had run it into the large dome-shaped copper and watched Ben add the carefully measured quantity of dried hops which would 'bitter' and clear the wort.

He stood beside the copper, anxiously checking the time with his watch. Ten-past-ten. Not bad at all!

He smiled at Ben, who grinned back. 'What d'you reckon?' Ben asked. 'How much longer?'

Bertie considered, his head on one side. 'Another forty minutes should do it,' he said.

The boy nodded, convinced by Bertie's calm manner. Then they would run it over the cooler and into the fermenting vessel. By which time, Bertie told himself excitedly, the worst would be over.

The small circular window in the side of the copper always reminded him of a ship's porthole. He stared in at the liquor which bubbled and spat; had they added *exactly* the right quantity of hops, he wondered, assailed by a momentary doubt. And the right amount of sugar? Yes, surely. He had checked and double-checked.

Once the beer was in the fermenting vessel he would add the yeast, most of which had been kept back from the previous brewing. Then came the agonising wait for the fermentation to be completed. Today was Monday, fermentation would be complete by Thursday afternoon – his train of thought was suddenly broken.

'Bertie!'

It was Bea, wearing her shawl, accompanied by a young man. Busy with his calculations, Bertie had not heard their approach but now he turned smiling, and held up his thumb to signify success to date.

'How's it going?' asked Bea.

'So far so good,' he told her proudly, 'but keep your fingers crossed. Another forty minutes, perhaps.'

He grinned at the young man standing beside Bea and pointed to the copper. 'Take a look,' he said. 'That's beer in the making. That's good beer – Harris's beer!' He laughed. 'D'you want to see it?'

The boy nodded.

'Then stand well back, both of you.'

'Is it all right?' Bea asked nervously, listening to the roar from within the copper.

'As long as you stay well back,' Bertie told her. He turned the handle of a circular metal door in the upper half of the dome and it swung open. Craning their necks, they could just make out the liquid which boiled so violently that hot drops of it were bounced out of the open door.

'Oh, do shut it again, Bertie,' begged his wife. 'Someone could get hurt. That's dreadfully hot.'

'It's *boiling*, I hope,' he corrected her.

The door clanged to and Bertie fastened it securely before turning enquiringly towards his wife.

'This is Alexander,' Bea told him, raising her voice slightly above the noise from the copper. 'Mary Bellweather's son.'

'*Adopted* son,' Alexander corrected her quickly.

'He has a letter from Vinnie, who told him to come and see you.'

'Me?'

Alexander said, 'I can explain, sir, if you will let me.'

As they shook hands Bertie regarded him closely. The boy reminded him of someone, but he could not think who it was. Not Mary Bellweather, obviously, if the boy was adopted. Bertie had heard Vinnie speak of Alexander, but while he and Bea had been at Foxearth, the boy had never accompanied Mary on her visits.

'I've plenty to do,' said Bea, 'so I'll leave him with you. When you've done talking, you can make yourselves a cup of tea if you like. I'm just off to the market to get a few bits of shopping, but I won't be long.'

Bertie nodded and when she had gone he led the boy into the comparative quiet of the small room which served as an office.

'Sit yourself down,' he said. 'Vinnie didn't tell me you were coming, so suppose you start at the beginning and I'll listen. Ben will keep an eye on things for ten minutes or so.'

They seated themselves one on either side of the table and Alexander told his story while Bertie listened with growing impatience. It all sounded very foolish to him, although he refrained from saying so since it was obvious that to the earnest young man it was a matter of tremendous consequence.

'Eva wrote to her sister-in-law,' Alexander concluded, 'and

Vinnie wrote back to me, saying she did not know how best to advise me but suggested I should come to see you. I hope you don't mind, sir? I really would be most grateful if you could advise me. I must get back to Sylvia again – she'll be so unhappy. When you love someone it seems for ever when you're apart.'

Bertie saw the anguish in the grey eyes and tried to remember what it was like to be – how old?

'How old are you?' he asked.

'Nearly eighteen, sir.'

'And Sylvia?'

'Just seventeen, but we're not children,' he insisted. 'We're not too young to know our own minds. Sylvia's a very serious girl – very grown-up for her age – so, Mr Harris, please don't dismiss us.' He clenched his hands as they rested on the table and Bertie saw the knuckles whiten. 'However it may seem to others – and I know Mary sees us as foolish – we do truly love each other and all we want is to be together. This holiday would be so perfect for us. I've been trying to find my real mother without success. Someone told me she had married and gone to America. I had hoped she might help me, but I'm not sure that she would want to know me now.'

'Why do you say that?'

Alexander shrugged wretchedly. 'She has never taken any interest in all these years, although she's lived in the neighbourhood.'

'She doesn't write to you at all?'

'Never! Mary says she may not be able to write – at least, not a whole letter – although I expect she can sign her name and so on. I don't know much about her except—' He broke off and shrugged again, not meeting Bertie's eye. 'I saw her once a long time ago. A woman kept waiting outside my school, on the far side of the road. I recognised her, but I was too ashamed to speak to her because I didn't want the other boys to know who she was.'

'Ashamed? Why ever should you be ashamed?' Bertie asked curiously. 'You had done nothing wrong.'

'The other boys said she was a whore, but I don't believe she was. Now I think they were just making boys' jokes, but I was worried about it at the time in case she was and in case she spoke to me. I didn't know what I'd say to a . . . to someone like that. I asked Mrs Markham (she's our housekeeper) about her – to know if it was true what the boys had said. She said she was 'a baggage' and then wouldn't say any more, but Mrs Markham is terribly loyal to Mary, of course. She's been with her for years.'

'Boys say things like that,' said Bertie, 'just to sound grown-up. I expect she just wanted to see you and be satisfied that you were in good hands. It's never easy to give up a child.'

Alexander sighed. 'Have *you* got any family?'

'No,' Bertie said. Changing the subject, he went on, 'I'm sure if your mother stayed away it was for your sake – so as not to upset you. She may have been wrong, but I'm sure she meant well.'

'Maybe,' he shrugged. 'Eva said you might know her.'

'*I* might?' He was genuinely astonished. 'Why on earth should I know her?'

'Because of the 'Barley Tap', sir. If my mother lived round here, then she's quite likely to have come in for a drink. You might have seen her without knowing her.'

'It's possible. What's her name?'

'Pett, sir. Mollie Pett. Or it was.'

It took a long moment for the significance of the boy's words to dawn on Bertie. Mollie Pett! The name had a familiar ring to it and yet he couldn't put a face to it. Mollie? Did he know a Mollie Pett? Suddenly, the name Dora sprang into his mind. Mollie and Dora! The two girls on that last night of their leave before the regiment embarked for India! But Mollie was no whore – at least, he amended, not at that time. She had given herself to him willingly and cheerfully, with never a mention of financial reward. God, that was a long time ago! Mollie Pett! He had a quick vision of the pert, freckled face with its mop of red hair staring up at him from the rumpled bed. She had glanced up at him sleepy-eyed in the early hours of the morning as he struggled back into his uniform, afraid of missing his ship. He heard again her reproachful voice – 'What, can't you stay for a bite of breakfast? Soldiers can't fight on empty bellies!' She had insisted on making him a dish of porridge, but he had taken only one spoonful when a thunderous knocking on the front door announced the arrival of Adam, straight from Dora's bed. There had been no time for an exchange of addresses and Mollie Pett had rapidly faded from his memory. No wonder the boy had seemed familiar! The likeness was unmistakable. Mollie Pett's son, here under his roof, after all those years! It was incredible!

Alexander said, 'Do you know the name? Have you seen her, do you think?'

Bertie pulled himself together with an effort. 'Mollie Pett!' he repeated 'Yes, I know the name. I met her years ago when she was not much older than you are now. She wasn't married then, of course.'

'She never was married, so Mary says.'

'Oh well, she's not alone in that respect.'

'Was she . . .' the boy hesitated. 'Was she respectable when you knew her?'

'Oh yes. Very respectable!'

'Not *that* sort of person?'

'Certainly not!' Bertie said quickly.

'I think,' said Alexander, 'that she would have married my father, only he was a soldier and he went away to war and disappeared. He didn't come back – my mother told me that when I was a child.'

Bertie's thoughts cartwheeled suddenly and he rose to his feet. 'Excuse me,' he mumbled, 'I must have a word with Ben. Just a moment.' Once outside the office, he glanced back through the window at the boy who sat disconsolately at the table, his chin propped in his hands. Mollie Pett's son! And his father was a soldier? How old had the boy said he was? Nearly eighteen?

Alexander turned his head and Bertie ducked out of sight and went over to stand beside the huge copper. He did not look

at it, however; he was not even aware of its existence. Mollie
Pett's son was nearly eighteen and his father was a soldier. Did
she still live close by? His thoughts flew to Beatrice downstairs.
She was childless and would remain so. How on earth would
she react to the possibility that – no, it was impossible, he told
himself. The boy could be anyone's child. Mollie had been as
wanton as the next girl. His recollection of the evening was
becoming clearer and the details were falling into place. He
and Adam had met the two women in a pub on the last night of
their leave. At closing time Adam had gone off with Dora, and
he had gone home with Mollie of the glorious ginger hair.

'Mollie Pett!' he whispered. Was it possible that he had left
her expecting his child? Surely she would have written to him.
No, the boy had said she couldn't write and anyway where
could she write to? She would have no idea how to trace him.
Surely Mollie would know who fathered the boy – or would
she? How many other soldiers had spent a night with her? How
many men had slept in that same bed during that very week?
He saw the room again, shabby but homely. What had she said?
'It's not the Ritz, but it's clean and paid for.' He had teased her
about the bed with its lumpy mattress. He could see Mollie's
glowing face with its frame of bright curls, her cheeks flushed
with drink, her eyes sparkling, her naked body relaxed and
eager. He remembered suddenly that she had been a seam-
stress of some kind – she had said she worked for a Jew,
machining blouses or skirts. A new thought occurred to him.
Was Alexander her only child? Had she ever married or had
she been forced on to the streets? And had she now gone to
America?

Once again Bertie thought of poor Beatrice. If Alexander
was his son, would she be pleased or angry? He thought the
latter most likely. And how on earth would Mary Bellweather
react? And Vinnie? If Alexander was his son, he was also
Vinnie's nephew. Louise, Teddy and James would have
another cousin. *If.* It was the not knowing, he thought, yet his
heart raced with excitement at the possibility that the charming
and earnest young man in his office might be his own flesh and

blood. If only he dared find out the truth! But who would be hurt in the process? Beatrice would never conceive, they both knew that. Perhaps she would find an eighteen-year-old step-son more acceptable than having no family at all.

'Are you mine, Alexander?' he whispered, 'and if so, what in God's name shall I do?'

Bertie wondered dubiously whether or not honesty really was the best policy. Suppose Beatrice could not bear the thought that he had fathered a child by another woman and one who was nothing more to him than a casual encounter – a young man's 'wild oats'.

He leaned back against the wall and covered his eyes with a hand that shook with suppressed excitement. How much time did he have before Bea returned from the market? She would take one look at his face and ask the reason for his agitation. Beatrice knew him very well; she was shrewd and perceptive and there was no way he could deceive her even if he wanted to. He decided to get Alexander out of the way. The boy must not be present when – *if*, he corrected hastily – he decided to confide his suspicions to Beatrice. If Bea rejected the idea, then no one else need ever know.

Bertie sighed deeply. Perhaps he should say nothing and get rid of Alexander before the boy could say something to alert Bea. Then he could try to track down Mollie. But was *that* a good idea? Mollie had no doubt changed over the years and might well be tougher, more mercenary. She could cause a lot of heartache for a great many people, not least Alexander. He jumped nervously as the young man appeared round the corner.

'Is everything all right?' Alexander asked, referring to the brew. Bertie tried not to stare at him. 'Yes, fine!' he said. 'I've been thinking about you and Sylvia. How would it be if I gave you the money for your fare to Switzerland—'

'No sir, I couldn't accept it,' the boy said firmly.

'Lent it to you, then – an extended loan,' Bertie amended. 'You can repay it at any time. Five months, five years, twenty years.'

Astonished, Alexander began to stammer his thanks, incredulous at this turn of events, his hopes soaring.

'No, please don't thank me,' Bertie told him.

Suddenly he knew he must get Alexander out of his sight before he, Bertie, was tempted to do anything rash. He must have time to think the matter out, but every minute that they were together made it harder for him to let the boy go. He was allowing himself to believe that Alexander was his son; allowing his eyes to see a similarity between the boy's colouring and his own; convincing himself that there was something in the voice, and a certain sideways tilt of the head when asking a question.

'Listen,' he said. 'I can give you twenty pounds in cash.'

Alexander's eyes widened. 'Twenty!' he gasped.

'And I'll give you a post-dated cheque for another twenty.'

'But, sir—!'

Bertie held up his hand. 'No arguments,' he told him. 'I was young myself once, remember, and I know you'll repay it eventually.'

'Every penny, sir! I most certainly will.'

'Of course you will,' Bertie laughed. 'One day when I'm on my beam ends and down to my last penny, forty pounds will suddenly arrive and I'll say, "Good heavens, young Alexander has come up trumps!" '

The boy laughed uncertainly, his eyes slightly narrowed, aware of a subtle change in Bertie's attitude towards him.

'Should I give you an IOU, sir?' he suggested. 'That would make it legal, wouldn't it?'

'Certainly not,' said Bertie. 'This is a transaction between friends.'

'Friends? But we hardly know each other.'

'Between gentlemen, then. A little arrangement between gentlemen of honour. I trust you and that's enough for me. Now come into the office.' Once there he took a key from the drawer, opened a small box and counted out four five-pound notes, brushing aside Alexander's stammered thanks. Then he wrote a cheque, folded it in half and pressed it into the boy's hands.

'Now you get along to the station and buy yourself a ticket,' Bertie told him. 'Then go home and pack your things. By tomorrow you could be on your way to Sylvia. And give her my best regards.'

He held out his hand and Alexander, dazed by his good fortune, shook it.

'I can't tell you how grateful I am,' he said. 'It's just so kind of you to help us. I won't forget it, ever. *Or* the money, of course. I promise, on my oath, to –'

Bertie held up a hand to silence him. 'Remember what I said,' he told him. 'It is an arrangement between men of honour. I don't need any reassurances because I *trust* you. Now go along – we're wasting time!'

Bertie led the way down to the yard, in a fever of anxiety in case Beatrice should return and discover what had passed between them. Forty pounds was a lot of money which they could ill afford to spare. He would have to find some way to explain it satisfactorily if Bea found out it was missing.

When Alexander had gone, Bertie sank down on to a chair in the kitchen, fighting down an urge to run after him and call him back. He felt lost, almost lonely. It was ridiculous and he despised himself for being so vulnerable. Restlessly he got up and put the kettle on the stove. A cup of tea, Beatrice had said – he could certainly do with one. He *must* calm down, he told himself, or she would ask him what was wrong. He counted slowly to ten, then began again. By the time he had counted to ten for the fourth time, his mood of exhilaration was giving way to one of panic. What had he done? He had given forty pounds to a young man he hardly knew on the assumption Alexander was his *son*. It would all come out and Beatrice would never forgive him. Or Mary or Mollie. Oh God! What had he done? He had been hasty and ill-advised. A few pounds would have been sufficient as a gesture of goodwill while he made some discreet enquiries.

'Bertie Harris, you're a bloody fool,' he whispered. He spooned tea leaves from the Jubilee caddy into the pewter tea-pot which Bea's aunt had sent them as a wedding present, and waited impatiently for the water to boil.

He would find out if Mollie Pett was still living locally, but he would be circumspect in his enquiries. Perhaps he would ask one of the mission people when they came back from Kent – Gareth Brooks might know something. Or Lydia Grant.

He made the tea and was pouring himself a cup when Beatrice arrived back with a loaded shopping basket which she dumped thankfully on the kitchen floor.

'No scrag-end,' she told him. 'I said to the butcher, isn't it time you – ' She broke off, remembering that she had left her husband with Alexander. 'Where's the lad?' she asked.

But her words had triggered a response in her husband. He snatched out his watch, glanced at it and then leaped to his feet, jarring the table and making the cups and saucers rattle.

'What on earth – ?' began Beatrice.

'The beer!' shouted Bertie as he raced for the stairs. 'Ask me about it later.'

In the excitement of Alexander's arrival, he had forgotten his very first brew.

CHAPTER SIXTEEN

Mrs Markham opened the door with trembling hands and a sinking heart. The mistress was going to blame *her*, she knew. The housekeeper had been watching for the past hour for Mary's cab to draw up outside; ever since their conversation on the telephone earlier, she had been rehearsing what she would say and how she would convince her mistress that Alexander's sudden departure to Switzerland was not *her* fault. Now the moment had arrived and one glance at Mary's expression told her that her worst fears would be realised – her mistress was *not* going to understand. Mary ran up the steps, her face white, her jaw set. As she swept into the hall with only a curt nod by way of greeting, the housekeeper's unease deepened – when Miss Mary forgot her manners, she was most definitely out of temper.

Mrs Markham said, 'Good afternoon, ma'am. I hope you had a good journey?' Normally Mary liked to be asked about her journey, but today she ignored the comment, pulling off her gloves and tossing them on to the hall-stand, then unpinning her hat.

'So tell me again,' she demanded, striding into the morning-room and leaving Mrs Markham to follow her. 'I want to hear it all again.'

Mrs Markham clasped her hands and prayed for the right words while Mary took up a position beside the mantelpiece, one elbow leaning on the shelf itself, her fingers drumming with nervous intensity.

'Please, ma'am it wasn't my fault!' the housekeeper burst out.

'I did not ask you whose fault it was,' Mary said icily. 'I am asking you to tell me exactly what happened. Your telephone message greatly alarmed me, but it was not convenient to discuss the matter over the telephone. Foxearth is buzzing with servants, all with their ears flapping. Just start at the beginning and tell me what happened. Has he definitely gone to Switzerland? You are quite certain of that fact?'

'Yes, ma'am. Quite certain. He said . . .' she glanced at the clock '. . . he said that by four o'clock he'd be in France and on his way to meet . . . ' She faltered.

'Yes? To meet what?'

'The girl he loved, ma'am. Oh Miss Mary, he's *so* in love with her! It made me feel all happy.'

'I'm not interested in your feelings, Mrs Markham – I want to know what happened. He took the Golden Arrow, presumably?'

'Yes, ma'am. He told me the exact time of departure, though I forget – but it *was* the Golden Arrow. Then he said he would get another train across France. With a sleeper, ma'am. A couchette, I think he called it. That's French, he told me.'

'I do know what a couchette is,' Mary said, a trace of weariness in her voice. 'Do get on with it, *please.*'

'Well, ma'am, like I told you, there was a knock at the door – bang, bang, bang at the knocker – and I opened it and there he was, smiling all over his cheeky face, bless him! So I said, "Master Alexander, you're a sight for sore eyes" – just joking, you see, not knowing what to say really. So what does he do but throw his arms around my neck and hug me until I thought my ribs would break.'

Mary swallowed hard, consumed with jealousy that Alexander should be hugging the housekeeper and not *her*. She bit back a caustic comment and said, 'Do go *on.*'

'Yes, ma'am. So I said, "Come to your senses, have you?" and he says "Mrs M." – you know how he will call me that – "Mrs M." he said, "I'm only here for ten minutes to pack a few more clothes and then I'm off to Switzerland!" Well, you could have knocked me down with a feather, ma'am. I thought,

"Where has he got the money to go to Switzerland?" and after what you said to him, ma'am, I was a bit taken aback. Dumb-founded, as they say. Well, he rushed upstairs two at a time, *whistling*, ma'am, so I called up, "Stop that! You know Miss Mary doesn't like you whistling".' She hesitated.

'Yes? Go on,' said Mary.

'I'm sorry, ma'am.'

'About what?'

'Him being so cheeky. "Blow Miss Mary," he said, and grinned the way he does.'

Mary nodded.

'So I went up and there he was, ma'am, throwing things into his case all higgledy-piggledy. "I'm going to see her again!" he said, over and over again. Just that – "I'm going to see Sylvia!" He's so in love with that girl, ma'am.'

'Yes, I know.' Her tone was changing, Mrs Markham noted with relief.

' "How do you mean", I asked him, "going to Switzerland?" Where did you get that sort of money? "From a friend," he said. "From a gentleman. We had a gentlemen's agreement – it's a loan and I shall pay it all back." '

'Who was it?' Mary demanded. 'Who gave him that sort of money?'

'It was someone called Bertie Harris who lives not far from here, according to Alexander, and this Mr Harris *knows* Mollie Pett.'

'Bertie Harris!' cried Mary. She sat down abruptly in the nearest armchair and looked up at the housekeeper with fear in her eyes. 'But how did he know? I don't understand how such a thing – '

'Well, ma'am, it was Vinnie Harris who sent him there,' Mrs Markham told her. 'She wrote to him telling Alexander to go and see this brother of hers and he would advise him.'

'Vinnie sent him?' Mary's face crumpled suddenly, but then she controlled herself with a supreme effort. 'Vinnie sent him to Bertie – oh God, how did she know, I wonder?'

'Know what, ma'am?' The housekeeper looked at her with

concern. 'Are you feeling all right? Shall I get you a cup of tea? You must be parched after all that travelling.'

'Not yet, Mrs Markham, but I will have one later. Just finish your account of what happened this morning.' She rubbed her eyes tiredly. 'You say Bertie Harris gave Alexander the money for his fare to Switzerland.'

'Not *gave*, ma'am – *lent*. Master Alexander was most insistent – said he was brewing beer in a big copper.'

'In a copper?'

'Yes, I know, ma'am. I couldn't understand him either, but that's what he said. Chattering away, he was, happy as a sand-boy and he would keep whistling. He was so *happy*, ma'am,' she added wistfully.

'That's good,' said Mary dully. Her eyes brimmed with tears. 'I wish I'd seen him,' she whispered. 'If only I had known! I had made up my mind to go to Bromley and ask him to come home. I was only waiting for the hopping to end because I didn't want to let the others down, and it's such terribly hard work even with four of us.'

'I'm sure it is, ma'am.' The housekeeper looked at her mistress with growing anxiety. All Mary's strength of purpose seemed to be deserting her. The lines of her face sagged with misery, making her look much older than she was. 'A cup of tea now, ma'am –'

'In a moment.'

Mary's eyes wandered round the room as though seeing it for the first time – her gaze resting on the Wedgewood vase, the cut-glass bowl, the circular wooden box. Finally her eyes returned to the housekeeper's face.

'Did he say anything else about Bertie Harris?'

'What sort of anything?'

'I don't know.'

'Only that they had this "gentlemen's arrangement" or whatever he called it, about the forty pounds.'

Mary's head jerked up. 'Forty pounds! So much?'

Mrs Markham nodded. 'I didn't know what to do, ma'am, so I just followed him round the house. He went into the kitchen and helped himself to a slice of Dundee cake. "Let me call Miss Mary on the telephone," I said. "At least you should talk to her and tell her what you're up to." "She won't understand," he said. "Well, write her a note then," I told him. I thought a note would be better than nothing, but he wouldn't. "Can't stop", he kept saying, "I'm going to see Sylvia." Every time he said her name, his face sort of shone. "So what's this young lady of yours like?" I asked him. Oh, that did it, ma'am!' Mrs Markham smiled at the memory. 'On and on he went about her – how gentle, what a sweet smile, so kind-hearted and what a pleasant family. All wide-eyed, he was – you know how he is, ma'am, when he's excited. The way he looked when you brought him his first pony. "Tell Mary I'll write to her," he said.'

'Did he leave an address?'

'No, ma'am. He wouldn't – but I did ask.'

'I see.'

The housekeeper hesitated. 'I don't think you do, ma'am, if you'll excuse me saying so. I know it's not my place to say, but I do want you to understand. It is not that he's against you or anything, he is just so much in love that nothing else matters to him as much as Sylvia. It's only natural in a boy of his age and it doesn't mean he doesn't love *you*.' She was picking her words carefully. 'Or that he doesn't care. He's not trying to hurt anyone – especially you, Miss Mary. He's just not interested in anything in the world except this young lady. I was the same over my first love. We all are really, aren't we? Not my husband, I don't mean, but my very first young man when I was only fourteen.' She chuckled. 'I thought he was the only boy in the world for me. John Leonard, his name was and I can still remember him. If he had said he was going to jump over Beachy Head, I'd have gone with him without a moment's hesitation. Oh, I would, ma'am! My father teased the living daylights out of me. Moonstruck, he called me, and "Here comes love's young dream" he'd say. John Leonard Woodham. That was it. He had a funny bit of white hair in amongst the brown. I thought it was marvellous, that bit of white hair. So distinctive.' She sighed deeply. 'He got killed on the way home from school one day – a horse-tram ran him down when the horse went out of control. It broke his parents' hearts and mine too, of course.'

'Yes, it would.' Mary shook her head dazedly. 'I don't know what to do. It's all happened so quickly,' she said. 'One minute he's a schoolboy, the next he's travelling to Switzerland on his own with borrowed money and thinks he's in love!'

'He *is* in love, ma'am,' the housekeeper corrected her gently. 'If only you could believe that, you would understand why he's acting this way. She sounds a very suitable young lady. Maybe if you met her – invited her here when their holiday is over – it would be like gaining a daughter. You know what they say?'

She looked hopefully at Mary, but her mistress's mood was already swinging back again.

'It's the interference I cannot tolerate,' she said. 'Bertie Harris had no right to lend the boy money. He was inciting him to defy me, encouraging him to go away like that, without a word to me. It was most irresponsible – and I blame Vinnie Harris, too, for writing to Alexander the way she did. It's unforgivable – quite unforgivable and I shall tell them so, both of them.' She stood up and seemed to be in control of her feelings once more, her face set in hard lines. 'And then he just left?'

'Yes, ma'am. Blew me a kiss as cheeky as you like and rushed into the taxi – '

'Taxi? You'd ordered a taxi for him?'

'No, ma'am. He had come home in it and left it waiting outside while he packed.'

'Good heavens! That doesn't sound like Alexander!'

'No, ma'am.' The housekeeper smiled. 'Being in love's changed him all right. He's very grown-up, Miss Mary, yet he's still our Alexander.'

'Is he?' said Mary with a hint of bitterness. 'It sounds as though he's Sylvia's Alexander.' She lifted her head and straightened her back. 'Well, that's that, then!' she said. 'Light the geyser, please; I should like a bath later. And bring me a pot of tea – I shall write a few letters while I'm waiting.'

'Yes, ma'am.' Mrs Markham moved to the door and then turned back. 'He will come back, won't he ma'am?' she said. 'Him and his Sylvia – it would be nice to see them together . . . ' She shrugged. 'I'm sorry, ma'am, only I'm that fond of the boy. I couldn't bear it if – '

'I know you are, Mrs Markham. Please don't upset yourself. When I have an address, I shall write to him and possibly – *probably* – I will extend an invitation to her family.'

'Oh, ma,am, that would be splendid!' Mrs Markham brightened visibly.

'I said "probably",' Mary reproved her. 'Now, please – I'm covered in dust and I would like that tea.'

When the housekeeper had gone, Mary sat down again and covered her face with her hands. 'Vinnie Harris!' she whispered. 'You hateful, interfering . . . ' She searched among the few harsh words she knew for the worst one she could find. '. . . bitch! You have everything you could ask for in *your* life, but you never stop interfering in mine!'

*

Meanwhile Dora sat propped up with cushions in her bed in the mission tent, the baby beside her in the crib which had once been used by Vinnie's children. Vinnie had offered a room to mother and child but Dora had declined, preferring to be within sight and sound of 'her own sort', especially Albert. She was thoroughly enjoying all the attention she was receiving and her only regret was that she had not given birth earlier on in the month. As it was, the last Saturday had come round all too soon and tomorrow she would be on her way back to London and all the responsibilities that awaited her there.

Even in Whitechapel, however, she would not be abandoned by the mission. Their interest in the baby was intense and plans had already been made for a supply of milk and eggs to be continued for a further two months after Dora returned home. Roland had been in favour of cash payments, but Lydia convinced him that this way they would be sure that it was Dora who benefited. The extra nourishment was for Dora and thus indirectly for the baby. Roland was also arranging to move the family to a small downstairs flat which had been empty for some months and was conveniently placed in the same street as the mission shed. This meant that while Dora was unable to work because of the young child, her family could receive a free breakfast each day and the mission members could keep a surreptitious eye on their general well-being. Dora's future looked surprisingly rosy, and not being religiously inclined she thanked her lucky stars for the propitious meeting with Albert on the station platform. Without Albert's encouragement, she would never have dreamed of jumping over a hop-pole, would never have tripped and would not have given birth in a moonlit hop-field.

Beside Dora was a small apple box containing a selection of very superior clothing for the baby, which Vinnie had given her. It had once belonged to young Edward Lawrence and Dora was inordinately proud of these clothes; she spent many pleasant hours admiring them and imagining how impressed her new neighbours would be when she paraded little Albert in his pram. She would never, she vowed, shorten his name to Bert, although she thought she might abbreviate it to Al when he was older. Her only regret – and it was a major one – concerned Albert Crittenden. She admitted to herself that they were a sight too fond of each other. He was as proud of the baby as though the child was his own and the thought of their imminent separation was a source of great misery to him. Dora worried about him. He was so young, so eager to please and would be so dreadfully hurt when she had to tell him the awful truth – that her 'husband' would not allow their relationship to continue. Ideally Sid Carter should never discover that a relationship of any kind had ever existed between them!

Promptly at one o'clock Albert appeared through the opening in the tent, a self-conscious smile on his face and a spray of hops in his hands. He stood blinking, waiting for his eyes to adjust to the gloom.

'Hullo, Albert,' said Dora.

'Hullo, Dor,' he said. He had taken to calling her 'Dor' and she found it rather appealing.

Albert glanced round furtively and then came forward to drop an awkward kiss on the top of her head. 'I brought these,' he said, 'for our little hop baby.'

He knelt beside the makeshift crib and draped the hops across the pillow. 'There's no insects or anything on them,' he assured her. 'I've washed them carefully – and dried them well, so they're not damp.' He clucked at the baby. 'Hullo, then, young Albert! How are you this morning, eh? Had a good bye-byes, have you?' He glanced up at Dora. 'Did he sleep well?'

'Oh yes, bless him, very well,' she told him. 'Not a peep all night until it was beginning to get light. I fed him then and he went straight back to sleep.'

'Did you go back to bye-byes then?' Albert cooed. 'Did you? Was you a good boy then for your Ma? Did you drink up your milk like a good boy? That's the way – soon be a big strong lad then.' He held a finger in the baby's hand and watched the tiny fingers curl instinctively round it.

'He knows you,' said Dora. 'I swear he does.'

'He does,' said Albert. 'He's smiling – Well I'm blowed!'

'Smiling? He never is. Babies don't smile so young.'

'He *is*, I tell you. And he's putting on weight. Don't you think so, Dor? I'm sure his little face looks fatter. More sort of round-looking.'

'I suppose so,' she said. 'Miss Grant'll be in later to weigh him again, then we'll know.'

'Six pounds isn't much for a baby,' said Albert. 'He must put on a bit of weight before the cold weather comes.'

He said it knowingly, his tone worldly-wise, but Dora recognised Lydia's words.

'And how's my Dora today?' Albert asked, settling himself on the camp stool beside her bed. 'Did you sleep well?'

'Like a log!'

Albert's cheerful smile wavered slightly. 'Well,' he said, 'today's the final day – it's come round at last. Only seems like yesterday I saw you sitting on the platform, all lonely and a face as long as a wet week.' He tried to laugh and failed. 'Well, it's been a good old month, hasn't it, Dor?'

'Yes, it has.' She took hold of his hand and stroked the long bony fingers which were scratched from the rough hop-bines and covered with small scars.

'What on earth do you do to your poor hands?' she asked him. 'All chipped, they are.' He tried to withdraw it, but she held on. 'They're nice hands – you should take better care of them.'

'They're just hands.'

'Oh, well – '

After a pause, they both began to speak at the same time and then both fell silent.

'Go on,' prompted Albert.

'I don't know,' said Dora. 'At least . . . I do, but – Albert, it's about when we go back to London. I know you won't like it but I've got to tell you. When we're back home you'll have to stay away from us. For good, that is!'

'How d'you mean?' he mumbled. She allowed him to withdraw his hand and he examined it nervously, frowning severely at the various blemishes.

'Just what I say, Albert,' she said gently. 'Honestly, it's the only way. My Sid'll go spare if you come round. He won't have it – he's terribly jealous and spiteful with it. You don't know him like I do. We can't go on seeing each other.'

'What, not see you *ever*, d'you mean?' It was even worse than he had expected.

'We daren't, Albert! Sid would just go mad if he knew about what we did.'

'How's he going to know that,' Albert demanded, 'unless you tell him?'

'He'll guess, if he sees us together. If he knows we were friends here, then he'll put two and two together and he'll *know*!'

'Just don't tell him anything, then.'

'How can I explain who you are if I don't tell him we got

friendly? It's no good, Albert – I've thought and thought about it and I can't see how we can meet each other again.'

'But I *must* see you, Dor! You know I must. You want to see me, don't you?'

'Course I do.' She sighed heavily without looking at him. 'I shall miss you, Albert, I'm not saying I won't. I really fancy you, but I'm married to Sid –'

'No you're not! Not legally.'

'Well, as good as.'

'It's not the same,' he insisted.

'It is to me and Sid.'

'But if he's nasty to you and hits you and all that . . . ' He stared out through the flap of the tent, his eyes full of misery.

'Look,' said Dora gently, 'it's not only young Albert here; I've got two other kids. Three kids and a wife – that's a lot for any man to feed and clothe. Sid's got a decent job and he's fond of us in his way. So I couldn't leave him even if I wanted to. He is the kids' father, after all. We're his family.'

'But if he's a brute, like you said –'

'So what? I never said he was a brute,' she protested. 'I said he's got a temper when he's had a drink or two, that's all. He doesn't mean to hurt me, but he just doesn't know his own strength – he's always sorry afterwards. We're none of us perfect, Albert. So he loses his rag sometimes, but he's got lots of good points. He's not tight with his money and I don't think he's ever looked at another woman – he's just jealous and a bit heavy-handed.'

Albert's expression changed slightly. 'Sounds like a blooming saint,' he muttered. 'Don't know why you wasted your time on someone like me.' Dora tried to take his hand again but he stood up abruptly and moved just out of reach.

'Albert!'

He did not answer at first; then he said suddenly, 'I know where you're going to live. I could come to see you when he's at work.'

'The neighbours will talk, Albert. Don't you dare!'

'I'm entitled.'

'Who says?'

'I reckon so.' As he turned, silhouetted against the light, she saw the slumped shoulders. 'Tell him I'm a friend,' suggested Albert desperately, 'and ask if I can call once a week. How's that? He can't object to that – not once a week. And fix it when *he's* there if you like, so he won't think we're up to anything. Is that too much to ask?'

Dora regarded him wearily. 'Yes, it is, Albert, because I know Sid Carter and I know how his mind works. He'll put two and two together and there'll be hell to pay – not for you, but for me.'

'But it was only once!' Albert shouted. Lowering his voice hastily, he repeated in a whisper, 'We only did it once!'

'And you did enjoy it, Albert. And you said you were grateful.'

'Well? So I am.'

'So show me how grateful you are by not making my life difficult when I get home.'

'Do you know,' Albert said slowly, 'I really hate your husband? I do, Dor! I've never met him but I hate his guts and that's the truth, if you must know.'

'I'd rather not, thank you,' said Dora. 'Look, this is all getting silly and sad and I don't know what else to say. I'm very fond of you, Albert, but I have got a husband and kids and there's no way you and me can be together. That's a fact and you have to face up to facts in this world, believe you me.'

'You sound like my mother!' he said bitterly.

'Well, thanks very much! And talking of mothers, can you imagine *yours* if you told her about us? A married woman with three kids! She'd half murder you – call you everything under the sun for being so daft. Albert, you're a very nice man and one day you'll meet a nice girl who will give you plenty of what I gave you that night. *And* a kid of your own to dandle on your knee. You'll meet someone else – you will, Albert, I promise you.'

He looked at her miserably. 'And I suppose you'll go home to Sid Carter and forget all about me?'

'I'll never do that, Albert,' she said. 'Even if I wanted to, I couldn't forget you. You've been real good to me and we've had some good times.'

'I shall look for another job,' he said. 'I'm sure to get a job some time. Soon, I expect. I'm strong and I can do anything. I'd look after you and the kids, if that's what's bothering you.'

'It's not,' said Dora. 'What's bothering me is – right's right and me walking out on Sid would *not* be right. Please don't make it so hard for me, Albert. Can't we say, "It was fun" and go our own ways? Look . . . ' She had a sudden inspiration. 'I know where you live, right? Now, when I can get Sid in a good mood I'll tell him you were a good friend to me while I was here. I could say you were passing by and happened to hear me groaning and you fetched the nurse and it was all thanks to you and so on. Then I'll say, would it be a nice idea if I invited you round so he could thank you. If he says "Yes" I'll write you a note and put it through your letter-box.'

Albert sat down again on the stool, a gleam of hope in his eyes as he considered this 'straw'. Dora saw the scrawny neck and the poor hunched shoulders, 'Strong!' she thought. 'He's as weak as a kitten', and she wanted to cry.

'That might work,' he said. 'It just might work. Oh Dora, that may do the trick. You promise you *will* ask him, Dor? You're not just saying that?'

'I'll ask him,' Dora promised, 'but it may be a week or two, so don't get impatient or think I've forgotten. I shall have to wait for the exact moment. Husbands are funny animals and you have to catch 'em just right. But if he says, "No" then that's the end of it. Let's enjoy our last day, Albert. No more cross words. What do you say?'

He looked down into her earnest face and felt a sudden rush of tenderness. 'I say "Yes",' he agreed.

She reached up, pulled down his face and kissed him soundly.

'That's for nothing,' she laughed. 'Now be careful!'

*

Vinnie had invited Philippe to stay at Foxearth until the spare parts for the damaged Voisin had been obtained from France. The wrecked plane had been carefully dismantled and transported back to the hanger at Leysdown where Armand, Philippe's mechanic, began the repair work.

To his surprise, and greatly to his satisfaction, the mechanic found himself working alone, since Philippe's passion for flying had given way to a passion for the mistress of Foxearth. Armand hoped fervently that the affair might be prolonged indefinitely and abandoned himself to the heady experience of bearing sole responsibility for the Voisin's resurrection.

Vinnie's guest had been given a bedroom along the passage from her own, but Philippe had so far restrained the impulse to cover the short distance between them. He was, however, finding it increasingly difficult to maintain the necessary degree of self-control, being a warm-blooded young man unused to the agonies of frustration. Being constantly in Vinnie's presence produced in him an acute awareness of her body and a growing desire to enjoy more than the kisses and fervent embraces which had so far been granted him when they said 'Good night' and went their separate ways to bed.

By the time the last day of the hopping arrived, Philippe knew that Vinnie's feelings echoed his own and he was determined to resolve the matter as quickly as possible. He made up his mind that they would sleep together and the decision, once made, eased him a little and allowed him to relax slightly and view the world more sanely while he waited for the night to come. He did not doubt for a moment that Vinnie would welcome his advances and return his passion. He was experienced in the ways of young women and knew also how to beguile those who were more mature into his bed, for he had long ago mastered the art of love-making and could excite a woman with a turn of his head or the tone of his voice. It was a matter of pride to him that he had never taken a woman against her will – that no matter how determined she might be to resist him, the moment inevitably came when she would surrender to his pleadings or more subtle persuasions. There were few, he believed, who regretted their final capitulation – and indeed the majority seemed very willing to repeat the experience. Philippe Delain found women captivating, exciting and vital to his happiness. Lavinia Lawrence, he promised himself, would have no cause for regret. There was a moment in all relationships when desires should be satisfied and that time, he told himself, was very near.

At seven-thirty he walked out on to the large terrace at the front of Foxearth, where the last evening's 'paying out' to the hoppers was in progress. A trestle table lit with two hurricane lamps had been set up and here Vinnie sat in solitary splendour with the large tin box containing the money in front of her. Standing on her left was Ned Bray, the chief pole-puller, a large leather-bound ledger in his hands. A queue of pickers stretched all the way from the table along the terrace to the far end of the house, and more waited on the lawn. Each one carried a small green card, grandly called 'The Hop Picker's Account Book', with his or her name on the front. Inside, the left-hand page was headed by the name of the bin-man who had supervised the picking, the picker's name being repeated on the top of the right-hand page. Below each heading, the page was divided up into columns – the date, six measurings, total, tally and the cash due. The total was the number of bushels picked, the tally being the price agreed for that year. On the back there were two sets of rules and regulations – one for the pole-pullers and the other for the pickers.

Most of the waiting pickers chatted among themselves but others, weary and with little left to say, read and re-read their cards or checked again the total number of bushels they had picked, gloating over the amount of money they would get. All of them had received some money on account each Saturday in order to pay their dues at the local shops or buy a few drinks; these 'subs' had been noted in the ledger and would now be set against their total month's earnings. As the queue shuffled forward, Vinnie took the profferred account book from the next picker, checked it and read out the final figure. Ned consulted his ledger and agreed or disagreed the sum owed. Most transactions went smoothly enough, but there were occasional disputes.

Philippe watched Vinnie glance up with a smile at the next woman and take the card from her. She was unaware of his presence and he was able to observe her without causing her any embarrassment by his scrutiny.

'Mrs Banks?' said Vinnie.

'Yes, ma'am – that's right, ma'am.'

Vinnie glanced at the card and raised her eyebrows. 'You've done very well this year – you must have worked terribly hard!'

The woman jerked her head towards a small girl who stood silent beside her, thumb in her mouth, one hand clutching her mother's skirt.

'This one helped me,' she said. 'She's a good little picker, is Em. Take your thumb out of your mouth and say "Good evening" to Mrs Lawrence.' The child scowled and buried her face in the faded cotton skirt.

'Oh, she's a soft kid and no mistake,' the woman apologised. 'Takes after me when I was her age. Wouldn't say "boo" to a goose, I wouldn't.'

'Em?' said Vinnie. 'Is her name Emmeline? That was my sister's name.'

'No, it's Emily really. Emily Agnes Banks – after my husband's mother, that is.'

While they had been talking, Ned Bray had worked out the sum due, noted it in the ledger and laid the book in front of Vinnie, his finger on the correct line.

'Two pounds seven shillings, Mrs Banks,' said Vinnie. 'Is that what you make it?'

'Two pounds and eight,' said Mrs Banks hopefully. It was her policy always to add on a shilling in the forlorn hope that one year she might be lucky and get away with it.

'Oh dear,' said Vinnie, recognising the ploy. 'Perhaps you should check it again?' She turned round the ledger and Mrs Banks made a pretence of checking the figures with her card.

'Oh, yes,' she said. 'It *is* seven shillings. I don't know how I got eight in me mind.'

'It's easily done,' said Vinnie kindly, proceeding to count out the money. 'There's two pound notes. Two florins and three shillings – and an extra penny for Em to buy some sweets. And thank you for all your work, Mrs Banks. I hope you enjoy the party tonight and we hope to see you again next year.'

'Oh I'll be back, don't you worry. *And* I hope the rains keep off for tonight. Say "Ta", Em, to Mrs Lawrence, 'cos she's give you a penny for sweeties!'

Em took the thumb out of her mouth and closed her hand over the penny.

'Say "Ta"!' her mother urged in vain.

'It doesn't matter,' said Vinnie. Her smile was dismissive and the next picker was already pushing forward. The last night party started at half-past eight and everyone was anxious to collect their money and begin the transformation from grimy picker to clean partygoer.

'Mrs Ellwood?' Vinnie began. 'I hope you enjoyed your stay at Foxearth . . .'

She reached out a hand for the green card and so it continued. Philippe was content to watch Vinnie as the little ceremony proceeded slowly but inexorably towards the last pickers.

He thought how splendid she looked in the creamy lace gown with its high collar and long sleeves. Her face was shaded by a hat of broad-brimmed cream straw with green silk leaves and bright red cherries which glinted in the wavering lamplight.

Nearly an hour went by and still half a dozen people queued at the table. Ten more minutes and the last picker, an old man, held out his card.

'Mr Dobbs?' To her credit, Vinnie's smile was as bright as it had been an hour earlier. 'Have you enjoyed your stay in Kent?'

'I have, yes, ma'am,'

'I expect you're tired?'

'I am, yes, ma'am.'

'Will you be coming to the party tonight?'

'I will, yes, ma'am.'

Vinnie caught Ned Bray's eye and hastily smothered her amusement. For a brief moment Philippe resented even that fleeting exchange of sympathy between *his* Lavinia and another man, but then he chided himself for being foolish. Tonight Lavinia Lawrence would be in *his* arms and she would want to be there more than anything else in the world. He tried to imagine her, excited by the party, probably a little flushed from the wine – he would see that she drank enough but not too much. He visualised her bare shoulders and slim pale arms, her rounded breasts and slightly curved abdomen. She was a mother to three children and no longer a virgin and such women were warm and sensuous, with none of a maiden's shyness. He could imagine her hair tumbled free, a halo of dull gold around her face and lower down, between her soft legs, a deeper gold, sweet and curled . . .

A voice beside him interrupted this vision and he was surprised to find Clive le Brun standing there. The two had not met since the unfortunate occasion when Philippe and Vinnie had missed lunch.

'I was at the flying ground today,' Clive said, 'and at Muswell Manor. I expected to see you around there.' His tone was a little cool but his expression, Philippe was relieved to see, was friendly.

The Frenchman smiled. 'But what am I to do there?' he asked. 'Armand is the genius. Armand is the man who can put my beautiful machine back together again. He likes to work alone and I can only watch him with admiration and envy. Lavinia invited me to stay at Foxearth until the—'

'You are staying at Foxearth?' Clive said, trying with some success to hide his displeasure at the news. 'I didn't realise that.'

Philippe smiled disarmingly. 'Just until the spares can be shipped across from Paris. Armand will let me know as soon as they arrive. The propellor was beyond repair and one of the rear wheels was badly buckled. While we wait, Armand is patching up the wings. Lavinia has been most generous and insisted on making a contribution to the repairs.'

'Did she now.' It was not a question.

'I argued, but she would not listen. She wanted to be involved. She insisted they were her hop-poles which caused the damage.' Philippe laughed. 'Will you be at the party tonight? The big Foxearth celebration to end another hop-picking?'

Without waiting for Clive's answer he went on, 'I have just been watching the "paying out"; it has been most enlightening.' As he spoke Mr Dobbs tottered away from the table and Vinnie stood up. Seeing the two men she hurried over, hiding the relief she felt that Clive had obviously forgiven her.

'Clive! How lovely to see you again,' she cried with genuine delight. 'You've been neglecting us.' She thought he looked tired.

'I'm sorry,' he said, 'but there was some more trouble at Hunton. That poor fellow never seems to get decent pickers. You are very lucky here at Foxearth.'

'I look after them,' said Vinnie, 'and they know it. Oh, I am glad that job's over. It's not so much sorting out the money as keeping the wretched gnats at bay. The lamps attract them at this time of night.' She smiled at Philippe. 'We tried holding the pay-outs in the morning-room but the carpets were in such a mess afterwards that I decided the gnats were the lesser of two evils.'

Clive said pointedly, 'I was at Leysdown today and everyone was asking after Monsieur Delain. The news of the crash had got around, of course. Everybody expected him to be busy on the machine, but poor Armand was all alone.' He was obviously implying that Philippe was neglecting his duties and the young Frenchman flushed slightly.

'I have already told Mr le Brun—' he began, but Vinnie forestalled him by slipping an arm affectionately through his.

'Blame me,' she told Clive. 'I refuse to let him go to that boring old hangar and work on that silly machine. I have told him: it's an omen. God didn't give us wings because He didn't mean us to fly in the air.' She laughed happily. 'Anyway, I'm sure Armande doesn't appreciate Philippe's company as much as I do. Philippe is teaching me French and I am teaching him to play Patience.'

Clive noticed the casually possessive way in which she held Philippe's arm and saw that Philippe did not seem to object. And Vinnie's reference to Patience? Did he detect a hidden meaning? Impulsively he said, 'I came to tell you I shall not be at the party tonight, I'm afraid. I imagine I was going to be invited?'

'Why Clive, of course you were,' said Vinnie, dismayed. 'Didn't I invite you? Surely I did. I mean, you always come. You don't need an invitation after all these years! I thought it was understood – isn't it?'

Clive shrugged and his smile was forced. 'Well, it hardly matters since I cannot be with you.'

'But why? Where are you going?' Vinnie protested. 'Not to another party, surely? Oh, do please come, Clive! It won't be the same without you.'

He saw that Vinnie was hurt, but he knew he could not spend the evening watching her and Philippe so obviously enjoying each other's company. He had fully intended to be at the party and had come to tell her so, but Philippe's permanent presence as a house guest had put a different complexion on the matter.

'I have promised to meet William and a friend,' he said. 'We're going out to late dinner in Maidstone. Don't ask me where, because I don't know.'

'William's friend?' queried Vinnie.

'A young man,' said Clive, 'who shall be nameless simply because I don't remember his name.'

He was angry with himself for these stupid fabrications and furious with Vinnie for provoking them. And that damned Delain looked so smug!

'I mustn't keep you,' he said. 'I only came over to help you with the paying-out really. William used to give you a hand and I thought you might need assistance. But I see you have Philippe and I need not have worried.'

'I did the pay-out all on my own,' said Vinnie, her tone indignant, 'except for Ned Bray with the ledger as usual. Philippe didn't help me at all.'

Philippe smiled deprecatingly and gestured with his hands. 'I am purely decorative, you see,' he joked. 'How do you say it – of no use for man or beast.'

'Of course you're of use,' Vinnie protested. 'You are good for me and I'm glad you are here – I love to have visitors.' She squeezed his arm affectionately and then turned to Clive. 'I have to make the most of him while he's still in one piece,' she said. 'Next time he crashes, he may not be so lucky.'

Philippe held up crossed fingers for luck. Vinnie, vaguely sensing Clive's disapproval, released the Frenchman's arm and held out both her hands to Clive instead.

'Please come to the party!' she said. 'Have dinner with us first and stay on for the celebrations. Who will dance the polka with me if you don't?' She turned to Philippe. 'Last year Clive and I stole the show. Oh Clive, it won't be the same without you here. Must you really go out with William?'

*

Clive gave her an intense look, ignoring her outstretched hands. 'I'm afraid I must,' he said, 'but I am sure Monsieur Delain will look after you splendidly. And now if you will excuse me, I must go. I do hate to be unpunctual.'

When he had gone Vinnie looked at Philippe and he saw that some of her earlier vivacity had faded.

'Oh dear,' said Vinnie, 'he seemed very prickly. I worry about that man. I've known him a long time, but I don't think I shall ever really understand him. I think I've offended him again somehow.'

'He disapproves of me,' Philippe told her. 'After all, you are alone in the house with me, unchaperoned – and what will people say? No doubt he is afraid for your reputation.'

'Oh dear,' said Vinnie. 'I suppose tongues will wag, but let them! Do we care?'

He held out both his hands, unconsciously echoing her appeal to Clive.

'No, we don't care,' he whispered and kissed her lightly on the lips. 'Tell me, Lavinia, that we don't care.'

Wordlessly she shook her head.

'Tell me,' he persisted, his lips moving down to her neck, setting her body on fire. 'Tell me that you don't care about Clive or anyone. Tell me that as long as we are together all the world can whisper.'

'But I *do* care very much about Clive—' she began, but he

drew her suddenly close, pressing his mouth fiercely against hers to silence her. Then she was kissing him wildly in return, and Clive le Brun was quite forgotten.

CHAPTER SEVENTEEN

It was eight-forty-five and most of the hop-pickers had already arrived and were surrounding the large trestle tables where the food was laid out. A trio of flute, drum and fiddle was providing lively background music and the scene was lit partly from the light of a huge bonfire and partly by dozens of candles, each one set in a jam-jar. Over the bonfire a large kettle was suspended, for tea and cocoa were being offered as well as the cider and beer over which Maisie Hunter presided at a separate table. The tables were arranged in a horseshoe, with the central one reserved for the members of the Lawrence family.

As Ellen Pitt surveyed the scene, it was a source of bitter disappointment to her that only Vinnie was there to represent the family. The doctor had not thought it wise to allow Colonel Lawrence down this year, although on previous occasions – warmly wrapped in blankets and furs – he had traditionally spent an hour with the revellers at the beginning of the evening. Julian Lawrence was dead, she reflected, and the handsome young master they had all so much admired and whose presence had graced so many hopping suppers would never be with them again. Eva – his sister and *so* like her mother Christina – was married and had a family of her own. Ellen sighed heavily. She had been such a bonny little girl – a 'bit of a madam' at times, perhaps, but then rich children were always pampered and it was not to be wondered at if they turned out precocious with their temper tantrums and airs and graces. Ellen could find it in her heart to forgive Eva such frailties, for Eva was a Lawrence and that was fair enough. Not that she was now, of course, but Gerald Cottingham was a good match for her – even Christina had approved of him – and that too was fair enough.

Tonight, to Ellen's chagrin, Vinnie sat with Philippe at the top table. Ellen did not quite approve of his presence. He was foreign and as such suspect in her eyes. Did he think he could ever be master and take Julian Lawrence's place? She sighed again, remembering the first time she had seen the two of them together – Julian, the son of the house, with his arm round Vinnie Harris, a poor girl from the London slums. They had made a handsome couple as they danced together – cheeks flushed, eyes glowing and so much in love, although no one ever knew what Henry and Christina Lawrence thought of the friendship. It was all so sad, Master Julian dying like that, but Vinnie had the three children, bless them, though even they were missing from the top table. It was a crying shame that they should miss the supper, but they were in Cornwall with Doll and likely to remain there for a few more weeks unless the weather turned cold. Since the Lord had seen fit to spare their little Louise, Ellen could not find it in her heart to complain if the convalescence took her away.

Her last hopping supper! She was glad in a way, for it was a time-consuming job and she was 'no chicken', as she had told Vinnie; the worry of it all was too much at her age, not to mention the arthritis which was 'getting a hold over her'. It was time to give up and let a younger woman take over – Maisie Hunter from the pub, most likely, or maybe Joan Tupp.

A middle-aged woman came up to Ellen with a half-eaten sausage in one hand and a hot potato in the other.

'You've done us proud again, Mrs Pitt,' she said. 'Lovely bit of sausage, this. Real meaty it is. We don't get 'em this good in London, not nearly so good.'

'I'm glad you like them,' said Ellen. 'They're made in Maidstone – Betts of Earl Street do them.'

'It's been a good season. Nice fat hops – a joy to pick.'

'Yes. They dried a treat, so my husband's well-pleased.'

The woman took another bite of sausage and mumbled,

'Keeps the old beer flowing, eh!'

Ellen laughed. 'Oh yes!'

As it was the last supper she would organise, Ellen had made sure it would be a memorable one. The usual sausages had been supplemented with small meat pies and as well as the jacket potatoes there were whole baked parsnips. She had also made six trays of thick bread pudding, served hot with cinnamon and nutmeg and full of currants. Later on there would be a side of beef – also provided by the Lawrences – which would be carved and put between slices of bread. The Lawrences, she reflected, were a sight more generous than most of the other growers – but then Vinnie Lawrence was sprung from the hoppers and was bound to be so.

In the old days the Colonel had counted the pennies although, to be fair, the side of beef had been his own idea. Still, if it served its purpose the same reliable pickers would return the next year, satisfied with their treatment and terms of employment. A trusted band of pickers was worth a mint of money and the price of a bit of beef was a small enough investment if it sent home the Londoners with a feeling of satisfaction and the knowledge that their labours had been properly appreciated. With a sudden grimace Ellen Pitt put a hand to her back, where the arthritis troubled her most. The doctor had told her to shed a few pounds of weight in order to take the pressure off her right hip, but she liked her food too well and, forced to choose between the two, would opt for the food and put up with the pain for as long as she decently could.

She glanced up at the oast-house. A face peered out of the window and she waved to her husband. He would rarely attend the supper for he was not a dancing man, but he liked to watch the proceedings from his vantage point in the drying-room. By now the last day's hops had been spread out over the horsehair blanket and down below another handful of sulphur had been added to the furnace to bring a touch of gold colour to the drying hops. She sometimes believed, though her husband would have none of it, that she knew as much about drying hops as he did!

Ellen had given him a plateful of the choicest food and a hunk of bread and butter, so he was happy. She turned her attention once more to the courtyard which was thronged with people, all eating. Some sat on the straw bales provided, others stood around and the children, deaf to their mothers' shouts, ran in and out with their mouths inelegantly crammed with food. Ellen walked round the tables, ensuring that they had been re-stocked after the initial onslaught.

'You'll want a few more sausages, Sue,' she said. 'I'll send Edie over with them. What about you, Joan? D'you need some more – whoops!' She steadied herself as a child cannoned into her, nearly knocking her flying. 'More butter?' she finished. 'It's on the end table under the blue checked cloth.'

She smiled at Vinnie who sat with Philippe beside her.

'It's very good, Ellen,' said Vinnie. 'Really first-class. Congratulations!'

'*C'est magnifique!*' Philippe corrected her and Ellen smiled at him dubiously.

'That's a compliment,' Vinnie translated with a laugh. 'It means that the food is magnificent. You see, I'm learning French. *C'est magnifique.* How's that, Philippe? Did I pronounce it properly?'

'*Par excellence!*' he told her.

Ellen Pitt pretended not to notice this second foreign outburst and wondered again about the handsome Frenchman. Opinion among the staff at Foxearth varied greatly and feelings ran high. Janet, Bertha and Edie all professed to find him wildly attractive, while Cook, Mrs Tallant and Doll acknowledged his good looks but found him a sight *too* charming; aware of Vinnie's obvious admiration for the young man, they confided their opinions only to each other.

Ellen moved on to check that the supply of cider had not run too low. The beer was purchased from the 'Horse and Cart', but the cider had been made a year since with apples from the small Foxearth orchard and set aside for this occasion. Glancing back to the top table, Ellen saw Philippe lean close to his companion and whisper something to her. Whatever it was made Vinnie jerk up her head, a blush spreading lightly over her cheeks.

Ellen pondered briefly about the prospect of Foxearth under a foreign master and didn't like the idea at all. Not that anyone would care a fig for *her* likes and dislikes – if Vinnie Lawrence took it into her head to marry this handsome foreigner, they would all have to like it or lump it. Steven Pitt's cottage went with the job.

Taking another careful look around her, she realised she could not see Clive le Brun anywhere. When she went back to the top table, Vinnie glanced at her enquiringly.

'Mr le Brun's late,' said Ellen. 'It's not like him at all. He usually has a bit of a word with my husband first, but we've not seen hide nor hair of him so far.'

Vinnie said, 'I'm afraid he's not coming, Mrs Pitt. I am sorry I didn't tell you. He's gone to Maidstone – he had to meet someone there.'

Ellen Pitt's face fell in dismay. 'What, *tonight*?' she exclaimed. 'The hopping supper? My very *last* hopping supper—' Frowning, she broke off in mid-sentence. 'But that can't be right. He told my husband a few days back as he'd see him here tonight, and Steven *told* me so himself. Mr le Brun would never miss my last hopping supper!' Her eyes met Vinnie's accusingly.

'I suppose,' said Vinnie awkwardly, 'it must be because of William. They always came together and now, of course, William probably preferred not to come.'

'I can understand *that*,' said Ellen, 'but Mr le Brun would never have promised to see Steven if he hadn't meant to be here. I do hope he hasn't had an accident.'

'Of course he hasn't had an accident,' Vinnie said, exasperated. 'I told you he said he had to be in Maidstone this evening – with William and a friend.'

Ellen folded her huge arms over her chest with an air of someone about to embark on a long argument, but fortunately for Vinnie Maisie appeared at Ellen's elbow to ask about another barrel of cider and reluctantly she moved away, muttering under her breath.

'So he *did* mean to come!' said Vinnie. 'Oh dear, something is wrong, I feel it. Poor Ellen! This is always her big moment and she thinks the world of Clive – so does her husband. They've worked together for as long as I can remember.'

Philippe put an arm round her shoulder. 'Don't worry, little one,' he said. 'Ellen will get over it. Life is full of disappointments and we must be philosophical. I am disappointed that my little Voisin is damaged, but I do not pull a long face. Forget them all, Vinnie. This is *our* evening, yours and mine. It is my first hopping supper, remember? Eat up and then later we will dance together . . .' He lowered his voice, 'and I will hold you in my arms again. You will soon forget the bad-tempered Monsieur le Brun and the sad Mrs Pitt also.'

Vinnie sighed. 'You're very kind,' she said. 'Am I being silly to worry about it? I'm sorry – I don't mean to spoil your evening.'

'You do not spoil it, you *make* it,' he told her. 'If I am next to you, then I am a happy man. Tonight we will forget everyone else and be just the two of us: Lavinia and Philippe. You and me. And I shall keep you all to myself. If you dance with anyone else, I swear I shall shoot myself.'

Vinnie had to laugh as he looked at her with an expression of exaggerated despair.

He raised his mug of cider. 'To my first hopping supper,' he said, 'and to the two of us. Will you drink to that?'

'Of course I will.' Vinnie lifted her glass. 'To the two of us,' she said and they drank deeply.

*

Less than five miles away in Maidstone, Clive le Brun sat alone at the bar in the Royal Star Hotel. He was not spending the evening with William and a friend and originally had fully intended to attend the supper at Foxearth. Declining to do so at the last moment had put him in a slight predicament; if he went home he would be alone, for William had accepted an invitation to another hopping supper at Laddingford. On the other hand, if Clive attended any of the other celebrations to which, as hop factor, he was regularly invited, Vinnie would almost certainly get to hear of it and would know that he had lied. In previous years he and William had regularly attended the supper and had slept at Foxearth overnight and stayed for lunch on the Sunday. This year, of course, he had known it would be different, for William would not feel able to attend even if he had wished to do so, but Clive had been looking forward to spending some time with Vinnie. He had hoped to find the opportunity for a game of chess on Sunday morning – or perhaps a walk along the river, weather permitting. Now the wretched Frenchman had taken his place and with hindsight Clive cursed the day he had taken Philippe Delain to Foxearth, for Vinnie's head was obviously quite turned by the young flier. Clive swallowed the last of the whisky and pushed forward his glass.

'Same again!' he said.

The barmaid, a woman in her thirties, smiled cheerfully at him and wondered why he looked so miserable.

'It's going to be a fine weekend,' she remarked. 'We've had a fine September, really.'

Clive nodded as she poured his drink.

'Mind you, we get spoilt,' she went on, 'and then when it turns cold we all moan. Anything in it, sir? Soda water?'

'No, thank you.'

'Yes, we get a spell of good weather and we start to take it for granted – then down goes the temperature and we're all taken by surprise. We lost four lovely geraniums last year. Frost got them – my husband was that upset! Lovely deep pink, they were. Are you interested in gardening?' She began to polish a row of newly-washed glasses, hanging each one on the rack overhead. Clive considered her dispassionately. She had blonde hair, not gold like Vinnie's. Her eyes were blue and slightly protruberant; Vinnie's eyes were grey and her lashes were long and he recalled how they fringed her cheeks when she cast down her eyes. The barmaid was tall and well-built, with shoulders that were too heavy and arms that were too full so that they strained at the sleeves. Vinnie's arms were slim and almost certainly pale, probably sprinkled with delicate white-gold hairs. Vinnie's shoulders were much narrower and she was smaller altogether ...

'I said, have you got a garden?' she repeated. 'Do you like gardening?'

'I'm sorry,' said Clive. He looked round the bar, which now was empty except for himself and two elderly men. 'Is it always so empty?' he asked.

'It's early yet and people are in the restaurant. It'll fill up later. You not eating?'

'Maybe later. I'm not hungry.' He drained his glass and as he pushed it forward imagined that she gave him a funny look – as though she knew too much about him. He put a hand to his head. Whisky was not a spirit he drank very often, preferring wine on most occasions, but tonight was different. Tonight he was alone when he ought to have been with Vinnie, sitting beside her at the top table in the candle-light, with the oast-house towering darkly above them surrounded by a sea of happy faces ...

'Are you feeling all right, sir?' the barmaid asked as a deep sigh escaped him.

'Of course I'm all right,' he snapped, then to make amends said, 'The same again and take one for yourself.'

'Oh, thank you sir, I'll have a small port and lemon if I may.'

'Whatever you like.'

He wondered what to do with the rest of the evening and the night. Damnation! He had forgotten the night. He had to sleep somewhere, but he did not want to go back to Harkwood because there he would be alone with his thoughts and in his present mood that would be unbearable. He took his drink and pocketed the change.

'Do you have a vacant room?' he asked.

'I don't know, sir, but they'll tell you at Reception, through there.' She pointed. 'We're not usually too busy at this time of the year. It slackens off towards the middle of September.'

Apprehensively, she noted the speed with which her

customer drank his third whisky.

'If you'd like me to book you a table in the restaurant . . .' she suggested but Clive shook his head.

'I don't want to eat,' he said, though what he meant was that he did not want to eat alone and that deprived unexpectedly of Vinnie's company, he had unaccountably lost his appetite. All he wanted to do was rid his mind of the unwelcome image of Vinnie and Philippe and survive the long hours until morning.

Eventually he went through to Reception and booked a single room for one night, slipping the room key into his pocket. Then he returned to the bar, asked for a bottle of their best claret and a glass and retired to a seat in the window from which he could survey the High Street and watch the lonely evening go by.

*

Much later that night Vinnie stumbled into her room, dazed with weariness and the heady cider. The hopping supper had been a great success, lasting until just after midnight when the last of the revellers finally made their way to bed. They had all been feasted and fêted and none of the hoppers was in any doubt that the Lawrences valued their loyalty and labour. Three ringing cheers had convinced Ellen that her last supper had been a resounding success. The few short speeches had been well applauded; the food and wine had 'gone down a treat'; the dancing had delighted and finally exhausted them and the final sing-song had inspired mixed feelings of cheerful companionship and regrets that it was all over for another year.

Vinnie and Philippe had stolen the show with their wonderful vivacity and humour and their obvious adoration for each other. The young women eyed them speculatively, hoping to be similarly blessed, while the older ones looked back to a youthful love that, in retrospect, now seemed equally glorious.

Vinnie did not bother to brush her hair. She kicked off her shoes, tugged off her clothes and tumbled face downward on to the bed, too tired to struggle into her nightgown and too carefree to worry about propriety. For a few moments she lay smiling into the pillows, so happy that she did not want to go to sleep – she wanted to stay awake and recall each word that Philippe had spoken, each gesture he had made. She felt deliriously content with herself, with Philippe, with her whole life.

'I love you,' she said softly. 'Philippe Delain, I love you. Do you love me?'

She rolled over and looked round the moonlit room, her gaze wandering to the window, to the picture on the wall, to the gas-jets above the mantelpiece. Gently she ran her hands over her body which, freed from the restriction of clothing, felt smooth and cool to her fingers. The moonlight fell across the carpeted floor, just catching the corner of the bed, and she wriggled down until her left foot was lit by the moonbeam. Yes, she thought, it was a nice foot. A neat foot. Philippe would like that foot when he saw it. She raised her left leg and admired that too. Yes, he would appreciate her legs, she thought. One day Philippe Delain would be her husband and he would see her in all her nakedness and he would love her. She let her leg fall slowly back on to the bed and closed her eyes in ecstasy. Tonight he had said the most wonderful things to her and had talked about his desire for her in a way that no Englishman could ever match. Philippe was right, she thought drowsily. Englishmen were so reserved – they did not know how to treat a woman. Mrs Lavinia Delain! It sounded quite perfect.

She sighed luxuriously, then whispered his name into the darkness. One day she would be his bride and her many fears and griefs would be of no significance. She would put behind her all the mistakes of her past life and her new life with Philippe would be full of love and warmth and shared joy.

Vinnie wondered about his family – but of course they would love her too. In France they would call her Madame Delain! Idly she reached up with her fingers to pluck at heavy strands of hair, arranging them round her head to radiate outwards like the rays of the sun, then laughed aloud imagining her face thus framed. She saw herself suddenly as a beautiful flower, her face framed by golden petals. She was beautiful, clever, amusing – all the things she wanted to be – she had only to look into his eyes to see herself as she had never done before. He made her feel like a desirable woman.

She sat up suddenly, hugging her knees, her head bent, letting her hair fall forward to brush softly against her naked body. Lavinia Lawrence was not just mistress of Foxearth, nor was she merely the children's mother, much as she adored them. She was not Eva's sister-in-law nor Julien's widow. Philippe had told her she was Lavinia Lawrence: a woman.

Realisation of what that meant swept over her, bringing a warm glow to her whole body, so that she hid her face in her hands as though to conceal the revelation from a jealous world.

Abruptly she jerked up her head, for someone was tapping at the door. Vinnie slid off the bed, stumbling in her haste to find her dressing-gown.

'Don't!' said a low voice. 'Don't put it on!'

She turned sharply to find Philippe already in the room, standing with his back to the door. Only a few yards separated them. He wore a dressing-gown, but his feet were bare.

'Philippe!'

'Let me see that beautiful body,' he whispered. 'Don't hide it.'

'Oh no!' She was fumbling to tie the belt. 'Not now! Not here.' He crossed the distance that separated them and stood so close that her senses swam.

'But whyever not?' he whispered. 'I told you how it would be – I told you we would lie in one another's arms.'

'I thought you meant . . .' Vinnie was confused. She did not want to reject him, did not want to send him away. More than anything in the world she wanted to lie with him, but she had not understood earlier that he had meant this to happen tonight. Perhaps she had misled him by her answers, and now he was here with his arms closing round her.

'Oh Philippe. I can't—'

His lips closed over hers gently but firmly. All his movements were so sure, she thought; she would trust her body to him without a moment's hesitation when they were married, but was sure she had not intended this to happen now. Almost sure.

Calmly he slipped her dressing-gown down over her shoulders and arms, imprisoning her. His lips caressed her shoulders and arms, his eyes caressed her breasts with an exhilarating intensity.

'You are beautiful,' he murmured. 'So much more beautiful than I ever imagined.'

'But Philippe,' she protested weakly, 'the servants! They will *know*.'

He shook his head. 'No one will know, Vinnie. In the early morning I shall creep away back to my own room. Don't send me away, little one. I thought you loved me – you told me tonight you did.'

'Oh, I *do*, Philippe—'

Her protests died as his experienced fingers moved slowly over her and the dressing-gown fell to the floor.

'Come here,' he said softly. 'Come into the moonlight. Ah! My beautiful Lavinia!'

Vinnie's doubts began to melt away as her body relaxed. It was so long since she had shared her bed with a man. William had never been her lover; had never seen her naked. But Philippe was lifting her into his arms and she was clinging to him, her head buried in his shoulder. His own dressing-gown had slipped undone and she caught a glimpse of his body and found it infinitely appealing. With a sense of shock she realised that she *wanted* him. Not only was she willing to surrender herself to Philippe, she actually *wanted* his body with an animal longing that was quite new to her. With Julian she had never felt that way. With Tom Bryce . . . perhaps, but then there had been no love between them and no joy. Here in the darkness with Philippe she experienced both the delicate joy of giving and the fierce instinct to take also. Locked in his arms, Vinnie's common sense deserted her and she surrendered eagerly to the urgent craving of her body and the wild beating of her heart, abandoning herself wholeheartedly to a newly-awakened passion. And to Philippe Delain.

*

Much later they lay together in a drowsy haze of satisfaction. Philippe's arm was round her shoulders, her head was on his shoulder and from time to time he kissed her hair or ran his hand tenderly over her back.

'Don't cry, little one,' he said.

'These are happy tears,' Vinnie whispered.

'Not tears of regret?'

'No, no, of course not! How could I regret it, ever? I love you, Philippe.'

'I love you, little one.'

'Do you mean it? Oh, say it again, that you love me.'

'I love you – and it was very sweet for me.'

'For me, too, Philippe. Unbelievably sweet! I can't tell you how wonderful it was – there are no words.'

'I am so pleased,' he said softly. 'You deserve such joy. You have been very lonely and that is such a waste. We should take our pleasures while we are young.'

'Youth is fleeting,' said Vinnie. 'I read that once, to the Colonel. I used to read to him; I still do sometimes, but mostly Janet reads to him now. I wonder what he'll say about us?'

'About us? But how will he know?'

'I don't mean about tonight,' said Vinnie. 'I mean later on. I wonder if he will approve of you.' Philippe was silent. 'I mean – when we tell him . . . Philippe, are you asleep? Don't go to sleep on me, please, darling. Not yet.'

'Don't talk about the future,' he said. 'Don't think about it, Lavinia. Enjoy the present and let the future look after itself.'

'Yes, sir. I will, sir,' she laughed.

'You're mocking me,' he said.

'Only in a nice way,' she told him. 'Oh Philippe, I want to keep telling you that I love you and that your body is wonderful and—'

'Ssh! If you let me sleep I shall wake up and then we can do it all again.'

'Again? Oh no, I couldn't bear it! Could someone die of

ecstasy, do you think? I suppose it would be a good way to die.'

'Don't talk of dying, little one.'

'I'm sorry.' She snuggled closer to him, listening raptly to the beating of his heart, rocked by the rise and fall of his chest as he breathed. 'The world can end now if it wants to,' she told him. 'I think at this moment I could bear it.'

He made a non-committal sound and she realised that he was nearly asleep. She propped herself up on one elbow and kissed his chest where she imagined his heart to be, then settled herself once more within the circle of his arm.

'Goodnight, my dearest love.'

He murmured wordlessly and she smiled.

*

The strident clamour of a bell brought them both to their senses an hour or so later.

'What is it? Oh God!' For a moment Vinnie could not marshal her thoughts but sat up in bed staring down at Philippe beside her. Remembrance flooded back, filling her with a deep sense of guilt.

'The front-door bell!' she cried. 'What's happening? It's still dark.' Slower to waken from sleep, Philippe sat up.

'But who can it be at this hour?' Vinnie cried. 'Oh, Philippe, the servants! You must go – go quickly! They'll all be awake and will see us together.'

He rubbed his eyes sleepily. 'See us? Why shouldn't they?' he said with a trace of irritation in his voice. 'I shall stay exactly where I am. They will not look in here if you go out on to the landing and close the door behind you.'

Vinnie put a hand to her heart. 'Oh yes, you're right. I'm being silly. But don't move from here, promise me, in case someone sees you leave. I'll go down and see what's happening. Oh, where's my dressing-gown? Where did I put it?'

'Shall I light the candle?'

'No!' she cried. 'I've found it now. Oh, stop ringing the wretched bell, whoever you are! There must have been an accident or something. My slippers. Where are they? Oh dear, I hope I look normal.'

Faintly amused by her confusion, Philippe slipped back between the sheets and closed his eyes sleepily. Vinnie ran out of the room closing the door firmly behind her and met Mrs Tallant on the landing looking white and frightened, her head covered in curling-rags.

'Whatever can it be, ma'am?' she cried. 'My poor heart's bumping away.'

'It's all right, Mrs Tallant. I'll go down and see,' said Vinnie. 'You wait here in case I need you.'

She ran down the stairs and crossed the dark hallway. With trembling hands she unbolted the door and cautiously opened it. A tall figure stood silhouetted against the moonlight. Vinnie clasped a hand over her mouth to stifle a scream and then recognition dawned.

'Clive!' she gasped. 'What on earth has happened? Are you ill? What on earth are you doing here?'

'I had to see you.' Roughly he took hold of her wrist.

'Clive, you're hurting me!' she cried. 'What on earth is the matter? It's the middle of the night!'

'I must talk to you,' he told her. 'You *have* to listen to me.' He seemed to sway slightly and Vinnie said, 'Clive, are you all right? Are you ill or something?'

He shook his head. 'No, I'm not ill.'

'But how on earth did you get here?' she asked. Even as she did so, however, she looked past him along the drive and could just make out the vague outline of a carriage of some kind. A horse whinnied, the sound eerie in the dark air.

'By cab,' he said. 'I told him to wait. I must talk to you – there's something I have to tell you.'

He swayed again and, releasing her wrist, put out a hand to steady himself against the door-frame. Astonished, Vinnie smelt alcohol on his breath. She stepped back into the hall and called up the stairs to the housekeeper.

'It's all right, Mrs Tallant. I can deal with it, thank you.'

'But what's happened, madam? Who is it?'

'It's Mr le Brun – with a message. Nothing to worry about. Please go back to bed, Mrs Tallant – I'll explain in the morning.'

As the housekeeper hesitated, Bertha appeared behind her. Vinnie hoped desperately that it would not occur to them to wonder why Philippe had not yet put in an appearance to find out the cause of the disturbance. Could they possibly believe he had slept through all that noise?

'Please,' she said sharply, 'go back to bed. I can deal with this.'

As they still lingered, she raised her voice. 'Are you *deaf*? I have told you to go back to your beds!'

'Yes, madam,' said Mrs Tallant, her tone aggrieved, and at last she retreated, pushing Bertha ahead of her. Vinnie heard Bertha's plaintive voice and Mrs Tallant's furious reply.

She turned back to Clive. 'You'd better come in,' she said, 'and I'll make you some coffee.' She held out her hand to him but instead he caught hold of it and pulled her out onto the steps. With her free hand she tried to tighten the cord of her dressing-gown.

From the waiting cab a man's voice called gruffly, 'How much longer, guv'nor?'

Clive roared back, 'You wait until I'm ready, damn you, and hold your tongue!'

Vinnie said, 'Perhaps you should go, Clive. He – ', but he interrupted her.

'Vinnie, I have to tell you something for your own good – about Delain. He's no good, he's not straight. I feel it here.' He put a hand on his heart.

'Philippe not straight?' cried Vinnie. 'What on earth are you talking about? Of course he is! Look Clive, where's William? What's happened? You said you were having dinner with him and a friend and now, here you are alone – I just don't understand what's going on.'

'He's no good, Vinnie. That's what I'm telling you.'

Vinnie hesitated, then hurried down the remaining steps and ran across to the waiting cabby.

'Just five minutes more,' she said. 'Please wait for him.'

'Right ma'am,' he grumbled, 'but it's double fare at this hour of the night. I hope he realises that.'

'Don't worry, I'm sure he does. You will get your money. Have you brought him from his home in Tunbridge Wells?'

'No, ma'am. From the "Royal Star" in Maidstone.'

'I see. Well, please wait a little longer. I think he's . . . a little unwell.'

'Unwell? If you say so, ma'am.' He laughed sarcastically.

'Yes, I *do* say so,' said Vinnie, resenting his insolent tone.

Shivering slightly, for she was wearing only her thin dressing-gown and the night air was cool, she went back to the steps where Clive waited for her. In the light of the lantern beside the door she saw that his face was grim.

'Clive,' she began again, 'we shall both catch our deaths if we stand out here. The servants have all gone back to bed and we can talk inside in private if – '

'Thank you, no!' he said curtly. 'Not while you and that damned Frenchman are – '

Vinnie stiffened. 'Don't speak of Philippe that way,' she said. 'He's my guest and is entitled to your respect. I don't know why you have taken against him, unless it was that wretched lunch for which I am so sorry, but I have apologised. I cannot undo what happened, and I'm surprised if you still bear a grudge for it was my fault as much as his – maybe more so. Philippe has never done you the slightest harm – in fact he thinks very highly of you.'

'He's clever enough to pretend so.'

'Clive!'

'He doesn't like me and I don't like him, but at least I'm honest enough to say so. He has wormed his way into your affections and now he's living under the same roof and compromising you in the eyes of the village, not to mention the pickers. God knows what's being said!'

He had touched a sensitive nerve and Vinnie reacted angrily.

'I don't care about the village,' she cried, 'or the pickers! I don't care what people are thinking. They can think what they like. Damn them all!' She stared wildly into his face and it was only her anger that prevented her from seeing the threat smouldering in his eyes.

'Does that go for me too?' he asked evenly.

'Yes, it does!' cried Vinnie. 'If you have the same spiteful thoughts as everyone else . . . if you choose to think so badly of me – '

He put out a hand, clasped her by the right shoulder and pulled her round so that her face was in the light.

'But how do you think of yourself, Vinnie?' he asked. 'What do you think when you look in the mirror? Because that's what really matters.'

His harsh words wounded her more than he knew. Sober, Clive would have heard the faint gasp that escaped her trembling lips, but his mind was still hazy with drink and he spoke with abandon, wanting only to ease his own sense of desolation.

Vinnie, forced to face up to her own sense of guilt, bitterly resented his interference but, aware that curious servants were no doubt doing their best to overhear, made a supreme effort to salvage the potentially explosive situation.

'Clive, please,' she said, 'let's not hurt each other like this. I don't think you really mean what you're saying.' She lowered her voice. 'You are not . . . quite yourself at the moment. Won't you go home now and we can talk some other time? Please, Clive, I honestly believe it would be best. The cabby's waiting and – '

Without warning Clive seized her, his fingers iron-hard around her upper arms. She could not help giving a sharp cry of pain and struggled to free herself. All her good intentions melted away.

'Clive! You're hurting me, damn you! Let *go* of me, for God's sake. What is the matter with you?' His fingers tightened and she cried out again. 'You're hurting me, I tell you, Clive! Do you hear me? Let go of me at once or I shall call Mrs Tallant.'

His face came nearer to her own and his eyes glittered

dangerously. 'Why not call the Frenchman?' he taunted. 'You know I'd really like that, Vinnie. It would give me a chance to tell him a few home-truths. Call him, Vinnie!'

'I will *not*!' she hissed. 'But I *will* call Mrs Tallant if you don't take your hands off me!'

She had no intention of putting her threat into operation, having no desire to let the housekeeper find them struggling together. Clive, however, took the threat seriously and released one hand in order to clap it over her mouth. He began to push her backwards down the steps and away from the house and Vinnie, unable to utter a sound, felt the first cold touch of fear. His strength surprised her as he half-pushed, half-carried her away from the light of the house, across the dark lawn and into the shadow of the trees. There he pressed her so roughly against the broad rough trunk of a tree that she felt the bark dig into her spine; burning tears of pain and rage sprang to her eyes and rolled silently down her face to trickle on to the hand that still covered her mouth. Clive snatched his hand away and stared at it as though the soft tears had burned his skin. Vinnie took a gulp of air and watched him fearfully. In spite of the damp night air, her body burned as though ravaged by a sudden fever. Emotions whirled in her shocked mind – fear, anger, disbelief and, subconsciously, a perverse triumph that she had unlocked in Clive le Brun a deep and powerful passion that she had never suspected. For a moment they stared at each other and in the shattering silence Vinnie heard the drip of dew through the leaves above her and the rustle of a small night creature in the undergrowth nearby. She heard his laboured breathing and saw that his chest heaved.

'Oh, Clive!'

It was her own voice that uttered his name in a whisper that seemed to echo and grow in her brain until it deafened her. She had not meant to say it, but now the name was there between them and she waited helplessly for his response, her eyes closed against the darkness and the sight of his anguished face.

Suddenly she felt his arms round her, pulling her fiercely

forward, and a moment later his mouth was on hers, bruising her lips. She struggled frantically in the fierce circle of his arms, so that when he did release her she staggered and almost fell.

She clutched at the tree to steady herself, but Clive was already striding back across the grass towards the waiting hansom. Vinnie watched his tall figure through eyes blurred with fresh tears.

'Damn you, Clive le Brun!' she sobbed. 'Damn you! Damn you!'

CHAPTER EIGHTEEN

By the time Vinnie awoke next morning Philippe, as promised, had slipped back to his own room. She rolled over, smiling as she ran her fingers over his pillow and the slight depression made by his head – the only evidence that remained to prove that she and Philippe had indeed been lovers. Then suddenly a harsher memory intruded into her thoughts and she sat up abruptly.

'Clive le Brun!' she whispered, remembering with great clarity their encounter in the early hours. 'How *dare* you, Clive, say such terrible things to me? How *dare* you kiss me like that? What right – ' There was a knock on the door.

'Come in.'

Bertha came in rather self-consciously, holding out a letter. She did not meet Vinnie's eyes and Vinnie recalled her own sharp tongue the night before.

'This was delivered by hand, ma'am,' said Bertha.

'By hand? What time is it? I think I must have overslept.'

'You have, ma'am,' said Bertha. 'It's just after nine o'clock. And Mr Delain said as I'm to tell you he's had a message about his flying machine from Armand and has gone to Leysdown and hopes to be back later in the day.'

'I see.' Vinnie tried to hide her disappointment. 'Thank you, Bertha. I shall be up shortly. Please light the geyser before you go downstairs, and tell Cook I won't bother with breakfast but we'll have lunch half an hour early if possible.'

'Yes, ma'am.'

Vinnie hesitated. 'And Bertha,' she added, 'please tell Mrs Tallant that Mr le Brun was unwell last night. Tell her when the two of you are alone and say that on no account is it to go any further. If the matter becomes local gossip, I shall hold you both equally responsible.'

'Yes, ma'am.'

A sullen look had settled over Bertha's face but Vinnie ignored it. When the girl had gone, she opened the envelope and drew out a sheet of notepaper bearing the heading of the 'Royal Star Hotel.' She recognised Clive's bold handwriting:

My dear Vinnie,

This brief note comes from the 'Royal Star' and is to apologise for my behaviour last night. I have no excuse to offer, but deeply regret any embarrassment or distress I have caused you. No doubt you may now decide to look elsewhere for professional advice, and I shall abide by your decision if that is the case. I intend to leave for Scotland later today for a long-overdue holiday. If on my return I find you have not contacted me, I shall assume our relationship is at an end.

Sincerely – Clive le Brun

Vinnie crumpled the letter and threw it on to the floor. He had behaved so badly, yet there was no humility in the letter – no excuses, no pleading. How like Clive, she thought angrily. Let him go to Scotland. Let him stay there! She could manage very well without Clive le Brun.

She was taking a bath when Bertha knocked on the door to say that William was on the telephone. Surprised, Vinnie promised to ring back as soon as she was dressed and did so promptly.

'William, it's Vinnie.'

It was strange to hear his voice after so many months.

'Hello, Vinnie. Nice to talk to you again.' His voice was polite and impersonal. 'I'm phoning about my father. It's all rather odd and I wondered if you knew anything about it. I haven't seen him since yesterday morning, but the housekeeper says he's gone to Scotland. This is the first I've heard of it and I wondered if he mentioned anything to you at the supper last night or if – '

'But William,' Vinnie interrupted, 'I saw Clive before the hopping supper and he said he wasn't coming because he was dining in Maidstone with you.'

'With me? But that's ridiculous! I told him I was going to the supper at Liddons – he knew that quite well. He was supposed to be at *your* supper. Where the hell is he? Apparently, he's been home but he was in and out again within a few minutes.'

Vinnie groaned inwardly; surely the whole sorry mess was not going to come out? She picked her words carefully. 'I've had a note from him this morning, saying that he's gone to Scotland for a holiday. I expect he wants to do some fishing. I'm sure there's no need to concern yourself; he just seemed a little confused, that's all.'

'My father doesn't *get* confused,' said William, a little haughtily Vinnie thought. 'He's as steady as a rock. And why on earth should he go to Scotland? He hasn't been for years, not since my mother died.'

'He didn't come to the supper, but he called in late last night,' said Vinnie cautiously. 'He seemed very tired and – I don't know . . . He said he needed a rest.'

There was a moment's silence, then William said, 'If he called in late last night, why did he send you a note this morning? What the hell's going on, Vinnie? It's all so unlike him. Is there something I don't know?'

Vinnie searched desperately for a way to explain Clive's behaviour without going into unnecessary detail.

'Look, William, we had a slight disagreement,' she improvised, 'but I don't want to discuss it with you. I'm afraid we parted last night on rather unfriendly terms.' He had begun to speak, but she went on quickly, 'I'm sorry, William, but I won't discuss it. It was a personal matter that concerns no one else. As far as I know, your father is perfectly all right and you have no need to be concerned about him.'

The little speech sounded pompous, but Vinnie had intended to sound unapproachable. She waited to see if it had had the desired effect.

'Then where was he last night?' asked William. 'He certainly didn't come home.'

Vinnie cursed his persistence. 'I haven't the faintest idea,' she lied, 'but wherever it was I'm sure it's none of our business. Clive is his own master.'

'But why go to Scotland on his own? I would have gone with him gladly.' William's tone was aggrieved.

'I really don't know,' said Vinnie.

'He might have had the decency to leave me a note –' William began, but Vinnie had listened to him long enough.

'I'm afraid I have to go,' she said. 'The mission's outing to Camber is today and I've been invited.' She chattered on in an attempt to change the subject. 'The horse-bus will be here very soon to take us to the station, and I'm not nearly ready. Tomorrow the pickers all go home. It's so quiet when they've all gone; I always hate it for the first few days. They're so looking forward to it – Camber Sands, I mean. I don't suppose they've ever seen the sea before . . . ' Her voice trailed away.

'Vinnie,' said William, 'I do hope you were not discussing me last night.'

'Of course we weren't. Oh, for heaven's sake, William! I don't think your name was even mentioned. Does that make you feel any better?'

'I don't know. Was it about Foxearth?'

'Mind your own business, William!'

She immediately regretted her words and said quickly, 'Look William, I'm sorry to be so sharp, but I don't want to talk about it and I don't suppose Clive does either. Surely you can understand?'

After a pause he said icily, 'I am trying, Vinnie, but I'm not having much success.'

Vinnie longed to shake him. Instead, after a moment, she said calmly, 'I really must go, William,' and hung up.

*

First thing the following morning after the last of the hop-pickers had left for London, the mission also packed up and departed. They were excited about their plans to supervise the removal of Dora and her family to the two-roomed basement flat which was only yards away from the mission's own premises, where it would be easy for Lydia to keep a concerned eye on Dora's new baby.

Tuesday morning found Mary in her study hard at work on the mission's accounts, for she had agreed, albeit reluctantly, to take over the task from Gareth who now had less time to spare. There was always plenty of money going out of their fund, but very little coming in. Donations were irregular, but occasionally Roland organised a small soirée at his home and friends and relatives of the mission members were invited to buy tickets. They had also raffled a particularly fine vase bequeathed to Gareth by an elderly aunt and this had fetched the princely sum of seventeen pounds.

Mary, her head full of figures, heard but did not register the sound of footsteps outside, but the jangling bell caused her to raise her head enquiringly for she was not expecting visitors.

'Please, ma'am,' said Mrs Markham a moment later, 'it's that Mr Bertie Harris and he'd like a word with you.'

All the colour drained out of Mary's face as the words echoed in her brain. Bertie Harris! That could mean only one thing, she thought faintly. For a moment she could only stare speechlessly at the housekeeper who, puzzled by her reaction, presumed she had not heard her the first time and repeated the name more clearly.

'I heard you,' said Mary.

'He's in the hall, ma'am. What am I to say?'

Mary rose to her feet, her limbs leaden. 'I know him, of course; we met at Foxearth. Show him in, Mrs Markham, and bring a tray of tea and some cinnamon biscuits.'

Bertie came into the room and they shook hands.

'Please sit down, Mr Harris,' said Mary. 'Mrs Markham will bring us some refreshment.'

'That's very kind,' said Bertie. 'Look, Mary, I won't beat about the bush. I suspect you know why I'm here?'

Mary nodded. 'I imagine you've found out about Alexander

– I have been expecting this to happen.'

Her apparent calmness impressed him.

'How long have you known that I am Alexander's father?' he asked her.

'Several years. I imagine you have only recently found out?'

'Just over a week ago,' he said. 'It was a bit of a shock, as I had no idea at all – I'd like you to believe me.'

Mary looked at him curiously; he was evidently very nervous. She searched in vain for a likeness between father and son, but found none.

'I believe you,' she said. 'You don't appear angry and for that I am relieved. I suppose you wonder why I didn't tell you before? The answer is that I felt it would serve no useful purpose now. Alexander is my legal son.' She pointed towards the desk at which she had been working. 'I had a letter from him this morning and it seems he is well and happy. I cannot thank you for lending him that money – you had no right to interfere without consulting me first – but now that you are here I can at least repay you. I shall write a cheque – '

Bertie held up his hand. 'I won't take it,' he said, 'although I do appreciate the offer. It was a matter between the two of us. He's not a child now, but old enough to make such decisions for himself. He'll repay me sometime – the money doesn't matter.'

'You had no right to give it to him,' Mary repeated stubbornly.

'And you had no right,' he countered swiftly, 'to keep from us what you know about our relationship.'

The colour was slowly returning to her face. 'From his letter this morning, it appears you did not tell him?' she said.

'No. I was tempted to, but then I thought you would want to do that yourself. He must be told, Mary – you know that, don't you?'

Mary rose and turned away to glance out into the street. Bertie stood up, also.

'Can you imagine how I feel,' he said, 'finding out after all these years? I didn't abandon her – Mollie, I mean. I didn't even know about the child. She didn't tell me – says she didn't know how to find me and I believe her. She seems rather irresponsible.'

Mary turned round to face him, startled. 'You have seen Mollie Pett?'

He nodded. 'It wasn't too difficult. She's very ill.'

Mary said, 'She's a thoroughly unpleasant woman. Please don't try to defend her to me. She is feckless, immoral, lazy, a liar and a blackmailer. I've tried many times to find *some* good in her, but I always fail.'

'She gave you Alexander,' he reminded her quietly and when Mary made no answer he went on, 'Look, Mary, I came here because we've got to talk. I also want to explain that so far my wife knows nothing about this and to be honest, that's partly why I gave the boy the money. I wanted him to go away – to give me time to think. It's a terrible thing suddenly to find out that you have a son. We have no children yet, you see, and maybe we never will. It will be a great blow to my wife to learn that I had a child by another woman all those years ago – she will be dreadfully hurt.'

'Must you tell her?'

'I think so. I would like everything to be honest and above-board.'

Just then Mrs Markham arrived with the tray and set it down on the small table. Sensing the tension between Mary and her visitor, she gave Bertie an anxious glance before leaving them again.

'Please,' said Mary, 'let's sit down again. I'm sure we both need a cup of tea – this isn't easy for either of us.'

He watched her pour tea and milk into bone china cups. This was an elegant home and his illegitimate son had been very fortunate.

'Mary,' he said, 'I'm very anxious that we shouldn't quarrel over Alexander. As you say, he is your legal son and I do not want to dispute that or take him away from you. If that puts your mind at ease . . .'

'It does.'

She handed him a cup of tea and offered the plate of biscuits which he refused. Bertie noted with relief that her initial coldness was giving way to a cautious warmth.

He said, 'I want to thank you for all you've done for Alexander. He is a fine young man and I'm sure you are very proud of him. You must be very fond of each other and I envy you that.'

'It *is* a close bond,' said Mary. 'That disagreement over the girl was nothing – all very foolish. I was very upset at the time, but this letter has resolved all that and now we are friends again.' She smiled. 'Sylvia's parents also wrote to me – a charming note. They have invited me to join them all in Berne for a short holiday and I have written back to accept.'

Bertie smiled. 'I'm so glad,' he said and Mary realised with surprise that his pleasure was genuine.

They sipped their tea, watching each other over the teacups, relaxing into the unfamiliar situation. Then Bertie said, 'We both want what's best for Alexander.'

Mary nodded. 'Of course.'

'We're both in a bit of a spot,' he continued. 'I have to tell Beatrice about Alexander and you have to tell him about me. We should help each other, for his sake.'

'We can try,' agreed Mary.

'He's been attempting to trace his mother,' said Bertie.

'I know. But he didn't find her and I don't want him to. You won't encourage him, I hope?'

'No. Mollie herself doesn't wish it.' Bertie explained the circumstances of Mollie's encounter with Alexander and went on, 'I hope we are doing the right thing. If Alexander finds out later on, if Mollie dies, he may feel terrible guilt and blame us for keeping the truth from him.'

'Dear God!' Mary burst out suddenly, 'I almost wish she would die! If only you know how I loathe and despise her. Oh, I know what you think,' she said, correctly interpreting the expression on his face. 'I belong to the mission and we do our best to help these people. Some of them deserve help and we give it gladly. Others abuse our kindness and take advantage of us. They laugh at us behind our backs – oh, I'm not blind! I see how they sneer at us even while they mouth those grateful phrases.'

He was taken aback by her sudden vehemence and said, 'Not all of them, surely?'

'Not all, but a fair number. People like Mollie Pett. I know you will make excuses for her and remember her as a young, innocent girl. But I don't think the Mollie Petts of this world are ever truly innocent. Greed, that's all that motivates her – something for nothing is all she wants.'

'Well, she won't trouble you much longer,' said Bertie. 'She looks terrible – pale and gaunt, with that sweet smell of disease about her.' He shuddered.

'Did she ask you for money?'

'I gave her a few pounds,' he said, evading the question. 'I felt sorry for her, whatever you may say. Her life can't have been easy with three children and no man of her own – '

'She has only herself to blame,' Mary snapped. 'Too free with her favours!'

'Men take advantage of women like that,' he said sharply. 'I did. She was young and pretty with cheerful lively ways and I was a lonely young soldier – these things happen all the time. You can't put all the blame on the woman.'

'*I can*,' said Mary. 'Unless she's being raped, a woman can say "No". Mollie and her kind are a sight too free with "Yes".' She made an effort to speak more calmly. 'But we're not here to concern ourselves with Mollie Pett – Alexander is our main concern. At least,' she corrected herself hastily, 'he's my concern.'

'I did think,' said Bertie, 'that if and when I can afford it, I should perhaps help financially . . . '

'No, Mr Harris, I will not allow it', cried Mary. 'I am his legal guardian and I will support him in every way. When I die, everything will be his – the house, all my money, everything. Meanwhile he has a generous allowance and will never want. Please keep your money; I am sure you can put it to good use. Another cup of tea?'

'No, thank you. Will you write and tell him?'

Mary considered for a moment. 'Yes,' she said, 'I shall tell him about you and remind him of your address. Then no doubt he will write to you. I must say,' she added, 'that he could have done a lot worse for a father. Until I knew it was you, I used to imagine the most unsuitable man appearing suddenly out of the blue to be a bad influence on him and ruin his life. You were a great relief to me. I suppose you will want to tell Vinnie?'

'Of course; I think she will be pleased.'

'I am sure of it – and when will you tell your wife?'

'Tonight.' He sighed. 'It won't be easy, but the longer I wait the harder it will become.'

As Mary raised her second cup of tea to her lips, he saw that her hands trembled. She set down the cup and for a long time said nothing, her eyes downcast and a slightly puzzled frown on her face. At last she raised her eyes to his and he thought how very vulnerable she looked.

'It's a strange feeling,' she said, 'suddenly to be discussing Alexander with someone else. All these years I have made decisions alone. I never realised how it helps to share the responsibility.' She smiled faintly. 'I dreaded you discovering the truth, you know, and yet now you have and here we are talking like two civilised people about someone we both care for. It was fear, I suppose, that kept me silent – fear that you would try to take him away. He is all I have in the world. Can you find it in your heart to forgive me?'

'There's nothing to forgive,' said Bertie. 'I admire you tremendously for the way you've cared for Alexander. I shudder to imagine what his life would have been like with poor Mollie. I keep thinking that I've missed all his childhood – you've been so lucky.'

'He's still growing,' said Mary, 'and I imagine you'll see him frequently when he comes back to England.'

Bertie wanted to enquire about Sylvia, but decided against it. Mary, he thought, had so far behaved very well towards him and he did not want to risk provoking her in any way.

'Well, Mary,' he said. 'We're on the same side, then?'

She rose to her feet and held out her hand. 'Yes, Bertie, we are.' She laughed shakily. 'Hard to believe, but there it is! We still have problems, of course and I do hope your wife will not be too upset. It will be a great shock to her and if there is anything I can do to help – if I can talk to her, maybe – please let me know. Sometimes two women can speak more easily together than a woman and a man. And I will write to tell your son – that sounds so strange – later today. I suppose you are looking forward to him knowing?'

'I am really. I just hope he can accept it.'

'Gaining a father must be rather exciting,' Mary mused as she walked with him to the door.

Bertie laughed. 'Gaining a son is terrifying,' he confessed.

Hearing them in the hall, Mrs Markham came out of the kitchen and handed Bertie his hat.

Impulsively Mary said, 'Mrs Markham, I know you're very fond of Alexander. I would like you to meet his father!'

'His *father*!' cried the housekeeper. 'But – oh, ma'am, d'you mean it?' She turned to Bertie. 'You're the boy's father?'

Bertie nodded and while Mrs Markham still reeled from the shock, Mary opened the front door. Bertie shook her hand and then turned to the housekeeper.

'I can see Alexander's been in very good hands all these years,' he told her with a smile. 'I must go now, but I'm sure your mistress will tell you all about it.' He turned to Mary. 'I hope to see you again before too long.'

He raised his hat and with a final wave, walked away down the street.

'His *father*!' echoed Mrs Markham. 'Sprung out of nowhere, just like that?'

Mary closed the door and leaned against it. Closing her eyes, she gave a great sigh of relief. Then she looked at the older woman and smiled.

'I think we have got something to celebrate,' she said slowly. 'If you will join me for a glass of madeira, Mrs Markham, I will tell you all about it.'

*

Beatrice cut three thick slices from the loaf and worried. Bertie had been to see the solicitors and had returned in a strange mood. She knew him well enough to recognise repressed excitement when she saw it, no matter how hard he tried to conceal it. Something had happened at the solicitors, she knew that much. So why, she wondered, was he keeping it to himself unless it was bad news? He was making great efforts to appear normal and unaffected and so far she had pretended to notice nothing out of the ordinary.

Bertie took a slice of bread and spread it generously with butter.

'We're not made of money,' Bea said pointedly.

He glanced at his bread guiltily. 'Sorry, love,' he said, 'I wasn't thinking what I was doing.' He scraped off some of the butter and pressed it on to the side of his plate.

'Do for the next slice,' he said, his voice artificially jovial. 'Is that still Foxearth jam?' He picked up the pot of strawberry jam and examined it with enthusiasm before helping himself liberally.

'It's the last jar,' said Bea. 'There's a bit of cheese left if you'd rather?'

'Too late!' he grinned, taking a large mouthful and apparently finding it more difficult than usual to chew and swallow.

'There's a couple of jars of honey and then it's all gone,' she told him.

'Good old Mrs Bryce, eh?'

'Yes.' And good old Bertie Harris, she thought. What on earth had he been up to?

'How did it go?' she asked at last.

Bertie's hand hovered half-way to his mouth with the bread and jam.

'How did what go?'

'At the solicitor.'

'Oh, that.' He took another large mouthful and began to chew, making quite a performance of it.

Bea watched him uneasily. There was more in his manner than merely excitement, she decided, but what was it? Fear perhaps, or guilt? But no, that was impossible. They were financially sound, and there was little room for disappointment or failure. Not rich on a day-to-day basis maybe, but certainly sound.

'So how did it go?' she repeated as he swallowed the bread. He took yet another huge mouthful and mumbled something inaudible.

'Bertie!' she cried, her patience evaporating. 'How did it *go*? I want to know, so stop stuffing your face with food and tell me. For heaven's sake! It's not a secret, is it?'

Bertie's feigned cheerfulness deserted him and seeing this, Bea's uneasiness became anxiety.

'Bertie, tell me what happened?' she insisted. 'What did he say? I can't bear not knowing.'

He reached forward to put a hand over hers, but she snatched it away.

'Tell me,' she insisted. '*Now!*'

He swallowed hard. 'Bea, it won't be easy for me – or for you . . . ' he began. She jumped to her feet and shouted, 'Just tell me!'

'Look, sit down, Bea,' he begged. 'It won't do any good to get all upset before I've – '

'*Bertie!*'

'Sit down and I'll tell you,' he repeated.

'Tell me now, for God's sake!' she begged. A dreadful thought had occurred to her. 'Oh Bertie, it wasn't the solicitor, was it? You went to the doctor! Bertie . . . '

Panic-stricken she sank down on to the chair. He was ill – Bertie was ill and he was going to die, and he had delayed telling her.

'It was *not* the doctor,' he told her. 'But it wasn't the solicitor either. It was – '

'Not the solicitor?' She looked at him, confused and afraid.

'I went to see Mary Bellweather,' he said.

'Mary Bellweather? But you said you were going to the solicitor.'

'I know I did, Bea. I'm sorry.'

'But you never lie to me,' she said. 'Never!'

'I know. This time . . . I was afraid to tell you the truth because I didn't want to have to explain it all before I'd seen her. It was about something that happened a long time ago.'

'To Mary Bellweather?'

'No, to me.'

She stared at him. 'You knew her a long time ago – is that what you mean?'

'No.' He sighed deeply. 'I'm not explaining it properly; I'll start again.'

He swallowed and she saw the constriction of his throat. He was not looking at her directly and she thought, 'He's going to lie to me again!'

'And no more lies?' she begged quickly.

'No, I swear it! It's all about Alexander,' he began. 'His mother is a woman called Mollie Pett.'

Bea looked at him blankly, then remembered the woman who had asked for a job as barmaid.

'Good heavens! *That* Mollie Pett? The one I told you about? The one who looked so ill?'

Bertie nodded.

'Good heavens!' she said again. 'What a small world!'

'Isn't it?'

'But why – I mean, what's it got to do with you? Why did Mary Bellweather tell you that?'

Bertie took a deep breath. 'The boy told me,' he said, 'when he came that day and you went out shopping.'

'Then why – '

'He told me about his mother – and his father.'

Beatrice waited patiently, but her husband appeared dumb-struck and he stared fixedly at the table.

'I still don't see what it's got to do with you,' she said. 'Let them sort out their own problems. Why drag you into it? Don't they think you've got enough worries of your own to think about, without expecting you to—'

She broke off in alarm as he suddenly covered his face with his hands and a slight groan escaped him.

'Bertie! What's up, love? You *are* ill!'

He shook his head. She went to him and tried to prise his fingers from his face, but he resisted her efforts.

'Bertie! Look at me!' she ordered.

'It's no good,' he said. 'I don't know how to tell you. I don't want to tell you, but I must.'

Beatrice took a small step backwards. 'Tell me *what*?'

'About the boy, Bea.' He moved his hands helplessly. 'He's mine, Bea. That boy Alexander – he's mine. My son!'

The shock was so great that for a moment Bea felt literally turned to stone. She could not think, hear or speak. The world around her became a total blank and she felt cut off, isolated. Then merciful oblivion gave way slowly to a painful reality as Bertie's words echoed in her brain.

'I'm sorry, Bea,' he whispered, his eyes wide and tragic. 'I didn't mean to hurt you this way. I didn't *know* about him – I haven't deceived you. I swear I didn't know. But now that I do know, I had to tell you. Oh, Bea, don't look at me like that. He's a nice boy, he's a decent lad. Mary has—'

'It's Mary now, is it?' Bea said dully. 'What happened to Mary Bellweather?'

'Mary Bellweather, then. What does it matter? She's not important. What matters is—'

Beatrice was shaking her head from side to side. 'Then that woman—' she whispered. 'That awful creature . . . Oh God, no! Not you and her, Bertie. You *couldn't* have!'

Unable to bear her accusing eyes, he stood up and turned away. 'She wasn't always like that,' he said. 'Once she was young and—'

'Don't!' she cried. 'I don't want to hear it. I don't want to know anything about you and that slut. I can't believe it of you, Bertie. Not you and her – ever. Oh, Bertie!' Her eyes filled with tears. 'I don't want to believe it. Tell me it isn't true. Not my Bertie and that awful – oh God, tell me it isn't true!'

'It *is* true!' he said sharply. 'I can't deny it, so don't ask me to. It was a long time ago and I will explain if you'll let me—'

'No!'

'Then you'll have to believe it, Bea. That boy is my son. There's no way I could deny it – even if I wanted to.'

Her head jerked up so that their eyes met squarely. 'And you don't want to deny it? Is that what you're saying?'

'Yes, Bea. I don't want to.'

'And Mary Bellweather knows all this? What on earth does she think about it?'

He nodded. 'She accepts it; she's known for some time.' He moved towards her with arms outstretched to enfold her, but she held up her hands as though to ward off a blow.

'Don't touch me, Bertie,' she whispered. 'Just don't come near me! I don't know what to say or do – I'm lost without you.'

'But I'm still here, Bea. I'm the same man—'

'You're *not*!' she cried. 'Of course you're not – you're a stranger with a son!'

'But he's a nice lad, Bea. You said so yourself.'

'I'm not saying he isn't, but *my* Bertie hasn't got a son! Don't you see? It makes everything so *different*. I don't know you, I don't know *me*. I don't know anything any more. I'm lost. Lost. Oh God, Bertie, how *could* you!' She began to sob. 'All these years . . .' The words came out in gasps, barely coherent. 'I've loved you all these years and now – look at us, Bertie. We're strangers. I can't bear it!'

He tried again to put his arms round her, but she pushed him away.

'Save your cuddles for *her*,' she cried, suddenly vehement. 'Your precious Mollie – the mother of your *son*!' Full realisation was slowly dawning and bitterness now mingled with grief and shock. 'All these years I've longed to give you a child. It's been so awful, Bertie, you'll never know. Awful for you, maybe, but so much worse for me. To be a failure – all these years I've felt so terrible, failing you, knowing you were childless. And all the time you had a child – and by that creature!'

'She was a young woman, Bea, that's all,' he said wretchedly. 'Not a creature. Not a slut.'

Bea jumped to her feet, her eyes blazing. 'Don't you dare defend her to me. Do you hear me, Bertie? Don't defend her.

Don't talk about her. Oh God, I wish she was dead, that's what I wish!'

'She will be dead soon; she's very ill.'

Bertie sat down slowly, looking tired and desperately unhappy. For a moment she pitied him and longed to take him into her arms, but almost at once the sense of betrayal returned and she hardened her heart. Then his words registered.

'How do you know she'll be dead soon?' she asked sharply.

'I went to see her. She's dying.'

'Good! Good riddance! Bloody good riddance!'

She seized a cup and hurled it across the room and it smashed against the wall, spattering the paper with the dregs.

He shook his head wearily. 'Please, Bea, don't go on like this. You'll make yourself ill and it doesn't help. I wanted you to understand – I hoped you would.'

'Well, I don't!'

'If only you would be calm and sensible, you might—'

'What did she say to you, Bertie? Did she say she was dying?'

'She didn't have to,' he said heavily.

'Well, I'm glad!' As Beatrice looked at her husband, her rage faded temporarily, giving way to malice. 'What does he think about it – Alexander? He knows you're his father, does he?'

'Not yet. Mary's going to write to him.'

'He might disown you,' she said spitefully.

'He might.'

'And Vinnie! Oh, poor Vinnie. She's got a bastard nephew! What does *she* say?'

'She doesn't know yet – I shall write to her.'

'Well, he's not coming here,' she cried.

'No. I don't think he'd want to leave Mary. That's the only home he's known since he was eight.'

'Fell right on his feet, didn't he?'

'I suppose so – but being illegitimate can't have been easy. Kids need a father as well as a mother.'

'You should have thought of that eighteen years ago!'

'I didn't know about him then,' Bertie protested.

'And if you had, you'd have wed *her*, I suppose?'

'I suppose so.'

Bea's eyes blazed again. 'Don't keep saying you suppose so!' she shouted. 'Oh, don't you see, Bertie? This makes it all wrong! Us, I mean – and it's never going to go right. How can it be? It can never be the way it was for us. Never, *ever* again!'

Despair swept over her and once more she crumpled into tears, but this time she allowed him to put his arms round her as her sobs increased to hysterical weeping.

'I want it to be the same,' she stammered. 'I want us to be the way we were, but we can't. He's spoilt it all. *You've* spoilt it all! Oh, yes you have, Bertie. You may not understand, but you have. It's gone, all we had – everything's gone.'

'We can start again,' he urged, 'make a fresh start. If you would only give him a chance it could be fun, the three of us. You always wanted a child and we can share him. He might come round and have tea with us – or we could go for an outing together. It could be *fun*, Bea, if you would let it.'

She raised her head and looked at him, her face blotched with tears, her eyes reddened, and shook her head.

'He's not our sort,' she said. 'You know he's not. Why should he want to come to tea with our kind? He's Mary's son, Bertie. He's what Mary's made him and it's too late.'

A small hope glimmered in Bertie's mind at her words. 'Then you would *like* him to come?' he asked. 'If he would, I mean?'

'No, I wouldn't.'

'But I thought you said—'

'I said he's not our sort. We're just ordinary folk.'

'There's nothing wrong in that.'

'But he's not ordinary, is he? He's one of them – you know what I mean'.

Bertie thought frantically. 'You liked him when he called in,' he reminded her. 'You said how pleasant he was and what nice manners he had.'

'I didn't know then,' she protested.

'But he's the same boy. Put yourself in his shoes, Bea. Think how upset and shocked *he's* going to be!'

'I don't want to see him, Bertie.'

'Well, it wouldn't be just yet. He's gone away.'

Her eyes snapped open. 'Gone away? Why? Who sent him away?'

'He's gone to Switzerland to stay with his lady friend's family. I told you – Sylvia, her name is.'

'Yes, you did. I forgot.'

'Mary's going over to stay with them. She will probably ask them all to England and maybe we'll be invited to meet them.'

He held his breath as Bea looked at him.

'What, go to Mary's house, you mean?' she said.

'Maybe. A sort of reunion. I don't know – I only said maybe. If they want to meet us, that is!'

'Why shouldn't they?' she demanded.

'We're not really their sort, you just said so yourself.'

'You're his father, aren't you?'

Bertie shrugged, afraid to say too much or hope too much. Beatrice sniffed.

'If they came to England,' she said, 'and didn't want to meet Alexander's father, I wouldn't think much of them. I mean, if this Sylvia's supposed to love Alexander and she doesn't want to meet his father . . .' Her indignation grew the more she thought about it.

'He seemed to like me,' said Bertie. 'We seemed to get along . . .chatting together.'

Beatrice sniffed again, took a handkerchief from her pocket and blew her nose loudly. 'At least,' she said, 'he's got a decent father. He might have had a drunkard or a thief. I wonder why Mary didn't tell you before?'

'I expect she was afraid that she would have to share the boy.'

'Well, so she should,' said Bea. 'She's only his adopted parent, but you're his real parent. At least the boy's old enough now to know his own mind and if he wants to spend time with you – with us – oh Bertie, I'm sorry!' Tears filled her eyes. 'I didn't mean all those things I said. At least, not all of them. But it was such a shock . . . Such a terrible shock, and Mollie Pett is so – no, I won't say it again. I don't want it to be different between us, Bertie. I love you and I'm so afraid.'

Gently he stroked her hair. 'It won't be,' he promised. 'I swear it won't make any difference. We still love each other – at least, I still love you. You're still my best girl and I think you've been so brave, so marvellous. I can imagine what a shock it's been.'

She flung her arms around him. 'And poor old you, with all that on your mind! You must have been so worried. I do love you, Bertie and we won't let it make any difference. Just don't talk to me about his real mother. Not ever! I didn't mean what I said about her dying, though. That was wicked of me.'

'It doesn't matter, she's not important. Oh, Beatrice Harris, I adore you but I don't deserve you.'

'You do!' she insisted, kissing him. 'We love each other and we deserve each other . . . Do you think we *will* be invited to Mary Bellweather's?'

'I should think so. You'd have to have a new outfit.'

'Oh no, Bertie, we can't afford it.'

'Of course we can!'

She frowned. 'Is he my step-son, then?'

'I suppose he is.'

'That makes him sort of mine, then?'

'Yes.'

'Maybe just a new hat, Bertie. That old straw—'

'A whole new outfit! It's not every day we find ourselves a son.'

'A good-looking son!'

'And maybe later on a daughter-in-law – and grand-children! What about grandchildren?'

'Oh, Bertie!'

Bea gave a squeal of excitement and as they clung together Bertie knew with a sense of overwhelming relief that the crisis was over.

CHAPTER NINETEEN

Daniel Smith, the wheelwright, was proud of the new box-waggon he was making for Foxearth. It was the first time he had been commissioned by the Lawrences and he hoped it would not be the last. The only stipulation they had made was that he should have the ironwork done by the Teesbury black-smith, instead of the smith at Barming with whom Daniel shared most of his business. Something about 'keeping it in the family', Mrs Lawrence had said, because Andy Roberts at Teesbury had married Rose Bryce, whose mother-in-law had looked after Mrs Lawrence when she was a girl. It all sounded very complicated but Daniel, a large, corpulent man with easygoing ways, told himself that if it meant good money in his pocket, he'd work with Uncle Tom Cobley if they asked him to!

The body of the waggon was finished and in a day or two he would begin to paint it in traditional Kent colours – buff for the body, with a scarlet undercarriage and wheels. The shape was also traditional, with the sturdy curves that had characterised the Kent waggons for hundreds of years. Now he stood in the yard at the back of the Teesbury smithy, while the fourth wooden wheel was clamped down on to the tyring platform – a circular area of metal set into the ground. Daniel was proud of his skill and hoped that his audience appreciated to the full all that had gone into the creation of the wheel. Andy Roberts had measured the wheel's rim, had cut a suitable strip of metal and was now hammering it into a circle inside the smithy.

Mrs Bryce, standing beside Daniel, put her hands over her ears.

'I don't know how Andy stands that noise,' she said. 'That banging goes right through my head. Can't do him any good, surely, that noise in his ears all day? Wonder he's not deaf with it. I'm sure I would be.'

Rose, with the wide-eyed baby in her arms, grinned at her. 'He says he doesn't notice it,' she said. 'I suppose you do get used to it. He gets agitated though if the baby cries, but that never worries me – had too many crying babies in my time, I suppose. It's the noise you're not used to that bothers you.'

Tommy Bryce, Rose's eldest son, helped Daniel Smith to settle the wooden wheel carefully into place. Tommy was keen to follow in his stepfather's footsteps. Daniel gave the clamp handle a final twist and then straightened up, tugged down his waistcoat and settled his cap more firmly into position.

'You should have been a wheelwright,' he told Tommy with a grin. 'It's much quieter than all that.' He jerked a thumb towards the smithy, then turned to Vinnie who was also watching the proceedings. 'That's a nice set of wheels, ma'am,' he told her. 'Very neat job, though maybe I shouldn't blow me own trumpet. Still, who else will if I don't? Seasoned elm, that hub is, and the spokes are heart of oak – I won't use nothing else – and all shaped by hand. You see there?' He leaned forward to describe his handiwork. 'A tongue in one end of each spoke fits into the hub, the tongue at the other end goes into a section of the wooden rim. A "felloe" we call it. First we tap all the spokes into place in the hub, then add each felloe until we've got a complete rim.'

'But how,' Vinnie asked him, 'does it all stay together?'

Daniel Smith beamed at her. 'Well now, that's where the smith comes in,' he said. 'He puts the metal tyre round it. Young Tommy here will tell you – he saw the other wheels done – ah, too late! Here comes Mr Roberts now. Stand well back, folks, because that tyre's been in the furnace and it's *very* hot!'

As though alarmed by this information, the baby started to whimper and Mrs Bryce held out her arms eagerly.

'Give the little pet to her grandma,' she said and Rose handed her over willingly.

Vinnie was watching the proceedings with interest, although she had come to the smithy hoping to find Rose on her own. Another message had awaited Philippe at Leysdown, recalling him urgently to France and he had crossed on the next boat. To her intense dismay, Vinnie had not seen him before he left England and had received only a brief note telling her of his departure. She wanted very much to talk to Rose about him, but instead had stumbled on the tyring ceremony. Now the wheelwright hurried over to help Andy carry the metal tyre, which smoked with the heat, and then the spectators drew back as it was carefully lowered into place around the waiting wheel.

'Get the water, lad!' cried Andy and, guiltily, Tommy rushed to refill the bucket from the nearby tap.

While the metal was still hot, Andy hammered it into place. As it cooled it would contract and exert pressure on the rim of the wheel, and it was this pressure which would hold it all together. If the spokes were not identical in size or one of the joints was poorly made, Daniel knew the wheel would buckle and break up.

'The moment of truth!' Rose whispered to Vinnie.

They all watched anxiously as Tommy splashed the hot tyre with water to cool it before it could burn the wooden rim. Andy waited also, his own skill being tested, for if he had over-estimated the circumference of the tyre then it would not grip.

'There she goes!' said Andy modestly, with a pleased nod of his head. 'I reckon that's fair enough.'

Daniel nodded. 'What say we let young Tommy douse this one? He'll never learn if he don't try.'

Andy agreed and Tommy, eager to demonstrate his own skill, carefully unclamped the wheel. To one side of the yard there was a long iron trough full of water; Tommy rolled the wheel over to it and lifted it in, submerging the outer half of the wheel and turning it slowly round so that the metal tyre cooled evenly.

Andy watched him with hands on hips and lips pursed, then

he and Daniel moved forward together to satisfy themselves that the finished wheel reached the high standard for which each man was respected.

At last Tommy lifted the dripping wheel from the trough and everyone gathered round for the final inspection.

'That looks perfect,' said Vinnie, feeling that her approval was required. 'A really fine wheel.'

Rose glanced proudly at her husband and her son, who exchanged pleased looks with each other.

Daniel winked. 'Teamwork, ma'am,' he said. 'You can't beat it! That waggon of yours is going to look a right winner. I'll get the paint on her and she'll do you proud.'

Mrs Bryce carried the baby back into the house and Rose and Vinnie prepared to follow her.

'If you men want to celebrate,' said Rose, 'there's one of last year's cider barrels just tapped. Why not quench your thirst? I'll make us ladies a cup of tea.'

Daniel looked at her admiringly. 'Now why didn't I marry a sensible lass like that?' he asked as he tugged at his waistcoat and adjusted his cap before following Andy and Tommy back into the smithy.

*

Half an hour later, Mrs Bryce volunteered to take the baby in her pram to meet the younger children from school, so Rose made another pot of tea and prepared to catch up on Vinnie's exciting news.

'Philippe is so *different*, Rose,' Vinnie told her earnestly. 'He's just not like an Englishman. Not that I mean anything against Andy or your Tom . . . or anyone . . . but I mean generally. You know how shy and reserved Englishmen are? Philippe is not a bit like that. He says the most wonderful things – oh, Rose, I'd be embarrassed to tell you. And his eyes! Rose, I can read what he's thinking in his eyes!'

Rose poured out a cup of tea for each of them and cut two slices of fruit cake. Ten minutes later Vinnie's tea was still untouched and she had taken only one bite from the cake.

'So, what's he doing now?' Rose asked when at last Vinnie paused for breath and began to stir her cold tea. 'Why has he returned to France? And more important,' she grinned, 'when is he coming back?'

Vinnie's expression changed as the excitement left her eyes. 'I don't know,' she said slowly. 'It was all rather sudden. He sent me a message to say he'd gone to Leysdown and would be back later in the day, and then another message that evening to say he'd had to go home – urgent family business, whatever that means. Oh, Rose, I don't know why he went, but I feel so terribly lost without him.'

'Poor Vinnie!'

'But he will come back.'

'Of course he will.'

Rose saw the doubt in Vinnie's eyes. 'Go on,' she said, 'finish the telling – and eat your cake. It's getting cold!' Her mild attempt at humour passed Vinnie by completely.

Vinnie looked down vaguely at the cake and then back at Rose. 'It was that very morning after we'd . . . well, it was the very next morning that he left. It was so dreadful, Rose; I just wanted to be in his arms. I just needed him so much and he'd gone. I don't know how I got through the day – except that it was that awful mission picnic at Camber Sands and I'd promised to go, so I had to. I had planned to invite him, you see.'

'I expect it helped to take your mind off things,' said Rose.

'That's just it, it *didn't*,' cried Vinnie. 'I couldn't bear it. I'd expected the two of us to be together there and I thought what fun it would be – and then I had to go on my own.' She stared earnestly at Rose, her expression anguished.

'Poor Vinnie,' said Rose. 'I do know what being lonely feels like. After Tom died, I was lonely. Even though I had all the kids, I was lonely for Tom.'

'Poor Rose!'

They stared earnestly at each other, commiserating, drawn closer by their common experience of loss.

'Dare I ask you something?' said Rose.

'Anything!' cried Vinnie. 'If you only knew what a comfort it is to have someone to talk to. I knew you'd understand! He went on Sunday morning and now it's Tuesday and there's been no word – not a telegram, nothing.'

'About the future,' said Rose, 'do you think you might marry Philippe Delain?'

'Marry him?' Vinnie's tone was agonised. 'Oh, Rose, I do hope so! I know it's sudden and I know he's a foreigner – and maybe he's a bit younger than me, I'm not sure—'

'Age doesn't matter,' broke in Rose wisely. 'Not when you're in love.'

'Of course it doesn't,' said Vinnie. 'And I do love him, Rose! I adore him – and I think he loves me. I was so happy; I never thought it would be like this!'

'What about William?' asked Rose. 'Wasn't it the same with William?'

Vinnie shook her head. 'Oh, no! That wasn't love at first sight. We sort of grew together, you know. Everyone expected it and William was so eager. I did love him but now, looking back on it, I think perhaps it was more in a sisterly way.'

Rose sat up suddenly. 'Vinnie!' she gasped. 'Philippe going off like that! Maybe he's gone home to break the news to his family? To ask his father's permission to marry you, or whatever they have to do in France! Because it *was* sudden, him going so quickly!'

For a moment Vinnie stared at her and then she covered her face with her hands. 'Do you think so?' she whispered.

'It's not what *I* think,' said Rose. 'It's what *you* think. I don't even know him and I've only seen him twice: that day when he crashed his machine in the hop-field and then at the hopping supper. Do *you* think that could be why he went home so suddenly? Look at me, Vinnie! What do you think?'

Slowly Vinnie uncovered her face and Rose saw the hope in her eyes.

'Oh Rose, I never would have thought of that, but you could be right. Maybe they didn't send for him – he just went home to tell them and wanted it to be a surprise.'

Rose clapped her hands. 'And when he's got their blessing, he'll come back and ask you and then take you to France to meet his family – oh, Vinnie, he might even bring a ring!'

'Oh Rose! It just could be.' Vinnie sighed. 'I feel so much better about everything now. I wasn't going to say anything but it did seem so unfeeling to just go away like that after everything that had happened. He didn't even wake me to kiss me good-bye – oh!' She clamped a hand over her mouth as Rose grinned, delighted by Vinnie's slip of the tongue.

'So *that's* what happened,' cried Rose. 'It's like a fairy story, isn't it? It's so romantic. Don't worry, Vinnie, I won't tell a soul, I promise. And don't you fret – I'm sure he'll come back.'

'Oh, I do hope so!' said Vinnie. 'I don't know what I shall do if he doesn't.' Impulsively she jumped up and moved round the table to hug Rose hard. 'And if he does ask me to marry him, Rose, you'll be the first to know!'

*

Janet always woke the Colonel from his afternoon nap at three o'clock, because she had learned by experience that if he slept for too long in the afternoon, he did not sleep well at night.

She had her own lunch in the kitchen with the rest of the staff, then took Cook's *Daily Mail* upstairs to read to the Colonel, for although he pretended to despise the newspaper he was always disappointed if she forgot it.

'Sir, wake up now!' she urged, shaking him gently by the arm. 'It's three o'clock, sir and I've brought up the *Mail*.'

There was no response, so she leaned over and spoke a little louder. 'Sir, it's three o'clock and you've had your nap.'

The eyelids did not flicker and the pale face remained expressionless against the lace-edged pillow. The Colonel's mouth was slightly open and his breathing was very shallow, so only an occasional rasping sound showed that his lungs were still functioning. Wispy white hair fringed his freckled bald head and his skin had a transparency that allowed the veins to show through.

One clawlike hand held up the blanket to his chin, while the other was hidden beneath the bedclothes. Janet looked at him closely, with the familiar prickling of fear. 'This is how it will be,' she thought. 'I shall try to wake him from his nap and he'll be dead.' She had tried to prepare herself for the day when this would happen, and it never occurred to her that it might turn out any other way.

'Colonel?' she insisted, gently pulling the blanket away from his chin. 'Wake up, sir!'

Each day it seemed more difficult to wake him, as though he slipped deeper into sleep and found it that much harder to return to consciousness. Did he want to die, she wondered. Did the Colonel feel that being alive was too much of an effort? In his frail state it would be so easy, so tempting, to let go. She was becoming obsessed with the possibility of his death and often lay awake during the long hours of the night, fearful at the prospect of losing him. Over the past few years he had become much more to her than a patient, although she would admit the fact to no one else. The old man had assumed the role of the father she could not remember and she had to be careful – when talking about him to other members of the staff – not to refer to him in a way that might appear over-familiar. The extent of her fondness for the Colonel was a secret even from the old man himself.

'Colonel Lawrence, sir!' She raised her voice slightly and patted the side of his face.

He spoke suddenly, in a whisper. 'Don't, Nursie! I'm sorry.'

Shocked, Janet looked at him, mistrusting her own hearing. The Colonel never called her anything but 'Janet'.

'Colonel, what are you saying?' she demanded. 'And who's this "Nursie"? I'm Janet – Open your eyes and see for yourself.'

He whispered again. 'I didn't mean it. No! Please!'

Her unease increased. Was he delirious, she wondered. How could he be delirious if he wasn't ill? He had no temperature.

'Sir, wake *up*!'

She shook him more roughly than she intended, almost

afraid of him in his semi-conscious state, and was relieved to see him open his eyes at last. Her relief, however, was short-lived for the old man stared round the room with an expression of great confusion and then put up an arm defensively as though to shield his face.

'Don't, Nursie! Don't!' he repeated.

A cold fear clutched at Janet's heart. 'Don't say things like that,' she said shakily. 'I'm not "Nursie". I'm Janet. You know me! I'm not going to hurt you, sir, and there's no "Nursie" here.'

His pale watery eyes looked into hers without recognition and she fought down a rising panic.

'Now sir, I'm Janet and I'm going to sit you up,' she said as briskly as she could, struggling to keep her tone and manner normal. 'Push yourself up – that's the ticket.' She began to tug him into a sitting position. 'Then I'll pour your medicine and read to you from Cook's *Daily Mail*. Up you come, now, that's the way.'

In spite of her urging, the Colonel made no effort to help her, but he weighed so little that she finally managed to get him into a sitting position and propped him up with the pillows. Then she looked at him anxiously and was relieved to see the confused expression in his eyes giving way slowly to one of recognition.

'Are you with me now, sir?' she asked. 'You must have been dreaming with your eyes open. Gave me quite a fright, you did, sir, calling me "Nursie" like that. Were you dreaming, Colonel?'

'I don't know,' he said weakly. 'She was here: she was so real.' He shook his head as he watched her uncork the medicine bottle, memories beginning to flow into his mind. 'She was so unkind to us,' he said, 'that nurse. We hated her, Janet, d'you know that? Yes, we hated that nurse.' He opened his mouth obligingly and took the proffered medicine. Swallowing it made him cough and splutter; Janet waited until he had recovered and then wiped his mouth and chin with a small hand towel.

'Unkind, sir?' she asked. 'In what way was she unkind?'

The old man looked vaguely around the room as though seeking an answer to her question.

'She bullied us, Janet, that's what she did,' he said at last. 'That's how she was unkind. She bullied us and she shut us in the garden shed. We hated that shed – it was so dark, you see. We were very young and easily frightened. "Nursie!" We had to call her that, but we hated her. No one could hear us, you see. The shed was a long way from the house and I used to think she'd forget me and leave me there all night. I can see her now!'

'You called me "Nursie",' Janet told him reproachfully. 'It made me feel all funny, you not recognising me. That nurse sounds like a monster. They shouldn't allow people like that to be in charge of little children. You should have told your parents.'

'We didn't dare, Janet. We didn't think they'd believe us and we knew she would most certainly deny it. But she left after about a year. Might have been longer. She went very suddenly and I remember we weren't allowed to know why. My mother was a very strict woman with very strong moral principles. Maybe the girl stole something, or was impudent or encouraged followers – that wasn't allowed, of course. Oh, dear me no. It might have been any of those things – or perhaps she was idle or not clean about her person. "Nursie," we called her, but she was such a bully.'

Janet pulled a chair close to the bed and unfolded the *Daily Mail*. 'Well, you forget all about her, sir,' she advised. 'It was good riddance to bad rubbish when she left, if you want my opinion. Nursie, indeed! And don't you go dreaming about her any more, sir! You gave me a real turn looking at me that way. I'm Janet, not Nursie, and *I* don't bully you!'

'You nag me, though,' he said with a twinkle in his eye.

Janet grinned. 'Only for your own good,' she told him. 'Now, let's see what the *Mail* has got to tell us today.' She ran her eye down the front page. 'There's a bit about the cost of living and something about that railway accident . . . A piece about the

murder in Stepney – another item here about the fishing
industry. Looks a bit boring—'

The Colonel shook his head to all these suggestions. 'I've
heard it all already,' he grumbled. 'It's all in *The Times* and they
do it so much better. Find the gardening column, Janet, there's
a good girl – and read it slowly. You know I can't follow it if you
gabble.'

She had just refolded the newspaper when there was a brief
knock at the door and Vinnie came into the room, waving a
letter and trying unsuccessfully to hide her agitation.

'Will you leave us, Janet?' she said and then, seeing the
alarm on her face, added, 'It's nothing to worry about. You'll
hear about it all in good time, but I want to tell the Colonel
first.'

'Yes, ma'am.'

Janet laid the paper on the bedside table and vacated the
chair. As she reached the door, she glanced back and saw
Vinnie at the foot of the bed unfolding the letter.

'I'm sorry to disturb you,' Vinnie told the Colonel, 'but I had
to see you right away. I've had the most terrible shock.'

The Colonel frowned. 'It's that young flyer,' he said. 'I knew
no good would come of encouraging a foreigner.'

'Philippe? Oh no.' Vinnie shook her head. 'It's nothing to do
with him – It's my brother Bertie. I can hardly believe it but
. . . ' She shrugged helplessly. 'He says in the letter that he's
just discovered that he had a child by Mollie Pett, of all people,
and – '

'Do I know the woman?' the old man asked. 'Mollie Pett? It
rings a bell.'

'That awful woman who broke the bedroom window years
ago when the hoppers were protesting about the old barn . . .
and Julian was so terribly angry and Mollie ran away.' Vinnie
paused for breath and then rushed on, 'She left a boy here,
Alexander. Oh Colonel, you must remember Alexander! He
hasn't been down for a few years now, but you used to say you
liked him and what a fine boy he was.'

The Colonel shook his head. 'Alexander? But he's Mary's

boy, isn't he? Mary Bellweather's boy. Yes, of course I remember him but – '

'That's right,' said Vinnie. 'Mary adopted him legally because Mollie Pett didn't want him. Now Bertie says in here' – she waved the letter – 'that Alexander is *his* son! Honestly, Colonel, I'm so shocked, I hardly know what to think. Bertie and that awful Mollie! I can't believe it; I don't *want* to believe it!'

Restlessly she turned and walked to the window then turned again and walked back.

The Colonel shook his head once more. 'I don't see it, somehow,' he said. 'I mean, dammit, Bertie's been abroad for years. India, wasn't it? It beats me how he can be the boy's father if he's been in India all those years. Bit unlikely, I'd say, wouldn't you? Got his wires crossed, I should think!'

Vinnie scanned the pages. 'Ah, here it is: "I spent one weekend in London with Adam before we rejoined our regiment and we met two girls. I spent the night with one of them. It was Mollie Pett." Oh, how awful! How could he have been so stupid?'

'A young man's fancy,' the old man suggested tolerantly. 'He was young and no doubt the woman was a pretty little thing then. A young soldier on leave is a good catch, you see, for a woman. Money in his pocket and wanting a good time. It's called wild oats, Vinnie, but you wouldn't understand. Women never do understand the way a young man's heart can be captured by a certain smile or the sight of a neat ankle. And what of it, eh? There's no harm done.'

Weakly Vinnie sat down in the chair. 'No harm done, you say? But poor Bea,' she reminded him. 'It must have upset her terribly. How can you say there's no harm done? And Mary Bellweather, too – it's such a dreadful shock for everyone.'

The Colonel chuckled at her dismay. 'Not so dreadful for Alexander, is it? The boy's found himself a respectable father after all these years – and a respectable aunt, too. He's your nephew, isn't he? I should think the lad's well-pleased. Nothing dreadful about it from *his* point of view.'

'My nephew!' Vinnie repeated. 'That means he's the children's cousin! Oh, it's all so . . . so unexpected. I don't know what to say.'

The old man was enjoying her discomfiture. 'Not a lot you can say, is there?' he said. 'The boy's found his father and that's how it should be. It could be a lot worse.'

'I suppose so,' said Vinnie. 'At least he's had a decent upbringing. Mary has given him everything. Poor Mary!'

'It's not "poor Mary" at all! She's had the pleasure of his company all these years, so she can count herself very fortunate.'

'But poor Beatrice!' Vinnie sighed disconsolately. 'That awful Mollie Pett!' she repeated. 'It's all her fault. Oh, don't wag your finger at me, Colonel! I know what you're thinking, but I'm sure she must have led him on. Bertie wouldn't have done a thing like that.'

'Of course he would, you silly girl!' laughed the Colonel. 'I've told you he was a young soldier in the big bad city on a few days' leave. It happens all the time, girl. Why should your brother be any different?'

'But whatever am I going to say to him?' cried Vinnie. 'To Bertie, I mean. I shall have to answer this letter.'

'Congratulate him on having a fine son and say you hope that in time he *and* Beatrice will find the lad a source of pleasure. Life's too short, Vinnie for recriminations. Remember . . . "There but for the grace of God, go I." '

Vinnie stood up, looking very unhappy and not at all reassured by the Colonel's attitude. 'Everyone will be laughing at us,' she said. 'And the hoppers will love it!'

'They'll gossip, of course,' the Colonel agreed, 'but they'll only laugh if they think that you're put out by it. Let them see that you're delighted – and proud of Alexander – and it will be a nine days' wonder soon forgotten. Anyway, you've got a whole year yet before you need to worry about the hoppers again. Oh, cheer up, Vinnie,' he said, 'and put a good face on things. It's not the end of the world. Think what fun it will be for the children to have a grown-up cousin! You'll have to write to Doll and break the news.'

He smiled as Vinnie's expression softened at the thought of the children's pleasure. She stood there for a long time, turning the letter over in her hands, busy with her thoughts while the old man waited. Abruptly, she looked up.

'You're right, Colonel,' she said. 'Yes, you're absolutely right and I'm being selfish and arrogant and silly.' She leaned forward and kissed him lightly. 'You've made me feel much better about it. I'm glad I came to you, and I'm beginning to feel happier already. I shall do as you suggest and write to Bertie straight away.'

The Colonel patted her hand. 'Yes, do that, my dear. We must all help them as much as we can.'

Vinnie laughed suddenly. 'I'm sure you're dying for me to go so that you and Janet can have a good chinwag about it?'

'You did say she'd have to know.'

'Yes, I did. Will you tell her? She'll be so surprised.'

'I'll tell her and gladly. You go along and write to that brother of yours. Send Janet back to me.'

'I will – and thank you again.'

After Vinnie had gone the old man settled himself more comfortably on the pillows, a broad smile on his face. When Janet came back into the room, she was surprised to receive a conspiratorial wink.

'Sir?' she said, sitting down on the chair and reaching for the *Daily Mail*.

Laughingly, the old man put out his hand and laid it over the newspaper. 'We don't need the gardening column today,' he told her. 'In fact, we don't need the *Mail* at all. I've got some news for you, Janet, that will knock the poor old *Mail* into a cocked hat!'

CHAPTER TWENTY

The kitchen at Foxearth was a gloomy place with Cook frowning over the puff pastry, Edie sulking and Mrs Tallant silent with repressed anger. When Tim Bilton put his head round the kitchen door, he took one look at the faces of the occupants and hastily withdrew without asking for a cup of tea as he had intended to do.

'What's up with him?' Cook demanded. 'In and out like a blooming yo-yo.'

'After a quick cuppa, I expect,' said Bertha, who was not herself in a bad mood but was being adversely affected by the mood of the others. She had tried unsuccessfully to lighten the gloom and had now relapsed into a more bearable indifference.

'Cadging, you mean,' said Cook.

Edie, peeling three pounds of cooking apples, looked up sharply to defend her father.

'My pa's not cadging. Who says he's cadging?' she demanded. 'A cup of tea's not cadging.'

'Who asked you to pipe up?' said Cook. 'You mind your own business and get on with your work.'

'I *am* getting on. I can talk and peel apples at the same time.'

'Don't answer back!' said Mrs Tallant.

Bertha, stung out of her apathy, said, 'Well, why does Cook have to pick on her? She's only telling the truth. She *can* talk and peel apples at the same time – anyone can.'

'See!' said Edie rashly, encouraged by Bertha's support.

Cook, with a muttered oath, snatched the peeler from her hand and then clipped the side of Edie's head.

'That's enough cheek from you!' she snapped. 'You can get

up to your room and stay there – and don't bother to come down for any dinner.'

Edie let out a loud wail and immediately burst into ugly, hiccuping tears. Mrs Tallant asked, 'Who's going to peel the apples then?' and Bertha responded, 'Don't look at me! I'm a parlour-maid, not a skivvy.' Then Cook cried, 'I'll do the bleeding apples myself!' and they all fell silent with shock because she had never before used such a word.

'Well!' said Mrs Tallant, who was the first to recover her composure. 'I think this nonsense has gone far enough. Edie, stop bawling and get on with the apples and don't ever speak to Cook like that again! Bertha, you should know better than to encourage her, but we'll say no more about it. We're all feeling a bit down in the dumps and we're getting a bit scratchy. Now I'll make a pot of tea and Edie, you pop down to the stables and tell your Pa he's welcome to a cup if that's what he wanted. Five minutes, tell him. He's got a lot on his plate now Young Harry's not here to lend a hand.'

Harry had been despatched to the cottage in Porthleven to be with Doll and the children. When the holiday season down there had finally ended, Doll had written to complain about the isolation of the cottage and Vinnie, sensing her nervousness, had decided she needed a man about the place to discourage unwanted attentions from any unreliable members of the community. Therefore Tim had to take over all Harry's tasks and as well as caring for the horses he was chopping wood, carrying coal and acting as driver and general handyman, which did not please him at all.

His grievance was real enough, but the rest of the staff were not being overworked. Their ill-humour was a direct result of Vinnie's deep depression, which made her impatient and irritable with everyone around her – a depression which was directly attributable to Philippe Delain who, having gone back to France at very short notice, had not yet returned. Nor had he written to explain his prolonged absence.

Vinnie lived from hour to hour, day to day, in a state of profound distress brought about by physical longing and desperate anxiety. Rose's innocent remarks concerning the possible purpose of Philippe's return to France had roused in her such heady anticipation that her subsequent disappointment was all the greater and an unspoken fear was growing daily in her mind. Her nerves were frayed with uncertainty and apprehension and her temper had suffered as a consequence. All the servants had either felt the lash of her tongue or had seethed under unfair criticism or an undeserved rebuke.

'I wish Doll would come back,' sighed Bertha. 'She's always so cheerful. I really miss Doll, don't you?'

She looked at Edie who, red-eyed, nodded and then sniffed loudly, still mortified by her recent ill-treatment and not prepared to be pacified too easily.

'I wouldn't mind being in her shoes, though, mind you!' said Mrs Tallant. 'A few weeks by the sea would set me up a treat.'

'What, with three kids to look after?' Cook protested. 'Not my idea of a holiday.'

'I've never been to the seaside,' said Edie.

They all looked at her in astonishment. 'Never been to the – what are you on about?' Cook demanded. 'You went to Camber Sands with the mission, didn't you?'

'What if I did?' said Edie.

'Well, Camber Sands *is* the seaside.'

'Is it?' Edie's face registered surprise and then disbelief.

'Well, of course it is, you silly goose!' Bertha rolled her eyes despairingly. 'It's sea, isn't it? All that wet blue stuff you paddled in. And the sand – that was *beside* the *sea*. Seaside!'

Mrs Tallant's grim expression relaxed into a grin as she tapped her forehead meaningfully. 'What on earth did you think it was, then?' she asked.

Edie shrugged 'How should I know if I've never been? They never said it was seaside. They said it was Camber Sands. How was I to know? No one *said*.'

'Well, you know now,' Bertha told her. 'So you have been to the seaside. You were lucky – no one else got to go except you.'

'And the mistress,' Edie reminded her.

'Let's not talk about her,' said Bertha. 'Old misery!'

'She's crossed in love,' said Cook. 'You'd be a misery in her shoes.'

'Crossed in love,' said Bertha. 'D'you really think so?'

Mrs Tallant spooned tea into the pot. 'Well, I reckon so after that night when Mr le Brun turned up – and we all know where Mr Delain was.'

'Do we?' said Cook. 'We know where we *think* he was.'

Edie giggled. 'In Vinnie's bed!'

Mrs Tallant cast an anxious look towards the kitchen door and said, 'Not so loud, stupid! D'you want her to hear you?'

'But – '

'But nothing! Just keep your voice down. And don't you dare repeat that outside these four walls!'

Cook finished rolling the pastry, draped it over a large tin plate and trimmed off the surplus with a practised knife. 'Have you finished those apples yet, Edie? This pie's for today, you know, not tomorrow.'

'I'm nearly done.'

Cook sat down to await the apples – elbows on the table, floury hands held aloft. 'I wonder,' she said, 'if she will marry him? She's got to marry someone.'

'Poor Master William,' said Bertha. 'I feel most sorry for him. He would have been a lovely master of Foxearth. You liked him, Cook, didn't you?'

Cook nodded. 'A really good match that would have been, but poor Vinnie can't seem to make up her mind. All this time since Master Julian died and she's still single. A good-looking girl like her – I don't understand it.'

Mrs Tallant pulled the knitted tea-cosy over the tea-pot and considered the matter thoughtfully. 'If she has her way, I reckon it'll be this Delain fellow. Really smitten with him, she is. She's breaking her heart over him, poor girl! Mind you, I'm not saying I approve of what they were up to – there's a right and a wrong way to go about things. If they're in love, then there's nothing to stop them getting engaged and doing the thing properly. A nice ring . . . '

'A piece in *The Times*,' contributed Cook.

'Piece of what?' Edie asked, handing over a large basinful of sliced apples.

'Not that sort of piece,' said Cook. 'I meant an announcement. You know: The engagement was announced today of Mrs Julian Lawrence to Monsieur Philippe Delain . . . '

The back door opened just then and Tim Bilton entered in his stockinged feet. Bertha put her fingers to her nose, but Mrs Tallant pushed them down again.

'You leave him be. I'd rather have cheesey socks than muddy boots. You don't have to clean the floor.'

Edie began to say, 'Neither do you', but then remembered the result of earlier impudence and swallowed her words.

'What's that about an engagement?' Tim asked.

Mrs Tallant collected the mugs and began to pour the tea. 'It's nothing,' she said.

'It's the mistress and the Frenchman,' said Edie eagerly. 'They're getting engaged – it's in the paper!'

'It's *not*!' cried Cook. 'Honestly Edie, you never listen. I only said that if they *were*, there would be an announcement in *The Times*. If they *were*, which they're not!'

'I'll be glad when Young Harry gets back' said Tim, losing interest in Vinnie's affairs. 'I don't know if I'm coming or going at the moment.' But it seemed no one was interested in Tim's problems.

At that moment Janet came into the kitchen.

'I swear you can smell tea being mashed' said Cook as Janet found herself a mug and held it out hopefully.

'It's not all I can smell', said Janet pointedly. 'I see Tim's got his boots off.'

Tim grinned amiably, ignoring her comment. 'I was talking to Mr le Brun the other day,' he told them. 'Senior, that is, of course. Last time he was here. He doesn't like the Frenchman, that's for sure. I could tell by the way he spoke. Doesn't like him at all.'

Cook looked at him, unconvinced. 'I'm sure Mr le Brun wouldn't confide in you', she said tartly.

'He wasn't confiding. More speaking his thoughts out loud.

I reckon he's jealous.'

They all gazed at him incredulously. Edie looked puzzled. 'What then?' she asked. 'Does Mr le Brun want an aeroplane? Does he want to be – ?'

'No, silly!' Janet tutted at her stupidity. 'Jealous of Mr Delain and the mistress.' She turned to Tim again. 'How could he be jealous? He's much older than her.'

'Not that much and what if he is? Lots of women like older men.'

'Well, I never!' said Mrs Tallant. 'Mr le Brun and the mistress.'

All eyes were on Tim, who said hastily, 'I'm not certain. I only said I reckon he's jealous.'

'The point is,' said Cook, 'does *Vinnie* like *him*? In that way, of course? I wonder.'

Mrs Tallant looked thoughtful. 'Something happened that night, you know. The night of the hopping supper. Between them, I mean. But don't ask me what. Vinnie came in looking very odd, sort of upset.'

'Funny, isn't it?' said Janet. 'We've never thought of her and him before, but they'd make a good couple don't you think?'

'I don't know really', said Mrs Tallant. 'He's certainly a handsome man and she's always had a lot of respect for him.'

'He's tall,' said Edie, 'and he's got nice eyes. And he's always polite to me – really polite, not like some people.'

The women looked at Tim, who shrugged.

'The trouble is,' said Cook, 'we've known him as a friend of the family for so long that it's hard to imagine him as anything else.'

Janet sighed. 'Perhaps Vinnie has secretly loved him all these years and we never guessed and *he* doesn't know either –'

'But if it's in *The Times*', said Edie and they all groaned, except Tim who said, 'Don't take any notice of them, love.'

'It would be rather romantic, wouldn't it, after all these years?' said Janet. 'She does seem to need him, if you know what I mean. Like when Louise was ill. She asked him to stay or else he offered, but anyway he stayed to be near her in her hour of need. It *is* romantic when you think about it.'

'You read too many novels,' said Mrs Tallant.

'What's wrong with that?'

'Nothing except that real life's not like it is in books.'

'Well, more's the pity then. I wish it was! What do you think, Tim? Let's have a man's opinion.'

'Let's have a bit of sense, you mean,' he grinned. 'Well, cut out the romance and look at it another way. Clive le Brun knows a lot about hops and horses. I'd like to work for him. I leave the romance to you women.'

'The Colonel thinks very highly of him,' said Janet thoughtfully. 'It would please him no end if they were to make a match of it. He'd like to see the mistress settled and he's not over-struck on Mr Delain. Little things he says – I can tell.'

'I think *I'd* like to work for Mr le Brun,' said Cook. 'As Janet says, he's a gentleman. He can be a bit stern, but he doesn't mean it.'

'I wonder . . . ' said Bertha. 'If he thought Vinnie was falling in love with the flyer – '

'Maybe that's why he didn't come to the supper,' cried Cook. She brushed the pie-crust with beaten egg-white and shook caster sugar over it. 'Blow it! I forgot the cloves,' she said. 'Let's hope she doesn't notice. All this cooking for one – it doesn't give you much heart, somehow. She nodded thoughtfully as she carried the pie over to the stove. 'Mr le Brun! I never would have thought of him, but the more I think about the idea, the more I like it.'

*

In the last week of October the weather began to deteriorate rapidly and Vinnie, waking to the sound of rain lashing against the window, made her first task of the morning a letter to Doll; she instructed her to give the landlord notice that they would be vacating the cottage at the end of the week. Harry was still there and Doll would have help with the children on the journey back to Kent. Then Vinnie rang for Bertha and asked her to give the letter to Edie, who would go down to the post-box with it.

Vinnie wanted the children at home for selfish reasons, too. She had still heard nothing from Philippe and now her misery was tinged with anger and her heart was heavy with dread. She waited in a fever of longing for a letter from him, yet feared what it might contain. She could not forgive him the long delay, nor would she forget his abrupt departure and if she considered these two aspects, she was forced to doubt his intentions towards her. Yet she had only to recall his words and the passion of their lovemaking to be reassured that no man could behave in that way without feeling a deep and genuine regard for the woman who shared the experience. The hardest thing to bear was the servants who, obviously aware of her apparent rejection, watched her with compassion in their eyes and treated her with an unfamiliar subtlety and gentleness. As though, thought Vinnie, she were a fractious child who might, if provoked, throw a temper tantrum. Somehow she managed to get through each day, but it became an increasing effort to do so. The hands of the clock hardly seemed to move at all. In her distracted state, Vinnie found the smallest problem enormous and fought down a desire to scream and shout or burst into luxurious tears. Neither of these reactions was reasonable, she knew, and she went to bed at night exhausted by the day-long struggle with her emotions.

Once in bed she lay awake for hours before falling at last into a heavy sleep, only to be a victim of horrible nightmares from which she awoke in the early hours, sweating and afraid. In the seclusion of her room she cursed Philippe Delain and berated him, but always afterwards she begged him to come back and tell her that he loved her, and promised her forgiveness. In spite of all the signs to the contrary, Vinnie still believed that he loved her.

So she wanted the children home to fill the empty house, to give her affection and to distract her mind from unpleasant thoughts. She had written a letter to Philippe, but having no address for him and being too proud to make enquiries, had been forced to send it to the Royal Aero Club at Muswell Manor, marking the envelope 'Please Forward'. In it she asked Philippe to telephone her or to write; she also reaffirmed her own feelings towards him and asked for reassurance that he had truly meant all that he had said to her during their brief courtship. For that was how Vinnie viewed their relationship. Sheltered from the harsh outside world by her early marriage to Julian, it had never entered her head that men might amuse themselves with women or pretend to feelings that did not exist. Nor did it seem possible that Philippe's passion might be real and heartfelt while they were together, but could cool to indifference once they were apart. She would not have denied that such shallow men existed, but would have wagered her life that Philippe Delain was not among them. He might have been detained for any number of perfectly satisfactory reasons – the illness of a member of his family; his own disposition (heaven forbid); a business crisis; more problems with the Voisin. But why did he not set her mind at ease when it would be so easy to do so? She tried to convince herself that he intended his return to Foxearth to be a wonderful surprise, and that at any moment he would arrive and take her in his arms, putting an end to all her doubts and fears. Vinnie rehearsed this scene many times in her mind, for to do so gave her brief comfort and held the dark thoughts at bay if only for a few moments.

'He *will* come', she told herself again and again, as though by pronouncing the words often enough she could make it happen. 'He will come and he will love me and he will never go away again.'

The hands on the mantelpiece clock were at ten-thirty-one and the whole day stretched ahead, black and uninviting. There was plenty that Vinnie could do, but she was not in the mood to concentrate on housekeeping bills, next week's menus or a temporary increase in Tim Bilton's wages. She decided to ring for *The Times*.

'Bertha,' she said, 'has the Colonel finished with the paper? It's usually down here again by now.'

Bertha avoided her eyes. 'It's on the hall table, ma'am. I don't know why.'

'Then bring it in, will you?'

'Yes, ma'am.'

Vinnie thought she was behaving rather oddly – but then all the servants were the same and she had only herself to blame, for she too was behaving oddly. The whole world was behaving oddly, she reflected wearily, and sighed heavily. Outside, the leaves were already red and brown and the wind and rain had torn them from the trees and scattered them untidily across the lawn. Autumn was a sad time of year, she thought, then shook her head. No, that was nonsense, for if Philippe returned – *when* he returned, she corrected herself quickly – Autumn would be the most glorious season of the year. There would be beauty in the lowering grey clouds and the earth would welcome the rain. The winds would blow and the crisp cold snows of winter would be eagerly awaited. *If* he returned!

Bertha came back into the room, set down the paper with clumsy haste and departed.

'Really,' thought Vinnie crossly, 'she makes me feel like an ogre. Anyone would think I bite!'

Idly she took up the newspaper and her eyes skimmed the headlines with disinterest. Then, as though drawn by magnets, they fell immediately upon a smaller item in the right-hand column.

FRENCH FLIER TO WED

It was announced today that Philippe Pierre Delain is to marry Lucille Marie Benoit, the only daughter of Viscomte Henri Benoit, after a short engagement.

The words blurred before Vinnie's eyes and a strangled cry escaped her. Philippe engaged? It was absurd! Impossible! It was another Philippe Delain – it must be a dreadful coincidence. She forced herself to read on:

The engagement, which was not expected until the spring of 1910, came as a surprise for many people. Philippe Delain is well-known in England as the keen flier who recently shipped his flying machine – a modified Voisin – to Kent in preparation for a further attempt at the cross-Channel flight so recently achieved by Louis Blériot. Monsieur Delain's attempt has been delayed due to a recent accident in which he crashed his machine – '

'No! This is nonsense!' Vinnie whispered as fear churned her stomach. 'It's not possible!' Against her will her eyes were drawn back to the final paragraph.

Philippe Delain has been staying at Foxearth in Teesbury in the Weald of Kent, the home of Colonel Lawrence, the well-known hop grower. He has also been a regular visitor to Muswell Manor and the flying ground on the Isle of Sheppey. The date of the wedding has not yet been announced, but close friends believe Easter may be a possibility.

A dark mist clouded Vinnie's vision and her left hand, which was clutching the newspaper, trembled violently. She shivered as a chill swept through her and for a moment she thought she was going to be sick as shock wracked her body.

'No.' she whispered. 'You can't mean this, Philippe. You can't do this to me! You wouldn't! How – oh, don't let it be true, Philippe. Please don't let it be true!'

Stunned with disbelief, she stared straight ahead seeing nothing, while the fingers of her right hand strayed to her mouth. She needed desperately to feel anger – it would be so much easier to bear than the overpowering pain of humiliation and loss. The terrible awareness of Philippe's deceit grew more acute as each second passed.

'You told me . . . ' she began again, then the paper slipped from her hand and she swayed and had to cling on to the chair to save herself from falling. A fine perspiration broke out over her skin and her limbs felt leaden. She realised that the Colonel and Janet would have seen the item already and suddenly she understood Bertha's reaction to her request for the newspaper. Doubtless everyone knew! She groaned aloud, but still could feel no animosity towards Philippe. Her mind simply refused to believe him capable of such treachery. After what seemed an eternity, she picked up *The Times* and re-read the offending item. Could he have whispered such wonderful things to her if he had been engaged to another woman? It simply was not possible.

'I don't want to hate you,' she whispered. 'I love you and you love me. You *do*, Philippe! Come back and tell me that this is all a terrible mistake.'

Perhaps she should send a telegram? She would find out his address from the Aero Club. In her imagination she saw his mother asking him about the telegram; heard her reproaching him; saw Philippe, appalled at what he had done. Yes, she would send a telegram asking for an explanation. As quickly as she had decided to do so, she changed her mind. No, she would not stoop so low. He might laugh at the telegram. Worse, he might show it to his fiancée. She visualised their two heads bent over the flimsy paper. No, she could not contact him. If he had rejected her, then the fewer people who knew the better.

'Oh Philippe, why have you done this terrible thing?' she cried. She wondered if his parents had arranged the marriage against his will and he had returned to find it a *fait accompli*. This was feasible but not very likely, and she knew that if they had done so, Philippe had only to refuse. He could tell them of Lavinia Lawrence, who had given herself to him so willingly, so trustingly.

And Clive le Brun! How he would gloat over her! She almost writhed at the thought of it. He could stay in Scotland for ever as far as she was concerned, for she never wanted to face him again and confess that his instincts about Philippe had been right after all. Philippe Delain was *not* to be trusted, it seemed He had deliberately misled her and she, Lavinia Lawrence, had fallen for his easy charm and had made a complete fool of herself.

Now she began to understand how William must have felt and a great wave of remorse seized her; it dashed her to even greater depths of despair to know that she had inflicted this same hurt on someone else. The thought was unbearable and she wanted to run to William and beg his forgiveness.

'I thought I knew what you were suffering,' she whispered, 'but I had no idea at all.'

A new thought occurred to her – that this was her punishment for the way she had treated William. Mrs Bryce used to say, 'God pays his debts without money' and maybe He was doing just that and it was a reckoning. She sat on the chair like a statue, longing for the relief of tears, but none came. Then the door opened and she heard Bertha say, 'Ma'am?', her voice hesitant.

Without turning her head Vinnie said, 'Go away, please,' and the door closed quietly.

Vinnie hurled the newspaper to the floor, then got up from the chair and began to pace restlessly up and down. She felt trapped, like a caged animal. She was surrounded by servants who would stare at her curiously as if she was a freak of some kind. No, a wounded animal – she *felt* like a wounded animal and wanted to crawl away and hide. Better still, she wanted to crawl away and die.

'I can't stay here,' she whispered through clenched teeth. 'I can't! I *must* be on my own.'

It came to her suddenly like an inspiration and she ran across the room and rang the bell. When Mrs Tallant came in answer to it a moment later, Vinnie managed a certain degree of composure, although the housekeeper noted her pale face and haunted eyes.

'I'm going down to Porthleven to the cottage,' she said, her voice brittle. 'I feel I have earned a few days' holiday. Tell Bertha to come up to help me pack and Tim can arrange a train and drive me to the station.'

*

For the first ten minutes of the train's progress through London, Vinnie's mind was mercifully distracted by a scrutiny of her fellow passengers who shared the sumptuous first-class carriage with her. After that, another five minutes was taken up with an appreciation of the comfortable armchairs upholstered in velvet, the deep pile of the patterned carpet, the decorative inlaid ceiling, wide-curtained windows and frosted glass lamp-shades. Cook had offered to prepare a small basket of food for the journey, but Vinnie told her she would eat in the dining-car. However, when the attendant came round to take orders for the first sitting, Vinnie declined, for she had no appetite and the thought of forcing down food she did not want among a crowd of strangers held no appeal for her. In her present state she felt insecure and loth to leave the more familiar surround-ings of her carriage.

Hence, when her fellow passengers disappeared in the direction of the dining-car, Vinnie was left alone and the unwelcome thoughts came crowding back into her mind.

During the hour that followed she surrendered herself to a succession of fantasies, all of which involved Philippe Delain and varied greatly depending on her mood, which fluctuated wildly from extreme dejection to barely suppressed rage. She visualised herself appearing like a spectre at the feast to ruin Philippe's wedding. She saw the young couple together at the altar steps, about to take their vows, when the door at the rear of the church opened to admit a distraught Vinnie. Then she pictured herself mingling with the guests at the wedding breakfast, arousing whispered speculation as to her identity until she was pointed out to Philippe who realised, too late where his heart truly lay. Better still, Vinnie imagined for Philippe a disastrous marriage. He would repent his folly, she told herself fiercely, and was at great pains to convince herself.

These flights of imagination served their purpose after a fashion, for they helped to restore Vinnie's shattered self-esteem and to persuade her that Philippe would regret his infidelity. Eventually, however, they lost their potency and she found herself once more face to face with reality and loss. Then more terrible doubts assailed her – of her own worth as a person and the consequent suspicion that she was not lovable. She tried to relate these ideas to her past experiences and was not encouraged. Julian had married her when he thought she was dying; Jarvis had tried to rape her; Tom had found her too compliant; Adam had played upon her loneliness and William . . . a deep regret swept over her as she remembered how she had hurt him. Perhaps she did not deserve love, she reflected anxiously. Perhaps she would never remarry. The thought of the long years ahead frightened her and a knot of despair formed in her stomach. Leaning back in the seat she closed her eyes, determined that she would not give way to tears; that relief must be reserved for the privacy of her own bedroom.

With an effort she thought of the three children, who had no idea that their mother was about to join them. At least they would be pleased to see her, she reminded herself. James, Louise and Edward loved her and she must be grateful for that, for she was not alone in the world and should thank God that He had sent her three healthy children. Of course they were more at ease with Doll, but that was because they spent more time with her than they did with their mother. That was only to be expected, but she *was* their mother and they *did* love her. She repeated this to herself several times. If she could not count on *their* love, she told herself, she certainly would be a pathetic and loveless creature.

'Well, that was very welcome!'

Startled, Vinnie opened her eyes to find the diners returning. The elderly woman occupying the seat opposite hers had spoken to her and Vinnie smiled politely.

'I said, that was very welcome,' the woman repeated.

'Oh, the luncheon,' said Vinnie. 'Did you enjoy it?'

'Very much indeed. They really do serve a most creditable meal. Are you not eating?'

'I'm not hungry,' said Vinnie.

The woman laughed, a false, tinkling sound. 'Oh, but my dear, you should!' she said. 'I'm never hungry, but I always eat. I enjoy my food and see no reason to pretend otherwise. Mind you, I don't run to fat like some unfortunates. I can eat whatever I fancy and I do have a very sweet tooth. And wine – I do think a good wine lifts a meal, don't you?'

Vinnie nodded, hating the woman for her self-assured

manner and wishing she would address herself to someone else.

'Good food and wine are my weakness,' the woman continued, settling herself into the chair and arranging a travelling rug over her legs with heavily-ringed hands. Seeing Vinnie's glance rest on these, she laughed again. 'Oh, and jewels, of course! Another of my weaknesses. My poor husband says that all my vices cost him money! And why not, I ask him. What's money for, if not to fritter away on life's pleasures!'

Vinnie looked at the pale blue eyes, long thin nose and petulant mouth, hoping her dislike would not show in her eyes.

'Good food and wine, jewels and furs – in that order,' the woman continued, apparently mistaking Vinnie's silence for interest. 'A good fox fur can be a woman's best friend, I always say. My sister argues in favour of the mink, but I make no apologies for my choice. A good fox, preferably red – '

She broke off as Vinnie stood up, unable to bear either the woman or her stupid chatter for a moment longer.

'Excuse me,' said Vinnie, 'but I've decided I will eat something after all.'

As she made her way between the chairs to the end of the carriage, Vinnie heard the woman's offended 'Well!' but she did not care. At any other time the thought of offending someone – even someone she did not like – would have been unthinkable, but now nothing seemed to matter and such niceties of manner appeared superficial.

Explaining to the waiter that she had changed her mind, Vinnie was shown to an empty table and while she waited for her meal to be served, she stared out over the hurrying landscape with a jaundiced eye. But the train was taking her away from Foxearth and her humiliations and for that reason, if for no other, she was thankful. The further the better, she reflected grimly. At least Doll and Young Harry knew nothing of Philippe's betrayal, and hopefully she could come to terms with the situation away from pitying eyes.

She dined in solitary splendour. No one shared her table and everyone else was concerned with their food, few of her fellow diners bothering Vinnie with a second glance. The soup was hot and full of flavour; the saddle of lamb succulent enough; the peas and roast potatoes were just as they should be. Vinnie enjoyed it in spite of herself, and felt vaguely comforted. The waiter, young and good-looking, was attentive and her confidence began to return, only to be dispelled almost immediately by a new and terrible thought. Suppose she had been pregnant! Thank God she was not expecting Philippe's child! Vinnie wondered frantically how she had omitted to consider the possibility before. A child would have been the ultimate disaster, the final degradation. Horrible visions filled her mind once more as she imagined herself giving birth to Philippe's bastard while he was married to another.

Then the young waiter was beside her. 'Is madam unwell?' he asked, seeing her agitation.

'I – I beg your pardon.' Her throat was dry and it was an effort to force out the words.

'I asked if you were unwell, madam? You look pale.'

'Yes,' she stammered. 'I mean, no. At least, I do feel rather faint.'

'A glass of cold water for madam?' he suggested briskly and she watched him retreat towards the kitchen.

Suddenly she remembered another train journey so many years ago, when she had travelled from Wateringbury to London at the age of fifteen. The parallel was so incredible that it almost took her breath away as she saw that her life had come full circle. Then she had been a mere child, her brief encounter with Tom Bryce having led to her expulsion from her home and all that she had ever known or loved. She had given herself to Tom in a moment of confused innocence. Now another train was taking her away from her home, but this time she could not claim innocence as her excuse, rather must she attribute her disgrace to a supreme error of judgement. Then she had been only fifteen, now she was twenty-seven and old enough to be held responsible for her actions. Then, unknowing, she had carried Tom's child . . .

To her surprise, the glass of cold water helped, stilling the shivering long enough for her to settle the bill and make her way back to her seat. She was glad to see that her neighbour was dozing, her head awkwardly askew, her mouth open. Vinnie wished she could sleep, but knew it would not be possible. She wished she could die, but that would be more difficult. Or too easy? No, with three children death was a luxury she could not afford. Whatever happened, she would suffer it to the bitter end. In the meantime, she was safe in her velvet chair, and she wished only that the journey could last for ever.

CHAPTER TWENTY-ONE

Sid Carter was not very bright, but he was a hard-working man and when he was in a good mood was marvellous company; yet he could also be morose and cantankerous and his temper was uncertain. He was not particularly fond of Dora, but he found it useful to have someone to wash and iron his clothes and cook his meals and he was inordinately proud of his children. He was what Dora called 'an independent sod' and so he was not entirely pleased when the Brothers in Jesus offered them a flat which, while not palatial, was far superior to the home he had provided for his family. Dora's enthusiasm irked him – it seemed to suggest that his own provision for the family had been inadequate.

He was also deeply suspicious of outside intervention in his affairs and feared that the interest shown by the Brothers in Jesus, while appearing harmless enough, might conceivably prove the thin edge of the wedge. It did not help when his workmates teased him on the subject and asked him to sing a hymn, or suggested that he prayed hard for the outcome of the three-thirty at Aintree. He did not like being singled out for special attention, although he could not tell Dora why this was, and he was also unable to think of a single reason to back up his decision not to accept the mission's offer of the basement flat.

'But it's going to be rent-free!' Dora exploded. 'Don't you understand, Sid? Rent-free and no strings. And it's got a garden where I can hang out the washing and the kids can play. A garden, for God's sake! Just think of that. No playing in the street for our kids.'

'It never did me no harm,' Sid protested. 'Nor you neither. All kids play in the street.'

'They do not,' said Dora. 'Only those with no gardens. We could keep a couple of chickens or you could breed rabbits – '

'Oh, thank you kindly! I don't want to breed rabbits and I don't fancy chickens. Anyway, I haven't got time to mess about with all that.'

'Well, grow vegetables then. We could have fresh vegetables – that would save a bit.'

'I don't want to save a bit – I don't need to,' he grumbled. 'And don't go getting fancy ideas about a garden. I work all the hours God sends and I bring home a fair whack. I just don't like handouts, you know that; I never have. This place has always been good enough so why do they have to go poking their noses in, giving you fancy ideas.'

'They're not fancy,' Dora snapped. 'There's just no pleasing you, Sid Carter. Any other man in his right mind would be pleased as Punch, but not you. Oh no! You have to take it all the wrong way and go and spoil everything. Sometimes, Sid Carter, I wonder what you've got in that head of yours. Sawdust, I shouldn't wonder. If you can't see how lucky we are – well, I just give up. Might as well save me breath.'

'I wish you would.'

'Right then, I will,' she said, her face like thunder.

'Is that a promise?'

'Yes.'

'Good.'

This argument, with a few simple variations, was repeated several times before Sid finally gave in. As a housewarming present, the Brothers in Jesus promised them a strip of new green linoleum for the passage and two second-hand armchairs in good condition for their living-room. Dora was beside herself with excitement and even Sid had to admit when he saw the flat that they would be very comfortable and that the money saved on rent would come in handy. However, he was not at all pleased when Lydia Grant called in to talk about the move and Roland Fry looked in again in the evening.

'We're not a bloody peepshow!' he shouted as soon as the door closed behind Roland. The new baby woke up with a start and began to cry – the thin fretful wail of a very young child which always grated on Sid's nerves. It aggravated him almost as much as being called 'Mr Wilks', because Dora had not liked to remind the mission that she and Sid were not actually married. Sid towered over her as she began to wash up the tea things, and wagged a finger menacingly.

'Now you listen to me, Dora, and listen hard because I'm only going to say it once,' he told her. 'Tell them to keep away! They don't own us just because they're going to pay the rent.'

'They don't mean any harm,' Dora told him mildly. 'You're behaving like a silly kid, Sid Carter, you are really. Them giving us that lino and them two chairs, and you can't even bear them to pop in and say "Hullo". They're friends of mine, Sid, don't you see that? They're fond of little Albert – well, that's natural enough, isn't it, after what happened – and they want to help us. I'm grateful for small mercies, I am, and there's lots of people would change places with us tomorrow if they could. But not you! Oh no, you have to be mean about it and go on and on and now you've woken up the little 'un.' She sniffed loudly. 'I don't know what's got into you, Sid, I really don't! Since I come home from the hopping, you've been like a bear with a sore head.'

'I never asked you to go hopping,' he reminded her. 'I can look after this family without anybody else's help, yours or theirs.'

'Well, you didn't say "No" to the new boots I bought you with the hopping money, I notice.'

Sid brought down his fist on the table and shouted, 'You can stuff the bloody boots for all I care! D'you hear me?'

The two other children, sensing danger, began to whisper and Dora said, 'Now look what you've done! Scared the daylights out of them.' She dried her hands hastily and went over to comfort them.

'Your Pa didn't mean nothing,' she told them. 'There's nothing to cry about, so hold your row.'

Then she went back to Sid who sat hunched and miserable at the table, fiddling with the salt-cellar. She put her arms round him; at first he pretended to shrug her off, but she knew his ways and persisted.

'Don't be mad, Sid,' she wheedled, kissing the back of his head. 'Let's not squabble. We'll have a nice little place and you bring in a good wage. More than most, I'll bet. Let's just enjoy it and all be happy, shall we? I really love you, Sid Carter, you know I do.' She moved round so that she could see his face. 'Come on, love, give us a smile. Give us a kiss and let's make up, eh? We've got each other and three lovely kids. That's a lot to be thankful for.'

'Well, just tell your fancy mission friends to stay away,' Sid told her. He swung round on the chair and Dora slid on to his lap. 'I don't want any more snoopers, Dora, so you tell 'em or else I will.'

'I'll tell 'em, Sid. They'll understand; they're nice people, really.'

'Then let them be nice somewhere else,' said Sid. 'The next person who just "pops in" is going to get a mouthful – of this!' He held up a meaty fist. 'I don't want to hear any more about the Brothers in bleeding Jesus or bloody hopfields. Nothing! Get it? And next year you can give it a miss. I mean it – you're not going down there again. So there's an end to it. Right?'

'Right, Sid – and you do love me, don't you Sid? You're not mad at me?'

''Course I'm not. And course I love you. Now get off me lap and fetch us the paper.'

*

Dora and her family moved into their new flat on Thursday and on Friday Sid's mother had the older children so that Dora could 'settle in'. By Friday evening when Sid came home from work, their few items of furniture had been tugged and bullied into place and the curtains had been hung at the front of the house. Delighted with their new quarters, Dora and Sid went round to collect the children, who were put to bed in their new bedroom which Sid promised Dora would have a 'lick of paint' by and by.

Saturday morning was Sid's morning: he always went to see his mother for half an hour and would then make his way to the betting shop. He did not spend a lot but enjoyed his 'flutter' and whether or not he won he would call in at the pub for a few drinks, eventually returning home with a bottle of stout for Dora. Dora did not begrudge him his few hours' relaxation, except on the occasions when he drank too much or quarrelled with one of his mates and came home in a mean mood. On this occasion, he had been gone less than an hour when there came a knock at the door. Dora crossed her fingers, hoping that it would not be one of the mission people, for she did not relish passing on Sid's message and had not had time to compose a suitably modified version. It was Mollie Pett who stood there, however.

'Mollie!' she cried with relief. 'How on earth did you find me here? We only moved in Thursday. Come on in.' She was delighted at the prospect of showing off the new flat.

'Your Sid home?' Mollie asked, stepping inside. 'I've never met him.'

'No,' said Dora, closing the front door. 'He don't go far on a Saturday. Pops in to see his Ma first. He'll be at the betting shop by now or in the pub on the corner. You might see him – he might be back.'

Mollie followed her into the living-room. 'I got to talk to a friend of yours at the "free bee" this morning – free breakfast to you. It was him that told me where you were.'

'How d'you mean? Who was it?'

'Funny little chap called Albert Something.'

Dora's expression changed rapidly from pleasure to alarm.

'Albert!' she gasped. 'Oh, he doesn't know where I live, does he?'

''Course he does or he couldn't have told me, silly!' Mollie stood in the middle of the room, her hands on her hips as she looked around. 'It's very nice, Dora,' she said. 'They've done you proud.' She looked out of the window. 'And a bit of a garden! Coo, you've really fallen on your feet, Dora Wilks! I wouldn't say "No" to some of your luck.'

Dora tossed her head. 'Look who's talking,' she said. 'You haven't done so badly out of them, all these years. They've looked after your three kids and kept you in fancy hats!'

Mollie decided to change the subject. 'Well, aren't you going to show me round?' she asked.

'Of course,' said Dora. 'Well, this is the living-room; I've got to shorten the curtains, then they can go up. The mission have given us a few things, as well as clothes for the baby.'

'Oh yes, the new baby. Albert told me about what happened. Quite a bit of excitement, one way and another. Don't I get to see him, then?'

'He's in the bedroom fast asleep, bless him. Sleeps right through the night, he does. The other two are next door with my neighbour. Mrs Sowby, her name is. Seems nice enough – she's got twins a bit older than Sam and she said as how mine could play with hers for a few hours while I get myself sorted out. Nice of her, wasn't it?'

'Very nice.' Mollie glanced at a tea-chest which stood against the wall.

'I'm still unpacking,' said Dora, a trifle defensively. 'A few more ornaments and the mirror. Some of Sid's tools. He's good with his hands, Sid is. Going to put up a shelf there . . . ' She pointed to a small recess beside the fireplace. 'And a cupboard in the kitchen. Come on, I'll show you.'

Trying to disguise her envy, Mollie followed Dora along the narrow passage. The walls were painted a light green and a strip of border in darker green had been added at shoulder height.

'Sid's going to paper over that,' Dora confided. 'He doesn't know it yet, so I shall have to catch him in a good mood. Here we are!' Mollie made admiring noises as she stepped into the small dark room.

'Sun gets round here in the afternoon,' Dora told her. 'Lovely in here then, it is. Really cosy.'

Together they inspected the gas-stove and the copper and

Dora pointed out where the overhead dryer would go for the washing, explaining that the cupboard would replace the dresser and take all the crockery.

'What's wrong with the dresser?' asked Mollie.

Dora shrugged. 'They collect dust, don't they? All it needs is a couple of doors. Sid's mother's giving us a cover for the table with all fringing round the bottom – you know the sort.'

Mollie nodded. 'Very nice,' she said. 'No wonder you look so smug.' She saw Dora's expression change and added hastily, '*I'd* look smug if I had a nice place like this.'

Dora's eyes had narrowed, but she made no comment. At last Mollie said, 'So let's have a quick peek at the little 'un. Right little charmer, according to your Albert!'

'He's not *my* Albert,' Dora said as she led the way to the bedroom. Not wishing to disturb the sleeping infant, the two women admired him in whispers and then tiptoed out again. The bed was still unmade and although Mollie did not comment upon the fact, Dora knew that she had seen it and felt mortified. It seemed to her that Mollie was deliberately not showing the amount of respect that the accommodation deserved and she led them back into the living-room with a growing sense of resentment.

Mollie perched herself on the arm of the chair and for a moment neither spoke. Dora felt a rush of irritation that she was not looking her best; her hair was uncombed and a grimy apron was tied round her waist. Wearing her outdoor apparel, however, Mollie looked reasonably presentable; only her face ruined the impression for, as Dora noted with grim satisfaction, this was haggard and grey and Mollie's eyes seemed to have fallen back into their sockets. Her cheekbones stood out sharply from the flesh and the tight-drawn skin made the jaw in turn look inordinately large. She had, Dora thought suddenly, the look of a skull about her. Mollie Pett's days, or weeks, were very obviously numbered and although Dora felt shocked she could not feel the compassion she knew was due.

Instead she heard herself say, 'So what were *you* doing at the "free bee" – you, with your rich doctor friend? Have you finished with him or something?'

'Yes and no,' said Mollie, after only the smallest hesitation. 'I haven't seen him for a week or so. His wife's threatening to divorce him, which will ruin him, of course – the scandal, I mean.' She swung one leg nonchalantly and Dora noticed that the once neat ankle was now bony and unattractive. She sat down in the other chair, unfastened the offending apron as casually as she could and tossed it aside before patting her hair hopefully without the benefit of a mirror.

'So, how's Albert?' Dora asked, eager to show Mollie that even as a wife and mother of three she could still attract the men.

Mollie laughed. 'Poor little cocker!' she said. 'Not a lot up here,' she tapped her forehead, 'but he seems a bit doolally about you. Says to tell you he'll be round to see you later.'

Dora's face fell. 'Oh no!' she cried. 'I've told him to stay away from me for the time being. Sid can be real nasty at times and he gets so jealous.'

'Oh!' Mollie's eyebrows rose. 'Like that, is it, you and this Albert? Bit young for you, isn't he?'

'I like 'em young,' said Dora, 'and they seem to like me. Not,' she added hastily, 'that there was anything between us. It wasn't like that at all. He was just kind when the baby came and that.'

'Don't bother to lie!' Mollie crowed triumphantly. 'He told me! I told him I was your best friend and he couldn't wait to tell me all about it. Proper high jinks, by the sound of it. Hoppers' wedding, my foot! Oh, don't worry,' she said, seeing Dora's dismay, 'I won't tell Sid – why the hell should I? And you called the baby after Albert, I'm told? Nice, that! He's certainly over the moon about you and the baby.'

After Dora's colourful account of young Albert's birth, Mollie produced *her* bombshell and Dora listened in astonishment as she explained how 'that young soldier, Bertie Harris' had reappeared in her life to 'claim his long-lost son'.

'Bertie Harris?' cried Dora. 'After all these years? How

romantic! But where on earth did he spring from, then? Oh, he was nice, wasn't he, Moll?'

'He owns the old "Barley Tap". Him and his wife.'

Dora's eyes widened. 'He owns it? Well I'll be blowed. Sid said it had opened again; he goes in there sometimes. And Bertie Harris owns it? Well, that *is* a turn-up!'

'I met his wife,' said Mollie. 'Funny little thing – very quiet. Mousy, almost.'

'And you go in there,' cried Dora, wide-eyed, 'knowing that – well, I mean, what on earth does his wife think about it?'

Mollie shrugged, trying to affect indifference, but Dora could see that she was embarrassed.

'I haven't been in lately,' she admitted. 'I only spoke to her once, actually, and that was before I knew who her husband was. I went after a job as a barmaid, but I haven't been back since. Haven't felt up to it, really. I get very tired these days, out of breath like. It's me lungs. They're – '

As though to demonstrate her point, she began to cough and went on coughing – doubled up, her arms crossed over her stomach, her face scarlet. Dora thought unkindly that a barmaid who looked the way Mollie did would drive away more customers than she encouraged.

'Well, what did Bertie say,' she asked, 'when he knew you'd dumped the kid? Didn't he mind?'

Mollie had come prepared for this question. 'Of course he didn't mind,' she laughed. 'I told him how I was desperate and couldn't give the boy a decent home. I told him I wanted Alexander to be a credit to his father. He thought I was very clever, the way I worked it, and he was really grateful to me. He said Alexander is a fine boy and I can be proud of him.'

Dora searched for words which – while avoiding an outright confrontation – would show Mollie that she did not believe this account. She thought it most unfair that Mollie should be claiming credit for her irresponsible behaviour.

'Well,' she said at last, 'at least the boy didn't starve, thanks to Miss Bellweather. I'm sure Bertie *was* grateful for that.'

At once she knew she had gone too far and regretted her

spiteful tongue, but it was too late. Mollie's expression hardened and she seemed to stiffen.

'Meaning what?' she asked, separating the words ominously.

'What I said,' answered Dora, her pulse beginning to quicken. 'You'd disappeared and the boy had no one in the world.'

'Exactly,' said Mollie. 'I knew Mary would look after him – that's why I went. It was for the boy's sake.'

'That's not what you told them at Sammy Tulson's,' said Dora indignantly. 'You told 'em there that you'd got into trouble – smashed a window – and had to run away from the police.'

Mollie was taken aback. 'Who told you about that?' she demanded. 'I never did.'

'I met Meg Wilson and she told me. They didn't think much of you, either, for what you did.'

Mollie's face flamed with anger. 'You cow!' she whispered. 'You sneaky cow! Talking about me behind my back to my friends. Oh yes, I should have guessed. That's just the sort of rotten thing – '

'I didn't ask her to tell me!' Dora snapped. 'She couldn't wait to talk about it. They all thought it was disgusting to abandon your own kid, if you must know.'

The two women faced each other furiously and Mollie stood up. 'Well,' she said, 'at least my son's enjoying a holiday in Switzerland *and* he goes horse-riding.'

'So?' Dora shouted. 'So what? No thanks to you, is it?'

'So,' shouted Mollie, 'he doesn't live in a dump like this, Dora Wilks! And he doesn't have the arse hanging out of his breeches, which is how your boys'll end up! *My* son – '

'*Your* son? I thought he was Mary Bellweather's son now. At least *my* sons have got a proper home,' cried Dora, 'with a mother and a father, *and* we all live under the same roof. That's what's called a family, Mollie Pett, just in case you didn't know!'

'A family?' cried Mollie. 'Why, you're not even married to your stupid Sid.'

Dora stood up and tossed her head with an incredulous laugh.

'Look who's talking. Pot calling the kettle black! Not married? At least my Sid's looking after us. You and your so-called doctor friend – who do you think you're fooling, Mollie Pett? There's no rich doctor and you know it.'

'At least I'm not carrying on behind a bleedin' hop-pole with a man young enough to be – '

Mollie began to cough and curse, holding on to the mantelpiece.

Dora looked at her dispassionately. 'At least I don't *charge* for it!' she said, determined to have the last word. 'Now you can just get out of my home, Mollie Pett, because you're pathetic – that's what you are. A pathetic, raddled old bag, fit for nothing and nobody.' Her voice rose. 'You can fool yourself maybe, but you can't fool anyone else. Cheap and nasty – that's what you are – and what you did to your kids stinks. You're no friend of mine. Now are you going or do I have to throw you out?'

Furious, Mollie tried to shout something but another paroxysm of coughing effectively prevented her. Her face was scarlet as she struggled for breath and her eyes streamed.

'You wait!' she managed at last, as she took a few unsteady steps towards the door. 'You just . . . ' She staggered and almost fell, but Dora made no move to help her.

At the front door Mollie turned. 'I'll make you sorry, Dora Wilks – ' she began, but at that moment Albert Crittenden arrived with a bunch of violets in his hand, the smile on his face fading rapidly as he looked from Dora to Mollie.

'Oh God!' said Dora. 'That's all I need!'

Albert was astonished. Less than two hours earlier he had been talking with Mollie, who had assured him she was Dora's best friend. Now it looked as though they would be at each other's throats at any moment.

'I just thought . . . ' he said. 'I thought, Dora, I'd bring you these . . . ' He held out the bunch of violets.

With a swift movement of her hand Mollie dashed the flowers to the pavement and then stamped on them. Dora gave a squeal of rage and wrenched Mollie's hat from her head, throwing it up the street and then pushing Mollie after it. Mollie lost her balance and fell sprawling in the road, but when Albert made a move towards her Dora hissed, 'You dare!' and he hesitated. Together they watched Mollie pull herself to her knees as a fresh burst of coughing racked her. When at last she struggled to her feet she gave Dora a look of pure hate before staggering away along the street to retrieve her hat. Dora and Albert watched in silence as Mollie, summoning what dignity she could, pinned on her hat and walked away without a backward glance.

Albert looked at Dora. 'I thought she was a friend of yours,' he stammered.

'Not any more,' said Dora shakily. She bent to gather up the spoilt violets and sudden tears spilled from her eyes.

'Don't cry!' said Albert. 'I'll bring you some more, I promise. And don't get mad at me, Dor. I know you said not to come, but I did so want to see you.'

Dora rubbed away the offending tears with the back of her hand. 'Well,' she sniffed, 'now you're here, I suppose you'd better come in.'

*

Mollie stumbled away down the street with murder in her heart. Her rage brought two spots of colour to her cheeks and each breath was an effort. Her lips moved soundlessly as she gave vent to her feelings in a stream of curses and a blistering description of Dora Wilks. Half-way along the street she faltered and nearly fell, but saved herself by clinging to a convenient lamp-post. With her right arm round the post and her left hand clutching her heart, she swayed for a moment, gasping with exhaustion and staring back up the street to Dora's front door. There was no sign of Albert Crittenden now and she imagined the two of them laughing together over her humiliation.

'Damn you to hell, Dora Wilks!' she muttered venomously. 'I'll get you for what you said to me. Oh yes, I'll pay you out,

Dora bloody Wilks, if it's the last thing I do.'

A fit of coughing seized her and as she bowed her head, the lamp-post knocked her hat askew. An elderly couple passing by stared at her and Mollie put out her tongue. 'Think you'll remember me?' she demanded. Hastily they looked away, but Mollie was loth to let them off too lightly. 'Stuck-up prunes!' she shouted, knowing how embarrassed they would be. 'Stupid pigs, the pair of you!'

The couple, stiff-necked, walked faster and she felt a small glow of satisfaction. 'Serves you bloody well right,' she told their retreating backs. 'Now you know how *I* felt!'

Slowly she was recovering her composure and blind rage was giving way to thoughts of revenge. She thought with disgust of the dingy attic room that was her home and could see no good reason why Dora Wilks should enjoy a ground-floor flat with a garden. Why should Dora Wilks have a man of her own to support her when Mollie Pett had no one? If only the fictional doctor was a reality! Mollie imagined herself, dressed in the height of fashion, driving past Dora's flat in the doctor's private brougham. She would stop the carriage and send the groom to knock at Dora's door. When she appeared Mollie would lean out of the window and spit – that would show Dora Wilks how little Mollie was impressed by her flat and her Sid and her screaming brats!

Thinking about Sid gave her the germ of an idea and suddenly Mollie stopped coughing and straightened up. What was it Dora had said about her precious Sid? That he would be in the betting shop or the pub on the corner. Across the street she saw the 'King's Head' – was that where Sid Carter was? But how would she know him? Damn! Frowning, she tried to recall anything Dora had said which might help her to identify him, but nothing occurred to her.

With an effort, Mollie slowed her breathing and with shaking hands smoothed her clothes and checked that her hat was straight. She tucked a few wisps of hair behind her ears and tried to erase the frown from her face. Once her looks and charm had been her fortune – now she would have to rely on charm alone.

'Right, you cow!' she whispered. 'Here's where you get what's coming to you!'

Fixing a pert smile on her face, Mollie marched across the road and pushed open the door of the 'King's Head'. The familiar smell of warm stale beer and pipe tobacco reminded her of the earlier, more cheerful days of her ill-spent youth and she felt her taut body relax slightly. The dim light and hazy atmosphere would, she knew, soften the harsh contours of her face and help to disguise her pallor. The public bar was full: mostly men, but here and there a few elderly women and also two dogs. The latter, a small Jack Russell and a whippet, eyed each other warily. The women sat in little groups, laughing raucously and nudging each other; the men stood with mugs in their hands or leaned across the counter. One man sprawled on the floor, with his back against the bar, ignored by everyone. Mollie hoped he would not turn out to be Sid Carter.

Humming cheerfully, she elbowed her way through the crowd until she was directly behind the row of men standing at the counter. She tapped one of them on the shoulder and a bull-necked man with very little hair turned enquiringly.

'Room for a little one?' asked Mollie.

'What?' he said suspiciously.

'I'm dying of thirst and who's going to see me behind all you big fellows?'

She smiled helplessly and saw his expression soften. Oh yes, Mollie Pett, she told herself triumphantly, you can still pull the men! The man said 'Here, push up a bit and let the lady in,' and the others jostled along until there was room for her.

The barman moved forward and Mollie said, 'I'll have half a stout, thank you kindly,' and began to fumble slowly in a rather grimy purse.

' 'Ave it on me,' offered the bull-necked man, and a roar of mocking laughter went up from his companions as Mollie rewarded him with a warm smile and a wink.

Mollie hoped this was not Sid Carter, for she did not plan to talk to him direct unless it was absolutely necessary. A bottle and glass appeared on the counter and Mollie's new-found friend poured it for her.

'Thanks,' she said. 'Here's health!'

'Likewise,' he said and they both drank deeply. 'Haven't see you in here before,' he went on.

Mollie giggled. 'Not surprising,' she told him. 'I've never been here before – only come in today to look for someone.' She glanced round.

'Who you looking for, then?'

'Friend of a friend,' she said, tapping the side of her nose mysteriously. 'His name's Carter, Sidney Carter. Don't know him, do you?'

He shook his head. 'But Dick'll know him. He's the barman and he knows everybody. Well, all the regulars, that is.'

'He's supposed to be a well-set-up kind of man,' she told him. 'Big muscles, broad shoulders and that. Same build as you, I should reckon.' He grinned self-consciously at the implied compliment, then he said, 'What d'you want him for? What's he done?'

'Him? Nothing,' said Mollie. 'It's not him who's done something; it's his wife. Proper little wotsit with the men, she is.'

'Go on!'

Mollie nodded and took another mouthful of stout. The man's eyes narrowed and he began to search among the crowd for a man who fitted Mollie's description.

'I feel sorry for him,' she went on. 'It's a crying shame to see a decent fellow done down.'

'You know his wife, then?'

'Sort of – she's a neighbour and they live over the street from me. I see it going on – as soon as he's out of that house, the boyfriend's round there. And Sid's such a decent bloke.' She smiled up at him. 'Shouldn't we get introduced?' she suggested. 'I'm Norah.' She held out a hand.

'I'm Alfred.' They shook hands with feigned solemnity.

'So why did you want to find him?' Alfred asked.

Mollie sighed. 'I'm not sure,' she said. 'I think I meant to tell him – you know, put him wise. I hate to see a decent man made a fool of. But now I'm here I'm not so sure. Maybe I shouldn't interfere. I don't know what to do – I'm only a neighbour.

Perhaps I should leave well alone . . . Mind my own business like.' She shook her head. 'But here he is, having a well-earned pint, doing nobody any harm, and she's back there having it off —'

'What?' he stared at her. 'Right now, you mean? Now? The boyfriend?' Mollie nodded and hastily finished her drink.

'What's his name again?' Alfred asked, wiping froth from his mouth.

'Sid Carter. Why?' She looked up at him innocently.

'Never you mind, love,' said Alfred. 'You just toddle off home like a good girl and leave it to me.' He winked slowly with ponderous meaning.

'What?' gasped Mollie. 'You mean *you'll* do it? Oh my Lord!'

He grinned. 'No skin off my nose, is it?' he asked. 'If I can do a chap a favour?'

'But he may not actually be here,' said Mollie breathlessly, unable to believe that her plan had worked so well.

'Soon find out then, won't we?' He leaned over the counter and beckoned the barman. The two of them whispered together and the barman jerked his thumb towards a man standing at the far end of the bar.

'That's him!' Alfred whispered to Mollie. 'But don't let him see you looking!'

Mollie looked at Sid from out of the corner of her eye and noted with some satisfaction that he had obviously drunk more than was good for him and was ordering another.

'Poor chap!' she whispered. 'Shame, isn't it?'

'Don't you worry,' said Alfred. 'I'll put him wise! Sooner he puts a stop to it the better.'

'Well,' said Mollie, 'maybe I'd best get back home then. I'm well out of it and she can't point the finger at me. Honestly, Alfred, I'm ever so grateful.'

'It's nothing. Be glad to help. We men have to stick together!'

'I'll be going then,' said Mollie. She held up crossed fingers. 'Good luck!'

'It's as good as done.'

Outside once more, Mollie resisted the impulse to cheer and set off at a quick pace along the road. She went past Dora's flat and waited at the far corner. Time passed and she was beginning to wonder if Alfred had failed her after all when she saw the unsteady figure of Sid Carter making his way home and watched with malicious triumph as he struggled to put the key in the lock of his front door.

*

Mary looked round the shed with a practised eye. The stove was switched off, the mugs and dishes stacked in the cupboard, the spoons put away in the drawer. The box containing sugar and porridge oats was closed securely and tied with string and the three wooden trays were propped against it.

'I think that's it for today,' she said.

Gareth closed the roof-light and checked that the windows were shut.

'This catch is very rusty,' he said of the last one. 'I keep meaning to mention it to Roland – we ought to replace it before it rusts away completely.'

Mary nodded, picked up the notebook in which they kept a record of the meals they served and wrote carefully:

Saturday – 17 (7 men and 6 women, 4 children) – Porridge and tea.

'I'll pick up tomorrow's bread if you like,' she offered. 'I can go that way home, past the baker's. What shall we serve tomorrow – dripping or jam?'

They tried to vary the breakfasts within certain limits – one day porridge with milk and sugar; the next, bread or toast with a spread of some kind.

'Neither, Gareth said now. 'My mother has made some marmalade and she's promised us two pounds of it.'

'That's very good of her,' said Mary. 'People are so kind.'

'She likes to feel she's helping,' he told her. 'If her arthritis wasn't so bad she'd be down here with us, pouring tea or ladling porridge.'

Mary looked round the familiar room and sighed. 'I would like us to find better accommodation,' she said, 'but that would mean moving away from the people who need us most. Some of the older ones would never make it any further. I noticed a small hall to let, but it's nearly a mile away from here. I did mention it to Roland, but he's not happy for us to move. I'd willingly pay the rent of it, but I suppose there's no point if people won't come that far.'

Gareth considered. 'Different people would come,' he said. 'So we would still be helping.'

'But what would happen to our people here – old Mary, for example, or Mr Tedder, or even old Miss Jay? She would never come all that way. No, Roland's right, I know; we're more use here. It just depresses me sometimes.'

Gareth laughed gently. 'It depresses us because we compare it with our own homes,' he said. 'It doesn't depress them – but if you like, we could put up some nice bright curtains or hang a few pictures on the wall.' He grinned. 'Or even bring along an aspidistra.'

Mary, laughing, began to put on her coat and he hurried to help her. Suddenly he took his courage in both hands.

'Mary, I was wondering – at least, we were, that is my mother and I – wondering if you would care to join us for lunch tomorrow. Mother would enjoy a bit of company.'

Mary, hiding her surprise, said that she would like to come. It was well-known, though never mentioned, that Gareth's mother was a very possessive woman.

'Please thank her for the invitation,' said Mary. 'I shall look forward to it. It's rather solitary at home at the moment, without Alexander.'

'But not for long, eh?' said Gareth. 'A few more days and you will be with him in Switzerland?'

'Another week,' said Mary and he saw that her eyes lit up at the prospect of the coming reunion with Alexander. 'I'm counting the days. It's silly of me to be so excited, I suppose, but I've always wanted to visit Switzerland and, of course . . . '
Her eyes darkened suddenly. 'To tell you the truth, Gareth, I

have missed him terribly. It's been quite a nightmare in some ways. All very foolish, but . . . ' She shrugged helplessly.

Gareth, greatly daring, put a hand lightly on her shoulder. 'Never mind,' he said. 'That's all over now. It was just a misunderstanding – the kind of thing that happens all the time. I've felt so sorry for you doing these last few weeks.' He looked at her earnestly and she was surprised by the change in his tone. 'I have wanted to help you, but didn't quite know how. I felt so useless, Mary.'

'There was no need,' Mary began, wary of his pity. 'Please don't reproach yourself.'

'But I *do*,' he insisted. 'I reproach myself severely for not helping you through a very anxious time. Caring for a child alone must be a great burden.'

'A burden? Oh no, Gareth,' Mary protested, 'it's never been a burden. I've been very fortunate in being financially secure, so for me it has been a joy.' She laughed. 'I can say that with hand on heart.'

'I am glad for you then,' he said and there was an awkward silence. 'I'm only sorry I didn't offer my help years ago when it might have been of more use. Alexander is almost a man and – '

'Please, Gareth,' she said, 'there really is no need to apologise for anything. I'm sure that if I had needed help I would have turned to you.' Her casual words had an immediate effect as Gareth seized her hand and gazed into her eyes. She might almost have found him amusing, except that his hand trembled and he looked so vulnerable.

'Dear Mary,' he stammered. 'I'm such a coward. Yes, it's true. All these years I have wanted to speak to you and never dared. I have come so close to speaking of what is in my heart, but never could say it. You must think me a terrible fool – no, please don't interrupt me or it will happen again.' Mary stared at him helplessly. 'Let me just say how much I admire you – you won't be offended, will you? – and that if ever I can be of any use to you I am here, waiting to be of some service.' He shrugged, at a loss for more eloquent phrases.

Mary opened her mouth to reply, but he rushed on. 'Oh, don't say anything!' Alarm showed in his eyes. 'I don't want you to say anything, I only want you to *know*. Please, Mary, think of what I have said and . . . and I'll see you tomorrow for lunch. You will still come, won't you? I haven't been too rash, have I?'

He seemed to realise suddenly that he was holding her hand and abruptly released it.

Mary smiled to reassure him. 'I am looking forward to lunching with you,' she said, 'and nothing you have said has disturbed me in any way. You have been very honest and generous and of course I look upon you as a very special friend. But now we ought to go or the baker will close and I shall have no bread for tomorrow. I'd like to call very briefly on Dora Wilks on my way – I promised Lydia I'd keep an eye on the new baby, although I get the distinct impression that Dora's husband is none too pleased to see me. No doubt thinks of us as busybodies, but there!'

She shrugged and after a last look round, they made their way outside and Gareth locked and padlocked the door.

'I must remember to buy a mousetrap,' he said. 'That poison we put down doesn't seem very effective. I'll go and get it now before I forget. Unless you would like me to come with you to Dora's?'

Mary shook her head. 'I shall just put my head in at the door,' she told him. 'Two seconds, that's all. And I shall come to see you and your mother tomorrow – what time would suit you?'

They decided on twelve-thirty and then went their separate ways, Mary stepping briskly towards Dora's flat while Gareth walking more slowly, paused at intervals to glance back at her. Buoyed up with elation, he smiled broadly at everyone he passed and gave a shilling to a beggar who stood in the gutter with a tray of boot- and shoe-laces suspended round his neck.

Mary reached Dora's house and put up a hand to the knocker. Suddenly she became aware of raised voices within and hesitated, assuming it would embarrass them to have a visitor at such a time. She was about to turn away when there was a loud scream, followed by rapid footsteps in the hallway and then, to Mary's astonishment, the door was pulled open and Dora flung herself out of the house. She narrowly missed Mary, who put out a hand to save her from falling.

'What is it?' cried Mary. 'What's happening?'

Dora's lower lip was split open and blood trickled down her chin.

'Stop him!' she sobbed frantically. 'He'll kill him! Stop him, for God's sake!'

'Who? Kill who?'

From inside the house there came the sound of a crash and splintering wood; then a cry of pain, followed by shouted obscenities and another crash.

'Albert! He'll kill him – and the little 'un's in there. I'm going for the police. Help!'

Mary's mind seemed to be moving in slow motion as she watched Dora running up the street screaming at the top of her voice for someone to find a policeman. For a moment she stood rooted to the spot, literally paralysed with shock, but then Dora's words about the baby startled her into action. Without a thought for herself, she ran along the passage and pushed at the living-room door. At first it would not open, but she heard a voice she recognised as Albert Crittenden's and banged on the door with her fists.

'It's me, Mary Bellweather! Let me in at once!' she shouted.

She heard Albert's terrified voice call, 'Miss Bellweather! He's gone mad! Get a policeman. He's . . . ah!' He gave a cry of pain which was followed by another crash.

'Oh God, help me,' Mary whispered, as the door suddenly swung open to reveal a scene of devastation. Her heart hammered with fear as she took in at one glance the broken window and the overturned table. Even as her eyes registered the awful scene, Sid Carter lunged towards Albert with a poker raised murderously in his right hand. Albert, trying desperately to avoid him, put up his left arm to shield his battered face while his right arm hung uselessly by his side.

'I told her I'd kill you and I bloody will!' cried Sid. 'You won't sneak round here again, you – '

By a miracle, Albert side-stepped the blow and it was Sid's turn to curse with pain as the poker, landing on the wooden arm of the fireside chair, jarred his arm. 'By Christ, I'll swing for you – ' Sid shouted, regaining his balance with an effort and turning to see where his victim had gone. Albert's right eye was closing rapidly and there was a bright red weal down his cheek. His face was ashen and he stumbled about the room, blind with terror and faint from the pain of his broken right arm. Mary ran in, seized his shoulders and pushed him towards the back door.

'Get out, for God's sake!' she cried. 'He won't hurt me. Go into the garden and leave him to me.'

He began to argue, but she pushed him through the door and then closed it and turned to face Sid Carter.

Controlling her voice with an effort, she cried, 'Stop this, Sid Carter! Stop it at once!'

Out of the corner of her eye she saw the baby lying in the pram in the corner of the room. She wondered frantically how she could get herself and the baby out of the house. Meanwhile Sid Carter swayed on his feet and stared at her in disbelief.

'Oh, it's you, you meddling old cow! What are you doing here, eh? And where's that bloody little Albert? I'll teach him to play around with my woman – ' He raised the poker again. 'Where's he gone, eh? Where's the little sod gone to? I'll break every bone in his – ' He swayed suddenly and fell forward into the armchair.

Mary seized what she thought might be her only chance and snatched up the child, but as she did so Sid staggered to his feet again. He placed himself between Mary and the door which led to the passage and with a sinking heart, Mary knew that her escape to the safety of the street was now cut off. She wondered frantically if she could follow Albert into the garden and elude Sid that way. For a terrible moment they stared at each other while Sid's fuddled brain reassessed the situation. He leaned back against the doorway and spread his arms, effectively barring her way. She glanced through the window into the garden, but there was no sign of Albert.

'Please get out of my way,' Mary demanded shakily. 'You have no right to keep me here.'

He leered at her drunkenly. 'Who's stopping you?' he demanded. 'I'm not. Go – I don't want you here. Bloody meddlers!'

'Then move aside,' said Mary, 'and let me pass.'

'You can go,' he said, stepping aside, 'but you're not taking my kid with you.'

Mary's arms tightened round the child, who now began to whimper.

'No,' she said as firmly as she could. 'I *am* taking him. You're not fit to look after him at the moment. I'll give him to his mother – ' She realised too late that mentioning Dora was a mistake.

'That little good-for-nothing slut!' he roared. 'I'll wring her bloody neck when I get hold of her!'

He levered himself away from the doorway and took two steps towards Mary, the poker held above his head. She could hear the sound of a policeman's whistle and confused voices from the street; in another moment she would be safe.

Sid heard the whistle too. 'Give me that bloody kid and get out of here!' he cried, but Mary shook her head – she knew there was no way she could hand over the child to his drunken father. She heard Dora's voice screaming from the street and then footsteps pounded along the passage. At that very moment, however, Sid leaped towards her and she turned to run for the safety of the garden. The poker caught her diagonally across the back of the neck and she heard rather than felt the soft crunch of bone as it bit deeply into the base of her skull. Mary felt no pain at all, only a shocked realisation that he had struck her. She clutched the baby to her as she slipped to the floor and was aware of a loud buzz of anxious voices; she could dimly see hands reaching down at her from all directions and then the light was blotted out by a circle of shadowy faces.

As she closed her eyes she heard Dora say, 'Oh, Miss Bellweather!'

Somehow she managed a faint smile, then she opened her eyes again and said, 'Alexander!'

Then Mary Bellweather died.

*

Panic-stricken, Dora snatched up the screaming baby, while around her people edged back from Mary's prostrate form.

'She's not dead, is she?' Dora whispered. 'Not really. Oh, she *can't* be!'

The young constable, kneeling beside Mary, tried unsuccessfully to find a pulse. Behind them Sid Carter leaned against the wall, his face pale, his mind confused and his eyes wide with fright. The poker fell from his hand with a clatter and alerted the constable to another of his priorities. Jumping to his feet, his fists clenched defensively, he rounded on Sid Carter.

'I'm going to have to charge you,' he began uncertainly. He had never before had to arrest a murderer. 'That woman – ' he pointed. 'I think she's dead, in which case you must have killed her.'

'No!' cried Dora. 'He never meant to. Not Sid! He wouldn't do *that*! Oh my God, Sid, say you didn't do it!'

Sid eyed them blearily, the alcohol in his blood still mercifully blurring the significance of what the constable was saying to him. The constable looked round hopefully to see if any of his colleagues had been alerted by his frenzied blasts as he ran towards the scene of the tragedy. Seeing no one who could help him, he repeated, 'Yes, that's it. I'm accusing you – no, I'm *arresting* you. Anything you say – '

'Stop it,' cried Dora, clutching his arm desperately. 'You can't arrest Sid – He didn't mean it, did you, Sid? It was an accident. Oh, please God, she's not really dead! She must just be knocked out.'

'He was going to kill *me*!' whispered Albert, who stood just inside the living-room door ashen-faced, supporting his broken arm. 'He said he was! He meant to kill me.'

Sid looked helplessly at the circle of faces all turned in his direction.

'I didn't – ' he stammered. 'That is – I haven't! I never meant to *kill* her. She wouldn't give me back my kid – I told her . . . '

'I warn you,' said the constable, producing a pair of handcuffs. 'I've told you – anything you say will be taken down and used in evidence. Now, hold out your hands, please sir. Let's have no nonsense.'

'Don't let him, Sid!' cried Dora. 'He's trying to arrest you!'

But without protest Sid allowed himself to be locked into the handcuffs; then he slowly slid down into a sitting position with his hands round his knees and his head bowed.

'We shall need a doctor,' said the constable, 'and reinforcements.' He pushed his way through the growing crowd of onlookers who now filled the passage and stepped out into the street. Desperately he blew several more loud blasts on his whistle and was very relieved to see a senior colleague approaching on a bicycle. An old woman stood on the doorstep opposite shouting, 'Murder! Bloody murder!' and the constable marvelled at the speed with which the bad news had travelled.

When the two policemen had re-entered the house, Mollie Pett moved cautiously forward from her vantage point on the corner and sidled up to the old woman.

'What's happened?' she asked. 'Who's been murdered?'

'The mission lady,' she was told. 'The one from the free breakfasts. Killed by the new chap – only just moved in, he has.'

Mollie stared at her in growing dismay. 'Mary Bellweather, d'you mean?'

The old woman nodded. 'Killed her stone dead,' she said with relish.

Mollie was seized by a terrible coldness as the old woman's words registered. 'Killed?' she echoed. 'Are you sure you've got it right?'

' 'Course I'm sure!' grumbled her informant. 'One of 'em

come running out shouting for another constable. Murder, he said, and I said "Who?" and he said her. I do know what I'm talking about. If you don't believe me, go and see for yourself.'

But Mollie shook her head fiercely at the suggestion and put up a hand to hide her trembling lips. She had seen Mary Bellweather go into the house after Sid Carter and before the arrival of the constable, so it was possible that the planned revenge had misfired. Mollie had hoped that with Sid alerted to Albert's presence, Dora would end up with a good hiding. No one was supposed to get *killed*.

'Perhaps she'll come round,' said Molly hopefully. 'Probably just a bang on the head.'

'I tell you she's dead!' insisted the old woman. 'Terrible thing, that! She was a good woman, that Miss Bellweather. I've had more'n one breakfast off that mission lot *and* a coat and hat. It's a terrible, terrible thing.' As Mollie began to cough, the woman moved back, eyeing her distastefully. Then she pointed triumphantly as a hansom cab drew up outside Dora's house and a middle-aged man climbed down.

'There you are!' she hissed. 'That's the doctor – see his bag?' At that moment Albert came out into the street and stood blinking in the sunshine. He leaned back against the wall and Mollie hastily turned away, fearful of being recognised and implicated, but the pain of Albert's arm absorbed his full attention.

'Here,' said the old woman. 'What say you and me pop over and have a look?'

'No!' cried Mollie, struggling to regain her breath. 'No, I don't want to.'

'Please yourself, but I'm going. Something to tell my old man – he's bedridden, poor old stick. Bit of excitement for him. He gets a bit fed-up sometimes, just lying there. Well, you would, wouldn't you? Stands to reason – hullo, now what's up?'

The doctor had come out again and he now addressed Albert, examining his arm; Mollie and the old woman watched as the injured man was helped into the cab and driven away. Then the senior constable emerged, mounted his bicycle and pedalled off furiously in the direction from which he had come.

'Gone for the Black Maria,' said Mollie's companion, 'and the young fellow's off to the hospital. Dear oh Lord, what a carry-on!' Without another word she waddled across the road and disappeared into the house.

Mollie remained where she was, horrified by the knowledge that she was largely to blame for the tragedy and weighed down with a deepening sense of guilt. People began to leave Dora's house and Mollie suddenly realised that Dora herself might come out at any moment and see her. Fright galvanised her limbs and she began to run.

Only later did it dawn on her that Mary Bellweather had been her main source of income and the full enormity of the situation swept over her with sickening clarity. By bringing about Mary's death she had killed her 'golden goose'! As she lay awake, staring up at the smoke-blackened ceiling, she began to comprehend the full extent of the disaster she had unwittingly brought upon herself.

CHAPTER TWENTY-TWO

The October sun lacked the heat of July and August but its brightness, contrasted with the dark shadows, remained undimmed. The beach at Porthleven was typical of the Cornish coastline, with small bays of fine sand beneath towering cliffs from which massive boulders had fallen on to the beach below – to sink into the yielding sand and become permanent fixtures. Around the base of each boulder successive tides had scoured out small pools and these provided a source of endless interest and amusement to the countless children who played on the sands. A rough cliff path wound up the face of the cliff to the narrow street at the top, and it was from this street that Vinnie and the children had descended to the beach for the last time.

'It's not fair, Mama,' wailed Louise, her face rebellious below the wide-brimmed hat. 'Why have *we* got to go home if you're not going?'

They crossed the beach in their various ways – Vinnie walking slowly and holding her daughter firmly by the hand; James running in circles round them; Edward striding forward, thrusting the heels of his left shoe deep into the sand at each step and using only the toe of his right shoe. From time to time he glanced back approvingly at his irregular footsteps.

'People will wonder,' he told Vinnie gleefully. 'They'll think a poor cripple boy walked over the sand and wonder who he was.'

'They won't, then!' said Louise scornfully. 'Everyone will know it was you. I expect they're all up there watching you and no one will wonder at all.'

'They will, won't they, Mama?'

Vinnie smiled. 'I think they will be rather puzzled,' she agreed. 'James dear, could you go round the other way for a change? You're making me dizzy.'

James laughed triumphantly. 'I always made Doll dizzy, didn't I, Teddy? Poor Doll got dizzier and dizzier and then she fell down!'

All three children giggled with delight at the memory of Doll's pretended collapse until Louise, recalling her grievances, reiterated her complaint.

'It's not fair! I don't want to go home. I want to stay until *you* go home.'

'Well, I'm sorry, but you can't,' said Vinnie, 'so that's settled – and stop tugging at my hand like that. I shall have one arm longer than the other soon.'

'But *why* can't I?' Louise persisted.

Out of the kindness of his heart, James paused in his play to explain to her.

'It's because we've had a long holiday already,' he said. 'Doll told us last week that we had to go home because the summer is over. Poor Mama only came down yesterday and she hasn't had any holiday yet.'

'But I want a longer holiday. I've been ill . . . ' his sister protested. Vinnie had been warned by Doll that Louise tended to exploit her recent illness to further her own ends and she refused to be impressed.

'It's *because* you've been so ill that you have to go back to Foxearth,' she said. 'The doctor told me that you should only stay while the weather is dry and warm. The weather is not so good now and we have to take care of our little girl. Cold air is no good for your lungs. You've had a lovely long holiday with Doll and now it's time for you to go home. You'll enjoy the ride on the train – '

'I won't,' said Louise, 'because I hate trains.'

'Oh, what a fib!' cried James, deeply shocked. 'You said you loved it when we came down here. You said – '

'Tell-tale-tit!' Louise stuck out a pale pink tongue. 'Your

tongue will split, and all the little puppy dogs will have a little bit!'

'That's quite enough of that!' said Vinnie firmly.

James, tired of running in circles, decided to be a horse instead and began to gallop, slapping himself on the thigh to urge himself to greater speeds. Suddenly he stopped and turned to Vinnie with shining eyes.

'Once Doll saw a mermaid!' he told her. 'She pointed to it and we all looked, but we were just too late – it had dived back under the sea. Mermaids are very shy, you see. And once she saw a wicked sea-witch riding on a dolphin!'

'Good gracious!' cried Vinnie. 'Doll certainly has got marvellous eyes. Did you see the sea-witch?'

'I sort of did,' said James. 'And I saw the splash as the dolphin dived back under the waves.'

'You didn't,' said Louise, 'because there wasn't any witch. Doll was making it up.'

'She wasn't!'

'She was!'

'Wasn't!'

'Was!'

Teddy looked at his mother. 'I think she really did see it,' he assured her, 'becase Harry saw it too.'

'How exciting!' said Vinnie. 'You've obviously had a wonderful time. Doll has taken good care of you – and so has Harry – and you are all to behave yourselves on the journey home. I shall telephone to Foxearth tonight and ask Doll if you behaved well.'

Teddy paused suddenly and held up a dead starfish.

'A starfish!' he cried. 'Now I can make a wish. Doll said that if you find a starfish on the right side of the moon you can make a wish.' Screwing up his eyes he clasped it to his chest – then opened his eyes again. 'Louise can have it,' he offered in an effort to dispel her ill-humour. 'Here, Louise, you can make a wish.'

Louise took it gingerly and looked up into Vinnie's face. Then she closed her eyes and said, 'I wish I could stay here until Mama goes home.' Teddy was outraged: 'Ooh, you horrid girl!' he cried. 'Now you've wasted the wish.'

Louise flung the starfish away. 'Why have I?' she demanded. 'Now I can stay – Doll said the wish would come true.'

The two boys looked anxiously at Vinnie, who somehow resisted the impulse to shake her recalcitrant daughter. 'Well, you aren't staying any longer,' she said calmly. 'So it must be the wrong side of the moon.'

Fortunately, before the little girl could find another argument. Teddy gave a shout and pointed to a figure about fifty yards ahead of them.

'It's old Samuel,' he shouted. 'Let's go and say "Good-bye" to him.' And without further explanation, he raced away over the sand to where a solitary fisherman splashed about in the receding tide.

'He catches fish,' James told Vinnie, 'and then he sells them. That's his barrow. Once he gave us a ride in it.'

He too ran off and Vinnie saw that Louise hesitated.

'Old Samuel likes *me* best,' Louise confided. 'He calls me his "little lady".'

'Does he?' said Vinnie. 'Then you should go and say "Good-bye" to him.'

Louise, her ill-humour forgotten, freed her hand from Vinnie's and went skipping demurely across the gleaming sand towards the group at the water's edge.

By the time Vinnie reached them she found that the tide had uncovered part of a long net and in its mesh a variety of fish flapped despairingly in the cruel air. The fisherman – a whiskered man in his late sixties – looked up as Vinnie approached. With a few deft movements of his hands he untangled a small plaice and tossed it to James who, with a squeal of excitement, caught it close to his chest and turned to his mother for approval.

'Well caught!' she cried obligingly.

Beyond him a barrow stood on the sand, its two rusty wheels partly submerged by the scurrying wavelets. The plaice was laid reverently on the old newspapers and sacking with which the barrow was lined. Already there were several other plaice, a dogfish and half-a-dozen mackerel.

By way of a greeting, the old man winked at Vinnie. 'Like mother, like daughter,' he remarked. ' 'Tis easy to see who they take after. They said as how you was coming down. So excited, they was, bless 'em!' He turned to Teddy. 'And where's that Doll of yours, then, eh? Left her behind, have you?'

'She's packing all our clothes and our books and our toys,' said Teddy, 'and Harry is helping her because Mama hasn't seen us for a long time and she wanted us all to herself because she missed us terribly. Doll told us.'

His innocent words pricked at Vinnie's conscience. Had she missed them 'terribly'? Or had she been so besotted with Philippe that she had scarcely given them a thought, merely congratulating herself that they were in safe hands? The doubts and fears from which she had struggled to escape threatened her once more.

But now it was Teddy's turn to catch a mackerel – or rather to drop it!

Samuel laughed. 'Slippery old devils, them mackerel,' he said. 'A sight more lively than a plaice, but they make handsome eating. You're staying on, I hear, ma'am? I'll give you a couple of mackerel for your supper and you'll see what I mean. Here, little lady, d'you want to catch one?'

Louise gave a firm shake of her head, saying, 'No *thank* you,' and Vinnie thought, 'She *is* just like her grandmother – she will be another Christina Lawrence.'

But Samuel found the child's reactions amusing and chuckled.

'Oh, they're all the same, the little ladies,' he said. 'Toss them a fish and they holler like a stuck pig. Don't want to get their pretty little hands messed up. Here then, James, it's your turn again.'

Teddy eyed the old man's waders enviously. 'I wish we had boots like that,' he said, 'then we could wade in the water. Could we next year, Mama? Could we have long boots like that?'

'We'll see,' said Vinnie.

James groaned loudly. 'Grown-ups always say "We'll see." Doll says it and Harry says it and now Mama's saying it.'

The old man wagged a finger at them. 'Ay, well, you mind your mother,' he told them. 'That's what mothers are for – for minding.' He winked at Vinnie. 'My old mother, God rest her soul, she had a way with words, she did. Box us on the ears, she would, when we ain't done nothing. That's for nothing, she'd say, so now be careful.'

The three children regarded him solemnly.

'For *nothing*?' said Teddy, aghast at this injustice.

'Aye, for nothing, young man.' He tossed two fish over their heads and they flew in a silver arc to fall neatly into the waiting barrow. 'Because she was a wise woman, my mother, and that way we never got to do nothing bad. Well, not as she ever found out!'

It took him another quarter of an hour to retrieve all the fish, then reluctantly the children said 'Good-bye' to him. As promised, the old man wrapped up two large mackerel and pressed them into Vinnie's hands, refusing any payment.

'A little gift,' he said. 'You'll enjoy those. When you've got shot of this little lot,' – he winked at the children – 'you pop them mackerel into a pan with a big knob of butter and I promise you they'll go down a real treat.'

*

At one-thirty Vinnie stood on the platform waving to the children with a lump in her throat. She watched the train pull out of the station, then as she began to walk back towards the ticket barrier a wave of desolation swept over her. If the weather had been better she would have been tempted to keep them with her, although she knew she needed to be alone. No one could help her, she reflected; for the first time since her marriage to Julian she had no one to turn to for help and comfort. Somehow she must come to terms with her grief and find a way to live with her deep despair. Having handed in her platform ticket, she walked back to the cottage and let herself in at the front door. When she walked through into the kitchen, she saw the mackerel lying on a plate covered with a square of muslin; after staring at them for a few minutes, Vinnie opened the food safe, put the plate of fish inside and closed the door.

Now, she knew, the bad thoughts would come crowding in. Now she was alone with nothing to distract her thoughts or dull the sharp edge of remorse. Somehow, she thought, wearily, she must get through the rest of the day.

*

Later that evening Vinnie walked on the beach. The sky was empty of clouds and a large moon hung there, rippling the sea with silver and casting great shadows across the cold grey sand. Vinnie began to walk eastward away from the village, a solitary figure on a wide, uncaring shore. She walked quickly at first, following a straight line except where she had to veer to right or left to skirt a rock pool or avoid one of the many large boulders that littered the beach. She intended to exhaust herself so that she would be more likely to sleep when at last she threw herself into bed. During the daylight she had felt unwilling to face such a walk, in case late holidaymakers still strolling along the sands might possibly greet her, hoping to engage her in a few moments of cheerful conversation. She guessed that the failing light would drive people back to their lodgings and was gratified to find her assumption proved correct. For the first five minutes she trudged along the beach trying to hide her nervousness from herself, but after ten minutes her eyes became accustomed to the gloom and the soft crunch of her shoes on the damp sand became a familiar sound which blended naturally with the gentle rush of waves breaking along the sea's edge. After twenty minutes Vinnie even began to take a perverse satisfaction in the discomfort of the chill night air on her face and hands, and a grim pleasure in the knowledge that she was walking away from civilisation. The latter seemed very apt. Whatever lay ahead was dark and untried – like the rest of her life, she thought ruefully. Behind her were the familiar landmarks, the mistakes and heartaches of her previous life.

But the joys and pleasures were there too; it had not all been bad, she reminded herself, and she *had* survived. But what of the future? In her present despair, Vinnie did not see a great deal to inspire her in the lonely years ahead. 'Except the children,' she said aloud. 'I have got the children.'

Abruptly she stopped and stared out to sea, trying to pierce the darkness and see beyond the gleaming water. Then she turned to look back at the village now far behind her, a mass of twinkling lights above the cliffs. Gazing out to sea once more, she cried, 'Philippe Delain, you have abandoned me. You have broken my heart!' The words rang out sounding absurd in the darkness. Was it absurd? She stared out across the moonlit water and thought, 'I could walk into the water and drown. I could die the same way my Ma did. I could float away on the tide and be swallowed up by the night.' The thought that her life meant so little saddened her. 'Philippe!' she groaned 'Why did you do this to me? How *could* you hurt me so much? Answer me, Philippe!'

She began to whisper his name: Philippe! Philippe! Then she shouted it at the top of her voice and, turning east again, began to run. Suddenly she tripped and with a short cry fell forward, lying there breathless for a moment while the coldness of the wet sand seeped into her clothes. She began to sob as she lay there, and then to curse, and then to sob again. At last, shivering violently, she pulled herself to her knees and then to her feet and ran on. Wildly she thought, 'I will never go back. Never! I'll just run on and on – '

Tears blurred her eyes but still she ran on blindly, stumbling heedlessly until a large boulder brought her once more to her knees. With a cry of pain she rolled over, doubled-up and clutching her bruised legs.

'You've done this to me, Philippe! You! Yes, you!' she sobbed, rage, pain and grief mingling indiscriminately. 'You've brought me so *low*! Do you see? You've hurt me, wounded me. But for all you care, I could well be dead. I *am* dead to you, aren't I? No more than a name to you now. I've been such a fool to think I loved you. You aren't the man I thought you were – no, not at all. Oh God, Philippe, you never could have cared for me. Never!'

She sat up, hugging her legs, her head on her knees, weeping bitterly – oblivious to everything except the slow and bitter realisation that what she had believed was a great love was nothing but a game in which she had been no more than a player. For a very long time her body shook with the violence of her tears, but her grief ran its course and was finally exhausted. Slowly Vinnie straightened her back and lifted her head.

'I must get back,' she said, becoming aware that her knees hurt and her body was cold and cramped. 'You've got to get up, Vinnie Harris,' she told herself. 'Get up and get on with your life.' Smiling shakily, she answered herself, 'Yes, ma'am!'

When she stood up and steadied herself, she felt tired and ill and swayed a little.

As she began to stumble back the way she had come, the cluster of lights that was the village seemed very far away, but she moved resolutely towards them. She had gone perhaps only fifty yards when suddenly a tall figure detached itself from the shadows and stepped into her path.

Vinnie froze in her tracks, too tired to run and too frightened to scream.

'Vinnie! Don't be alarmed!'

Incredibly she recognised the voice. 'Clive!' she gasped. He came towards her somewhat hesitantly, stopping a yard or two in front of her.

'Clive! What on earth? Oh, God, I was so frightened!'

'I'm sorry,' he said.

'But where did you come from? I mean, you are the last person I expected to see.' She was ridiculously pleased that now she need not tramp the dark beach alone.

'I've been following you,' he admitted. 'I thought you needed to be alone, but I didn't want you to come to any harm.'

'You've been *following* me?'

Dismayed, Vinnie thought back on her hysterical behaviour. What *must* he have thought of her, she wondered.

They looked at each other warily, still separated by several yards of darkness, then she took a long shuddering breath that was half a sigh.

'It doesn't matter,' she told him. 'Nothing matters any more.' But she thought, 'He heard me crying and calling for Philippe. He saw me fall. He could have comforted me when I cried, or picked me up when I fell, yet he did nothing but watch and wait for me to work through it all.' She felt awed by his wisdom.

As though he read her thoughts, he said, 'Did you hurt yourself?'

'I am a bit shaken,' she confessed, 'and my knees and shins are sore, but it's not too dreadful.'

'Shall we walk back together?'

'I'd like that.'

They walked side by side, not touching each other. At first there seemed no place for words, but as Vinnie's spirits began to rise her curiosity got the better of her.

'What are you doing down here, Clive?' she asked. 'I thought you were still in Scotland.'

'I heard what had happened and wanted to see you.'

'About Philippe, you mean? That he's . . . gone?'

'Yes.'

'That's all in the past now,' she said with as much conviction as she could manage.

'I'm glad to hear it,' said Clive.

From the corner of her eye Vinnie watched him as he strode along beside her and saw that he made a deliberate effort to slow his pace to match her own.

'Did you enjoy your trip to Scotland?' she asked.

'No. But Scotland was not to blame – the fault was mine.'

Vinnie decided it would be wrong to enquire further, so said instead, 'Where are you staying?'

'The "George".'

'When are you going back?'

He laughed. 'Are you so keen to get rid of me?'

'Of course not; I didn't mean it to sound that way.'

'I shall stay until tomorrow. I thought we might travel back together?'

Vinnie hesitated. 'I don't think I'm ready to go back,' she told him.

Clive made no comment. Vinnie stopped for a moment, clutching her side.

'I have a stitch,' she said. 'Just give me a minute to get my breath back.'

'Only another half-mile or so.'

'Clive,' said Vinnie, 'I want you to know how sorry I am about that night. I have to . . . no, I *want* to tell you that you were right and I was making a terrible mistake.'

'It's all in the past,' said Clive. 'Let it go.'

'Not without apologising,' said Vinnie. '*Now* I can let it go!'

'I've made my share of mistakes,' said Clive. 'Everyone does. It's how we learn from them that matters.'

Vinnie nodded. 'I feel a hundred years older,' she said with a faint smile, 'and incredibly wise.'

Clive laughed and held out his hand. 'Come on! I want to get you home and into bed with a hot drink. I don't want you going down with pneumonia.'

A strange thrill went through Vinnie as his hand closed over hers and the bitter taste of the past few hours began to fade as she walked beside him with a feeling of increasing serenity. The friction of his hand as it moved carelessly against hers began to absorb all her attention and they trudged on in silence for a while. The lights in the village grew more distinct and the small sounds of civilisation came thinly through the darkness: the rattle of wheels on a rough road and the barking of a dog. As they drew nearer to the cliff steps, Vinnie was seized with a fierce reluctance to exchange the wide brooding beach for the narrow streets with their flickering gas-lamps.

Clive, sensing her reluctance, stopped. 'What is it?' he asked.

'I don't know,' she faltered with a shake of her head.

After a moment he said, 'It's easier to hide in the dark.'

She was astonished by his perception and could only nod. But it was not only the darkness, she knew; it was her sense of one-ness with Clive le Brun. On the beach in the darkness they had been two mortals, joined by clasped hands into one: one speck of humanity in an alien environment. At the top of the steps the real world waited to separate them again.

Vinnie sighed deeply. 'I can't explain,' she said. 'I would like to, but I don't think I can find the right words.'

Clive said 'Vinnie . . . ' and then stopped. 'No, this is not the time or place.' He wanted to say, 'I came to tell you that I love you,' but he had heard her anguish as she hurled Philippe's name into the darkness.

'You must change out of those damp clothes,' he said. 'Everything else can wait until the morning.'

'Everything else?'

Tomorrow he must break the news of Mary's death, but now he considered her in no fit state for further shocks.

'All the news,' he amended. 'You know the kind of thing – bright conversation over the breakfast table?'

It took a moment for Vinnie's tired brain to register his meaning. 'Over breakfast!' she exclaimed.

'Oh, don't worry! he teased. 'I won't burn the toast. Here, take my hand. These cliff steps are none too easy at night.'

So was Clive going to stay overnight at the cottage? Vinnie hoped desperately that he was.

'But the "George"?' she asked.

'I shall cancel my breakfast when I get back,' he said, 'and I shall be knocking on your door at nine o'clock sharp.'

Vinnie hoped he could not guess at her disappointment. 'My Ma used to burn the toast,' she said, 'and Bertie would scrape it for me. She used to boil the eggs hard, too, when we had them. I didn't know there were such things as soft-boiled eggs.'

Hearing his low laugh she thought incredulously, 'I have taken him for granted all these years. He's always been around – Julian's adviser in those early years, and since then a good friend for me to turn to in time of trouble. Oh, Clive le Brun, have I ever really *seen* you before tonight?'

She wanted to say, 'Stop Clive, let me look at you! I can see you clearly now for the first time in my life.' But he was moving on up the steps ahead of her, guiding her, his grasp on her hand firm and sure.

Suddenly the steep steps proved too much for her waning strength and Vinnie's legs buckled underneath her. Without Clive she would have fallen.

'I'm sorry – ' she gasped. 'My stupid legs . . . it's my own fault . . . '

'It's all right. Take it slowly.'

Somehow, with Clive's help, she reached the top of the cliff and stood thankfully on the road once more, but the climb had drained her remaining energy and left her weak and trembling with exhaustion. In the light from the street-lamp Clive saw her pallor and knew that she had reached the end of her resources. Without a word he picked her up, ignoring her half-hearted protest, and carried her back to the cottage.

There he left her to undress while he heated a mug of milk to which he added a generous dash of brandy. He found her in bed, propped up among the pillows.

'Well, Mrs Lawrence,' he said with mock severity. 'I hope you have learned your lesson. No more night-time jaunts. You obviously don't have the stamina for it.'

Vinnie smiled faintly as she took the proffered mug. A great weight of weariness had settled over her and her limbs felt leaden. The mug seemed almost too heavy to hold, but under Clive's watchful eye she sipped it gratefully until it was empty.

Then he took it from her and watched her settle down in the bed with an expression she could not read. Bending down, he kissed her forehead.

'Goodnight, Mrs Lawrence!' he said. 'Sleep well – and remember. Nine o'clock on the dot!'

He turned out the gas and then he was gone. Almost immediately Vinnie found herself sliding into a deep and welcome oblivion, carrying the memory of Clive's kiss with her into her dreams.

*

True to his word Clive le Brun was knocking at the door of the cottage at nine o'clock sharp, but Vinnie was already up and dressed and preparing breakfast.

'I don't want you to think I'm useless,' she laughed as she showed him into the kitchen. The sun shone through the small latticed window, making the room bright and cheerful. There was a red checked cloth on the table and Vinnie had picked three late rosebuds and put them in a glass vase. A bowl of well-whisked eggs stood beside the stove and thick slices of bread waited under the grill. On the table stood a dish of butter and a jar of honey. Vinnie was glad he could not know how early she had risen and how impatiently she had watched the hands of the clock. Chattering as casually as possible, she poured him a cup of tea to drink while he waited.

For his part, Clive was pleased to see how well she had recovered from the previous night's ordeal, but his response to her cheerfulness was tempered by the knowledge that he had bad news for her. He had intended to wait until they had finished breakfast but Vinnie, her senses finely tuned to his every word and look, soon became aware that something was troubling him.

'Is something wrong, Clive?' she asked when at last they sat down to eat. 'You seem rather thoughtful.'

'I'm afraid so,' he told her. 'It's rather sad news – oh, no one too close, so don't take fright. But it's Mary Bellweather; there was an accident – at least, no one is quite sure how it happened, but Mary was killed.'

Vinnie stared at him, wide-eyed with shock. 'Killed? Oh no! That's not possible. Clive, how? When did it – ' She shook her head in disbelief. 'Who would kill Mary, of all people?'

'It was some kind of brawl,' expained Clive. 'I heard it at second or third hand, and the details always get distorted in such circumstances, but I understand there was a fight between one of the pickers and another man and Mary tried to separate them.'

'One of *my* pickers?' cried Vinnie. 'Oh, how terrible! Which one, Clive? Do you know his name?'

'I forget his name, but he was somehow connected with the girl who had the baby.'

'Dora Wilks! Oh, then it was Albert! But he wouldn't hurt a fly! Not Albert Crittenden! There must be some mistake, Clive.'

'It wasn't him,' Clive reassured her. 'It was the husband – I'm afraid it looks like a murder charge. I thought I would come down and tell you myself, knowing how concerned you would be and guessing that you'd want to get back to Foxearth.'

'Yes, I must, of course.' She pushed away the remains of her breakfast. 'And poor Alexander!' she cried as the full enormity of the situation began to dawn on her. 'He's in Switzerland – or is it Italy? I suppose he's been told. And Dora! If her husband is in prison – what will become of her and the children? Oh, I must get back!' She rose in great agitation, but Clive put out a hand to restrain her.

'I'm sure everything is being done for her,' he said. 'The Brothers in Jesus will take care of them. Sit down, Vinnie, and finish your breakfast.'

'But I –'

'Please sit down, Vinnie. There really is nothing you can do at the moment.'

She sat down with some reluctance and Clive pushed her plate towards her. 'Be a good girl and finish your breakfast,' he said. 'The world will get along very well while you eat those last mouthfuls. I haven't come all this way to sit by and see you starve yourself.'

To humour him, Vinnie cleared the plate while Clive poured them each another cup of tea.

'Poor Mary,' said Vinnie. 'What a terrible time to die.'

'Is there a good time?'

Vinnie shrugged. 'I suppose not. But to be killed! Did he mean it, I wonder?'

'I believe he was the worse for drink. These things happen.'

'Poor Mary!' said Vinnie again. 'After all that trouble with Alexander and Sylvia – it's all so dreadfully sad.'

'Try not to distress yourself, Vinnie,' Clive told her sensibly. 'You've had your own share of sorrows. We all do. If we suffer for each other as well as for ourselves . . . ' He shrugged, leaving the sentence unfinished.

Vinnie nodded. 'I know, but it's hard to stand by and not be moved by someone else's tragedy – though I know you're absolutely right. But poor Dora! Perhaps I can find some work for her and somewhere for her to live – ' She stopped as Clive began to laugh. 'What have I said?'

'Vinnie, you're incorrigible, but I won't try to change you. I – ' He meant to say, 'I love you the way you are,' but checked himself just in time.

Vinnie was too preoccupied to notice anything. 'I *will* travel back with you, Clive,' she told him. 'Luckily I never finished my unpacking. I wonder if they have fixed the date of the funeral? And where will it be?'

'Near her parents, I imagine,' said Clive. 'Roland Fry is sure to know what is best and Mary has probably left a will. Mrs Markham will – '

'Oh, *poor* Mrs Markham!' exclaimed Vinnie. 'I'd quite forgotten her. Clive, I just can't believe that Mary is gone. Just like that, from one day to the next.'

'Life is very fragile, Vinnie,' said Clive gently. 'We should not take it for granted the way we do. We ought to make the most of our short time on this earth, but I doubt if many of us do so.'

They regarded each other soberly. 'What a sad subject,' said Vinnie. 'What a sad breakfast.'

'I'm sorry I had to tell you now,' said Clive. 'Last night was not the time to do it either, but there is never a good time for news like that.'

Vinnie pushed back her plate and stood up, looking down into Clive's clear grey eyes and remembering how he had carried her the night before; she had felt so very safe in his arms. Her gaze moved over the strong lines of his face – from the thick well-shaped brows and nose to the mouth which had kissed her twice, once so roughly and last night so gently. He returned her gaze levelly.

'I want to ask you something, Clive,' she said at last. 'Will you answer it honestly?'

'I'll try.'

'Why *did* you come to Porthleven? Was it because of Mary Bellweather?' He hesitated.

'*Honestly*, Clive,' she reminded him.

'No, it wasn't because of Mary. It was because of you.'

Vinnie said nothing, waiting, her eyes fixed on his face.

'I heard about Philippe's engagement,' he said, 'and I guessed what it would do to you. I was afraid you might take it too hard and perhaps ... ' He shrugged expressively, long fingers moving in agitation. 'I was afraid you would try to kill yourself,' he said, 'and I could not allow that to happen.'

Vinnie swallowed hard. 'So you came all this way, not knowing what sort of reception you would get after our last meeting!'

'I thought I'd risk it!' he said with an attempt at lightness.

'I think that was very fine of you, Clive,' she said, unsmiling. 'I want you to know that I'm very grateful. Your appearance last night was timely, I think that's the best word. Because of the children I would not have killed myself, although I have to admit that the idea crossed my mind.'

'I'm glad you dismissed it. No one is worth throwing away a life for.'

'No.' Vinnie sighed. 'I don't remember now exactly what I said out there on the beach, and I don't know how much you heard, but whatever it was I want you to know that Philippe now means nothing to me. I think I have exorcised that particular demon. Do you understand, Clive? Whatever he once was to me and whatever delusions I may have had – it's all in the past. Over! I want you to believe me.'

'I believe you, Vinnie. Thank you for telling me.'

Vinnie could think of nothing else to say, so she began to clear the table. Her movements were clumsy and she knocked over a cup, spilling the dregs of tea on to the cloth and giving an exclamation of annoyance.

Clive put a hand over hers. 'It doesn't matter,' he said.

'It *does*,' she said stubbornly, angry with herself for revealing the extent of her agitation.

He stood up and took both her hands in his. 'No, it *doesn't*,' he countered. 'All that matters is that you and I are friends again.'

*

The churchyard was crowded with mourners as Roland Fry spoke a few final words over Mary Bellweather's coffin. Immediately around the newly-dug grave stood those who had been closest to her. Mrs Markham, her face blotched with tears, was supported by Alexander – his face pale, his eyes large. Sylvia stood on his other side with her arm linked through his; she was fair-haired, with a sweet face, and Vinnie found herself wishing that she and Mary had been brought together in happier circumstances. Roland's wife Emily stood beside Dora Wilks, who looked drawn and ill and fidgeted constantly with a posy of violets tied with a thin black ribbon. Unaccountably, William and Clive le Brun had not arrived, but Lydia Grant was there and so was Gareth Brooks. The rest of the people were hop-pickers, all of whom Vinnie recognised. Albert had insisted on attending and stood next to Dora, his splinted right arm in a sling. Mollie Pett, to Vinnie's great relief, had not put in an appearance.

'Mary meant something different to each one of us,' said Roland in his clear, calm voice, 'and we will all remember her in a different way and for different reasons. Alexander, who has been a son to her for so many years, will remember her great capacity for love and the generous way she opened her home and her heart to him when he was quite alone in the world. For a single woman with no children of her own, that was a tremendous act of faith, even courage, and I am pleased that Alexander gave her so much love in return. He knew her as a wise mother and loving companion and today we all share his grief at her untimely passing. To Mrs Markham, her loyal and trusted housekeeper, she was a considerate mistress. Mrs Markham told me earlier that Mary Bellweather was a lady in every sense of the word and she had been proud to serve her.'

He paused to look towards the housekeeper and give her an encouraging smile. Deeply affected by his words, however,

Mrs Markham began to cry and after a few whispered words, Sylvia changed places with Alexander and put her arm protectively around the old lady in an attempt to comfort her.

Vinnie felt a lump come into her throat and again Mary's own words came back to haunt her. 'You have ruined my life, Vinnie Harris.' Vinnie knew that they were wild words, spoken in the heat of the moment, but it distressed her nonetheless to think that she had – albeit unintentionally – caused Mary grief.

Now Vinnie closed her eyes and prayed: 'Please forgive me, Mary. Look right into my heart and you will see that truly I meant you no harm.' Perhaps now, she thought hopefully, Mary could see everything clearly and would know the truth. She felt slightly reassured as she opened her eyes again and turned her attention once more to Roland's address.

'To most of you gathered here to pay your last respects, Mary was known as a member of the Brothers in Jesus. As the founder of that brave little band, I am privileged to have known Mary since its inception, many years ago when we met in a small hall to try to find a way to help those in need. Mary had been an inspired and inspiring member of the group ever since that day, giving unstintingly of her time and energy. You all know that for yourselves . . . '

There was a murmur of agreement at this point and one of the women called out, ' 'Ear, 'ear!' and another, 'Bless 'er 'eart!'

'We shall all miss her,' Roland continued with a catch in his voice. 'We will miss her kindness, her honesty, her generous spirit and her unfailing love of humanity. Mary Bellweather was an example to us all and we must treasure the memories we have of her. These London streets will be poorer without her presence and she will be sadly missed from the hop-gardens at Foxearth. We all know the tragic circumstances of her death and I will not dwell on them here. I will say only this – that Mary Bellweather gave her life, as she lived it, to help others.'

Vinnie's eyes roamed over the crowd which, as Roland's address drew to its close, now pressed forward. There was still no sign of Clive or William and her anxiety grew. She had not seen Clive since they had travelled back to Kent together, but she had spoken to him on the telephone and they had expected to meet at the funeral. She was beginning to wonder if there had been an accident. Mary and Clive had not been close, but at one time William had been very fond of her and Vinnie was sure he would regret missing the funeral service. Nothing of a trivial nature would have prevented them from being present.

Vinnie's parting from Clive, when he delivered her safely to her home, had been very difficult for her and she was proud of the tight rein she had kept on her feelings. During the few hours they had been together in Porthleven and on the journey home, Vinnie had discovered a growing need for the man she had once so lightly described to Philippe as 'just a very good friend.' In his company she felt complete. Without him she felt unfinished and since his departure had been sick at heart; only the prospect of seeing him again had sustained her. Now it looked as though the le Bruns were not coming and Vinnie struggled to hide her disappointment.

Roland Fry had concluded his farewell speech and the vicar stepped forward to pronounce the final words.

'Ashes to ashes, dust to dust . . . '

As the coffin was lowered into the grave Dora stepped forward, kissed the bunch of violets she had been holding and tossed them down on top of the polished wood. Alexander scattered the first spadeful of earth on to the coffin and then stood staring down into the grave, shaking his head as though in bewilderment, a look of deep sorrow on his young face. Suddenly, astonishingly, a woman at the back of the crowd began to sing:

'For she's a jolly good fellow – '

The solitary voice, tuneless and quavering, sang the next line but then a second voice joined in softly and reverently, followed by several more. The vicar looked startled.

'For she's a jolly good fellow – '
And so say all of us.'

Soon all the hop-pickers were singing and the familiar words rang gently and sorrowfully across the open grave.

'And so say all of us, and so say all of us . . . '

Vinnie and Roland exchanged wondering looks as the chorus finally ended and the pickers' spontaneous and moving tribute wavered into a protracted silence.

Then it was all over. Mrs Markham, Alexander and Sylvia were first to leave the graveside and Dora, Albert and the Brothers in Jesus followed soon after. Their space was taken by the pickers, who respectfully pushed forward to stand for a moment gazing down at Mary's coffin before making way for those behind them. Vinnie walked through the churchyard still desperately searching for a glimpse of Clive or William, but there was no sign of them. She was becoming increasingly alarmed by their non-appearance and as soon as she caught up with Alexander she asked him if she could make a telephone call from the house. There was no answer from Clive's home and she replaced the receiver with a feeling of unreasonable panic. Roland Fry came into the hall, saying, 'Ah, there you are!'

'I'm trying to reach Clive le Brun,' Vinnie told him. 'I was expecting them to be here, but as they haven't turned up I'm getting a little worried about them. There's no answer from their home, so something must have happened – some delay or maybe even an accident. I don't know what to do.'

'I thought it strange that they weren't at the service,' he said. 'I do hope nothing has happened. Give them a little while longer – the train may have been delayed, although I admit that's not very usual. Come in and have something to eat. Alexander and Sylvia make a charming couple, don't you think? A rather nervous host and hostess on this sad occasion, but very charming.'

Against her better judgement, Vinnie allowed herself to be drawn into the dining-room where Mrs Markham had earlier prepared fresh salmon, salads and a mouthwatering selection of home-made desserts. Under the influence of good food and wine the sadness of the occasion inevitably receded and the conversation grew more animated. Vinnie however could eat nothing; the glass of wine which Alexander insisted she should drink merely seemed, on an empty stomach, to heighten her already considerable anxiety. She telephoned Harkwood again and this time spoke to Clive's housekeeper; she had just arrived home from her weekly shopping trip and told Vinnie that earlier on Clive and William had left for the station in the brougham to catch the London train. She was disturbed to learn from Vinnie that they had not arrived at their destination.

Vinnie determined to leave for home at once and, explaining her anxiety to Alexander, made her excuses and left the house.

The train journey from London to Maidstone seemed interminable and when she finally arrived she hired a hansom cab to take her home. Once there she would telephone Harkwood for news – if there was none, she had made up her mind she would contact the police.

Dismissing the cab, she ran up the steps. Tim Bilton called to her from the direction of the stable, but she did not catch what he said and rang the bell firmly.

Bertha opened the door. 'Has there been any message?' cried Vinnie, snatching off her gloves and hat.

'No, ma'am,' said Bertha, taken aback by Vinnie's obvious agitation, 'but Mr le Brun is in the morning-room. He said – '

Vinnie whirled round. 'He's here? Clive le Brun? Oh, thank heavens!' She ran along the hall and burst unceremoniously into the room where Clive stood at the window, looking down on to the front terrace.

He smiled and came forward. 'I thought I heard a carriage,' he said. 'I was just – '

'Clive!' cried Vinnie in anguished tones. 'What happened to you? I was terrified. I was so sure . . . ' She stopped, not daring to move towards him, convinced that even now he would hear the beating of her heart and see the joy in her eyes.

'I'm so sorry, Vinnie,' he began. 'I tried to get in touch as soon as I could, but it's been the devil of a morning. Vinnie, are you all right?'

'Yes,' she nodded. 'Yes, go on, Clive.'

They stood facing each other, separated by the length of the morning-room. Vinnie felt weak with relief; she just wanted to look at him, to listen to his voice and to know he was safe.

'Aren't you going to sit down?' he asked.

Vinnie shook her head. 'I've been sitting down for ages on the train. Just tell me what happened, Clive?'

He shrugged and himself remained standing. 'We left in the brougham in plenty of time for the train, but half a mile along the road we saw a rather nasty accident. A motor car had run out of control on the hill and mounted the pavement. It ran into a group of people who were walking up the hill – a family with five children. Naturally we stopped to see if we could help. The mother was unconscious, the father very dazed and one of the children had a broken leg; they were very lucky indeed it was no worse. The police came of course, and as witnesses we had to make statements. By the time all that was done we had missed our train. The next train would have got us to London in time to join you at the house after the service, but the police asked if we would take the remaining uninjured children to their grandparents in Sevenoaks. It seemed the least we could do . . . '

Vinnie nodded, unable to speak, not hearing a word he said. She was shaken to discover the strength of her longing for Clive le Brun. All her senses cried out for his touch and the sudden memory of his kiss in the bedroom at the cottage set her body on fire with desire. If only he would keep on talking, she prayed. He must not guess at the conflicting emotions that threatened to overwhelm her.

'I went down to the police station and telephoned the Bellweather house, but there was no answer and I realised that by then you would all be at the church. Vinnie?'

'I am listening. Go on – please!'

She could not explain her feelings. 'He must go on talking,' she thought desperately. But when his account was ended, what then? Her throat and mouth were dry, her rapid breathing seemed frighteningly loud. He must surely guess! Suppose he came any nearer and looked into her eyes!

She said hastily, 'And I was ringing you at Harkwood. I thought – oh, Clive!'

'So I thought I would come over to Foxearth and wait for you here. Are you sure you're all right? I had no idea you would be so worried . . . Vinnie?'

As he moved towards her, Vinnie's heart seemed to somersault within her. She backed away until she felt the door behind her and then pressed herself against it.

'Clive,' she said faintly. 'Don't . . . '

She saw his expression change as he drew near enough to read what she knew was written in her eyes, but he ignored the trembling hand she held up to keep him at a distance. Without changing his pace he came right up to her, pulled her away from the door and into his arms and in the brief moment before he began to kiss her, she saw her own desire mirrored in his eyes.

'Oh Vinnie! My God, I love you, Vinnie!' he murmured and to her astonishment she realised his passion matched her own. 'I have waited too long for you, Vinnie, much too long. I think I've always loved you.' He was kissing her frantically and his arms imprisoned her. 'Tell me that you love me, Vinnie. Say it!'

'I love you, Clive. I didn't know it at first, but now I do. Oh my dearest Clive, I adore you!'

After a moment he pulled away from her, breathless, and she saw the excitement in his eyes. Suddenly he took a few paces away from her; when he turned back he said simply, 'So are you going to marry me, Vinnie Lawrence?'

'If you're asking!' cried Vinnie.

He held out his arms to her and Vinnie ran into his ecstatic embrace. 'I am asking,' he whispered. 'Oh yes, I'm asking, Vinnie! You will never know how hard it's been during these past few years. I thought you wanted William and I could not stand in his way. Oh God, Vinnie, I've longed for this moment. I can hardly believe it!'

Vinnie looked up at him with shining eyes. 'It's true, Clive,' she told him. 'I, Vinnie Lawrence, do take thee, Clive le Brun, to be my lawful wedded husband' – my darling Clive! I'll do my best to make you happy, I truly will.'